Praise for Julia Glass's

And the Dark Sacred Night

"Breathtaking. . . . Heartfelt. . . . What makes this novel so fresh is its notion that the need to know where we come from isn't limited to our formative years. And that all buried secrets are bittersweet when revealed."　　　　　*—Star Tribune* (Minneapolis)

"An exquisitely detailed novel."　　　　　*—O, The Oprah Magazine*

"An engrossing read."　　　　　*—Newsday*

"This memento mori is as much about the teeming, glad business of life as it is about grief—'the bright blessed day,' as the Louis Armstrong song puts it, as well as the dark sacred night."
　　　　　—The Washington Post

"Glass's prose is so lovely and filled with felicitous phrases and insights that when she orchestrates a family reunion, the reader is apt to just follow along like Kit, knowing the music is bound to enthrall."　　　　　*—The Dallas Morning News*

"The delight of reading Julia Glass turns out to be the connections we make with her generous characters, who become as endearing—and exasperating—as the people we love in real life."
　　　　　—The Miami Herald

"Wretched and wonderful—indeed, dark yet sacred."　*—BookPage*

"Glass explores the pain of family secrets, the importance of identity, and the ultimate meaning of family. . . . [A] lovely, highly readable, and thought-provoking novel."　　*—Booklist* (starred)

JULIA GLASS

And the Dark Sacred Night

Julia Glass is the author of *Three Junes*, winner of the 2002 National Book Award for Fiction; *The Whole World Over*; *I See You Everywhere*, winner of the 2009 Binghamton University John Gardner Book Award; and *The Widower's Tale*. Her essays have been widely anthologized. A recipient of fellowships from the National Endowment for the Arts, the New York Foundation for the Arts, and the Radcliffe Institute for Advanced Study, Glass also teaches fiction writing, most frequently at the Fine Arts Work Center in Provincetown. She lives with her family in Marblehead, Massachusetts.

And the Dark
Sacred Night

And the Dark Sacred Night

A Novel

JULIA GLASS

Anchor Books
A Division of Random House LLC
New York

FIRST ANCHOR BOOKS EDITION, JANUARY 2015

Copyright © 2014 by Julia Glass

The Library of Congress has cataloged the Pantheon edition as follows:
Glass, Julia.
And the dark sacred night / Julia Glass.
pages cm
1. Unemployed—Fiction.   2. Family secrets—Fiction.
3. Birth fathers—Fiction.   4. New England—Fiction.   5. Domestic fiction.
I. Title.
PS3607.l37A83 2014 813'.6—dc23 2013024331

Anchor Books Trade Paperback ISBN: 978-0-307-45611-3
eBook ISBN: 978-0-307-90863-6

Book design by M. Kristen Bearse

www.anchorbooks.com

Printed in the United States of America
10 9 8 7 6 5 4 3

For Elliot:
the brother I always wanted . . .
and found out I had all along

Every knot was once straight rope.
　　　　　　—*James Lapine,* Into the Woods

And the Dark
Sacred Night

S HE SAW HIM THROUGH THE TREES, and she almost turned around. In just eight days, she had come to believe that this wedge of shore, tumbled rock enclosed by thorny juniper and stunted saplings (but lit by the tilting sun at the western side of the lake) was her secret. Each afternoon, it became her refuge—just one brief measure, *a piacere*, of solitude—from another attenuated day of rehearse, practice, and practice even more; of master classes and Popper études, hour after hour of Saint-Saëns and Debussy; of walking over plush lawns, passing adults who spoke zealously, even angrily, in German and Russian; of waking and going to sleep in a room shared with three other girls.

Not that this life wasn't precisely, incandescently, what she had craved, dreamed about, most of all worked for. How funny that all this discipline and deprivation rewarded Daphne with the headiest freedom she had ever known: freedom, to begin with, from her mother's vigilance and her brother's condescension, from another summer mixing paints and copying keys in her father's hardware store.

During Afternoon Rest, some campers retreated to their rooms to write letters or take naps. When the rooms were too hot to stand, they spread beach towels under the estate's monumental trees—or on the sliver of sandy beach. Others loitered at Le Manoir, though nobody called it that. They called it HQ. There was a games lounge with a moth-eaten billiards table; you could play Monopoly, backgammon, chess. They took turns using the pay phones on the porch.

But Daphne came here: sometimes just to sit, sometimes read, more often to gaze at the water and let herself wonder at . . . well, at the *hereness* of here. To reassure herself that it was real. To be alone.

Except that today she wasn't.

Malachy, first flute, sat on her favorite rock facing the lake. She recognized him right away, because just that day, standing behind him in the lunch line, she happened to notice the distinctive swallowtail of his tame brown hair as it forked to either side of his narrow neck. (His close haircut seemed almost affected; most of the boys had mussed-up manes, Paul McCartney hair.) His posture, typical of flautists, was upright, attentive. He wore his T-shirts tucked into the belted waist of loose khaki shorts. And like his hair, his shirts were defiantly square: no slogans, tie-dyed sunbursts, silhouettes of shaggy rock stars, or sly allusions to other music camps. That day his T-shirt was orange.

"What, not practicing?" she said.

He did not jump, nor did he stand. Waiting till she stood beside him, he looked up and said, "If it isn't the swan herself, come to test the waters."

Daphne's swimsuit was a navy-blue one-piece chosen by her mother. She wore shorts as well, book and towel clasped against her chest, yet she blushed.

"You don't suppose," he said, "that Generalissima has spies in these woods? I've heard there's a flogging room in the cellar of HQ."

Daphne laughed.

"Not kidding," he said.

"Yes you are."

Malachy's prim expression broke. "Pretty martial around here, don't you think? And can you believe all the Iron Curtain accents?"

"What did you expect, the cast of *Captain Kangaroo*?"

This made him laugh. "Maybe *Hogan's Heroes*."

"You mean, we should dig a tunnel and escape?"

"We could steal those little mallets Dorian uses to play his glockenspiel." Malachy had swiveled to face her. He sat cross-legged, his calves pale and sparsely freckled, his bare feet long and bony.

He shaded his eyes. "Sit, or I'll go blind. And then I won't be able to see my music, and my brilliant symphonic career will flash before my irradiated eyeballs."

She unrolled her towel and sat, facing him. He had no book or other obvious diversion. Was he there to meet someone? What a perfect place for a private meeting.

"So are you aware," said Malachy, "that Rhonda would pay me a nice reward to drown you here and now?"

Daphne laughed nervously. She and Malachy played together in Chamber One; Rhonda was her counterpart, a cellist in Chamber Two. Openly and cheerfully competitive, she'd announced at their first dinner that anyone assigned the swan solo in the Saint-Saëns was clearly the director's pet. (Daphne might say the same of Malachy, chosen to play "Volière.")

"I just got lucky," said Daphne.

"No false modesty allowed," said Malachy. "They decided our parts based on our auditions. Nothing here happens by accident. You know that."

"I guess." She didn't like talking about the ranking they all deplored yet knew had to be a part of their lives forever if they wanted to succeed. "So are you from one of those musical families where everybody plays something different?"

He smirked. "Like the Jackson Five? There's a picture to savor. No, I'm it. The one who got whatever genetic mutation makes our subspecies behave the way we do. My brother and sister see me as the weirdo. The family fruitcake. Which is a huge relief to them. They get to be the normal ones."

"So maybe I've got it, too. The mutation. Mom plays piano, but Christmas carols. Hymns. She subs for the church organist. Actually, I'm not sure how I got into this place."

"Give it up, Swan. They've got their eye on you here. I saw our taskmistress *smile* yesterday in the middle of your solo. For about a tenth of a second. I didn't think she had those muscles in her cheeks." Natalya Skovoroda, the conductor of Chamber One, was Ukrainian, with a dense, porridgelike accent. Her face—a prime object, morning after morning, of Daphne's most devoted concentration—was as round and pale as a dinner plate, mesmerizingly smooth for someone who scowled so much. Beneath that scowl, Daphne and her fellow musicians had grown close to one another quickly, like a band of miscellaneous hostages.

Malachy leaned toward Daphne. "You have that cello stripped naked."

"Is that a compliment?" Because he sat almost directly behind her during morning rehearsal, she hardly ever saw his face. It was long and serious, his eyes a frosty blue that made him look all-seeing, older in a way that was spooky but cool. Across his nose—narrow like the rest of him—a scant dash of freckles stood out sharply, distinct as granules of pepper.

A speedboat careened raucously past, skimming the water, passengers shrieking as it bounced up and down. For a moment, they let it capture their attention.

Daphne started to stand up. "I should go wait for a phone. Haven't called home in a couple of days."

"No," he said. "You should stay and listen to one of my limericks."

"Limericks?"

"I'm working on a suite of limericks about our wardens."

Daphne shifted on her towel. "Well. Sure."

Malachy cleared his throat and sat up even straighter. He cocked his head at a dramatic angle toward the lake, as if posing for a portrait.

A Soviet chick named Nah-tail-ya
Said, "Eef you play flat, I veel flail ya,
But come to my room
Vare I'll bare my bazoom.
Maybe let you peek at holy grail-ya."

Blood rushed to Daphne's face. She felt both thrilled and appalled. He turned to her, widened his eyes. "Svahn? May vee haff your creeteek?"

She covered her mouth, trying to repress the spasms of laughter. "Oh my gosh, that is so . . . obscene!"

"Uh-oh. I've shocked you. See, I told you I'm a weirdo."

"Oh my *God*."

"Here, I'll give you something just a bit tamer. Appetizer to next week's celebrity recital." Again he struck his pose.

There once was a diva named Esme
With a lengthy and worldly résumé.
Listed way at the end
Was her tendency to bend
Quite far over and trill, "Yes you may."

"You are horrid!" Daphne cried. But she couldn't stop laughing.

Somebody to Love

I T IS THE TIME OF YEAR when Kit must rise in the dark, as if he were a farmer or a fisherman, someone whose livelihood depends on beating the dawn, convincing himself that what looks like night is actually morning. His only true occupation these days, however, is fatherhood; his only reason for getting up at this dismal hour is getting his children to school.

The morning after Halloween is always difficult, if predictably so. Oversugared, ill tempered, Will and Fanny wake more reluctantly than ever. Will is still wearing his Eli Manning getup, minus cleats and helmet. Fanny, who walked the streets as Cleopatra, now looks more tawdry than regal, eyes deepened and blurred by her mother's mascara.

Will insists on wearing the jersey to school. Kit, giving in, peels two flattened candies, fluorescent and gummy, from the hem.

At breakfast, Fanny announces that she has decided to become a chocolate-eating vegetarian.

"That's dumb. Vegetarians *eat* chocolate," her brother informs her.

"Like you'd know anything about it."

Sandra tells Fanny that her brother is right; she tells Will not to call his sister dumb. "What about vegans?" Fanny wants to know. Sandra asks if she knows any vegans; Fanny names a girl who, though homeschooled, attends her Saturday dance class. In private, Kit and Sandra refer to this girl's large, progressively minded family as the Naked Hemp Society. (All summer long, Fanny's fellow ballerina and her siblings are frequently glimpsed romping, without a stitch of clothing, through the sprinkler in their backyard.)

"They have babies. How do you raise babies on a diet like that?" says Kit, realizing too late that by joining the conversation he has merely increased the risk that Will and Fanny will miss the bus, sentencing him to a long wait in the drop-off line at their school, where no amount of intellectually skewed radio can ward off emasculation by the surrounding battalion of soccermobiles, their exhaust fumes colluding in a cloud bank that threatens to engulf his lowly antiquated Civic. The occasional Mini does nothing to assuage his gloom.

Sandra, clearing plates, declares that though she will support Fanny if she wants to follow the "usual vegetarian restrictions," veganism is another matter. While urging the twins toward brushing their teeth, she points out that vegans do not wear wool or leather, meaning that Fanny would have to give up her favorite purple sweater and the purse that her grandmother bought her at the crafts fair in Maine.

Kit gets them to the bus just in time, one child an aspiring quarterback, the other resembling a small punk musician the morning after a three-set gig. Please let that not be *her* aim in life, he thinks as he waves at Fanny through the passing window. Given the choice, he would prefer the crush of a murky, airless rock 'n' roll dive to that of a football stadium, but boys who like the tough sports—boys who are virtually nursed on that potion of hustle, slam, and grunt—they're the ones with the best chance in life. He believes this now, though with more resignation than zeal. Kit has even begun to admire the beefy dad who coaches Will's football team, lingering at pickup time to thank him for his efforts, laboring at small talk. Lame, he knows, but Will is the one whose passions should call the shots (so to speak), whose wants Kit should also want for him, no matter how far they seem from Kit's desires. Illogically and prematurely—and absurdly, considering his own predicament—Kit has begun to brood about what his children will "be" when they grow up.

Returning to the house, he notices that one of the jack-o'-lanterns by the front door was savaged by squirrels and that the leaves he has yet to clear from the lawn are membraned with frost. In the kitchen, Sandra idles at the sink, eating yogurt from a bowl, looking intently out at the yard.

"Should have cut back the butterfly bush before now. And that rose by the shed. Snow will break those canes—look how tall they've grown." She speaks with a tone of regret—rare for Sandra—and Kit knows she's worried because the peak season for her work is over; no one will be hankering after new bushes, new pathways, arbors, or flower beds for the next several months.

He waits a careful moment before saying, "Interesting—if Fanny really does give up meat."

"Not a bad thing," says Sandra, still focused on the garden. "Will's been brainwashed by the notion that athletes eat steak for breakfast. Something he read in a magazine at the dentist." She knocks loudly on the window. "Away from there, you fiends!" Squirrels: Kit knows without looking. "Maybe," she continues, "we should get a cat."

"Fanny would be thrilled. Though cats are meatatarians. Potential conflict of interest."

Sandra smiles at him. "Meatatarians. They certainly are."

Kit coined this term for members of an Inuit community they visited back in his grad-school days, a place where the body shape of everyone over twenty tended toward spherical—somehow, pleasingly so—and the oldest people had bronzed moonlike faces, cheeks taut and lustrous from all the animal oils and blubber they consumed. That was well before children, before the Jersey suburbs, before they could imagine a spectrum of tribulations ranging all the way from the vandalism of squirrels to the whims of professorial committees. Days of whales and ice floes, Sandra calls the time they were crazy in love. And they were. (But what couple, nowadays, does not have a history of crazy-in-love? Arranged marriages, shotgun marriages, marriages by mail order—all such unions persist, but among the people Kit knows, everyone chose freely after a long leisurely dance of passion and deliberation.)

Sandra sets her bowl in the sink and fills it with water. She turns to the counter, where yesterday's mail still lies in a pile: catalogs yet to be recycled; envelopes opened, the contents perused but unfiled—uncensored, Kit realizes as Sandra utters the words he's come to dread from her more than any others.

"What is this?"

Sometimes the stress changes (What is *this*? *What* is this? Or even, though this variation is sometimes a sign of amusement, What *is* this?), but whether she is looking at an overdue bill or a magazine whose subscription was supposed to be canceled or a package containing an unnecessary book he ordered, the person required to answer the question is almost always Kit, even when the answer is plain as frigging day.

This time she's addressing a sheet of paper she has just removed from the dignity of its envelope. Without looking over her shoulder, he knows exactly what it is: notification that he's being denied an adjunct position because his file is incomplete, the deadline past. There would be no letter, of course, if Kit did not know someone at the school in question, a school where he has no desire to teach, mostly because it lies across two rivers, so far out in Queens that it might as well be in Montauk.

"It wouldn't have worked. It was one course."

"Which could have led to more," says Sandra. "Would have, once they saw you in front of a class. You can't afford to be so picky. I don't need to tell you that, do I?"

He doesn't want to talk about what he, or they, can or can't afford.

"Didn't Ian write a letter to that guy he knew in Chicago?" she asks.

"I've asked enough of Ian already. And Chicago? Would you really, honestly consider moving to Chicago?"

She refolds the letter, puts it back in the envelope, and says conclusively, "Oh, Kit." Sandra doesn't waste energy on arguments she's had before. Yes, she might have reminded him, she *would* move to Chicago. Children change everything. Long stretches of unemployment, too.

She goes upstairs to dress. When she returns, she tells him she's going to the garden center to pick up salt hay, which goes on sale once Halloween scarecrows have served their purpose. Would he deal with the children's bathroom sink, which isn't draining properly? Would he transfer the clothes from the washer to the dryer when the cycle is done? Would he please rake?

He doesn't answer. The assumption (even his, if briefly) is that he will.

Kit does the autopilot things: puts dishes in the sink, turns off the coffee machine, turns off the lights they switched on two hours ago when they woke in the thick residue of night. (Soon, once the clocks change, the sun will rise before they do. That will restore at least a degree of normality to their lives.)

But when he hears the car recede from the driveway, he sits down on a stool at the counter facing the window to the yard. He watches a brawny-looking squirrel attempt to flatten its body just enough to shimmy under the door to the shed, where Sandra keeps the birdseed. It tries for a good long while before it gives up, thrashes its tail in scorn, and sprints up the nearest tree.

Theatrically, Kit shakes a finger toward the upper branches. "That's what you get for eating my daughter's pumpkin, fatso." His teaching voice. A voice he hasn't used in a classroom for ages.

The children's sink, he tells himself. The leaves. The clothes in the now-silent washer. He rises and moves toward these tasks, but he pauses at the kitchen table, where he sits again. There is no newspaper to reach for; he canceled their subscription to the *Times* a month ago. The only available text is Will's forgotten math homework, a sheet of penciled scrawl that feels, in Kit's hands, like a permission slip for despondency.

When he hears Sandra's car pull in, he knows he could make a dash for the second floor or the backyard—grab a plunger, seize a rake—but he doesn't. Sandra enters the kitchen and stops. When he looks at her, she is unbuttoning her long green sweater; her bushy peat-colored hair cleaves to the hood. The room is so quiet, Kit hears the prickle of static.

"Could you at least," she says quietly, "carry my bales of hay from the car to the shed? I'd be grateful for that."

"Sure thing," he says. Being outdoors in the chilly sun feels hopeful, wakes him up all over again. But when he goes in to take care of the laundry, Sandra's done it. Over the purr of the dryer, the intermittent clicking of a zipper against the metal drum, he hears her raking leaves.

He goes upstairs, finds the bottle of drain opener in the linen closet, takes it into the children's bathroom. He pours a slug down the drain and listens for the hiss of decomposing hair balls. Stepping into the hall, he glances through the door of the front bedroom. He happens to notice that the air conditioner is still in the window and, to his own surprise, feels the urge to take it out—as he should have done weeks ago.

He fetches the necessary screwdriver, along with a flattened cardboard carton from the recycling bin, something to protect Sandra's favorite kilim from the corroded seams of the metal box. He has no right to feel proud of himself, but he does, just a little. (How pathetic is this, congratulating himself for doing a task that Sandra did not ask him to do?)

Once he's wrestled it out of the window frame and onto the cardboard, once he's lowered the three storms in the wide bay (another unbidden chore, one to be repeated throughout the house), he goes into the hall and pulls the cord that summons the ladder of stairs leading into the attic—an act that once delighted the twins, who would shout "Presto!" every time they had occasion to witness this quaint open-sesame feature of their home. They are not allowed in the attic, where nails protrude, porcupinelike, from the underbelly of the roof. But when they were small, they would watch Kit ascend, eagerly awaiting his reappearance, as if he were Jack climbing down the beanstalk to bring his family a pouch of gold coins. (Oh, for a pouch of gold coins from on high.)

"Presto," he says to himself as the spring in the trapdoor yields to release the stairs. "Presto change-o. *Molto* change-o."

He carries the air conditioner braced against his torso, which is softening ever so gradually since he lost privileges at the college's weight room. He maneuvers it up by hefting it from one tread to the next. At the top, he will slide it straight back to its appointed place against a wall, cover it snugly with a thick plastic bag.

Kit has not climbed into the attic since midsummer, when Sandra was sure she heard wasps through the ceiling. They do not store many possessions up here, because this is the only house they've ever owned: furnished from scratch, as Sandra likes to say. She is a bargain huntress, a follower of haphazard handwritten yard-sale signs, an agile hoister of armchairs and tables onto the roof of her station wagon. A morris chair here, a ship's lantern there; a set of horn-handled steak knives, a tablecloth printed with lobsters, even—a triumphant find, a nod to their courtship—a small hooked rug depicting a polar bear beneath a crescent moon. One practical yet artful possession at a time, Sandra filled their house, each new object an unmeasured though rarely impetuous risk; nothing was saved if it didn't work.

Ten years ago, pregnant with the twins, she came home one day with a hexagonal deco mirror, its frame inlaid with ivory. "Front hall!" she exclaimed with fierce delight as Kit unwrapped it on the kitchen table.

"A find," he said, holding it at arm's length to reflect his upper half. "A little scary, though. Like the gravestone that reads AS I AM NOW, SO YOU SHALL BE. But maybe that's the idea. Take our vanity with a dose of humility. Mortality."

"What are you talking about?" Sandra's face entered the frame from behind his left shoulder. For an instant, it felt as if he were holding their wedding portrait. A portrait by Grant Wood.

"Earth to Sandra. It's shaped like a coffin." A coffin for a small child.

In the mirror, she stopped smiling. She stepped out of the picture.

"It's beautiful," said Kit. "I'm not superstitious, and neither are you."

"Speak for yourself. I don't know if that's true anymore about me." She spread her hands across the prow of her belly.

So away the mirror went, even though it could not be returned to the consignment shop where Sandra had found it, by accident, on her quest for a bureau to hold the babies' clothes.

In summer, the attic is unbearably hot, but on a cold bright day in the fall, it hoards a genial warmth from the sun pressing down on the shingles. The window in the rear gable presents a view of the small wood behind their yard. A patch of four acres became a park—pretentiously called the Green Sward—when the farm that once occupied this land was sold and divided into house lots in the heady 1960s. Reportedly, the park was a simple meadow back then, but since it lacked the amenities of modern recreation—no baseball diamond, no swings or climbing structures—few people used it, and random saplings took hold. (It is now a breeding ground for the villainous squirrels: a parallel development of sorts.)

Kit and Sandra's house, at the end of its cul-de-sac, stands out from the curving rows of ranch houses (some sullen and faded, others preened and sprawling with twenty-first-century additions). Though the developers razed the main farmhouse (reputedly riddled with termites), they spared a second, smaller dwelling. "Back in the day," the broker said, "this would have been a house for the help." She sounded confessional, even guilty, when she told them that it had been built in a modest, even miserly fashion for a house in 1910, "but by today's standards, it's a classic. Solid as you please—I mean, look at these floorboards!—and charming in the most totally understated way. Don't you think?"

She kept laying her palms on the walls and windowpanes, even stroking them, as if she were selling a horse or a gown, something far sexier than a tall but compact three-bedroom house with burlap-colored walls, gray carpeting, and appliances so heavily veneered in cooking oil and cigarette smoke that you couldn't tell if they'd once been yellow or pink—or might, if you bothered to scrub rather than discard them, turn out to be white.

"We can do it" was Sandra's way of telling Kit, back then, that they could do more than merely afford the house: they could make it perfect. Or (he knew this full well, and so did she) Sandra could.

The broker raved about the "possibilities" of the attic—"Pop out a couple of dormers, put a bathroom here, and you'd have the dream master suite!"—but Kit and Sandra knew they would never have the means to turn it into anything more than what it already was: an oversize, inconvenient closet; a rarely visited limbo between their sleeping selves and the sky.

So each time Kit goes up, he gives the place a brief inspection. He has never, even when Sandra thought she heard wasps, found anything amiss. The house has no fireplace and hence no chimney running through the open space, but a previous occupant built a cedar closet beside the front window. Casting a glance toward that end of the attic, Kit sees a long water stain stretching from the top of the closet all the way to a cardboard carton against its side.

The stain runs down the closet wall like the map of a rambling stream. Its source is a visible lesion at the apex of the roof where it meets the front wall of the house. The carton beside the closet, dry but warped, is labeled TAX RECEIPTS '03–'08. Kit pries it open. The stench of mold rises from the clotted mass of pulp within.

He opens the closet, which contains mostly woolen and down-filled coats not yet retrieved for the coming winter—and also, segregated to one side in a clear garment bag, the wedding dress worn by Sandra and, before her, by her mother. Fanny already has fantasies of wearing it herself.

The dress, like the box of receipts on the other side of the closet wall, is saturated with water. Its thick folds of satin, cocooned by its confinement, are no longer ivory but a mottled brown, as if the dress has been marinated in coffee.

"Christ," says Kit. "Fuck."

He hurries down to the second floor, as if there is still time to prevent this small calamity. He doesn't even bother to take the steep stairs backward, as he should, and he stumbles forward into the hallway, his momentum carrying him through the door to the master bedroom and almost onto the bed. Grasping one of the tall bedposts to regain his balance, he looks up at the ceiling near the bay window, the space beneath the cedar closet.

The paint is unblemished, blank as ignorance.

"Fuck," he says again. Because now he must decide whether—or shouldn't it be when?—to tell Sandra . . . who wondered, a year ago, if it wasn't time to think about a new roof. Back then, even Kit believed there was no way he wouldn't be working full-time again by now.

Out front he sees Sandra, wearing his work gloves, packing great cushions of leaves into the paper sacks she must have remembered to buy at the garden center. He imagines her, one morning or night in the next few weeks, lying in bed and pointing up at the stain that will inevitably, water having its meddlesome way, penetrate the ceiling. "What is that?" she will say. But she'll know. A leak in the roof they cannot afford to replace or even patch—unless one of them learns how to do it.

In the small room off the kitchen that Sandra and Kit share as an office, the phone rings. He starts toward it, but he stops before descending and sits on the top stair. He lets the answering machine take the message—a muffled female voice—and then he stands. Gently, he lifts the attic stairs until the spring takes over and the ceiling reclaims them. He watches the cord sway in an oval until it comes to a halt. "Presto," he whispers.

He will make lunch for both of them: grilled cheese, a salad. He will tell Sandra he missed a call that was almost certainly for her. Then he will go online and cruise the various sites that he knows will never yield real work.

A month ago, at the open house in the twins' school, he overheard two mothers discussing a fantasy site called Second Life, where people create alternate existences, just for fun, with dream jobs, dream spouses, dream houses or apartments furnished with a giddy selfishness, their spacious closets filled with clothing in dream sizes, sleek equipment for dream sports. In such a place, however virtual, Kit could write his dream book and teach his dream students (all tall, big-chested women who do not giggle or speak in a language as sparse as Morse code or pierce their tongues or text every minute they're not required to make eye contact with grown-ups). He could report to a dream department chair, drive his dream car (maybe one of those snotty little Coopers; why the hell not?), drink his dream beer in his dream bar (no giant screens showing Eli Manning at twice his already massive size).

Would Kit be allowed to keep his own, actual children, or could he do better than Fanny and Will? According to those mothers at the open house, the father of one of their children's classmates had left his wife for a woman he met online in that other, orchestrated life. Later, Kit wondered if maybe that man's first life, the one he actually lived, had begun to feel adulterous. Kit knows what it's like, in a different way, for life to turn itself inside out.

Downstairs, he finds that Sandra has driven off again. He could call her on her cell phone and ask where, but he won't. He makes himself a peanut-butter-and-honey sandwich. He drinks a glass of low-fat chocolate soy milk. When Sandra has still failed to return, he goes into the office—ignoring the blinking numeral on the answering machine, fending off the specter of Sandra's ruined wedding dress—and scans the *New York Times* online. He checks the five-day forecast. Very little chance of rain: one small gift.

The children return before their mother, entering the house cranky and hungry. Fanny is accusing Will of having stolen the Almond Joys from her trick-or-treat bag. She checked that morning. She knows there were two.

"I stole them," says Kit, "and promise to replace them." He's happy to be the brunt of a rage stirred by something as minor as a candy theft.

"Dad, you're just covering for him. Will is the one, I know it."

"Innocent before proven guilty!" says Will. "Unless you're from someplace like China."

Kit tells them it's time for a snack. He takes the last apple from the fruit bowl and goes to the fridge for the peanut butter.

"So tell him what you *are* guilty for, show him the paper," he hears Fanny say to her brother, sounding like a child whom Kit would gladly exchange for another, given that Second Life.

Will calls his sister an asshole. Kit scolds him for using such a word (which he's sure his son heard, uncensored by any adult, on the football field).

"Tell him," says Fanny. "You have to, you know."

When Kit delivers their plates to the table, Will hands him a note from his teacher. For the third time in two weeks, he has failed to turn in his math homework on time. Also, his subject binder is "unacceptably messy." Would a parent please e-mail or call to arrange a meeting so they can "coordinate a strategy" to improve Will's organizational skills? Before Kit can respond, Fanny flourishes a note of her own. This one informs him that she's been cast as a Sugar Plum Fairy in the school's *Nutcracker* ballet. Would a parent please sign the permission slip committing her to after-school rehearsals for the next six weeks?

Kit has no choice but to congratulate her, though it feels as if he's rewarding her for hitting her brother over the head. When, as quietly as he can manage, he tells Will that he and Will's mother will discuss consequences for his chronic failure to remember his homework, the boy breaks into wretched sobs and declares himself the "dummy of the family, the stupidest, stupidest one of all." When Kit reaches to comfort him, Will runs upstairs and slams his bedroom door.

"He'll get over it," Fanny says in a smug, pretend-adult voice.

"You need to be more sympathetic," says Kit. "Your brother has a harder time with schoolwork than you do. It doesn't mean he's less smart."

"Boys usually do. That's just the way it is."

Kit wants to be appalled by her attitude, but he knows she's aping something she heard from an adult—maybe even Sandra or himself when they thought they were out of earshot.

What, he sometimes wonders, if one child grows up to be a success and the other falls by the wayside? He once had stepbrothers, with whom he's lost touch, and he has a half sister who's little more than half his age, but he's always been, at heart, an only child. Learning that he would have two children at once was thrilling news—they'd been through so much to get Sandra pregnant—yet it filled him with panic to think of all the extra things he would have to learn along with becoming a father, things familiar to people who had real, life-long siblings.

Sandra walks in the door and stops. She can hear her son wailing from his room. "What's going on? You're both just standing here? Why are you letting him cry like that?"

Fanny, still eating her snack, says, "He's sad because he's in trouble." As she licks her fingers, Kit realizes that he did not ask the children to wash their hands, which reminds him that he never flushed their bathroom drain with water after filling it with whatever toxic potion eats through ossified toothpaste. He imagines a hole corroded in the pipe, which in turn recalls the leak in the roof. He says to Sandra, "There's just a lot going on right now." He picks up the note from Will's teacher to show her, but Sandra is sprinting upstairs. Kit sighs.

"Dad," says Fanny, "can I read you a new poem?"

Of course she can, he tells her. Fanny has fallen in love with memorizing poems. She begins by reading them aloud, several times, to her parents. Kit sits across the table from her and listens to the words of Edna St. Vincent Millay and then of A. E. Housman. The Staten Island ferry; English cherry trees in redolent bloom. So much exquisitely phrased nostalgia. For now, Kit assures himself, he can let go of the fear that she will become a punk rocker.

After reading the two poems twice—an encore for Sandra, who comes downstairs followed by a defeated-looking Will—Fanny turns automatically to pulling her homework from her (exceedingly well-organized) binder. Sandra sends her to work upstairs in her room while Will sits at the table, waiting for his parents to decide his fate. Kit, feeling as if his own crimes are yet to be revealed and judged, lets Sandra do the talking.

Is it the trick of dwindling sunlight that makes late afternoons in the fall pass more quickly than they do at other times of the year? Or is it the way in which school, still new, greedily consumes the prime of nearly every day? By the time both children are silently working and Sandra is in the office, it is dark. Kit turns on the radio to hear if a new war has begun or another oil tanker's split open; no hurricanes this late in the year, no significant elections in the offing, no movie stars falling off the wagon. He prepares to chop an onion, wash lettuce, grate cheese. He feels a measure of calm.

For dinner, Kit makes a risotto that includes the sun-dried tomatoes he found on sale at the supermarket. The children hate the taste and claim that it ruins the flavor of everything else, even the peas and the cheese.

"Too salty," says Fanny.

"Don't we get chicken or something *real* with this?" demands Will, restored to his formerly imperious self. "Is this because *she's* a vegetarian now?"

When Sandra offers to open a can of chicken-noodle soup, Kit shouts, "No! This is dinner, this! It's a perfectly fine dinner. Eat it or don't. Or just eat your salad and go to bed hungry. This is not a restaurant, in case nobody noticed."

His wife and children stare at him, as if he's turned into a werewolf.

All conversation is stifled. The children look at the risotto and pick at it, sulking. Fanny pushes the dried tomatoes into a neat pile on the side; Will eats almost none of it, leaving a plate of cratered soggy rice that Kit will later be tempted to scarf down, just for the brief comfort of starch, but will ultimately scrape into the garbage. When everyone has finished eating, Sandra orders the children to their rooms: time to read. "Will, you especially. And let's double-check your assignment book."

"I do the homework! I just forget it," he whines.

"Then you have to find a way to remember to remember." Before she follows him upstairs to get him settled and focused, Sandra tells Kit, with a decorum he finds almost creepy, that she liked the risotto very much and wishes the children had, too. She doesn't mention where she was for most of the afternoon, though her absence usually means she's with a client.

Kit checks the laundry; well, at least he can sort and fold the clothes Sandra put in the dryer. As he places them in the basket, he feels like a child hoping to gain favor with a parent—or like one of his mother's high-school students, working toward extra credit (except that his grades, if he were a student, would not be good to begin with). Upstairs, he hears Sandra cajoling Will toward a shower. Reluctant to join the bedtime fray, he leaves the basket of clean clothes on the dryer and wanders into the living room. It's dark and cold, the only light in the room cast by the ring of streetlights around the asphalt loop in front of the house.

He turns on a lamp, sits on the couch, and peers at the stack of books on the wooden chest that serves as a coffee table. When was the last time someone actually opened one of these books—weighty volumes on Italian gardens, trees and shrubs of the northeastern United States, the photographs of Julia Margaret Cameron? He frees the atlas from the bottom of the pile and opens it to North America.

He still does not fully understand what drew him to the art of people who live in so vastly different a world from his—though most people would say, *Well, of course that's it: the differentness. That's what you love.* Yet except when sunk in the pages of a book and looking at gallery walls, Kit has always thought of himself—not proudly—as clinging to the familiar. Canada and Mexico are the only other countries he's seen, and only at the urging of others. He had been studying the art of the Inuit, from Cape Barrow to Baffin Island, entirely in books and dusty anthropology museums when one of his professors challenged him to get off his curatorially lazy arse. With money he'd saved from art-handling jobs over college summers, Kit flew to Toronto, rented the cheapest car possible, and embarked on a journey along the coast of Hudson Bay to Umiujaq, Akuliviq, and Quaqtaq, places whose names he now touched in the atlas, one finger tracing an itinerary defined by a hard edge of water.

After poring over the map for a while, he realizes that the house has grown quiet. In the empty kitchen, he listens at the foot of the stairs: silence. Once in a while she goes to bed early after getting the children settled with books for their bedtime reading. But she almost always comes down to say good night. Kit is the family owl.

Never mind; just as well. He returns to the living room and pages through a book of Monet's Giverny paintings: old friends from way back. Neighbors' house lights go out, but the streetlights keep their vigil. He feels the artificial heat retreating from the room, the timer on the thermostat quelling the furnace.

The dishes in the sink, he tells himself.

He is most of the way through rinsing when, tired and careless, he drops a glass on the soapstone counter. It shatters with surprising drama, and when Kit turns off the water to clean up the glass, he hears Sandra get out of bed.

When he stands up from sweeping the shards into the dustpan, she is leaning against the kitchen table, facing him. "All day," she says, "I've been thinking hard."

If he were to say *About what?* he would sound like a fool. He sets the dustpan full of sharp fragments on the counter, rather than cross the kitchen to dump it in the garbage.

"You know I'm doing everything," she says, "not to go out of my mind these days. Not to lose it completely. Don't you?"

He nods.

"And I've started therapy again. I know we can't afford it, but I need . . ." She takes a deep breath, as if she's pulling in air after sobbing. "You know what, Kit? It's time for you to go. Go and find out."

"Find out what?" he says, but timidly.

"You know what I'm talking about."

Her arms are folded, her bare feet pressed arch to arch on the cold stone floor: Sandra as monolith, a deity robed in flannel, possessed of the truth. Behind her, from one end of the table to the other, lies a shadowy clutter of objects, Dutch still life rendered suburban: three geraniums in off-season bloom, a tumbled stack of schoolbooks, a wineglass bearing a ghostly halo of milk, two yellow pencils (one stippled with tooth marks), a pair of drugstore reading glasses tossed on an open magazine—no, a gardening catalog, a grid of green photos—and a wooden bowl holding a cantaloupe, a red pepper, an acorn squash, and three bananas past their prime.

Kit focuses on this random composition rather than on his wife's face. He does indeed know what she's talking about, and he has no viable protest to offer—unless he wishes to tell her once and for all that his mother's feelings come first, which would give any woman reason to send a husband packing. In a way, Kit has to wonder why they haven't arrived at this place long before now. Yet if he were to reach across the counter and switch on NPR (which Sandra believes he does by habit in order to shut the world out, not welcome it in) and if one of its many placid voices were to announce that the planet has just ceased spinning, he would believe it.

And supposing the earth stands still just now—if he does not move or speak—will she reconsider, modify her terms?

But what she says next is "I do mean *go*. Actually. Physically. And you know what, Kit? I need a break from this . . . inertia of yours, and I think you need to *move*, I mean pry yourself free from a place that's become so familiar you simply can't see it."

Is she telling him he has to pry himself free from *home?* Will she now say something about loving people by setting them free? (Of course not. Sandra is immune to bunk.)

This is it, then: the edge of the cliff. He will jump, or she will push. He's the guy in that overwrought painting by Friedrich, the framed poster that his least favorite colleague hung in the unisex bathroom between their offices, back when Kit had an actual office. That guy in black, gazing off into the roiling mists—though Kit doesn't share his gothic panache.

Look at the situation objectively, like an umpire, and Sandra is right: it's time. Kit has struck out. Fouled out, to complete the metaphor. Blown all the chances he's had—most of which he has probably failed to notice.

"Kit!" she insists after a moment, the way she might call out one of the children's names after saying it three or four times without getting a response.

"Sandra," he answers quietly. "I'm listening, Sandra." Even when he says it in fury or exasperation or disappointment, he loves the sound of his wife's name.

Her voice, reflecting his, softens—or maybe she's afraid the children might hear. "You can't keep telling me that you're struggling with it. Kit. Honey. You could have solved the meaning of *life* in all the time you've insisted that's what you're doing. You could have gone off and gotten a second Ph.D." *Could have finished your book,* she very kindly does not say.

She sighs. "The point is, you can't *not* do this. You have no idea what it's doing to you. What it's doing to *us*, this . . . blind spot of yours." Her gaze shifts down, to her feet—which must be awfully cold by now. Sandra is not a wearer of slippers. She does not, ordinarily, spend any time around the house in a state of undress. When she looks up again, she says, "Kit, I don't think you've come close to trying."

Now she pauses deliberately, even generously. He knows she's expecting him to argue, giving him time to make his case. Another silence widens the gulf between them—or no; the ice maker clatters forth a new batch of cubes, a sound that somehow embarrasses Kit, as if a bystander is chuckling at his plight. Shaking her head, Sandra says, "Look at you. It's like this doesn't even move you. Like you're paralyzed. You're breaking my heart, do you know that?"

She could have made her accusation, the part about paralysis, ten years ago—when he had just landed his first teaching job, when Will and Fanny were beginning to differentiate inside their mother's belly, when everything looked as rosy as Sandra's much-admired complexion—and even back then, Kit would have seen the truth in it.

One a.m. now, and here they stand in the kitchen, the pulsing heart of their small house, a room that Sandra painstakingly stripped of cheap varnishes, retiled, and repainted over several years during rare, brief intermissions from raising twins and (because raising twins cost more than they had expected, never mind conceiving and bearing the twins to begin with) landscaping other people's lives. It's a lovely kitchen now, a place guests are reluctant to abandon for the living room or the dining room (though Sandra has made those rooms lovely, too). It's a kitchen they might have to abandon, soon and permanently, if Kit can't find more than the fleeting adjunct position—*for God's sake, sweetheart, any real-live job,* as Sandra put it the last time she opened a credit card bill.

Does she mean any real-live job he could bluff, bribe, or cajole his way into? Kit is no more a bluffer or a cajoler than Sandra is a wearer of slippers. He's past forty, qualified to teach not software design or even auto repair but, and sometimes he wonders if this much is true anymore, the *history of art.* His mother warned him about the arts when he was in college, warned him from a position of knowing firsthand. (Never mind that she makes a decent living out of her affinity for music.) She had suggested to Kit that he major in economics, engineering; how about geology? As if he could suddenly flip a switch and become the kind of guy organically adept at numbers and charts. Did she think some specialized male hormone would suddenly suffuse his system at nineteen or twenty, flood his head with quantitative mojo?

The only light in the room glows from inside the hood of the stove. "Since you won't answer me," says Sandra, "I'll just barge right ahead and make a suggestion here. Go see Jasper. Go visit the only guy who ever came close to being your father. I know he knows. How could he not? And honestly, how could he possibly be expected to keep it a secret from *you*?"

"I could do that," says Kit, though he doesn't know if he can.

"At this point, you need to do just about anything."

"Well." He laughs. "Anything?"

"Don't be sarcastic."

Kit looks at the dustpan, the remnants of the busted glass. He thinks, for the hundredth time that day, of the leaky roof, the stained dress. He wishes he weren't the sort of man to see metaphors everywhere around him. He says, because he knows he has to say something, "So this is it then."

"Yes," Sandra says with an almost-cheerful decisiveness, "but you're the only one who can say what 'it' is."

"Let's not be coy. The big *it* is my paternity. My father. My *real* father. Right, Sandra?"

"Kit, I'm not the only one who wonders, am I?"

It isn't easy to be married to someone who knows the right answer to nearly every question, someone who appears irritatingly dominant to half the world at large yet who deserves to dominate, if only because she happens to be so damn smart. Even in the midst of a heated argument, she makes space for others to speak—you *can* get a word in edgewise with Sandra, as many words as you like—because, or this is how Kit sees it, she knows there is no debate she can't win, no matter how long it takes.

But that's his mother, too, isn't it? Almost his mother. Almost.

Kit's mother married for the first time when he was nine years old. Jasper Noonan was a widower with two sons, Rory and Kyle. Fifteen and thirteen, they were decent to Kit—they never complained, for instance, that while Kit got a room of his own, they had to move in together—but they were a club whose membership had closed at two. His mother's certainty that they would become Kit's "instant brothers," typical of the aggressively sunny outlook that seemed to steer her through life, soon proved a benign illusion. At least Kit's Lego castles and army formations, laid out like a red-and-white Bauhaus military encampment, deployed from bed to bureau, from closet to bookcase, remained as secure from destruction as they had in the apartment from which his mother moved them a month before the wedding.

Kit's mother had never been shy or defensive about what she called her "unweddedness." She might have chosen to settle them in a good liberal New England city—New Haven or Portland—where her single status wouldn't stand out so much, but she couldn't afford it. As Kit knew, this was the story: he had been born in the same hospital where his mother had been born, in Hanover, New Hampshire. For the first four years of his life, Kit and his mother had lived with his grandparents, in his mother's childhood room, while she earned a college degree in music education. Once she started teaching at the high school, giving cello lessons on the side, she and Kit moved into an apartment, close enough to Kit's grandmother that she could continue to help her daughter raise a son. After all, Nana had raised Kit's Uncle Andrew, who was (in her words) "successfully launched." Only in his twenties did Kit look back and catch the implication in his grandmother's metaphor, the image of his mother as a rocket that had fallen prematurely back to Earth.

Early on, Kit had come to believe that he and his mother were, much like those instant brothers, a closed society of two. She had introduced him to a couple of "special friends" before, but not until she became engaged to Jasper, not until Kit noticed the shimmer in her eyes whenever she looked from her sapphire ring to the face of her fiancé—a word she uttered with so much obvious pride—did it occur to him that maybe she had been looking to find a husband all along, all the way back to his birth. Kit's mother had been eighteen then. He didn't need math to figure this out. She was prone to saying things like "If I could grow up fast enough to be a solo mom at an age when most of my friends could barely drive a car, then I'll bet you can strike out on your own to nursery school at four. Just look in the mirror: is that boy ready to make his way in the world? What do you say, Kitten?"

That was the year he'd first asked about a father; every other child in his nursery school appeared to have one. Dads showed up in drawings, in stories told at circle time, and, in the flesh, just about whenever Miss Kannally invited another parent to take a turn in the "What Do Our Parents Do All Day?" spotlight. Kit's mother (who had played her cello, beautifully, in that spotlight) liked to recall that he had asked her not why he didn't have a father but simply whether he did. She'd seen this as a positive sign, proof that Kit did not feel deprived just because his friends had something he didn't. In fact, she would remind him, what had surely compelled him to ask was the persistent curiosity of a girl at whose house he frequently played. (Girls, she pointed out, her tone mildly accusing, were always the curious ones.)

"It does take two people to make a baby, one male and one female," Kit's mother told him—her hands, two vertical planes facing each other though not touching, as if she were measuring something, expressing a distance. "So yes, there was a second person who made you, along with me. But he was a boy, not a man, and boys can't really be fathers."

When Kit asked her why not, she said, "Because they aren't ready."

What about her? Was she a girl—or a woman? She told him that having Kit, becoming a mother, had made her a woman.

Then why hadn't it made the boy into a man?

"That's a good question," she'd told him. "But that boy, the one who could have grown up to be your father if he'd wanted, went away and made other choices on his way to becoming a man. He never became a father. And that's never made me sad. I've been very happy to have this family be just the two of us. We do perfectly fine, wouldn't you say?"

Kit had agreed with her. He hadn't missed the part about how that other person *could* have been his father *if he'd wanted,* but he also knew that this person had never met him. If he had, Kit told himself—if the boy unready to be a man had met the baby that turned his mother from a girl to a woman, maybe things would have been different. For a while, he found some comfort in this thought. At any minute that man might show up, recognize him, and step into the greatcoat of fatherhood. But then, along came Jasper Noonan.

Jasper adopted Kit. To Kit's relief, all this seemed to involve was signing papers, not sitting through promises to God and a big loud party like the one after the wedding. A quintessentially paternal figure, Jasper spoke, and loved to sing, in a deep sawtooth voice. He sang Johnny Cash, Woody Guthrie, Marvin Gaye, and sometimes, when he didn't know he wasn't alone, church songs rigged with words that had no place in church. He was so tall that he ducked when he came in the door of their apartment. His strides were twice as long as Kit's. A silver whoosh of hair, standing thick and high above his oblong ruddy face, made him look as if he had just stepped from a speeding convertible. Kit's grandfather had hair the same color. "Is he as old as Papa?" Kit asked.

His mother had laughed. "Oh no, sweetie. Jasper's what you call prematurely gray. It makes him look distinguished. Jasper's just the right age, young enough to be youthful, old enough to be wise. He's the right everything. Definitely the right guy for us."

Jasper owned a "mountain sports" shop. The goods he stocked would alternate, seasonally, between ski equipment and gear for camping and biking. All winter long he gave skiing lessons at the local mountain and then, whenever the snow finally melted for good, led day treks for hikers and cyclists. He lived off a dirt road at the foot of a nameless hill not quite large enough to rate as a mountain; locals simply knew it as the hogback. Jasper's house was a jumbled mosaic of windows, panes of different sizes and shapes framed by planks of wood so dark that the house looked as if it had survived a fire. By day, the windows mirrored the bluish pines that flanked three sides of the house and defied the wind that hurtled through the valley. At night, the house became a cubist shadow box, tossing triangles, squares, and trapezoids of gold across the meadow it faced. In winter, the longest season by far, fresh snow transformed the meadow into a vast tablet of paper, the lamps from the house casting on its surface a giant's geometry proof. There were no curtains because, said Jasper, there were no neighbors. "A house without shame," he'd say.

"A house he made *all by himself,*" Kit's mother bragged.

At first, for Kit, it was a startling, unnerving place to live. It contained but a few interior walls, which leaked light through the seams between their knotty boards. They gave just enough privacy to define three bedrooms, two bathrooms, a mudroom, and a few closets. Most of the ground floor was open. The entire structure appeared to be held up by several rustic flights of stairs, without banisters or risers, that shuttled to and from these various rooms, each on its own discrete level. From the doorway to Kit's room, the highest of all—the crow's nest, Jasper called it—he could look down and see, through the cat's cradle of stairways, clear to the bottom, where a stone chimney rose from a redbrick floor. At night, if he opened his door just a crack, he could peer down at his mother and Jasper as they sat together on the couch across from the fire: her head a smooth yellow orb, his a scribble of silver. Rarely did Kit hear their actual words, but he heard their laughter. How easily and often, for the first few years, Jasper made Kit's mother laugh.

Jasper had no living parents, no siblings. "I fly out front, point man, clear sky all around me," he'd say, spreading his long arms backward like the wings of a jet. When people who had never met him before asked what he did for a living, he described himself as a disciple of the elements, a scholar of snow. "Work that depends on outguessing the weather: never a dull moment there."

That first winter, Kit learned to ski. Jasper honored his anxiety, along with his self-consciousness at finding himself on the Junior Hill with children half his age: five-year-olds who rocketed past them again and again, greedy for speed. "They are fearless, and I mean that literally," said Jasper. "Okay for now, but Lord help those who still have no fear when they're old enough to drive a motor vehicle, move to the city—hell, to kiss a girl." He grinned at Kit. "That's right, boy; you had *better* blush."

Kit grew into skiing without ever welcoming that sense of risk. He would clutch his poles a little too tightly, squint so hard against the glare that later his eyes would ache and twitch. Each time he reached the bottom of a slope, he would expel all the breath he'd held in his lungs for the entire descent, one enormous visible cloud of relief. (In his twenties, having weathered a couple of implosive romantic entanglements, he realized that he enjoyed skiing the way you might enjoy the company of a charming but temperamental woman: careful never to let down your guard, to fall in love, because of what you stood to lose. You felt the true exhilaration of her company only after you said good night.)

But Kit understood that skiing was the best way to grow closer to Jasper, and it was also the best way simply to be with Rory and Kyle, whose lives beyond school were so crowded with friends, hockey, and homework that two or three days might pass in which Kit saw them only when he waited his turn for the bathroom before school. On winter weekends, the older boys taught skiing alongside their dad (their pupils the five-year-old rocketeers), but every so often Jasper would ask one or the other to "peel off" and take a few runs with Kit. Rory or Kyle would share the chair to the peak with Kit, then escort him down the cat track, the slow circuitous route around the backside of the mountain, with the best views and the least experienced skiers. Kindly if condescendingly, they tutored Kit, improving his turns, encouraging him to compress his posture, to build up speed for longer stretches. Of his two stepbrothers, Kit preferred the elder: the greater difference in age made his patronage less awkward. Rory treated him like a protégé, not a younger sibling. "Let go a little," he urged Kit repeatedly, never losing his patience. As Jasper would say in his pep talk to adults, "There comes a moment when you just let good old gravity have its way. And eureka. Know what, folks? That's the moment you become a skier."

Well, good old gravity had its way with Kit when the academic dean and his department head, Clifford, decided to turn him out with the wolves. Sometimes he wonders if finishing his book on schedule would really have made a difference. Kit wasn't good at committee work or forging ties with other institutions. (Cliff's personal coup had been a student internship program at the Whitney Museum.) The part of his job that Kit liked was the teaching. Would most of his students go on to be curators, art critics, arbiters of taste in the self-important cultural circles of New York, Los Angeles, or even Houston? Maybe one or two or three would live out such dreams.

But that wasn't the point of teaching what Kit taught, not as he saw it. The point was to give his students hours of indulgent yet rigorous thought about things made by people relentlessly withstanding the riptidal pull of moneygrubbing, disciplining children, growing old, worrying oneself sick about everything from traffic jams to terrorist attacks. Kit's closetlike office at the university had only one window: a narrow rectangle no bigger than a gunport, high in a corner, impossible to open without the aid of a step stool. So over his desk, centered above his computer screen, he'd tacked a large glossy photo of his favorite piece, the picture he imagined as the cover of his book: a Nunavik sculpture formed from a magnificent caribou antler. All along its sinuous, wavelike surface, the artist had coaxed from the bone a hunting expedition: five bundled men pushing forward through deep snow. How astutely the sculptor's tools had rendered not just their harpoons, tiny as toothpicks, but the bristled fur on their miniature hoods and even the gently collapsing boot prints defining their wake. Ahead of the men, out of sight around a turn in the antler itself, a family of seals crowded around a break in the ice, engaged in their own hunting expedition, oblivious to their imminent end.

A casual observer passing this piece in a museum might make the mistake of assuming that it was an artifact of "another time," some imaginary capsule of virginal disconnectedness from so-called civilization. Leave aside that such disengagement from time and workaday pressures had never existed; this object had been made fewer than twenty years ago, its maker someone who might well have hunted seals but who might also have car payments, a mortgage, concerns about his cholesterol level or a child's dismal grades in school or a wife's addiction to mail-order shopping. The deepest source of marvel, to Kit, was how the artist, in spending hour after hour after hour in the making of this object, was in fact *defying* gravity—a gravity far more cunning than the elemental force that pulls you swiftly down a mountain.

Except that this romantic vision of his—the artist at work despite the pressure of material demands, of ordinary economics—wasn't entirely accurate, either. Two decades ago, after falling for the austere quirkiness of the newest work he saw, Kit attended a lecture by an anthropologist who described how, in the 1940s, the Canadian government began relocating Inuit tribes to fabricated villages, forcing them to lead "modern lives": lives dependent on money, packaged foods, and compulsory education insidious to the knowledge that had always connected them to hunting, fishing, and the other ways they'd made a collective living. They found themselves disoriented, rootless, and poor.

They began to make and sell art as a new way of feeding their families. If tourists (or opportunistic curators) wanted to poke around their streets and towns as if perusing dioramas at the natural history museum, they would want to take home souvenirs. In this case, art answered the call of materialism rather than defying it. The sculptures of seal hunting took the place of seal hunting itself. Whales were rendered in polished soapstone rather than butchered on a vast sheet of ice. Not that these fabrications were any less worthy of the label "art" than altarpieces commissioned by fourteenth-century burghers in Antwerp.

So when, alone in his office, Kit opened the e-mail informing him he was to be cast out alone on the professional tundra (Ian, his one real friend in the department, had done him the brave courtesy of warning him), he had no window out of which to gaze in despair and dread. He had only this picture to stare at, this painfully apt story about the plans we make for the future and the sudden surprises sprung by fate.

Briefly, he had envied those tiny hunters their simple, attainable goal: find and kill those seals, get them home to be skinned and cooked. Feed your family, sell the pelts. Sharpen that spear and start all over again.

He remembered the title the artist had given this work: *On the Way Out.*

He stood up from his desk and circled the small room. If he were brave, he would leave right then, for good. But instead he sat down again to finish grading papers on contemporary American sculpture. At the top of the stack before him lay an essay titled "Richard Serra, Man of Steel." Oh to be a man of steel.

After Sandra goes upstairs, Kit sits at the kitchen table for another half hour. It's as if she is literally correct and he is indeed paralyzed. He does not read or straighten up the clutter. He does not drink, if only because Sandra will know that he did—she knows these things, instinctively—and will see it as further evidence of his withdrawal. (And she would be right.) He tries not to think about his options as narrowed by his wife. So he thinks about his children. Is it true that something as murky as his refusal to confront his mother about his father's identity could affect the lives of nine-year-olds who care more ardently about football and ballet, about fourth-grade fashion dictates, about Halloween costumes, than they care about the grandparents they do know? Forget about phantom relatives they never *will* know.

That's hardly the point, Sandra would say. The point is that Kit is missing something crucial, like a limb or one of his senses. "It's as if you don't know that you should be in mourning, because you don't know who's died," she said to him in the couples counselor's office. (They saw the woman for three sessions: all they could afford.) The counselor suggested that Kit find a support group for adult adoptees working through the difficult emotions of finding their biological parents; she promised to e-mail him a list of websites. Kit did not bother to remind her that this wasn't his situation. He has a "real" biological mother, and isn't she enough? Have people forgotten, in this needy, narcissistic world—to quote a song his mother used more than once in her favorite class—that you can't always get what you want? Maybe Fanny and Will should grow up understanding that less than everything is often enough, even plenty; that you can be a fully dimensional, well-grounded, largely content adult being without knowing everything you can possibly know about your "roots" (your pedigree back to the ark; your connection to early American history or British monarchs; your past lives, if past lives there are, and who's to say otherwise?).

Yet now this is also true: after so much endless talk about this mystery father, the shadow he casts across Kit's life has grown to the size of a monster storm cloud, a cumulonimbus. (Nor does it help that meanwhile the life over which that shadow looms appears to be shrinking.) At his angriest moments, Kit feels as if Sandra has willed into existence his own desire to find out.

Like any prudent and inadequately published academic, Kit applied for other jobs while going up for tenure. He was short-listed for a job in Tallahassee, and he had an offer in Las Vegas. He and Sandra tried to talk themselves into accepting such a move, though they knew they would pine for their respective coasts. While in Vegas for the interview, he was shocked by the alien quality of the air; was the imprecise yet omnipresent odor of photosynthesizing trees more essential to his well-being than he had ever known? (So much for falling in love with "differentness.") Back then, Sandra felt it was better to gamble that he would land something just as good in the education-besotted cosmos of New England and New York. If she wishes now that they had made a go of the desert, she would never say so.

———

It wasn't as if Kit grew up unaware that when you choose to teach, one way or another you are choosing a life of compromises. Once Kit and his mother moved in with Jasper, he saw a lot less of her during the school year—because when she had accepted Jasper's proposal, she had also accepted moving an hour away from the high school where she taught—and where, two evenings a week, she stayed late to direct the band and the chorus. Her new life was based in Vermont, but she commuted back to New Hampshire five days a week, as if constantly revisiting the past.

Jasper was the one to help Kit with his homework, to make sure he did his chores: setting the table; feeding Jasper's large, bearlike dogs (two huskies and a malamute); filling the bird feeders surrounding the house. Jasper was also the one to drive the three boys into the village, where Kit and Kyle attended the elementary school and Rory caught a bus to the regional high school. For the entire summer after the wedding, Kit had feared the change of schools—but Jasper's small-town fame bestowed a certain stature on Kit as well. After taking attendance for the first time, his fourth-grade teacher announced that the new pupil among them had the grand privilege of living with Ski Bum Number One. For an instant, the laughter was terrifying—until Kit saw the looks they'd turned in his direction. Nearly all his classmates skied; nearly all had been taught by Jasper, who, in the eyes of the town's youth, was kin to Daniel Boone.

On the three weeknights when Kit's mother made it back in time for dinner, she was worn out. The return route took her nearly due west the whole way, so in the warm months she had to drive straight toward the sinking sun. In the cold months, when it was dark by four-thirty, the final stretch of road, winding into the mountains, was often slick with ice. She was elated to reach home. She would hug Jasper and Kit before so much as setting down her satchel with its freight of rosters, songbooks, and stray recorders. Monday through Friday, Jasper made dinner. His meals were plainer than the ones Kit's mother made, and vegetables were scarce. "A man cooks as a man likes to eat," he declared when she wondered aloud whether all the broccoli, peas, and beans in the world had withered away. The next night, he served beans from a can.

It took Kit a few months to notice how much less frequently his mother played her cello, the instrument he thought of as her other child: mute, undemanding, assured of her devotion. The way she leaned in so attentively as she played, the way she nearly cradled its robust yet fragile body, looked so much like the physical affection she gave to Kit as well. He saw this, from an early age, as a source of comfort, not envy, a broader canvas for his mother's intent, expressive love.

When she and Kit had lived together, just the two of them, she often played after putting him to bed; three or four afternoons a week, she also gave lessons. Once, after he watched her play, alone, for some time, she told him that the cello was a way of bringing happiness into her life every single day. "Happiness doesn't come easily, just because you want or even deserve it," she said. "I don't think you're too young to know that. So you've got to find your own way to let that happiness in. Sometimes, when it threatens to get away from you, you have to reach out the window and pull it in, like capturing a bird."

On the occasions she did take out her cello, its solemn voice filled the lofty reaches of Jasper's house much the way it had filled Nana's church when she played for Uncle Andrew's wedding. He wondered what it meant that his mother did not play as much as she used to, but maybe this wasn't cause for worry. Maybe what it meant was that now happiness *did* come easily to her. Now she had Jasper to love, as well as Kit. She was busier; she was less lonely.

But by the time Kit entered high school—Rory gone off to college, Kyle soon to follow—he began to perceive his mother's life, nine months of the year, as an emotional balancing act between gratitude and fatigue. Her laughter seemed less spontaneous, more like a performance. Summer was her season of renewal, a season of long mornings savored in bed, meals and baths taken slowly, afternoons spent gardening and cooking. She baked elaborate pies and cakes until the heat of July suffused even the cellarlike shade at the base of the house, forcing her to abandon the oven.

Yet even then, on the long days she could fill as she wished, she rarely played her cello. And after the first two or three summers, when she had gladly followed Jasper on the group hikes he led through the mountains, she stayed home, reading in the hammock on the deck or playing cards with Kit when he returned from day camp.

She did play music on the stereo—not just the classical pieces she knew so well as a musician but jazz and rock and newer, stranger kinds of music: Kit would always remember the first time he heard reggae, when his mother brought home *The Harder They Come,* and the day she put on Talking Heads, an album one of her students let her borrow. Though she could listen to Bach or Debussy for hours on end, still as a stone, face peaceful, eyes closed, fingers flickering on her lap, the class she loved teaching best was The Modern Song, one of those electives so popular at her school that only the oldest, smartest students made the cut. Each year, for the fall semester, she chose ten songs for these students to interpret and compare; each year, the selection changed. In the months leading up to the school year, she would listen closely to a few dozen songs, over and over, to decide which ones were worthy. She chose classics, like Billie Holiday's "Strange Fruit," Joni Mitchell's "All I Want," Hendrix singing "All Along the Watchtower," Dylan singing "Tangled Up in Blue." Most of the time, she included something by the Beatles or the Stones, by the Dead or Pink Floyd, by Patsy Cline or Elvis; but she'd be sure to throw in songs or performers that no teenager in rural New England in the 1970s or '80s would know: Jack Teagarden, Johnny Hartman, Bob Wills, Tom Waits, Cole Porter singing obscure Cole Porter, Björk before she'd worn a stuffed swan to the Oscars.

Sometimes Kit's mother drove the household crazy; Jasper said it was like living with an amateur deejay: "Almost as bad as a one-legged dancer."

She let the rest of them make suggestions. One time, Jasper hauled a box from the back of a closet: it contained the records his first wife had banished from their mingled collection. Eagerly, Kit's mother flipped through them, pulling out a dozen or more. "God, I forgot about Jefferson Airplane," she said. "Who could forget about Jefferson Airplane?"

She slid the record from its brittle paper sleeve, tipped it toward the light to look for scratches, and placed it on the turntable. She leaned close, aiming the needle at a particular song; as soon as it began, she sang along with a passionate abandon that made the rest of them laugh. She altered her tone to emulate the lead singer, a woman with a voice as hard as flint, sparking with rage.

Kit had heard the song before, probably on the car radio, but he hadn't liked the aggression of the singer's voice. It was the voice of a woman trying to be a man. But as he listened to his mother sing the song, he heard more than bitterness and anger, or even the vehement longing to be loved; he heard a strange, almost vengeful threat in the words.

Don't you want somebody to love? . . . You better find somebody to love.

So what if you didn't? What then?

His mother raised the needle from the record when the song was over. She was out of breath from trying to match the emotion. "Grace Slick," she said.

Jasper's smile was sly. "I remember *that* summer, Lordy do I ever. I did not behave my age. Vivian almost left me."

Kit's mother returned his smile, but then she looked away. "I remember it, too." She pushed the box toward him and said, "You choose something. Something I wouldn't expect from you."

"Jefferson *Airplane,*" sighed Jasper, shaking his head, looking pleased.

"Something else," said Kit's mother. "Play me something else. From another summer. No more summer of *love*, please."

At three in the morning, he takes off his shoes and walks upstairs in his bare feet. Sandra's sleep, unlike her conviction, is fragile.

Without brushing his teeth or undressing, Kit slips into Will's room. Will, like his father, could sleep through a tornado. On the lower bunk, Kit shoves aside the stuffed animals gathered there in a sort of purgatory: too babyish to rank as sleeping companions yet spared, so far, from a box in the attic. A snowy owl, a parasaurolophus, Maurice Sendak's Max, SpongeBob, and half a dozen of the amoebalike creatures known as Uglydolls. How much more specific and peculiar are the stuffed animals modern children collect than the ones Kit owned (generic bear, generic horse, generic mouse). "Over, Uglies," whispers Kit as he pulls a fleece blanket out from under the menagerie, spilling several plush totemic beings onto the floor.

He lies down and pulls the blanket over his shoulder; still he shivers. To save money on heat (telling the children they are living greener lives), Kit sets the thermostat to sixty-five by day, fifty-five by night. In two and a half hours, the furnace will grumble back to life, begrudging them those ten degrees. Fanny complains that she can't dress "like a girl" in a house this cold.

It is entirely Kit's fault that he lost his job—or, really, failed to keep it. His students showered him with praise on their teacher evaluation forms (making him vulnerably smug), but he did not meet the deadline for his manuscript, the fattened-calf version of his Ph.D. thesis on the use of antlers in Inuit sculpture. He had collected permissions for all the illustrations—the art in the book would have been glorious—but he felt as if he'd said all he really wanted to say on this subject. What he wishes, in retrospect, is that he had taken what his colleagues (some condescendingly) would have called a "folkloric" approach, collecting stories along with the images. Bringing a culture's oral and visual customs together is all the academic rage. By nature, Kit scorns anything remotely fashionable—but to what end? Purity? Integrity? Look at him.

Kit met Sandra on what he now thinks of as his youthful "drive-about." He had stopped in Churchill to see the Eskimo Museum. The otherwise forlorn-looking town was crowded with tourists, yet the museum was virtually empty. For most of their time in the galleries, Kit and Sandra were the only visitors. Finally, they looked at each other and laughed. "Where is everybody?" said Kit.

"Bird-watching," said Sandra. "Or beluga watching."

"But not you."

"And obviously not you."

"I guess we don't give a hoot about the wildlife." It surprised him, how quickly he was flirting.

"Speak for yourself," she said. "I'm just taking a break from the sun."

Over dinner, Sandra told him that she was from Eugene. Friends of her parents who were moving had paid her to drive their second car to Montreal. She had decided to "see a bit of the way-up-north" on her trip home, a relay of bus and train. "What would ever bring me here again?"

Kit told her he would be driving even farther north. He had a list of artists' cooperatives, craft galleries, places to see the art he was writing about. They hadn't finished their main course when Sandra said, "Need a navigator? Hire me on spec. Free, I mean. You can boot me out anywhere."

"Deal," he said, then realized she wasn't joking. He also realized that she had mistaken him for a genuine adventurer. He wished it were true.

Tall and wide-boned, her limbs long, her feet large, Sandra made the rental car seem even more compact. Her knees nearly met the dashboard, and her voluminous hair clung to the fabric lining the roof. Within a week, they were sharing not just a car, and then a room, but a bed. How strange it felt to become lovers in a place where the sun shone through most of the night. "Do you think too long a period of nightlessness," mused Sandra, "could drive you insane, the way they say sleeplessness can?"

He objected, though of course he was flattered, when she called him "an academic Kerouac." He did like driving through the wilderness, through the brief, bright flowering of the tundra. The monotony of these spaces did not put him off, nor the hardscrabble roads, but when it came to striking up a conversation with the artists he met, asking them to talk about their work, he turned shy and formal. He learned little beyond what he needed to know.

Kit had no clue how to ask the startling question that would yield the unexpected revelation. He would never have made a good collector of folklore. He didn't have that investigative edge, what an anthro professor in college dubbed "intercultural moxie." Art history, he claimed, was where you belong if, despite a yearning for "the other," you lack the requisite shamelessness for probing into things like the sex lives of strangers. True to such predictions, that's where Kit ended up. Or thought he ended up.

If he'd had a "real" father from the very beginning, Kit sometimes wonders—though casually, not as part of some existential crisis—would he have been discouraged from pursuing such an impractical, vaguely effeminate path? Would such a path never even have occurred to him? Would he have hung out more often in locker rooms, developed ambitions for scoring goals, winning contests, closing deals, finding work where adrenaline mattered?

He doesn't even ski anymore. He could have blamed this on the job he landed—though blame of any kind was moot, back then, in the face of his good fortune. Emerging from the perpetual gridlock of too many smart young scholars, he landed a tenure-track position not just anywhere but at a college within view of the Manhattan skyline. From their house in suburban New Jersey, you can drive for a weekend to Vermont, even the baby mountains of the Berkshires; but life became too homebound once the twins arrived—even before the twins arrived, when he and Sandra found themselves tethered to the cycling of hormones, natural and then induced.

Not long ago, they would remind each other how lucky they were. Sandra still misses the latter-day hippies of Eugene, where her father owns a nursery. (Until a few years ago, when he finally understood how settled they were, he hoped that she would come home to run the business once he retired.) But she found a part-time job at a fancy nursery in Saddle River. After giving up on trying to get pregnant the "normal" way—she began to bracket the word with her fingers, in fond imitation of their fertility doctor—she decided that the logical, backhanded antidote to entering the IVF gauntlet was a return to nature, if only in the form of landscape architecture courses. By the time she was solidly pregnant, Sandra had a master's degree. "Talk about silver linings," she said. Kit had never seen her so happy.

After the amnio came back "normal" times two (the air quotes now a mimed stand-in for the word itself), after the morning sickness (blessedly severe) had passed, they felt giddy, shamelessly smug. They had no intention of trying for more children, no intention of moving, no intention of changing their jobs. They referred to their imminent babies as the two great unknowns. When these invisible creatures began to exert their eight limbs inside the chamber of her body, Sandra called them the two rambunctious unknowns. "Except I know this much: they're training for the frigging Tour de France." During the last half of her pregnancy, Sandra reveled in baby books; Kit's appointed challenge was to make giant strides on writing his own book, racing ahead of himself in an effort to outpace the time he would have to steal from his work life the minute he became a father.

The night of Kit's graduation from eighth grade, Jasper and his mother took him out for dinner at a starched-linen restaurant. No sooner had they placed their orders than Kit's mother proposed an idea she was certain would, as she put it so cheerfully, so succinctly, "simplify everyone's life." She leaned toward Kit. "Next fall, suppose I could rent a tiny apartment near my school? Near Nana and Papa. You could go to school with me, and we'd stay there four nights a week. Fridays, we'd come back here." Her smile swiveled toward Jasper.

Jasper gripped a roll in one hand, a knife in the other. He looked at Kit. "I'm not crazy about this notion your mother's cooked up, but I said she could try it out on you."

Kit said, "Well, no. No, I'd rather not."

His mother frowned. "Rather not? Why not?"

"Come on, Mom. I mean, I have this life here, at school. My friends. My team. Like everything is here." Kit ran cross-country. He liked hanging out with his teammates. He also liked a girl named Madeleine. At the big table in art class, they pulled their stools close, their bodies exchanging a mutual electricity. Madeleine admired the rickety cartoon strips he drew whenever the teacher let them indulge in "free drawing." Except for science, Kit liked just about everything related to school.

"But Kyle's leaving the high school here. It'll just be you," said his mother.

The regional high school would be a big change, he knew that, but this time he looked forward to the change. He and his local friends would travel together on the bus. They would still have one another.

"I vote no," he said. "Sorry, Mom."

She looked at Jasper. "Don't you see how this makes sense?"

"Things that make sense don't always make sense." Jasper shrugged. "I'd rather have you both here as much as possible, you know that. Weekends, I'm working more often than not."

"I can't be here as much as even I would like!" Kit's mother said, her sudden sorrow jarring.

Kit knew he was hurting her with his refusal, but she was the one who'd brought him to Jasper's remote house and sparsely populated town, and now that he liked it, the life she had chosen for both of them, he had no desire to trade it for yet another.

"Daphne, darling." Jasper cleared his throat. "I'd like to say you could quit your job, and I reckon that if I get ahead on the boys' college loans, then in two or three years—"

"Two or three years is all I have before Kit's gone, too! And Jasper, I like my job. You know that. What would I do all winter here, all day long—or should I say all day *short,* considering how soon the sun sets behind that mountain?"

"Bake your splendid pies?"

Kit saw, as soon as his stepfather made light of her disappointment, what a mistake he'd made.

"Five months of the year I take my *life* in my *hands* on that drive—the mud and the sleet and the snow. I do that to make this family possible! I want this family to *stay* possible." Was she threatening that somehow it wouldn't?

Jasper and Kit looked at their plates; for the first time, with a stunning surge of guilty pleasure, Kit was aware of a distinct alliance between them.

Jasper reached toward Kit's mother, laying a hand over hers. In the nicked, sun-spotted skin of his stepfather's massive hand as it engulfed his mother's fine fingers with their painted nails, Kit recognized something else: the acute difference between his mother and her husband—not just in age but in the habits and passions that had shaped those hands. "This family," said Jasper, "wouldn't be much of a family with you two gone half the time, now would it?"

Kit's mother shook her head, though it wasn't clear if she was disagreeing with Jasper or trying to shake free the delusion that her idea would "simplify" anything at all.

"I bet there's a plum job for you somewhere in this neck of the woods," suggested Jasper. "All your experience, that's got to be golden."

"All my experience is what gives me the seniority I have where I'm teaching now. *That* I am not giving up. And forget the problem of reciprocity between states. None of the schools here have the funding that makes my job what it is. You know that. The arts are diddly-squat out here in the boonies."

Kit stared at her, but she was focused entirely on Jasper. She seemed to have forgotten Kit was there, too. Was she saying that his art classes, his art teacher, his drawings and cartoons, were "diddly-squat"?

They ate in silence for a time, until the hostess—yet another past pupil of Ski Bum Number One—stopped by to ask Jasper what brand of hiking boots she should buy as a birthday present for her son.

And so, over the next three years, their routines remained the same, though now, at least through the cooler seasons, only the three of them shared the house—which made it seem larger, colder, and more a place of separate privacies than open-aired, communal living. Over these years, Kit discovered sex (with the admiring Madeleine) and the pleasure of being just the right degree of drunk. In Jasper's beat-up Rover, he learned to drive. He learned to paint with oils and sculpt wood. He made a few pieces of thick but useful furniture. In his sophomore year, he failed chemistry (retaking it over the following summer), but he won an award in a juried art show for students from all across the state. The following winter, he helped Jasper train their first team of sled dogs, to add another tourist attraction to the business. For good money, he helped a friend of Jasper's build a toolshed and a sugarhouse. Over these years, it was Jasper's approval and praise he sought, more than his mother's.

But Kit and Jasper weren't close, or not in any singular way. With Rory and Kyle weaned (as their father put it)—Kyle at the University of Vermont; Rory leaving college, midway through, to teach Outward Bound in Colorado—Jasper still cooked breakfasts and dinners, but in those margins of time when he and Kit were alone together, Kit's mother on the road or working late, he did not make much effort toward fatherly small talk. He kept a weather radio on at all times, sometimes stopping in the midst of an indoor task (caulking a drafty seam on one of the many windows; filling the firewood bin; unpacking groceries) to listen and comment on approaching changes.

"Sunny weekend, there you have it. Bonanza."

"That's not what the barometric pressure tells me, buster."

"Two feet of powder, Santa: that's right there at the top of my list."

Kit began to do his homework at the kitchen table rather than up in his chilly room. Jasper's periodic remarks on the changing climate became a companionable source of amusement to Kit, commercial breaks in the slog of history papers and cramming for Spanish or algebra tests.

His mother, meanwhile, seemed less amused by Jasper; by everything, really: by Garrison Keillor, by the dogs' antics in the first snowfall, by sharing songs on the stereo. She began to voice regrets: that she had never made Kit persist with piano beyond a single year's lessons, that they had never traveled outside the country together, that she had never searched out fellow musicians to form a local chamber group. On the occasional weekday afternoon, she'd call from work to say that she was staying overnight with a friend; she was just too tired to make the drive. When summer arrived, she did not appear to savor its freedoms. As if she were the budding adolescent, the restless, disdainful teenager, she seemed to prefer her own company to either Kit's or Jasper's. She hiked alone and read a great deal. She played her cello more often. When Kit told her how glad he was to hear her playing again, she gave him a skeptical, almost cautionary look. "Not a lot else to do around here, honey."

The second time Kit asked his mother about his phantom father was at the beginning of his senior year in high school, when she told him she would be moving out—and expected him to move with her.

He had stayed late on the second day of classes to attend the first cross-country meeting. It was nearly dinnertime, yet as he approached the house, he saw Jasper heading toward the trail that wound to the top of the hogback. When Kit asked where he was going, he said, "Gotta seize the last long days of summer, seize 'em by the throat." But he looked grim, as if someone had just seized him by the throat.

In the kitchen, Kit's mother waited at the table with two glasses of iced tea. She did not ask about his day. She said, almost before the screen slid into place behind him, "Kit, sweetie, I've made a big decision. I'm moving back. I can't make this long-distance thing work anymore. I'm worn to the bone. If it feels like I'm letting you down, I'm sorry." She spoke swiftly, breathlessly, clearly having rehearsed her lines, fearful of interruption.

Kit hung his pack on its hook and faced her across the table. "But you'll be back for weekends."

She looked at him for a moment, as if making up her mind just then. "No. I don't think so."

"Don't think so?"

"No. I won't be. We won't be."

"We?" Had Jasper agreed to move, too?

"Please sit," she said. Reluctantly, he obeyed her. Immediately, she reached across the table. When he kept his hands in his lap, she withdrew hers.

"Kitten," she said, "I shouldn't have let the decision wait so long. I know you've started your classes. But you and I are both moving back. You'll do fine. There's a place for you on the team, I've already made sure of that." She smiled proudly. "Your times are better than most of the best boys they already have."

"Moving *out,* you mean," he said. "Well, I'm not."

"Sweetie . . ."

"I'm not! I don't have to. I don't."

The look she leveled at Kit was half threat, half fear. "You're my son, and I'm your mother."

"And Jasper's my dad." Why wasn't he part of this conversation? Kit remembered the argument three years before, practically the very same one, at the restaurant. Jasper had made her see sense.

She looked at the stove, as if remembering a pie or a cake that might be done. Kit followed her gaze; the oven wasn't on. She said, "He's not your father as much as I'm your mother."

Kit felt his legs shaking. His voice shook, too, when he said, "Since when is it like some kind of quantitative thing? We're not talking math."

"It's not math," she said quietly. "It's . . . biology. You were born to me, not to Jasper."

"Did Jasper say I have to go?"

"Kit, you are almost an adult. But not yet. This decision is mine."

"Why not Jasper's, too? I'll bet Jasper doesn't want us to move."

"He doesn't. You're right. But this has to do with me." Hastily, she added, "And you. With us."

"I'm not talking more about it till he gets back," said Kit.

His mother regarded him as if he had slapped her, as if her pain were physical. Kit felt himself grow harder, not softer. He willed himself to stop shaking. "So if Jasper's not my father, then tell me who is. Tell me once and for all who is. Or who was. Or could have been. What*ever*."

She closed her eyes and stood. She took her empty glass to the sink. Without turning around, she said, "You're right. Let's wait for Jasper to return. You need time to absorb this. I should have made this decision a lot sooner. That's my fault. I understand your anger."

No, she didn't. Of course she didn't. Kit left the kitchen quickly. He took the stairs two at a time, all three flights leading to his room. He wished he were wearing boots, not sneakers, so his footsteps would sound vehemently through the echo chamber of the house, proxy to his protest. He lay on his bed, listening to his mother move pots and pans around, turn the water on and off, open and close the fridge. He heard the crinkling of foil, the percussive assault of a knife on a cutting board. She did not put music on, the way she normally would have.

When she called him to come down and eat, he ignored her. He heard her start to climb the stairs, hesitate, descend. He lay there, hungry, angry, determined to listen for one thing only: Jasper's return.

Jasper returned at nine; the numbers on Kit's alarm clock glowed in the dark. He rose and rushed out his door, down the many stairs, as if afraid that Jasper might go out again, this time for good.

His mother and stepfather stood in the kitchen, facing each other across the table. "I'm not moving," Kit said to Jasper. "Am I?" He refused to look at his mother.

"Oh, sweetie," she said. "I know how upset you are . . ."

"He's not the only one," said Jasper.

Kit's mother started to cry. "I have tried. God knows I have tried."

"Tried what?" said Jasper. "To have your dandy cake and eat it, too? None of us gets it easy, Daphne. Not me, not you. Not even good old Kit here."

"This isn't talk for him to hear."

"Why the heck ever not?" said Jasper. "He's no tender edelweiss. He's not your precious baby, not anymore, no ma'am." Jasper turned to the stove and ladled soup into a bowl. He set it on the table, loudly. He looked at Kit, his gaze stern. "That's for me. You want some, too?"

Kit nodded. "Thanks."

As Kit's mother stood to the side and watched, the boy and the older man sat down to share a late dinner. After a few spoonfuls of soup, Jasper looked up and said to her, "He stays. If he wants. Absolutely. Up to him is what I say. And I am—legally, by the way—his father. Guardian, what have you. And guard him I will, from this nonsense if nothing else."

This time, she was the one to leave the room abruptly, flee up the stairs. Later, from his crow's nest, Kit heard her crying. He could tell that she had retired to the empty room once shared by Rory and Kyle.

But she did move, the following Sunday. She hired one of her seniors to drive a small truck in tandem with her car; Kit recognized the boy from a band performance he and Jasper had watched the previous spring. Every morning before the move, Kit could see that she'd been crying the night before. But he said little to her, nothing to appease her or mislead her into thinking he would join in her betrayal of Jasper. That's how he saw it.

He said nothing of consequence to Jasper, either. The night after his mother drove off (her cello case propped in the front passenger space, the child who would never have refused to go, even if it had a voice of its own), Jasper made steaks on the grill. He said to Kit, "Next weekend, I'll drive you over to stay with her." He aimed a forbidding look at Kit. "You'll go every other weekend at the very least. If it means missing meets, dropping the team, that's what you'll do. That's the sacrifice you'll make for her, and you will not complain. I'm glad you're staying—I think it's best, no matter what your reasons—but you won't break her heart completely. Enough of that goin' on around here as it is."

That was the last time Kit heard Jasper say more than a sentence about his wife, who was already, though Kit didn't know it, filing for a divorce. There was so much he pieced together later: years later.

The following week, Kit dropped out of cross-country. By the third weekend he spent with his mother, he figured out her real reason for leaving (or her incentive): Bart, the principal at his mother's school, a guy who had shaken Jasper's hand dozens of times at all the concerts, plays, and graduations they attended with Kit's mother. That Christmas, after she invited Bart to come along to Nana and Papa's for the caroling and the eggnog, she announced to Kit, in the privacy of her old room, where coats were stacked high on the twin beds, that as soon as the divorce came through, she and Bart would be getting married. Nothing fancy, she assured him; just a civil ceremony (as if he could possibly care how big a party there'd be, what his mother would wear, what vows she would say in front of what higher power). And then she would move into Bart's house. "And that will be your new home, too, whenever you come back from college. Bart is very fond of you. Bart has the makings of a terrific dad."

Which he would be to Kit's half sister, June, who was born just after Kit's freshman year at Beloit. His mother was thirty-seven years old, a perfectly normal age, by the standards of her generation, at which to have a baby.

Soon after hearing that she was pregnant, after piecing together his mother's actions and what he could decipher of her emotions, he understood—as he had when she became engaged to Jasper ten years before—that this was something for which she had been hoping all along. Now, looking dispassionately at his mother's life, he can see how she must have spent most of her young adulthood trying to compensate in deliberate choices for the accident that produced Kit.

Each time Will turns in his sleep, Kit sees the mattress shift overhead, hears the slats creak faintly. In the past year, Fanny has surpassed her brother in height, but he's grown stockier. His body has begun to look distinctly male in its dialogue with the ground. On the soccer field, he plays low and fast; his feet, small for his age, are nimble.

Will is the age Kit was when his mother married Jasper. Twenty years in the future, Will may tell a serious girlfriend, *I was nine when my mother made my dad move out. She couldn't stand that he never found out who his real father was. She thought it would make him stronger.* (Or *She thought it would fix their marriage.*) Just as Kit had told his own comparable story to Sandra, and to a few girlfriends before her. It will be late one night, Will and the girl—the young woman—leaning shoulder to shoulder on a lumpy futon after a party (or, face it, in a tousled bed after sex). They will be adding beads and charms, even precious stones, to the complex chains of their respective autobiographies.

The childhood stories Kit has told about himself most often feature, among other milestones, the move after his mother's marriage to Jasper, the calm he discovered in running, his pride at learning how to train and then drive a pack of sled dogs (though he hasn't driven a sled in decades), and his shock, during his first year away at college, when he found out his mother would be having a baby.

There is also the story he tells if someone asks, *Why art history?*

Unusual for a guy, isn't it? Sometimes he suspects that what they mean is *Unusual for a guy who's not gay*.

Twice, before Jasper, Kit's grandparents gave his mother, as a birthday present, a weekend in New York City. Her birthday is in November, so both times she chose the weekend adjoining Veterans Day, allowing her time to travel by bus. The first time, Kit was four or five; this was first time his mother was away from him overnight—three nights at that. Nana let him eat foods his mother refused to buy: Cheetos, Froot Loops, Fresca, Devil Dogs. The conspiracy they shared (enhanced by the metabolic joy of so much sugar and salt) took the edge off his anxiety. Nana let him sleep in a cot next to the bed she shared with Papa.

The second time, when Kit was eight, his mother took him along. That Friday was cold: flurries mottled the windows of their bus as they traveled south through Massachusetts, arriving in New York after dark. Kit's first clear visual impression of the city was Port Authority, by far the largest enclosed space he had ever seen. A pigeon—indoors!—swooped back and forth over their heads as they made their way down several escalators and out toward the street.

The taxi with its black interior; the long vertiginous sweep of the avenue carrying them forward, straight as a ruler; the chain of traffic lights unreeling rhythmically, red to green to yellow again and again, as far ahead of them as Kit could see through the plastic partition behind the driver; the tall brick house that claimed to be a hotel, the flowery room at the top of three long flights of stairs: every bit of it was new. Like snapshots tucked in an album, these experiences are still in sharp focus when Kit calls them up.

His mother had tickets for two concerts and a musical play. One of the concerts was in a small theater, not much larger than the auditorium in Kit's school, but the other one took place in a hall higher than it was wide, nearly as vast as the bus station. They sat in seats so far up that to look down toward the distant stage, at first, made Kit feel as if they must inevitably fall. Surely they would be sucked into the vortex by the pull of all the bodies tiered beneath them. Leaning even slightly forward made him feel dizzy. But when the music from the orchestra rose, with astonishing clarity, it seemed to still the spectators all at once, to pin the audience firmly in place.

His mother's sense of enchantment was contagious. Just as the first instruments spoke up, Kit could feel her arm, against his, trembling. "This is Brahms," she whispered. "Beautiful, beautiful Brahms."

That night she wore a red dress Kit had never seen, with lipstick to match. She had twisted and pinned her hair tight against the back of her head. Kit had watched her do this in their hotel room, her arms bent unnaturally over her ears. She had sighed with exasperation as she did it. Now, each time he looked at her face, he was startled by her bright mouth and darker eyes, the jewels swinging from her shapely translucent ears.

At the intermission, she insisted they return all the way to the bottom. "Let's look at the people!" she urged. What a dense crowd it was, and what a din they made. Kit was too short to see much more than a shifting collision of jacketed and sequined torsos. His mother held his hand, but she didn't speak to him. She looked in every direction, as if she expected to meet someone. She did this at the end of the concert, too, when once again they joined the chattering perfumed wave of bodies flowing down the stairs.

She behaved the same way in the neighborhood where they were staying. Their hotel stood on a street of similar buildings, brick houses joined side to side, with tall windows and absurdly small front yards bordered by black iron fencing. Here, the trees stood higher than the buildings, sometimes touching above the narrow streets. On Saturday morning she announced, "Let's do some wandering, Kitten. This is such a perfect part of the city just to explore, just to see what we might see." It was sunny, noticeably warmer than it had been in New Hampshire, but Kit grew tired of zigzagging to and fro, without a clear destination. His mother looked constantly at street signs, as if to keep them oriented—yet they passed along the same row of shops three times.

Kit pretended his toes were cold and asked if they could go inside somewhere. They had eaten breakfast, but he was hungry again before noon. So they sat in the window of a tiny restaurant with dented tables and wooden benches, eating pastries and drinking cocoa. While Kit's mother reminisced about a field trip she had taken to New York City with her high-school orchestra ("We sang in a concert hall that I don't think exists anymore"), she looked past him out the window.

All of this Kit still remembers clearly, more than thirty years later, but what he remembers best is their visit to the Metropolitan Museum of Art.

"I say we head for Egypt," said his mother, once they had climbed the gargantuan stone staircase and entered yet another space made for giants. (Was it the quantity of air so many people required to breathe, was that why these places were so huge, bigger even than any of the churches Kit had seen in New Hampshire?)

"Here come the mummies," she said as she led him down a series of windowless halls. "I read that they have just about the world's most amazing collection of mummies. Outside Egypt, I guess."

Kit knew plenty about the pharaohs and the pyramids from social studies. He wasn't wild about any of it. It seemed as if all that remained of those people was everything to do with their death, not their lives. Now, in this extraordinary place that so obviously thrilled his mother, he was reluctant to hurt her feelings by saying that he didn't really want to look at mummies.

He asked her, "What else do they have?"

She stopped and looked down at him. At first he worried she was angry, that mummies were the only reason they had ridden the subway for so many stops, walked so many blocks, to come here. But she laughed.

"Kitten, what *don't* they have here!"

Was that a question she expected him to answer?

But then she said, "They have pictures and sculptures and jewelry and rooms full of furniture, and—wait, I almost forgot—they have suits of armor. Armor! Do you want to see armor? I think they even have armor for horses."

He didn't care for war much more than he cared for death, but he agreed to look at the armor. Armor for horses: that had a certain appeal. On the way to the armor, however, his mother became lost, and they found themselves in a room filled with brightly colored pictures of fields, rivers, flowers in vases, boats on the sea, people with faces of scarlet or blue or painted as a tumult of purple and orange. Kit slowed, arrested by the force of all that color. And here (unlike the halls of the mummies), sun was permitted to enter. Light soaked the room from a wall of windows, making the color even richer, even more mesmerizing.

Kit's mother let go of his hand. He walked from picture to picture, around the entire room, not missing a single one. She followed. For the first time, she didn't try to explain or tell a story about what he was seeing. Finally they stood, side by side, before a picture showing cyclones of paint in every conceivable shade of violet and green, with quavering slashes of blue and buttonlike blotches of red.

Kit was unsure whether he thought the picture was good—you couldn't call it pretty, and it didn't look terribly "real"—but he couldn't stop looking at the colors, at the way the paint stood out from the surface of the picture. The paint looked wet. Was the painter crazy in some way? Possibly a little blind, like Papa when he couldn't find his glasses?

"Mownay," his mother said.

Kit thought she must mean a particular way of using paint. He did not match the word *mownay* with the name of the painter on the label. He didn't ask his mother any questions; her world was music, not art. She seemed as surprised by the mownay as he was.

They never made it to the armor, but on the way back out, they passed through another room where Kit wanted to linger. Drums, masks, and clumsy-looking jewelry filled the room, but all this visual clutter was decidedly upstaged by the coarse-haired, bullet-breasted, bug-eyed, howling-mouthed figures lined up along one side of the gallery. Raised on white pedestals, they were made of old, decayed wood—split by long cracks, eaten away by insects. Some were missing limbs, fingers, noses. Some had large penises that jutted like boughs from a tree trunk. One had thick rusty nails for hair. They should have been ugly, if only for their complete lack of color—the opposite of the mownay pictures he'd liked so much—yet gathered together, each one standing in a column of light, they had a powerful collective personality, like a conference of warlocks. They reminded Kit of the dancers at a Christmas pageant he had gone to with his mother one year: the Mummery, it was called.

"They remind me of Christmas," he told her.

"Now that's an odd association," she said. "I'm glad your Nana's not around to hear that." But his mother seemed pleased with his reaction.

In the museum shop, she told him to pick out some postcards—not to send, she told him, but to keep as a reminder. "In your room, you can create your own museum. In miniature."

He did just that, and he would add to it whenever he had a chance to buy postcards of pictures and objects he liked. When they moved to Jasper's, he took down each one, meticulously peeling away the tape that held it to the wall. Up in the crow's nest, he reconstructed his gallery above his desk. He had thirty-five postcards then. By the time he left for college, he had close to three hundred.

After more than an hour of shivering among the Uglies and their cohorts, Kit rolls out of the bunk, careful not to strike his head on the frame supporting the upper mattress. He stands beside the bed for a moment, just to look at his son. Will is turned toward the wall, only a tangle of dark hair (Sandra's hair) visible above the quilt.

She thinks this is about you, he might say—and could say, without waking the boy, if he wanted. *And she's wrong,* he would like to say—and to believe.

Not finishing his book in time for his tenure review had nothing to do with not knowing the source of the genes carried on his Y chromosome. Even Sandra would concede that. But two full years of no secure employment (his book dead in the water, most of his academic friendships shriveled) have failed to produce enough motivation in Kit to spur him toward something else. And it's this—this inertia, as she called it—that Sandra feels certain is aggravated by the ancestral mystery. "To change direction, to go somewhere entirely new, maybe you need to know exactly where it is you came from in the first place. A secure foothold. Don't you think?" That's what Sandra said in the counselor's office. The counselor answered, "You phrased that so well," and asked Kit what he thought. "Sounds a little too pat," he braved. "But what do I know?" Would it have felt different if the counselor had been a man?

He wraps the fleece blanket around his shoulders and leaves Will's room. He stands in the hall and considers the three other doors, all slightly ajar but none beckoning: his daughter's room, the bathroom, the room where he should be sleeping beside Sandra. Briefly, he feels defiant: *I will not let you tell me how to live my life. I will not let you run the goddamn show.* He imagines entering their room and standing by the bed to make this statement. She will wake up instantly. She will have to accept what he says; she cannot evict him from his house.

But he goes downstairs.

In the dim kitchen, he mutters to the geranium plants, "Time for breakfast?" To the refrigerator, "Am I in the mood for Grape-Nuts? Toast? Yogurt?" He thinks of the cinnamon Pop-Tarts he and Jasper used to share, toasted and slathered in butter. Sandra, he's sure, has never bought Pop-Tarts.

The furnace startles him with an answer. It is time, if not for breakfast, at least for the heat to push its way through the pipes all over again.

He goes into the office, sits at the bulky outdated computer: one more thing that needs to be replaced. Without turning on the lamp, he wakes the monitor from its cryptic facsimile of slumber.

His in-box contains one new message: Ian, the only colleague with whom he's remained friendly, has chronic insomnia. The e-mail was sent at 3:12 a.m. It's short: *you up by any chance? staring at a stack of papers on public art in nyc. if this won't put me to sleep, what will?* After Kit packed up his office and left the college, it took Ian about a year to forget not to complain about work, to remember how lucky he is to have been anointed worthy of sticking around for good. Kit wishes he could put aside the envy; whatever his flaws, Ian is loyal.

He closes his e-mail and wanders across the lower screen to Safari, the same way a child might wander from one friend's house to the next when the first one isn't home. Besides, Google has an answer— a completely impartial answer—for everything. He types in *searching for my father*. The pinwheel spins, an elfin roulette. The first links are myheritage.com and mylife.com, followed by peoplefinderchat.com. Bleakly, Kit scans the screen and spots the query *I am trying to find my father but am not adopted. . . .* His heart lurches as he clicks on the link.

The questioner's tone and diction suggest someone young and helpless—and, he's not sure why, female. Or maybe it's the tearfulness that comes across. Her mother won't tell her a thing about her father, and his name is not on the birth certificate she found by snooping through her mother's files. Half a dozen indignantly supportive people have answered the query. How dare the mother withhold a part of her child's very identity! What country does the writer live in? Might there be a good excuse for the mother's secrecy? (Perhaps the dad is serving a long prison sentence for being a child molester.) Can she afford a private investigator?

Kit laughs quietly. He'd never thought of that option. He tries to picture a PI taking on this task—and doing what? Following Kit's mother everywhere, hiding behind bushes, driving several cars behind her as she shuttles about from teaching to rehearsals, from Trader Joe's to CVS? Or would he simply take her hostage for a few hours, throw her in a trunk and drive her to a desolate warehouse or storage pod, tie her to a chair, and scare the information from her? Kit derives a moment's perverse pleasure from this vision of his mother. So Sandra's right again: he *is* angry. But there is nothing like being out of work, out of civilized purpose, out of ego, he thinks, to make you feel a sweeping rage, as broad in its reach as a beam from a lighthouse.

He scrolls down and stops at a tiny photo, a video freeze-frame of a young boy next to a YouTube link; the expression on the boy's face is pleading. The video has actually been rated: five stars. As if it might be an Oscar contender.

"Jesus." Kit goes back to the search field and types in *waylaid dads*. At the head of the queue, Google offers him this nugget of farce:

The Kitchen Bitch Ponders: Waylaid *I seem to have been* **waylaid** *by events beyond my control, I must, must. . . . Oh the Ignominy of It All—This is a phrase* **Dad** *said a lot . . .*

Yes, indeed, the Ignominy of It All. The World Wide Web, almost telepathically, understands him perfectly. What human being, stuck in the labyrinth of mind and soul, could ever come up with *About 288,000 results* in 0.45 seconds?

Kit stares at the endless list of absurdities before him: *Waylaid in TEXAS, Waylaid by a waitress, Waylaid by the Flu Bug*. Heat emanates from the radiator against the wall beneath the desk, warming his feet, encouraging him in his flippant search for the paternal grail.

Soon after the twins were born, Kit pressed his mother for the third time; afterward, he knew it had been the last. She had driven down from New Hampshire to meet her grandchildren, to spend a week helping the new parents (one of them frantic, terrified, and doing his best to fake a sense of calm) cope with two babies at once. Before she arrived, Sandra had impressed on Kit how knowing the identity of his father would be essential to having a full picture of their children's medical history. "What if he had diabetes—or high blood pressure—or severe asthma? Conditions with early warning signs. Or think about preventive measures."

"Why would she know these things about the guy? That is so unlikely."

"Come on," said Sandra. "It's so obvious she knows more than you want to give her credit for."

"Obvious how? You've never even talked to her about this stuff."

Sandra regarded him with a tender pity. "Kit, anybody could tell from the way you describe her reactions in the past that she has strong feelings about this guy, or who he was to her. He wasn't some boy who picked her up in a bar."

"Sandra, she was seventeen. She wasn't hanging out in bars."

"I'm sorry. You know what I mean. But I'm sure that if it had been nothing more than a one-night stand, a blunder on an adolescent date, she would have confessed that to you by now—told you when *you* were an adolescent going on dates. And she grew up in this reasonably small town with upstanding parents. I mean, all the families knew all the other families, wouldn't you guess?"

Kit's brooding had led him down all these byways, a hundred times over. He thought of his grandfather, who owned a hardware store, and his grandmother, who, before having his uncle and then his mother, had taught in the local first grade. They hadn't rejected their pregnant daughter, thank heaven, but surely they'd have wanted to exact some kind of recompense, if not responsibility, from the "guy" Sandra referred to so casually. They hadn't been rich, and even if they had . . .

Now something almost insupportable occurred to Kit. What if his mother had been raped? Or seduced by some older man, a married man or a man simply passing through town on business—the textbook traveling salesman? What if his father hadn't been a "boy" at all? What if that allusion was the easiest excuse? He couldn't believe he'd never thought of these possibilities. To the extent that he had received a "facts of life" lesson from a relative, that relative had been Jasper—who gave him the brief speech, clearly canned, that he must have delivered twice already. *Respect girls etc. Resist urges etc. Exercise self-control etc.* But what if Jasper had been assigned this task not because he had done it before but because Kit's mother was traumatized when it came to teenage sex?

Sandra, ever vigilant, saw his expression. "What did I say?"

"It's not you. I'm just—overwhelmed. By this," he said, gesturing impatiently at the drifts of tiny clothes, tiny blankets, tiny nursery accessories littering every piece of furniture in sight. "Sorry."

"Nothing to be sorry about. Let's just be more direct with her, that's all."

"I'll talk to her. I promise. Let's not make her feel ganged up on."

"Two of us would hardly constitute a *gang*," said Sandra.

Kit conjured, then, the horrendous notion of a gang rape. Maybe, for the most ominous reasons, she didn't know who his father was. "Jesus," he whispered, and before Sandra could question this exclamation, William or Frances began to cry, setting off the other one, too. They tended to cry—to do everything, from eating to defecating—in tandem. They were so young then, barely a week, that Kit still had trouble telling them apart in an instant. They had yet to earn nicknames, to stop squinting at the brilliant, otherworldly light. They had only just shed the grisly knobs of tissue that remained of their umbilical cords, proof of their first dependency, on Sandra alone, on unimpeded access to her blood, her hormones, her oxygen; her body at work or rest, eating meals, taking showers, pruning trees, shoveling mulch, talking on the phone, reading books. Sandra had been their safe haven, their crib, their hometown, their entire civilization; now they were out on the wild frontier—of which Kit was the most prominent feature.

He waited until the third night of his mother's visit, by which time she had coaxed their lives into semiroutine. They sat at the kitchen table, finishing the bottle of wine opened at dinner. Kit held Frances; his mother held William. They were feeding the babies Sandra's milk while Sandra slept upstairs.

"Mom, that dinner was amazing. Sometimes I really miss your pies."

"Sandra's no slouch in the kitchen."

"No," said Kit. "But there are some things you make that always take me back. You know? Those summers you baked all the time: bread, muffins, two or three pies a week. Those blueberries from that field just up the hogback . . . remember how you used to take me picking, how you'd pretend to hear bears?"

They spoke in raised whispers, even though the babies were awake, sucking hard. The idea was that they would drink themselves to sleep, give Sandra two or three more hours of rest. When either twin so much as whimpered, Sandra would wake, no matter how exhausted she was.

"It's a treat to bake for you," said his mother, almost primly. "Bart has very high cholesterol. No more butter for him." She didn't want to talk about those summers, the years with Jasper.

It was now, thought Kit, or possibly never.

"Mom."

After a moment, during which he struggled with what exactly he should say, she looked up from William to Kit. "Sweetie?"

"Mom, I've never stopped wanting to know. About the other genetic half of me. I know he wasn't a father, not in the sense of a presence, but still . . ."

Kit's mother focused intently on the baby in her arms. With the expertise of a longtime parent, she used a corner of the cloth hanging over her shoulder to blot milk from William's cheek. "Water under the bridge, Kit. So far downstream by now. Out to sea. Can't you let it go?"

"Not now that I *am* a father."

"But you, Kit, are a true father."

"I don't understand why you have to keep this to yourself. I think you forget I'm no longer a child. If it's something difficult or traumatic, something you worry would shock me, I'm sorry, but I hate the possibility that maybe you were *hurt* and you keep it to yourself because . . . that maybe you were . . ."

"Of course I was hurt"—her voice rose to a hiss—"but only by my own foolishness. It's not something I discuss with *anyone*. Not Bart, not your sister. No one. I've said this before. You came along, and you were wonderful. I was never lonely again, once you arrived. I never looked back. That's what matters."

Kit felt absurdly young, but he couldn't surrender yet. *You can't take no for an answer this time,* Sandra had told him the night before.

Frances had fallen asleep in the crook of his left arm. Carefully, he withdrew the bottle and set it on the table. Frances's mouth continued to pulsate, fishlike; a small amount of milk seeped from her lips, soaking into Kit's shirt. He felt the intimate warmth of Sandra's milk against his belly. Though he continued to whisper, he enunciated carefully, to make it clear how serious he was. "Sandra wants to make sure we know everything we can about the babies' family histories. Medical . . . predispositions. Chronic illnesses. Things like that. We need to know these things, Mom. I agree with her."

Kit's mother had made a slope of her body against the back of the chair and laid her grandson along her slim torso, belly to belly. He looked boneless, his tiny body subsiding into hers. She stroked his back, pressing upward with the flat of her hand; Kit realized he had forgotten to coax the gas from his daughter. His mother's eyes were closed, her cheek against William's porcelain scalp.

"There's nothing alarming you'd need to know, I'm quite sure of that. I'd have told you if there was."

"But Mom, how do *you* know?"

She raised her face and looked at him, her beaded earrings capturing light from the candles that still burned at the opposite end of the table. "Because I do."

Both babies slept. Kit knew they should move the twins to their crib upstairs; Kit, too, needed whatever sleep he could bargain from theirs. So this was it: the same impasse all over again. He was trying to think of a new angle, to think like Sandra, who would have known how to maneuver out of this corner, when his mother said, "You should know that the man you're wondering about is dead. Even if I told you who he was, if it made the slightest difference, you couldn't search him out. You couldn't meet him." Her expression was miserly, not kind, and though she kept her voice low, her next words came out like a threat. "You need to leave it alone. Just believe me."

"He's dead?" Kit looked at her, and before he could think, he said, "God, Mom, I'm sorry, but that is the oldest line in the book. Do you expect me to believe that? Do you expect me to stop being curious even if it's true?"

Kit's mother pressed her lips together. She readjusted William in her arms, stood, and started toward the stairs.

"Mom?" Kit said fiercely, trying not to shout.

She turned around before she got to the staircase. "You do not get to know everything just because you *want* to know it. Did some 'counselor' give you this idea, tell you you're *entitled* to know? I am not impressed by this whole psychotherapy fad, this let-it-all-out philosophy that's got some kind of stranglehold on your generation. I am insulted that you're calling me a liar, but I understand. If that's what you choose to think, there's nothing much I can do about it, is there? But I *can* go to bed. You should, too."

Kit lay beside Sandra that night and did not get the precious sleep he craved. The twins slept for a rare stretch of four hours, during which he thought about his mother's angry speech. He realized, sadly, that when she mentioned Kit's "generation," she was talking about a broad population that, at one end, might have included *her*, Daphne Rose Browning Noonan McCoy, if she hadn't been forced to become older than she wanted to be—forced by Kit, even if he was blameless. He would bear whatever disappointment Sandra felt in his failure to "find out the truth." This quest, he thought, is over—if it ever really began.

Upstairs, the alarm clock bleats. Kit hears it cease quickly; Sandra is up. (Sandra does not believe in the snooze option.) She will shower and dress before waking each child, a kiss with a ten-minute warning. She will come downstairs to make coffee for Kit, tea for herself, and prepare whatever healthy breakfast she has already planned: halve grapefruits, measure oats, slice a loaf of whole-grain bread, stir farm-share honey into the Greek yogurt of which she is lately enamored.

Sandra's papers, divided into folders labeled with her clients' names, occupy a rack to the right of the computer. To the left, in a jumble that appears belligerent by comparison, lie sheaves and scraps of information exerting pressure on Kit's immediate future: a reminder from the dentist that it's time for a cleaning; a request for a recommendation from a student he taught three years ago (the young woman somewhere out west, ignorant of Kit's rudderless state of disemployment); the program from a poetry assembly where Fanny recited "Dover Beach" and three haiku by Basho (can they afford to send Fanny to a special after-school theater workshop?). Here, too, is a review clipped from the *Times*, praise for an exhibit of Tlingit drawings he wanted to see; it ended a month ago. Buried beneath these items, but not forgotten, are envelopes containing applications for two jobs at private high schools in the city. Sandra's idea. "You know," she remarked late one night, making this suggestion out of the blue, "I'll bet some of the precocious teenagers at those schools are every bit as articulate, and possibly more passionate about learning, than the—I mean, you've said so yourself—than the mostly average students you had at the college." Understatement of the century.

Right again, Sandra. Fucking right again.

Outside, the sky has lightened from cobalt blue to cinder-block gray, the default hue of an early November sky at 6:32 a.m.

Will (Kit can tell from the blunt tread on the stairs) is coming down first, before his mother. This is rare.

He comes straight into the study. "Dad," he scolds, "did you sleep in my room? There's like a huge mess on the floor."

"I needed guy company. SpongeBob and Max did the trick. But are you aware that the Uglies snore?"

Will gives him the *Dad you're like totally insane* scowl, a foretaste of adolescence.

"Go make sure your sister's up. Help your mother by setting the table."

"Can't do both at once, Dad."

"Exercise free choice," says Kit. "Prioritize."

Sandra's in the kitchen. The coffee grinder roars. He sits still for a moment, waiting to see if she'll come into the study, now that Will has returned upstairs. He hears cupboards opening and closing, the loose-change clatter of flatware being removed from the bin in the dishwasher.

He pulls up Google Maps, clicks on *Get directions*. Though he hasn't been to Jasper's house in more than a decade, he could find his way there by memory, but he wants to see the journey quantified in miles and times, as a series of dots connected, the zigzag of thoroughfares linking Kit's cookie-cutter cul-de-sac to that long dirt road. Perhaps the road has been paved by now; it pains Kit to think that some of the surrounding land might have been sold to developers, that the pine forest might be pocked with turf clearings and houses appointed to look like somebody's misguided notion of grand.

Will Kit actually drive down that road? Will Jasper have him? Is

Jasper healthy, still working, still skiing—still teaching? (Till now, he hadn't thought of their connection through teaching. Daphne, Jasper, Kit: all teachers.) By e-mail, a year ago—or, he cringes, possibly two—Kit had sent photos of the twins to Jasper. Jasper had thanked him, had said (hardly for the first time) that they would always be welcome; that it was high time those children learn to ski.

Sandra heads upstairs to tell those children it's time to get up for real, time to face the day: the fortifying meal, the gathering and packing of worksheets and books, the finding of hats and gloves; the catching of the school bus; and then, just an hour from now, the daily effort (for Will) and inspiration (for Fanny) of navigating school itself. Kit, as a small child, was more like Fanny: loved the lure of stories, basked in his teachers' approval, studied his times tables and spelling lists without much nagging. His heart goes out to Will, for whom the soccer ball and football are siren song and gospel alike.

Kit hears Sandra call the children's names. "Waffles, anyone? Banana waffles with yogurt?"

In stereo, small cries of pleasure. This is a treat. This is, and Kit knows it better than they do, a special morning. A distinctly different morning, that much at least. Mentally, he packs the suitcase he hasn't used since the last conference he attended. The suitcase will have gathered dust.

Now Sandra comes into the study. "Waffles?" What she means is *We have an agreement, but do we also have a truce?*

He thanks her. "But syrup for me, not yogurt."

"Have you seen the price of maple syrup?" she says, though her voice is cheerful. "There's jam."

She's looking over his shoulder at the computer screen. She says nothing, too smart (and kind, really) to let on that it looks like she's won.

"I need to tell you," he says, "that there's a leak in the roof. Up front."

He hears her sigh, but she doesn't tell him she told him so. "I can deal with that, call somebody. It's no reason to put this aside."

He continues to stare at the map on the screen. "So. What if I find out nothing?"

"You'll find out something."

A s they filed into their dedicated section, they laughed at one another and made faces. This was the season's opening concert; only at concerts were they required to dress up. The girls, as discreetly as they knew how, struggled in vain to make peace with their garter belts and scratchy nylons; the boys moved their necks to and fro like turkeys, agitated by the confines of collar and tie. Daphne had chosen the yellow minidress with the square neckline and the long bell-shaped sleeves, one of two bought just for this summer. Her mother said it matched Daphne's hair. Combed out loose, it felt almost like someone else's hair; for the very first evening among these new friends, she would not be playing her cello. Campers did not take the stage until later in the summer, when the first of their collaborative pieces would be, as Natalya put it, "enough ready to pass for art."

The camp's performance structure, its one extravagant nod to modernity, was quaintly known as the Silo. The stage, a perfect circle, protruded from a tall curved structure painted a classic barn red. Overhead, a web of steel cables and baffles fanned out above the near portion of the audience. Spectators with the expensive tickets sat in folding wooden chairs that were stored beneath the stage between concerts. Those farther back sat on blankets in the grass. The ground was more forgiving than the chairs, but the acoustics were inferior—and the bugs were merciless.

Daphne sat between Malachy and her roommate Mei Mei. The campers' chairs were close to the stage but off to one side, the sight lines less than ideal. They would be looking at the back of the pianist, the singer half-hidden in the curvature of the instrument. Esme McLaughlin, the season's opening act, was a Scottish soprano renowned not just for her exceptional range but for the covers of her record albums, on which she reclined in verdant Gaelic settings wearing scanty evening gowns and shamelessly expensive jewelry, not a musical prop in sight. Her pianist, a married man, was allegedly her lover.

As the campers gossiped and fussed, their anticipation kinetic, Daphne noticed that the adults seated in the center rows stared openly at them, smiling, as if they were an exhibit at a museum. Malachy waved to an older couple who called his name. "Too many people know my father," he explained. Of all the campers, some of whom came from as far away as Europe, Malachy was the only one from Vermont, his home less than two hours north. He made fun of his father, a successful lawyer, but Daphne could tell that his scorn was just a veneer.

Together, they read the program. "If this concert had a title," Malachy said, "it would be 'Dare Me to Sing It and I Will.' All she's missing is something from the Supremes." Esme would begin with two Negro spirituals and an Appalachian folk song, followed by a trio of Schubert lieder, a Handel cantata, and, to leave her audience longing for more at intermission, Cio-Cio-San's farewell aria from *Butterfly*.

She came onstage wearing a gown that looked as if it were made of gold leaf. The skirt billowed dramatically from a cinched waist—the colored spotlights flashing on its folds as she moved—but the strapless bodice was so tight that Daphne wondered how the singer's lungs could take in the air they required to produce such a powerful voice. Between each song, after the applause faded, the sound of crickets was urgent and vivid—yet every time Esme opened her mouth, Daphne's ears shut out everything else, even the piano.

At the intermission, as spectators rose to stretch out the kinks from an hour of sitting on their punishing chairs, she felt as if she couldn't move, as if she'd become, literally, "all ears."

Malachy stood. "I'd better go find those friends of my dad."

Mei Mei wandered off as well, so Daphne was alone, glad for a chance to collect her emotions. She looked up at the lighting cables and the night sky beyond, then back at the deserted stage. Only now did she notice the blue Oriental rug on which Esme had stood. The piano gleamed like a Cadillac waiting by a city curb to carry its privileged owner somewhere important.

It occurred to her that this was part of what they were being shown that summer: The Life. They were there to be drilled and tested, to learn that it could never be easy, and maybe to be noticed or even discovered, but they were also catching a flashy glimpse of the rewards for those who excelled. Daphne felt, for a moment, as if Esme were performing for them alone. The rich patrons with their city clothing, Esme's fellow "artists" with their bloated egos, the locals with their picnic baskets way at the back of the field: all these people were merely set dressing, like the blue carpet, the potted gardenia plants flanking the stage, and the champagne bar at which the wealthiest ticket holders were toasting one another and scanning the crowd for celebrities. Daphne spotted Natalya, their dour taskmistress, in a short hot-pink dress, talking to the camp's director, Antony Carpenter-Rhodes, and a handsome platinum-haired man in a plaid jacket. Natalya looked *giddy*; she was laughing, her magenta mouth wide open to the sky. She looked like a wax version of herself, a doll.

"You haven't budged. Esme put you in a coma?" Malachy was back, handing her a paper cup of water.

"Just taking it all in."

"Yeah, this is the night we get it that we're actually *here*. At this mind-blowing place with all these mind-blowing people. The fame! The glory! The girdles about to burst! Like, pinch me, man."

"Did you see Natalya?" asked Daphne.

"You mean her benevolent twin? Do not be fooled, Swan!"

He sat and opened his program. Side by side, they read the next round of songs they would hear.

The lights dimmed and swelled. Spectators reseated themselves. Throats cleared; shawls were adjusted; the shushers shushed. Antony Carpenter-Rhodes stood and beckoned the campers to stand as well. The rest of the audience applauded them politely, briefly. Daphne felt herself smiling inanely. Malachy murmured in her ear, "How does it feel to be among the chosen people?"

Their wooden chairs creaked awkwardly as they sat down.

The air grew swiftly chilly, and Daphne wished she had remembered a sweater. She leaned toward Malachy, who did not pull away. The stage lights bloomed. Once again, silence fell, though only to be broken by a collective sigh when Esme appeared wearing a different but equally revealing dress, this one a column of pleated gauze, pink infused with silver. She gave them hymns, arias, a ballad from *West Side Story,* Mozart, and Ravel. Through all of her nimble, radiant, flawless singing, Daphne became increasingly conscious of the heat she felt through Malachy's sleeve.

When Esme finished, the audience stood abruptly and roared. Flash-bulbs popped. One man stood on his chair and shouted *"Bellissima!"* at the top of his lungs. The singer bowed, blew kisses, applauded her accompanist. He was handsome, with cascading black hair and a beatnik goatee, but he was slight in build, and when he stood beside Esme, he looked like a page to her warrior princess. They held hands and bowed together. The applause did not fade. Then she spoke into his ear and, as he returned to his gleaming instrument, gestured that the audience should sit.

Like a roomful of children promised sweets by their teacher, the hundreds of spectators became instantly still and took their seats. Esme watched her pianist until he nodded. The piano began slowly, the notes sparse and halting; Esme's voice emerged with a sleepy languor. She sang, *"J'ai compris ta détresse, cher amoureux . . ."* In its first lines, the song sounded decorous; Esme's smile was coy.

Glancing down, Daphne saw that her left hand was only an inch from Malachy's right. She returned her attention to Esme. The song began to unfurl, its tones warming in response to the passion in its plea, like a dress being gradually unfastened. Esme's French was so pristine that Daphne could hear every word, could even translate most of the lyrics. *"Loin de nous la sagesse, plus de tristesse."* Far from us wisdom, farther still sadness.

Carefully, she allowed her hand to roll sideways until it rested against Malachy's, in the narrow cleft between their thighs. If she were a fool, he would snatch his hand away. But he didn't, and while his entire focus remained gravely on Esme—Daphne glanced side-ways for only an instant—his hand lay against hers for the remainder of the song.

I surrender to your wishes, sang Esme, leaning down toward the audi-ence so that her breasts, barely contained, must have been almost entirely visible to those in the front center rows. *Make me your mis-tress,* she beseeched the handsome man in the plaid jacket, who hap-pened to be in the front row. Then she leaned back, eyelids lowered in rapture, as the song rose to a rapid crescendo and plummeted to its blunt finale.

Esme bowed sharply the minute the pianist played the last note, and once again—more hysterically, if possible—the audience exploded. But this time the pair of performers, in single file, left the stage.

Daphne's and Malachy's hands had risen instantly to join the applause, but Daphne's held the memory of his (so much warmer than hers). What a relief that her virulent blush might honestly be seen as a response to the performance.

"What was that song?" she asked him when the applause had faded just enough to permit conversation. (It continued for a long time beyond Esme's exit. Daphne's palms were so sore that she had to press them against her hips.)

"I have no idea, but man, whatever it was, it ought to be a controlled substance. She'd better lock her door tonight." He laughed briefly. "Or not."

They filed out of their row and walked side by side on the pebbled path that led toward the girls' dorm and, farther along, the estate's old dairy barn, where the boys endured primitive sleeping quarters in scarcely converted stalls.

"I feel like my ears caught fire," he said. "Like I need to put them out."

"I know what you mean," she said.

They walked fast, arms folded tight against the chill, silent till they reached the fork in the path. *Now*, she thought. She didn't have to stretch far to kiss him on the cheek. When he reacted by stepping backward, off the path, she was mortified.

He looked at the ground, but when he raised his face, his expression was happy. He stepped close again and kissed her back, on the cheek, startling her almost as much as she had startled him. "That's her effect on us, isn't it?"

"I don't know," Daphne said. She willed herself to hold his gaze. Their arms were still folded against their bodies, both of them visibly shivering.

"Night, Swan," he said, almost a whisper.

2

Coming in From the Cold

THREE KNOCKOUT SURPRISES in one blessed week. Possibly a threat to Jasper's heart, and what's going on here anyway? Has he landed smack in a fairy tale? Not three gold coins or three dancing princesses, no such luck, but three tasks for the would-be hero. Two of them obvious in their solutions—but both hard, neither pleasant, one a point-blank tragedy. Difficult, unpleasant tasks are otherwise known as ordeals. Ergo: two ordeals followed by a wild card.

First, the biggest of the pines came down. Not like he hadn't been warned of its demise. Hadn't looked healthy for years, that tree, so maybe it succumbed to one of the dread blights spreading north with warmer winters. (Rumor has it the maples are already toast.) More likely it was crippled by the natural decay of aging; Jasper can sympathize there. It fell hard, shearing off the northeast corner of the house, gashing open his bedroom and the living room below. Came down, on a day of wicked wind, while he was at work, or no doubt his wonky ticker *would* have slammed to a halt. He dragged out the big ladder, yanked off dangling boards, and managed without breaking his neck, God knows how, to staple plastic tarps across the splintered wounds. Not good how touch-and-go his breathing felt after climbing that ladder a dozen times. Not good at all. Now he has to sleep through the flapping sounds, the sneaky drafts, the weird blue glow pulsing across his bed at dawn.

Second: no more Pluto.

Four days ago, the dog stopped eating; wouldn't touch the chicken cooked up with rice. Day before yesterday, he stayed inside the shelter, wouldn't get up. He was panting heavily, eyes oozing, ears limp. Without wasting the time to make an appointment, Jasper carried the dog to the truck, all hundred-some pounds of that almost-wolf, drove him over to the vet in Rutland, the space-age clinic with the fancy-pants diagnostic machines.

He got the one he thought of as the Baby Vet: how old was she, twelve? And those frosted nails, for God's sake; did she come to work expecting to type and file? But Jasper had no choice. He watched her listen to Pluto's heart, her brown ponytail twining around the cord of her stethoscope. She frowned. "Sounds like it's beating behind a pillow. He's what"—she glanced at the chart—"eleven? That's pretty old for a working husky, a dog this big." She stroked Pluto's thick fur and crooned, "Handsome guy, you are. Handsome, handsome guy. Sweet fella." When she scratched the magic zone behind his ears, he registered no pleasure. Miserable, that's all he was.

X-rays, as Jasper had feared. He sat in one of the hard plastic chairs, desperate for distraction, though fat chance he'd pick up magazines called *Cat Fancy* and *Bird Talk*—or pamphlets urging him to brush his dog's teeth, buy something called the "gentle leader" (Obama springs to mind), consider the wisdom of pet insurance. (Ha. Deductible, at least, the bills for a working dog's health.)

When Baby Vet called him into the room with the machine, she stood in front of a computer screen showing the image of Pluto's organs and bones. The tense set to her Bazooka-pink lips telecast the verdict. "Mr. Noonan, I am so sorry. Pluto's heart is encased in fluid. There's a massive growth in his thoracic cavity, and whether or not it's benign, I'm afraid . . ." She stood in front of the screen, arms crossed. Did she think him too dim to look at the evidence himself?

She read his expression. "Do you want to look?"

"I most certainly do."

She turned to the computer and, with one of her pearly nails, tapped at the alien shape, a cloud of smoke confounding the clean arc of Pluto's rib cage. No mistaking the abnormality, its fatal placement.

"There's a cardiologist up in Burlington," she said. "I could shoot these over to him. But honestly, Mr. Noonan?" She looked genuinely mournful, as if she knew what a hard worker, what a profoundly good dog, this animal was; as if she had the faintest notion what Jasper would be losing.

She told him Pluto would die on his own in the next day or two. He wasn't getting enough oxygen; he would suffocate. "I can be blunt with you, I'm guessing," she said. "Euthanasia is what I'd recommend."

"Ain't no youth to it," he muttered. "Oughta call it decrepitasia. Endatheroadasia."

Her anxious smile tipped toward a smirk. You could bet she had a boyfriend, this twiglet of a girl: likely another vet, a muscular type who doctored boutique dairy cows or pleasure horses, hobby livestock of the New Vermont. Once they had babies, she'd devote herself to them. The manicure told you as much.

"Do you want to be alone with Pluto?" she asked. "You can take your time. All the time you need to say good-bye."

As if he'd never been through this before, the holding of a sick or maimed dog, too big for a lap, down on the cold steel table. The one-two punch of the drugs. The brief spasms, the palsied letting go of every ligament and muscle. Followed by the absurd request about cremation, ashes to take home in a carton or urn like some morbid souvenir. Jasper mourned his dogs when they died, he damn well did, but put them on the mantel or bury them in a childlike cemetery plot? What sort of treacly pantomime was that?

"Prolong his pain?" Jasper shook his head. "Fetch the drugs." He resisted calling her *honey*. Loraina had set him straight on that. ("I can call *you* honey—or buster or boss—but not vice versa, hon," she had informed him the day she started work at the shop.)

Like his teammates, Pluto was a kennel dog, but this did not mean that a great deal of love talk and physical affection hadn't passed between Jasper and Pluto, all the way back to puppyhood: training, working, pulling cart or sled up and down the mountain trails, over logging roads, through meadows feathered with Queen Anne's lace one season, pillowed in snow the next. Pluto's death meant more than sorrow, however; more than reminders of Jasper's own less-than-reliable heart. It meant, to begin with, the cancellation of that bachelor party over Thanksgiving. Jasper needed two full teams, with two solid leaders, for a gig like that. He'd have to return the deposit, tell Jim he'd have one less job. Could he offer those rich boys an alternative? A midnight ski party? Unlikely. Unwise. The boys would want to be drunk as bees on thistle. That was the nature of these rituals. Some things change too fast to keep up with, others not a whit. Knuckleheaded customs tend to stay the same.

Third, and this surprise was of a different order, the wild card: Kit had sent him an e-mail. Jasper found it when he returned from putting an end to Pluto, after he greeted the other dogs in the kennel, promised them a run before dark, told them that no, Pluto hadn't returned from town, wouldn't be back. "He's gone, crew." Jasper would fry up a couple of steaks, spread the drippings on their kibble. Steak sandwiches for a week: to hell with doctor's orders.

Now, Jasper realized, he'd have to make the decision he'd been putting off: whether to roll up his sleeves for a new batch of pups or let the veterans dwindle into retirement—something Jasper himself should consider, according to Dr. Forster.

But Kit. Kit was asking to visit—alone, no wife, no kids. Just "taking a break." (Who was that boy fooling? He had to be getting the boot.) The professor professed he'd be happy to help Jasper around the house, make himself useful. He felt guilty they weren't in better touch, wanted to amend that.

Kit belonged, in Jasper's life, to what he wryly—not bitterly; never bitterly!—called the Daphne Decade. Of course it wasn't the boy's fault that his mother had fled, decamped, traded Jasper in for the younger model—leaving Jasper with the awkward dilemma of a mostly (but not entirely) grown child whom he had actually adopted, had partly (well, half attentively) raised through the bumpy years, the ones you dream will be easy when you're up all night with bawling babies, assuring yourself, *This is the hard part, it's all downhill from here.* Downhill via slalom and a few rocky drop-offs that first steal your breath, then slam you down hard. Avoid an avalanche, you're lucky.

Kit still carries Jasper's name, whatever that's worth. But the boy's mother did a job on Jasper. "A snow job and an ax job, neatly rolled into one," declared Rayburn, Jasper's best friend. Poor Kit was caught in the middle, and with the intuition of a Sensitive Guy (this was how Jasper thought of young Kit, not a scrap of disrespect intended), he clearly understood the damage his mother had wrought. Jasper remembers hearing about Daphne's pregnancy with his replacement, barely a blink after hearing about the marriage. Had to get the withering news from poor Kit, who was visiting Jasper for a week at the start of his first college summer, en route from Wisconsin to a job at a museum in Boston. Christ: the look on that boy's face as he explained how he'd argued with himself for the whole drive east whether Jasper needed to know. Of course he needed to know, Jasper told him; even thanked the boy. They left it there, end of pathetic story. (Or the end of it as shared by them.)

Through the rest of his time at college, Kit came back to visit Jasper for a week or so each summer, till he went off to graduate school in California. Then he wrote a postcard every so often, cards with pictures of Indian masks, beaded relics, totem poles, these things he claimed to be "studying." One day, Jasper opened a thick blue envelope, his name in a handwriting delicate and foreign, and pulled out a wedding invitation. Along with the card linking the name of the lucky, hopeful young woman with his, Kit had enclosed a note. He couldn't wait to introduce Jasper to Sandra, but Oregon was clearly a long, expensive haul from Vermont, so Kit would understand perfectly if Jasper chose to decline. And it would be a *small* wedding, the boy just happened to mention. . . .

Small. Code for awkward up the wazoo and beyond. How infuriating to find that Daphne could wound him all over again, even from a distance of years and miles, from across the border between their sister states. (In some ways, she'd never fully traversed that border, had she?)

So Jasper met Sandra a year later, when she and Kit were driving to Maine for a summer vacation. A pillar of a woman, handsome as a Greek statue, meet-your-eyes-every-minute direct in her manner. The sort who might wrestle your arm to the table, then help you kindly into the sling.

He answered Kit's e-mail right away, not wanting to dither or brood. *Sure thing. Come anytime. Do expect to work however. I'll take you up on that offer.*

The computer made its pneumatic Ricochet Rabbit noise: SENT!

He called the best man from the rich boy's wedding party, left a message with the numbers for two other dogsledding outfits, promised the refund on the deposit. He put off the call to Jim. He'd have to say he was sorry to withdraw the few hours of work that gig had meant (never mind the kind of tip those trust-fund boys were taught to leave): no chump change to Jim, a guy with three little kids and no prospects of a regular job. Last week he confided to Jasper that he was thinking of enlisting. God help these young people over at that jackassed conundrum of a war. Though maybe his son Kyle should have joined up years ago; maybe he'd have been shaken straight, scared clean once and for all. Or maybe not, maybe the reverse. You read about all the suicides of the boys returning home. Such a befuddling mess. On the way to the clinic with Pluto, Jasper had passed two young bucks in desert camo smoking outside a narrow saloon, the kind without windows, wedged between two sad-sack storefronts that might or might not have tenants. They looked unsteady, rootless, antsy for a brawl. Well, who was Jasper to judge from a glance—judge at all? Kyle was twice the age of those fellows, wasn't he? And maybe their futures were brighter than his.

So now Jasper stands between the rupture to his house and the toppled tree, contemplating both. Here's a mess that can be handled, has a tidy end in sight. For starters, hire Jim to cut up the tree. Jasper knows enough not to handle a chain saw at his age. Okay then, two problems solved as one. The call to Jim will be a good-news-with-the-bad.

But the repair of the house. Well, he thinks, let's hope that boy Kit (though he isn't in earshot of boyhood anymore, is he?) means what he says about pitching in. Despite all his soft bookish years in the Jersey suburbs, maybe he still knows how to handle a hammer and saw. As a teenager, he wasn't half bad.

Jasper looks at the sky, blue as blue can ever be. "You up yonder there. How about a fourth surprise? Snow the first week of November, that too much to ask? Just gimme ten inches."

Quoth the actress to the bishop, Rayburn would have quipped.

Christ does he ever miss Rayburn.

As Kit stands in the kitchen gushing on about how good it feels to be there, how Jasper hasn't changed a bit, how he's glad to see the dogs are still in the picture—and wow, so many!—Jasper tries to unite the jittery middle-aged man before him with his memories of the boy, even the younger man. Last time they faced each other, Kit was new to fatherhood, taking a detour en route to Christmas with his mother.

His hair is still Daphne's, still blond and curly though thinner, fogged with gray. He wears brittle wire-frame specs that do little to hide the fatigue laying claim to his eyes. But he's still fairly slim, maybe still in shape despite the scholar's life. (Probably frequents some gym in a strip mall.) Jasper notes the barely scuffed work boots, the good intentions (and lack of use) they show.

"Hungry?"

"Sure." Kit offers eagerly, "I'm up for cooking."

"No need. Chicken's in the oven."

"Chicken's great."

"Chicken and potatoes. Nothing out of the ordinary here. You remember."

"I always liked your meals."

"Short on green, that's why." Jasper puts away the few dishes in the rack by the sink. He doesn't bother with the dishwasher anymore, except when Rory comes with his kids in tow. In other words, once in a polka-dot moon.

"Take either bedroom. Big one's warmer, but maybe you want your old lair up top. Sheets in the bathroom closet."

"I know where everything is." Kit laughs. "Well, I used to."

"Unpack, have a shower. Water still takes its own blessed time getting hot. Dinner in half an hour, that good?"

"That's perfect." Kit lingers, his eyes moist behind the glint of his lenses, his hands seemingly trapped in the pockets of his jeans (urban issue, same as the boots). They hadn't hugged when Kit arrived; is he waiting for a gesture like that?

Jasper moves toward his former stepson and puts a hand on one of his shoulders. "Christopher, I'm glad to see you. Glad to have you here. I am. And I'll make good use of you, too. No idle warning."

"Bring it on." Kit looks grateful, anxious to please.

They smile stiffly at each other for a moment, then Kit pulls a phone from his pocket. "Just let everybody know I arrived."

Jasper points at the phone on the wall. "Best resort to prehistoric connections. Reception here's spotty at best. Outdoors if you're lucky. Give 'em my number as the way to reach you."

"Later's fine." Kit pulls his suitcase toward the stairs. Hard to tell, though it's fairly small, how long a "visit" the boy has in mind. Does it matter? Jasper may take pride in self-sufficiency, but he likes company, too. This arrangement will be better, far less difficult, than Kyle's random drop-ins. As if to grasp for an antidote, he glances at the latest picture of Rory's little clan, magnetized to the door of the fridge. Rory's golden wife, two golden girls, a boy like the proverbial cherry on the sundae, spoiled sweet by all concerned.

At least one child turned out happy, one out of two.

And Kit, does he count as maybe half a child to Jasper? And is he happy—maybe half happy? Jasper has a hunch he'll be finding out the answer to that one.

The upstairs shower goes on, the pipes thudding briefly in protest. Everything in the house is deferring to gravity in brand-new, unsettling ways. Awakened at dawn that morning, his room glowing a lurid blue as sunlight hit the tarp, Jasper noticed that one of the beams above him was starting to bow, ever so slightly. Too much heavy snow on the roof this winter and it will crack. But then again, too much snow—business thrives on that. Rory tells Jasper he's too old to keep up a house like this. Had the balls to suggest that Jasper move into one of those condos near the slopes, the units that look like ice-cube trays.

When Kit comes down, yet again he stands uncertainly beside the table, now set for two.

"See I forgot something," says Jasper. "You're hoping for a beer or an honest-to-God drink. I been warned off that habit by my doctors. And then I'm afraid there's Kyle. Here's a story you don't know, and I wish I didn't have to tell you. I'll give it to you in a thimble—or should I say a shot glass. Kyle's had what they call substance issues. Shows up here, time to time, no warning, so I don't run the risk of temptation any longer. He's been on the wagon a good few months—last report, at least—and once again I got my fingers crossed. But pick up a case or a bottle tomorrow, go right ahead. Don't mean to be inhospitable. 'Specially if I'm putting you to work."

"No!" says Kit. "I'm fine with coffee. Water. I mean, I'm sorry about Kyle. I had no idea. The last I knew, he was going back to finish college."

Jasper laughs. "That was a good dog or three ago. And he did, you know? He did finish. Even had a good job for a stretch. Real estate. Which is a no-brainer business in these parts. Or was until recently."

Kit looks miserable, poster child for foot-in-mouth.

"Sit," Jasper says. "I'll wait on you tonight. Tomorrow, your turn. Freezer's full of meat and make-believe ice cream. I am pathetically dependent on soybeans masquerading as pleasures I once took for granted."

Kit takes his place. "The chicken smells amazing."

"I'd be a dunderhead not to have that one down cold. How many chickens've I roasted by now?"

Roast chicken, baked potatoes with pretend butter, forget gravy (for which Jasper has found no decent consolation). Quarter heads of iceberg lettuce. Fat-free dressing with Paul Newman's mug on the label, its texture disturbingly akin to mucus.

"Tell me about Rory," says Kit. "Where's Rory these days?"

Jasper tells the easy story about his older son. The only hard part is that he chose to stay out west after meeting Kim at that sports-gear company in Boulder. In a previous era, he'd be the son to take over his father's business. In the current era, he has the once-you've-skied-out-west-no-turning-back excuse not to do so. (Not like Kim has family there; she's from Minnesota.) Easy to see, when Rory brings the family out, that Kim and the oldest girl are mildly bored with even the double-diamond runs on the mountains hereabouts. Rather than condescend to these lesser slopes, they take to cross-country, tolerating its tamer pleasures. "Sort of like," he tells Kit, "if you can't have the very best steak, you'll take the meat loaf. When I'm feeling sorry for myself, I try to figure out what I might've done different. As if it's personal, his making a life so far away."

"I always thought you were a great dad," says Kit.

"I was around the place some. That's nine-tenths of it, I think. Being present when needed." He sighs. "It's how the planet spins these days. Families splinter apart and spread. Bounce around like beads of mercury. Probably good for the master gene pool, in the scheme of things. Hybrid vigor."

Kit asks about the business. Jasper tells him about moving the shop from the village to the slope, his bargain with the particular devil who came north from Atlanta to buy up a mountain or two. "They're always getting us back for that war. One day I expect to find a Confederate flag flying from the lodge."

Kit nods and laughs. "Oh, I had a colleague like that from Charleston. He hummed while grading papers. 'Swanee River,' I am not kidding."

Jasper finds himself gratified to describe to a sympathetic outsider the ups and downs of recent winters, the influx of yoga-minded folks who show up in slinky outfits to commune with the "spirit of place" or restore their chakras.

"First time I heard that word, I took it to be the national currency of Tibet," says Jasper. "Frankly, I don't lead too many hiking trips these days. Today's small talk is a foreign language to me. Hired some Bennington grads who riff that woowoo jazz like Miles Davis. I still do the sledding runs, though. The day I stop working the dogs is a sorry day indeed." He thinks briefly, mournfully, of Pluto. The other dogs clearly miss him. Against common sense, Jasper could swear they regard him with a suspicious, quizzical look every time he goes out to the kennel now. *Where'd you hide our leader?*

Maybe he should breed Trixie the next time she comes in heat. If the litter's a good size, he can make a couple thousand selling the extra pups as pets.

Between them, they finish off the chicken and the potatoes; normally, Jasper gets two meals from one. Kit offers to wash up. Jasper goes into the living room and turns on the TV. When Kit joins him, he's looking at the forecast, searching the televised map for dandruff, a cloud of graphic snowflakes. Lucky stiffs, out there in northern Idaho.

"Where's your weather radio?" asks Kit.

"Now that's *Flintstones* technology. Please! These days I have a 'snow alert' on my computer. When there's even a whiff of snow in the forecast, it makes a goofy twinkling sound, what the computer folks imagine a shattering icicle sounds like. Or a snow fairy spreading her pixie dust. Gives me a start every time. Like something delicate fell off a shelf." He gestures around the room, at its few shelves of dusty objects: Rory's and Kyle's ski trophies, a Coleman lantern, a few paperback mysteries. "See anything delicate round here?"

"Other than me?" says Kit.

They laugh.

"We'll just see about that, won't we?" Jasper clicks through the channels. "I think that detective woman's on now. The daughter of the actress beheaded by a truck. Jayne Mansfield. Why do I remember her name quicker than the names of my grandkids?"

"Memory's mysterious that way, isn't it?"

"More like fickle. Devious." Jasper thinks of Rayburn, which hurts worse than thinking of Pluto. Sometimes he forgets that Rayburn isn't dead, but pretty soon he may be worse than dead: alive but totally absent. Not yet, however, and Jasper is overdue to pay his friend a proper visit.

They watch the beginning of the show, the discovery of a corpse under a bush in a city park. You have to give this show your full attention from the start or you are lost. Jasper wonders when, and how, he will ask why the boy is really here. He has a feeling Kit's purpose is thwarted by something. *Delicate,* he called himself a moment ago; thinks it's something for which he needs to feel apologetic. Ah, set the boy right, thinks Jasper, but now here's that dame detective with the perpetually alarmed expression on her face, mouth set sour and slightly agape, as if no joke will ever make her laugh again. Looks like she just took a slug of vinegar. Honestly now, who finds that appealing? But then there's the way she unholsters and flashes that gun whenever she senses danger. And how about the tight blouse? Definitely appealing, that.

The next day is sunny, good for the too-many tasks at the house if not the onset of another ski season in central Vermont. Jim's begun his deafening dissection of the tree, Kit's prying broken boards off the corner of the house. Jasper sets them up with a thermos of coffee, a box of doughnuts. When Jim opens the box, Kit looks at the doughnuts as if they are raw chicken livers.

"What, you jonesin' for colored jimmies?" says Jasper.

"I haven't had doughnuts in ages."

"Forbidden food? Listen up. Stick around here, you better lose the wife on the shoulder. I got my doctor spying on my diet from afar, and that is bad enough."

Jim laughs. "Not so easy as you think, Jazzman. You've been free too long to remember what it's like."

"Boy, that wife of yours keeps you out of trouble and *alive.*"

Ten years back, when Jim was in high school, he worked summers clearing trails on the mountain for Jasper. He talked about going to college, ambitious for the son of a short-order cook and a drugstore salesclerk. Then, senior year, he got Debbie pregnant. But Debbie's a good girl, not a tramp. Jasper thinks she keeps Jim straight; maybe he'd never have stuck out college in the first place. For a couple years, he had a full-time job on maintenance at the slope, but then came the layoffs.

Satisfied that the young men know what they're doing, speaking the same language (more or less), Jasper drives to the shop. Time to inventory everything, shift the balance of merchandise from hike and bike to ski and skate. Three years ago, the outfit that manages the slope (aka, the devil from Atlanta) bought a plot of adjoining land and built an indoor rink; they offer hockey clinics all year long. Somehow, it's all the rage with women. Like boxing, Loraina says. Seems as if no sport remains sacrosanct to men. (Sumo wrestling, maybe? Discus throwing?) Women want to punch each other black and blue or lose their front teeth to a puck, it's no skin off Jasper's back. Just perplexing. All that padding to rent, as well as the sticks and skates; that part of it's good. Loraina thinks they ought to sell little figure-skating outfits, sequined tutus. Too much, too fussy, Jasper argues. He is not running a boutique here. He'd have to add honest-to-God fitting rooms. Right now, you want to try on a pair of ski pants, Loraina clears you a space in the stockroom behind the register.

"Not a word about this mayhem," she says when he walks in. She stands between a huge carton of jumbled ski boots, flotsam from the previous season, and a series of rows she is constructing, pair by pair, like an army from the knees down. "And I have to warn you, we are out of coffee. I'm a dragon."

You might say Loraina is always a dragon. He calls her greeting the Daily Don't. Once in a while, she greets him as anyone else would, but usually she starts with a warning. *Don't tell me it's getting icy out there. . . . Do not talk to me about those SOBs in Congress. . . . On pain of slow death, do not walk with those muddy boots across the floor I just mopped.*

"So send Stu to the deli," says Jasper. "What do we pay him for?"

"Stu is out sick. I think I know what kind of sick. Stu was sighted at the Loft last night, after midnight. Wobbling to his truck. From which I assume he wobbled to bed and passed out. Speaking of pay, I do not make enough money to do work this stupid."

"I have urged you often to retire."

She glares at him, her blue mascara embellishing her scorn. Her doctor, like his, has probably made the same suggestion. She may, in fact, be older than Jasper. Hard to tell, even naked. She's in pretty good shape for however old she happens to be. Helps that she never had babies.

Loraina's crankiness is a shell. It's been more than a year since the last time she came home with Jasper, just another of so many random nights when they decided they might as well spend it together. So maybe he'll get to enjoy her cranky-sexy presence in his bed again, her grumbling generosity, the heat of her surprisingly muscular legs, but he doubts it. Those days in their relationship are probably over, for reasons no more definable than a change of seasons.

Jasper depends on Loraina. Not just on her business sense but on her knowing him so well that she does and does not call him on his quirks. Jasper wouldn't want to marry again—twice was plenty—but he needs various partnerships, however casual, simply to keep on going. The dogs are one kind of alliance; Jim (mostly due to his various skills) is another.

Jim has become, it's clear, a surrogate son. As for the real sons, one is too far away, the other too mulishly helpless, as if stuck to the bottom of his own shoe. (Jasper's recently wondered if he's turning Jim into a subconscious do-over there. Would that mean he's given up on Kyle?)

Loraina, mind reader that she is, says, "Your stepson get here?"

"Last night. I got him working on the hole in my house."

"What kind of hospitality's that?"

"He should what, lie around the house and read?"

"If that's how he likes it. I'd guess he's here for R and R."

"He offered to pitch in. He's got Jim for company."

Loraina has a brittle, crinkling laugh, like dry leaves. She smokes too much, one thing about her that worries Jasper. She says it's what keeps her "thinnish," and thinnish, she points out, is healthier than fattish.

"Jim for company's like cereal for dinner," she says.

"You know what?" says Jasper. "You are mean."

"I am truthful. You like that about me, remember?"

Jasper crosses the store and looks out the picture window that frames a postcard of the main run, the one that had better turn a glistening white within the next two or three weeks. Fake snow's expensive, never as good as the real thing. Last weekend, a good swath of Maine got six inches. Sugarloaf is up and running. He takes the binoculars down from the hook. He spots a pair of hikers near the brink of the hill.

"They're off to camp," says Loraina, standing behind him. "Fools from Rhode Island with backpacks as big as the state."

"We equip them?"

"They stopped in for energy bars, water bottles. Matches," she says.

"Vegetarian jerky types, I bet."

"We stock such a thing?"

Jasper snorts. "You'd be the one to know that."

Their conversation lopes along—weather forecast, rental fees, new vendors, Stu's work ethic (lack thereof)—until the door opens to the next few customers. They hesitate at the sight of all the ski boots; Loraina hastens to assure them that yes, the shop is open. Can she help? This is the slowest time of year, the stretch between Halloween and Thanksgiving. The fuss over foliage is past, and even if it snows like blazes, only the diehards show up so early. Even people who like the great outdoors take their weekend leisure in the city now: theater, museums, exotic meals. For Jasper, it's a season of too much time to think. Good thing, perhaps, that Kit's shown up now. Though it means there will have to be talk about Daphne.

"That's what you get for meeting a dame at a funeral," Rayburn said at the earliest signs of trouble. But even Rayburn had thought she was a find, a don't-let-this-one-out-of-your-sight, the first two or three times he met her. Pretty, talented, smart. Not, like other women who'd fallen into her fix, bitter. Packaged with just the one well-behaved son: meaning (or so she assured Jasper when they got to that stage of their courtship) she was done with babies.

Maybe the problem was that he hadn't set out, like a mission with a well-defined map, to find his own boys a New Mother—which is what some people had actually advised him to do. Rayburn's wife, Sharon, told him, "Make a list with three columns: 'Must-Haves,' 'Might-Haves,' 'No Way in Hell.' Stick to it." Starting about the minute Vivian was in the ground, there were fix-ups, one bust after another. As Rayburn put it, women willing to be fixed up generally remind you of hounds: so eager on the scent, you'd swear you see a wagging tail.

The first time Daphne met Rory and Kyle, she impressed them with her youth, her closeness to their age rather than to their father's. She was almost midway, in years, between Rory and Jasper: twelve years older than the son, eleven younger than the father. Watching her banter with his sons about music—the boys' music, not the music he'd heard Daphne play the day he met her—gave him a moment's pause, a chilly doubt, but she had been a mother for nearly ten years, and didn't that tilt her toward an older generation, give her an extra five years or so? Besides which, he *needed* a woman who knew how to be a mother. If he'd gone and made Sharon's list, wouldn't that have fallen under "Must-Haves"?

Daphne's search for a mate probably was a mission. She did nothing to hide it. And why ever should she? Single mother of a boy, earning a living as a public-school teacher and occasional church musician: good Lord, she'd have been a fool not to look for a man like Jasper—settled with kids of his own, cleanly widowed rather than divorced. The sheer suddenness, the fluke of how Vivian died—cerebral aneurysm, alone at home—had left Jasper in a semipermanent state of shock, more open to any woman than he might have been had he gone through the drawn-out campaign, the hardening wretchedness of nursing a spouse through a terminal illness. That kind of loss was in fact a release, he learned in later years, watching couples go through the hell of cancer. Losing your spouse to cancer might break your heart several times over, but from what Jasper's seen, it leaves you feeling as free as you feel bereft, like a diver breaking the surface of a lake after a drowning scare. You're more careful about what comes next.

Rayburn was at that funeral, too. It was for their friend Litch, who went down in his plane heading north to fish. Litch's wife, who taught at the same high school as Daphne, asked her to play at the service. So she was there in the church—in that dark blue velvet dress, her long sunstruck hair clipped back from her face with those flashing jeweled butterflies, clasping that cello like a brawny lover between her legs, playing those notes of a sorrow so elegant you almost felt glad for the occasion—and then, to Jasper's surprise, she was at the reception, too, putting platters of food on the table, peeling off Saran wrap with the same willowy fingers that played those notes an hour before, the music that gave nobility to grief, that made you stop thinking, for a minute, *Litch, you cocky bastard, they predicted that goddamn monsoon!*

"We know her?" Jasper asked Rayburn that day in the church hall, already wolfing the deviled eggs she'd just uncovered.

"We'd sure know it if we did. And know her we soon must. Or you, you lovelorn wifeless lout. You lucky stiff. The other *kind* of stiff." Rayburn chuckled. "Quoth the actress to the bishop." Rayburn, who'd barely survived his second tour in Vietnam, would have joked his way through Armageddon.

Vivian had been dead for two years. Jasper had discreetly sampled a few women in that time, most of them hardly candidates for moving into his bed on a permanent basis.

Sometimes he wonders whether, if he'd met Loraina back then, he might have considered her instead. But parallel to that point in Jasper's life, Loraina had been married, living in upstate New York, drunk for the half of every month she knew she wasn't pregnant. That was her tale about where she was back then.

How easy it was to fall for Daphne. Daphne deserved to be fallen for, let that be said. She, in turn, genuinely fell for Jasper. Even in the cracked rearview mirror, no doubt about that. Sweet, those first few years. They made each other sweet; they made each other clever, funny, alluring, sexy as hell. Gave each other energy to spare, to love the children through years when the children feigned indifference and scorn. They made each other bulletproof when it came to tough emotions. What was that if not so-called true love? Who said true meant forever?

"The best kind of blindness, that's for sure" was Rayburn's assessment in hindsight. Rayburn was still married to his high-school sweetheart (still is). He expressed the crude opinion that love, as a concept, was akin to cancer. Not that it was a disease, or even that it stood a fair chance of killing you (though it could), but that it was a force whose complexities couldn't be understood from the outside. It had an octopus nature, he said. It was, in fact, nowhere near a single entity. "Oughta be several dozen words for the different species of love, just like the Eskimo words for snow," he offered as an aside. But then he hewed back to its kinship with cancer. Love was manifold, and it was cunning in its unpredictability. Sometimes it was invincible, even in the face of dire threats; other times easily poisoned. Ask Rayburn about love vis-à-vis his own marriage, to Sharon, and he would say, "Trying to figure out if you're still in love after so many years is like trying to remember the misery of heat when you're suffering the misery of cold. Or vicey versa. Inconceivable."

Rayburn had opinions, even sermons, on every subject under the sun. He'd been lucky enough to stumble on a gift for elocution while cursing out the torment of physical therapy following service in that earlier pointless war. Severe burns over his left arm and torso put him out of commission for any kind of hard physical work—specifically, work in his father's auto-body shop.

Until recently, he had a radio show out of Woodstock. Rayburn loved to hear himself talk; good thing others did, too. He still does, but he doesn't make quite so much sense. A couple years ago, he started getting large blank spots in his memory. "Holes in my ozone layer," he joked when it began. "First signs of my fatal brain tumor": that was another of the many ways he made fun of suddenly not knowing where he was driving; or putting the butter away in his toolbox; or turning on the shower, then heading downstairs to open the mail, standing around buck naked in the kitchen while puzzling over utility bills.

Rayburn's grown children, who live in Chicago, Las Vegas, and on an army base in Guam, convinced Sharon to send him to a place that would make sure he couldn't drive off to nowhere or fall down the cellar stairs thinking he'd opened a closet to get a coat. Sharon goes to see him nearly every day; Jasper has to kick himself to visit once or twice a month.

"How's your friend, the deejay?" Kit asks midway through dinner.

"Gone around the bend," says Jasper. "Not to be irreverent. Alzheimer's, it looks like."

"Was he diagnosed?"

"Not sure it matters," says Jasper. "Senile is senile."

"There are new treatments for Alzheimer's. Versus dementia. Things they're trying, at least."

Jasper shrugs. "He's still got a wife who loves him. Not my place to butt in. Sharon's the type who'd research these things." He doesn't confess, because he can't even level with himself, that basically he's said good-bye to Rayburn. He can't relax when he visits that place, "nice" though it is. (Poor Sharon must be draining their savings account.) Pretty soon, he's sure, Rayburn won't know him from Loraina. When that happens, he knows he'll stop going. Selfish, okay, but he just won't be able to bear it.

"Rayburn was a character," says Kit. "That is so sad."

"Don't let's dwell on the gloomy stuff," Jasper says. "Tell me about your kids. I'm still hurt you won't bring them up for lessons from the master. Before the master's gone senile, too. What will they do for fun when they grow up? Move to Florida and golf?" He laughs derisively.

Kit gives him a pair of well-practiced thumbnail portraits: a girl's girl who loves to act and sing and (no doubt to her grandmother's delight) is beginning to play the flute. The boy, equally true to gender, does the sports thing on a couple of teams, roots hard for the Yankees (forgivable at that age), desperately wants a dog. Daphne's pushing Kit to give in; she and Bart are contemplating a dog themselves. (*Probably one of those poodle-doodles,* Jasper almost says.) But there it is: the woman who links them, who's been hovering nearby since Kit's arrival, plunks her trim butt (probably still trim) right down at the table.

"How is your mother?" Jasper makes his voice cheerful. Get this part over with; might as well.

"Good," says Kit. Jasper can see him trying to figure out how much to say. He speaks quickly, also pushing for upbeat. "Still teaching. In the same house. Playing in a chamber group that's actually pretty impressive. A couple of faculty members from Dartmouth—music faculty—plus someone retired from a big-city orchestra. They've put out a couple of CDs. I mean, you know, that they sell at their concerts. A hobby, really, though she'd kill me for saying so out loud."

Or saying so to me, thinks Jasper.

Kit insisted on shopping for groceries that morning, then making dinner. They're eating spaghetti with clam sauce and the kind of modern salad that Jasper thinks of as rich people's weeds: a frilly jumble of teeny-tiny leaves, pink and purple as well as green, that catch too easily in your teeth. Kit brings with him the convolutions of the modern world, from its novel medical theories to its new-fangled foods. (This much garlic, thinks Jasper as he wipes his plate with his whole-grain roll, is going to wake him up in the middle of the night.)

Kit bought a six-pack of Bass ale; he's on his second one and seems to be letting down his guard. It helps that Jasper was pleased—surprisingly so, and it probably showed—at the work Kit did on the house that afternoon. Jasper will join in tomorrow, oversee the repair that takes more craft and finesse, replacing the insulation and the timber. Lifting and nailing the timber is a two-man job, three if Jasper's wise. Sometimes, in the midst of a physical task, his right hip cramps up and locks. (Damned if he'll go for that replacement his doctor keeps suggesting.)

"Your sister, how about her?"

Kit hesitates before answering, probably wondering why Jasper would go this far to be polite. He's never met June.

"She got married last year. She met the guy at a craft fair where he was selling jewelry. He's a silversmith. They live in Bath."

"Maine."

Kit nods. "I think she might be pregnant already. Mom's hinted. But they have this . . . girl kind of secrecy between them."

"Girls do that. Make sure men *believe* they've got secrets, whether or not they do. Don't you think? Part of what keeps us wanting more, looking for hidden treasure." Jasper means this lightly, talk as filler, but all of a sudden Kit's looking frightfully serious. Divorce, thinks Jasper. Here it comes.

Saved by the phone, thank God. He leaps up and practically sprints to answer it. At first, he mistakes the small voice as that of his grandson in Colorado: "Hi. Can I speak to my dad?" In the background, a woman admonishes the boy for not identifying himself. "This is Will Noonan," he says quickly. "Is he there please?"

"A minute, young man." At which Kit is the one to vault from his chair. "Your boy." Though the boy, thinks Jasper with ludicrous pride, has *his* name.

"Hey there, you!" Kit says into the phone. Jasper is almost embarrassed by the change in his manner, his sunny, eager voice. He sounds like a prison inmate allowed one conversation with the outside world. But is Jasper any different when Rory calls out of the blue?

He stacks dishes in the sink, sponges off the table and counter. He can't help eavesdropping. Kit talks a good long time with each of his children; then his voice stiffens up, just enough to notice, and it's clear he's talking to Sandra. They talk practicalities: the children's homework habits, the state of the car, something about a computer, something about a call Kit needs to make (a call he's clearly been putting off). The bureaucracies of family and household. The bureaucracies of two people standing on either side of a barbed-wire fence.

When Kit returns to the kitchen, Jasper says, "Home fires burning bright?"

"Yeah." Kit nods emphatically. "Sandra's a marvel when it comes to maintaining order. I think she does it better when I'm gone."

"You make her sound like a civil servant." Jasper opens the freezer and searches the contents longingly. A pint of Cherry Garcia would be heaven. Instead, he contemplates low-sugar Popsicles and Tofutti Cuties, tiny imitation-ice-cream sandwiches that vanish down his gullet in two bites.

"Well, without those skills of hers, I'd be lost," says Kit.

"She has other skills, I presume."

"Many. Too many." He looks more rueful than proud.

Jasper fishes two Cuties out of their soggy, frost-encrusted carton and offers one to Kit. "So I'm getting the drift that you're not here because you're in some kind of trouble. Like, running from the law." He laughs, to make sure that Kit (who seems a shade humorless) knows he's joking.

"*Trouble* isn't the right word." The tiny package gives the boy something else to focus on.

"But you're not here on a lark."

"A lark? Nothing's a lark these days. I don't know what the fuck I'm doing with my life, if you want to know the truth."

They unwrap their miserly portions of pseudo–ice cream.

"I do want to know the truth. In part because I'm nosy," says Jasper.

Kit bites into the sandwich and makes a face.

"I know. Tastes like old snow between wafers of drywall."

"Good Humor bars don't taste a whole lot better. I've tasted them in recent years," says Kit. "They're not like we remember."

"Very little is." Jasper waits for Kit to finish eating.

Kit folds the wrapper into a square the size of a nickel. "The kids think I'm up here looking for a job."

"And you're not. Or are you?"

"No."

"But you could use one."

"Look. I came here to see *you*, Jasper, but I also came to find something out that I couldn't bring up on the phone. Especially since I haven't talked to you in so long. Which is totally my fault, and stupid."

"Because I have so much wisdom to impart."

"Don't underestimate yourself."

"Hold that thought." Jasper gets up. The urge to pee is typically sudden. In the bathroom, his face appalls him yet again as he confronts it in the mirror over the toilet. Daphne made him put the mirror up, and he's never bothered to take it down. He got rid of most things she left behind, but this thing he'd anchored good and fast to the wall. She didn't realize what it's like for a guy to take a piss while confronting how he looks to the world at large. Of course, thirty years ago the spectacle was, in retrospect, merciful. Tonight there's a grease spot, a bull's-eye of sloth, in the center of Jasper's shirt and a swipe of chocolate on his scruffy chin (or the swag of flesh that claims to be a chin). He hasn't shaved in two days because he keeps forgetting to buy new blades, and the light overhead exaggerates the crater in his nose where they dug out that sinister mole. His eyebrows look like they're trying to send up smoke signals. Christ, it might be better to head the same way as Rayburn, losing touch not with people but with actuality. In actuality, Jasper looks one step shy of homeless.

Back in the kitchen, Kit hasn't moved from the table. He's unfolded the Cutie wrapper and smoothed it out. He's trying not to look anxious.

"How about I make us a real fire," says Jasper. "Temperature's dropped these last few nights. You warm enough up top?"

"Yes." Kit follows him into the living room, settles into the couch. He spreads his hands across the worn cushions. "Everything's so familiar. The way I remember it, but it's still so strange to be here."

"Yeah, same old same old. One day I'll sink so far down in that old thing I just won't be able to get up. They'll find my skeleton gazing into a fire that burned out years before."

Jasper wonders how well Kit remembers the house when its crude wooden surfaces were tempered and brightened by Daphne's collection of concert posters, watercolor landscapes, and the flowery rugs hooked by her mother, all the "homey touches" that had replaced his first wife's similarly inessential things. The only nod to decor in the entire room is a gigantic topo map of the Green Mountains hanging over the mantel. Laminated but never framed, it's an item they couldn't sell at the shop, not even half price. One night Loraina drove it over in the back of her truck. "It spoke to me," she said. "*Hey, it called out as I was leaving. Give me to the clueless dude with the bare walls.*"

Jasper kneels by the fireplace and shoves kindling under the logs he laid in place that morning. "Let me guess. You suddenly remembered the adoption and came to see if I'm leaving you my vast fortune when I croak."

Kit doesn't laugh. Jasper rolls the Sunday sports section into a cone, lights it, holds it above the logs to prime the flue. A greedy draft sucks the flame up the chimney. He lights the kindling.

As he rises from his haunches, his hip kinks. When he finally joins Kit on the couch, he's shocked to see how fearful the boy looks. "Will you just get that anvil off your chest?" he says, trying for paternal wit.

Kit persists in looking at the fire. He speaks in a clogged tone, like he's confessing a crime. "I came here wondering what my mother might have told you about my father—the guy who got her pregnant. I know you might not know who he is, but Sandra swears you must. It sounds ridiculous, to sit here and ask you something like that after all these years, after . . . and it must seem ridiculous that I'd care at this point, because—"

"Your mother must have told you something," says Jasper, cutting short the boy's apology. Jasper hates cowering in people as much as in dogs.

Kit groans. "Nothing. She's refused to tell me every time I've asked. Not that I've asked so often. But still. I mean, it's like she's *offended*."

Jasper prods a log that threatens to tumble forward. He'd guessed several reasons for Kit's visit, not a one of them close to this. He grapples toward memories, barely in reach, of the evening on which

Daphne, quite formally—banishing all emotion—told him the story of the summer she became pregnant with Kit. She and Jasper had been seeing each other once or twice a week for two months, and though it loomed overhead that whole time, like a demolition ball suspended from a crane, Jasper had been careful not to broach the hot-potato question that Rayburn had already posed to him: *So who begat the brat?*

Once she told him, Jasper came to realize that his "discretion" might have looked to her like some cruel sort of test. As he waited for her to volunteer the story, it never occurred to him how terrified she might be that once it was out in the open, the reality of the details might make her seem tawdry, chase him away. So her confession only drew him that much closer; made him want to protect her from everything, even her past mistakes.

Looking at Kit, at the blatant fear of rejection in a face shaped just like Daphne's, fair and freckled too, Jasper recalls that that conversation occurred in this very room.

"I've lived forty years without knowing," says Kit, "and in a way, what the hell difference could it possibly make, right?"

"She never told you, all this time? That really so?" Jasper is genuinely amazed.

"Did you *know* she wouldn't tell me? Or did you assume I knew all along?"

"At the start—when you moved here, the two of you—I knew she wanted to keep this to herself. Needed to. And she wanted you to feel a part of us, mix it up with Rory and Kyle. Made sense to me. Back then it did," says Jasper. "Your mother had a lot of . . . I guess you'd call it pride, when it came to this detail—pretty thorny detail—of her life. Acted like she didn't give a hoot what people thought. What they might imagine."

"But she had to," says Kit. "How could she not?"

Jasper shrugs. "On the one hand you are talking the sixties. The days of anything-goes. But you're talking rural New England, too. Place of keep-it-zipped. Well, at least your mouth."

The fire cracks loudly; a log releases a pocket of sap, sizzling.

Jasper stands. "You don't mind, I'm going to have one of those beers you bought. Want another?" He heads for the kitchen.

Daphne made Jasper promise—swear, guarantee, on pain of losing every pleasure she could give—that he would never tell Kit what she told him that night. He wasn't lying when he told Kit that her secrecy made sense at the time. He's stunned, though, to know that she continued to withhold this simple bit of knowledge from Kit all the way into his life as an adult, as a father of his own children. Jesus but the woman could be cruel. This he knows. But he made her a promise, and almost out of brutish superior pride (not to be outdone by hers), he still feels bound to keep it—at least as long as there's the risk she'll find out he went back on his word.

Which only goes to show, he can hear Rayburn say, *that she still has a hold on your gullible, lamebrain heart. Other parts of your anatomy, too, buster.*

To buy time, Jasper speaks slowly. "You know, Christopher, I remember when I met you, that day we went to the state fair, rode the bumper cars, walked through the dairy barns, ate the cream puffs. Remember that?"

Kit forces a smile. "Do they still make those cream puffs?"

"Damn right they do. Had one this summer. Two. Take that, Dr. Forster."

Kit waits, his respect for Jasper calming him down. And yes, thinks Jasper, here is the very thing about Kit's nature that summoned this particular memory.

"What struck me first thing about you was your patience. Little boys aren't patient like that. We waited in line after line, and it was the worst of August days, Christ it was miserable out there in the sun. But you just waited like some little . . . mystic or I don't know what. And there was Kyle, jumping from foot to foot, whining about thirsty, hungry, boring—normal obnoxious behavior. Rory, I don't recall where he was, but he wasn't with us that day.

"But you. Never a complaint or a sign of losing your little temper."

"I was probably too scared to act impatient," says Kit. "Scared of you and Kyle, what meeting you meant. I had a good idea, even though Mom just called you 'new friends.' I do remember that day."

"Yes." Jasper smiles at Kit; blushes, too, unable to dodge the smaller pleasures emerging from the memory (that skimpy dress of Daphne's, her green eyes and their recurrent promise of *later*). "I couldn't help sizing you up, maybe just as scared as you. If I married this woman, you'd be my responsibility, too, and just who were you?

Come right down to it, I'd be marrying you, too. So I had an eagle eye on you those first few times we met. And I thought to myself that not only were you patient, but it's like you were waiting for something. And listening. You were a listener, that I picked up on. Some patient people are just plain out to lunch. Cows waiting for the call at milking time. None too sharp."

Kit laughs.

"Not you, though. Nothing got past you, was my impression. You were taking it all in."

As if he's doing that very thing now, Kit continues to smile at Jasper but makes no reply.

Jasper's running out of distractions from the much more urgent subject at hand. Turning to the fire, he adds two logs, bullies them into position with the poker. "I like this wood," he says. He points out the window, into the dark void beyond their reflections. "Old apple tree, from the end of the meadow. You boys liked to hide up there at chore time. Finally gave up the ghost. A shame. Fruit trees don't live forever." He gestures at the gash in the corner of the room. "Guess the big old pines don't, either."

Silence. Kit, ever the listener, is still waiting. When he gives in, his voice is barely audible. "But you know the answer. Right?"

"In part," Jasper admits.

"One thing I've been afraid of is that Mom . . . is that it wasn't something she . . . that she might have been forced."

"Raped, you mean?"

Kit nods. His eyes shine.

"Not at all, no," Jasper says. "No, it was normal, healthy teenage lust. A two-way burst of passion. The old firecracker. Ordinary that way."

Kit wipes his eyes on a sleeve. "Oh." He laughs nervously.

"Your mother was in control—or thought she was. Like so many smart girls think. Boys, too. When they give in to their wildest urges despite the best of advice." Jasper thinks of Kyle's impulsiveness, his perpetual resistance to good advice; at least he never got a girl pregnant (though would Jasper know if he had?).

"So who was the guy?" Kit's voice splinters with emotion.

"Hold on. Here's where I have to tell you I never learned his name." Kit's expression turns bitter. Jasper leans toward him. "God's truth.

As your mother said, what use was that information to me, the name of a fellow I'd never meet, a fellow she hadn't seen since it happened, had no intention of seeing again?"

"So in fact you don't know anything more than I do. You know nothing."

Christ, if looks could freeze-dry your innards.

"Hold on. It's not so black-and-white. She told me a couple of things."

"What things?"

"She had some contact with the family."

"What family? You mean my father's family?"

Here is where Jasper must tell or part ways with the truth—maybe just take a minor detour? Daphne told him that she had a relationship of sorts, for a few years, with the mother of the impregnating fellow; Daphne referred to her, coldly, as the Other Grandmother. The one thing he remembers is that the woman was married to someone distinguished. That name he did know—used to know—and with some effort he could probably jimmy it loose from the lower mine shafts of memory. But surely the woman's dead by now. What is the point?

"Christopher, by the time I met your mom, this was old news. She'd lost touch with those people, or so she said, and I had no reason not to believe her."

"Lost touch? *Lost touch?*" Half plea, half accusation.

"Listen. Jesus." Jasper contemplates pretending he has to pee again, giving his cowardly self the third degree in Daphne's goddamn mirror. "Listen. The way I saw it, seemed a good bet her memories of that fellow—the one who got her in trouble, and believe me, it was trouble with a capital *T*—looked to me like those memories weren't something she wanted to press in an album."

"So he was some kind of hoodlum?"

Jasper sighs loudly. "Give me some oxygen here, would you?"

"Sorry."

"He could've been a friggin' Eagle Scout. That is not the point. Again, please, we are talking late sixties. 'Choice,' to the extent women had any choice, you are talking a whole other kettle of fish than today. Kettle of sharks."

Kit thinks about this for a moment. "Do you think she was sorry?"

"Sorry?"

"About me. Having me. Because she had *no* choice."

Jasper wonders if this is the first time Kit has ever thought of his existence as something other than a free, all-things-being-equal proposition. "No way did she regret you. No way. That's certain. She could've put you up for adoption. That *was* a choice lots of girls made back then. You know enough to figure that."

Jasper finds Kit's naïveté surprising, even a bit silly. Rayburn says their children are all so damn spoiled—by the times, more than the parents—that they have yet to face the no-fun, no-justice, ice-water facts of adulthood. This daisy chain of thought returns Jasper, predictably, to Kyle. Stop! he scolds himself.

Maybe Daphne has resisted Kit's questioning (her stubborn streak deep and wide as a ravine), but hasn't he ever snooped through her drawers and closets, the way most kids would do? Is Daphne really so cunning at hiding secrets?

Well now. Is she indeed. Jasper would have a good long laugh if he were alone. All those nights, the last year or two, when she called to say she'd be staying over with a "friend," not making the drive home because she was dead tired or the rain was too heavy—or, gosh, it was somebody's birthday. . . .

Kit frets with the afghan on the sofa, a relic of Jasper's mother. (All these doggone mothers!) He pokes his fingers through the apertures in the yarn. He lets out a shaky sigh. "It must seem like I'm here just to pry something out of you. I'm sorry."

"I have a child who comes by mostly looking to pry loose my money. Or my sanity, not sure which. Family secrets are a good deal more fun."

"Fun? I wish."

Can Jasper ever get it right, the dad thing—the almost-dad thing in this case? "Now I'm the sorry one. I don't mean to get coy about this. I am dead tired and sore as all get-out after that work today. You did more than your share, and I'm thankful. I was going to make a joke about your not going soft after all, but that would fall flat, too. So I just say let's sleep on it. I honestly need to think. Reconnoiter with this stuff I haven't thought about in ages."

Kit nods, drained of anger. "Go to bed. I'll follow you soon."

"Watch TV if you like. I'll conk out dead as a granite slab." He labors to stand. "Alley-oop and upward!"

Kit makes himself smile. "See you in the morning. I'll be ready to get back at it."

"Better be," says Jasper. He forces himself to turn away from the pitiful sight of that boy, looking so forlorn, so . . . in fact, so like a *boy*.

Christ but that woman's reach is long.

He thinks of a fancy phrase Daphne once used: *filer à l'anglaise*. She told him it meant to depart from your hosts' home without a proper good-bye. Not quite Jasper's act, but still. He didn't sleep well, and when the sun began to ooze through the tarp (a problem they'd better amend today), he crept downstairs (funny to creep in a house you rarely share), ate a fat-free muffin with his coffee, and then, out of guilt but with vicarious pleasure, cooked a panful of bacon for Kit, pouring off the grease to save as a treat for the dogs. He left the strips draining on a paper towel, alongside a note saying he'd be back after lunch to resume work on the house. Jim could help Kit set up the sawhorse and tools.

Driving through the village, he stops on impulse at the bakery and the mini-mart—and still he arrives first at the shop, pleased that his early arrival will startle Loraina. Maybe he should plan a Daily Don't to drop on *her* when she walks in the door.

No messages on the answering machine (the phone's become disturbingly quaint), but he has to sift through twenty-some e-mails, only five related to booking lessons. Some guy's looking for an ice-climbing jaunt at New Year's, a daffy-sounding gal wants yoga while her husband skis; out of luck, these two. He clambers around a pile of empty cardboard cartons—which Stu is supposed to flatten every day before closing—to get a pot of coffee started.

His good years with Daphne he wouldn't trade for anything: nights of drinking wine, that meek Italian stuff Daphne liked, while listening to records and taking the risk, three boys sleeping above them (often snoring audibly alongside the music), of stripping off their clothes and making love everywhere from the couch by the chimney to the deck overlooking the meadow, its surface so dense with fireflies that it resembled a vast sheet of golden foil, a mirror to the starry sky. Daphne was, no matter what else she turned out to be, damn fun.

Vivian he'd loved, and a painful vacuum still forms in his chest when he pictures her body on the living room floor, the swarming of the ambulance crew, the pointless rush to the hospital, how his voice had threatened to quit when he told the boys . . . but Vivian had been the kind of woman you choose when you're ready to settle down, as sensible as she is warm, more circumspect than sexy. Daphne was an older version of the girl you choose halfway through high school, the kind who doesn't mind when you drive too fast late at night, aimed at no particular destination, whooping out the window at all the sedate housebound citizens who frown at your shenanigans while secretly wishing they had your crack-the-whip spontaneity. It occurred to him, a month or so after they married, that for Daphne this was effectively a do-over. It was Jasper's second go-round at marriage, while it was far more than Daphne's first: it was the kind of beginning she didn't get to have when she ought to have had it, ten years before. *I am so completely yours,* her every kiss, her every loaf of bread, her every combing of her sex-tangled hair said to Jasper. Not like he'd "saved" her, no, but like he'd opened the lockbox containing her heart.

He had been obtuse to think that she held no grudges about being weighed down early and alone by motherhood, especially a girl with so much talent and spunk. He liked her parents, and boy did they ever like him back, but to hell with how "nice" they were. Daphne's whole life had stalled when she stayed home to have a kid and care for it in her childhood bedroom while her friends went off into the wider world—a place, back in the late sixties, of tumult and color and high-minded, footloose defiance. Before Kit, Daphne had hoped to try for a career as a performer in, say, a small-city orchestra. She'd been offered a scholarship at a music school in Boston.

All of that she surrendered for Kit, though of course he wasn't yet Kit, he wasn't anybody definitive, when she made up her mind to do so. Jasper had no firm beliefs on the morality of abortion; he wasn't religious, and he was of the mind that it was women's business, deciding "when life begins." And who could ignore that governments sanctioned the taking of lives under a Chinese menu of special situations?

Not that such noble or ignoble questions had much to do with Daphne when she was pregnant. Or so he could only gather. There was, to Jasper, a kind of no-fly zone around that time in her life. He respected the selective silence she chose to maintain, chalking it up to "dignity." But how could she not have been angry, sorry for herself, felt like she deserved some kind of compensation from fate? (How vainly Jasper had actually believed, early on, that *he* was that compensation. Fate had a thing or two to show him in return.)

In the cramped corner of the stockroom that serves as a kitchen, Jasper rummages in the cupboard till he finds a tray. He rinses it in the sink, dries it with the hem of his shirt; does the same for a cream-and-sugar set so dusty it looks medieval. He dumps the basket of strawberries into a bowl (no woman around to insist on the ritual of washing fruit), puts the warm scones on a plate.

On cue, he hears Loraina's key, the confusion of someone trying to unlock a door already unlocked. When she steps inside, he grins at her. "Whatever you do, do not tell me I am the best boss in the universe."

She tries not to smile and almost succeeds. "Okay. Won't do that. I'll tell you instead that you need to start taking your shirts to the cleaners. The rumpled look isn't working."

He looks at his shirt. It's flannel, for God's sake. Who irons flannel shirts?

Loraina sees the tray beside the register. "What's this, *Masterpiece Theatre*?" She looks around. "Where's Alistair Whosieface?"

Jasper fills a mug for her.

"Let me take off my coat." She heads to the stockroom, fusses in back for a minute, reemerges. "And the occasion would be . . . ?"

Jasper sits on the bench for trying on ski boots and skates. "None, darlin'. The scones are my insomnia talking."

Leaning on the counter, Loraina eats two strawberries, puts milk and sugar in her coffee. After taking a sip, she says, "Is your insomnia talking to me in particular? I'm not sure I'd buy that." She picks up a scone and examines it. She knows better than to even suspect it was made by Jasper.

"I do miss your coming over."

"I think I need a real invitation to do that."

"You never did before."

Loraina shrugs. "Things change. As we of all people should know."

"I see," says Jasper. This isn't a discussion he'd planned. Actually, he hadn't planned anything. He knew she'd make him talk, that was all.

"Okay then, you see. Glad we're straight about that." She eats a few bites of the scone, staring out at the empty ski slope, a dreary swath of frostbitten grass. "Well, good news on that front," she says, baffling Jasper completely.

"What front?"

"Didn't your computer sing its twinkletoes ditty this morning?"

"Snow?"

"Late tonight, if the temperature drops as expected."

"Much?" Anxious to get out of the house, he hadn't checked the weather.

"A good start. If we pray to the right gods. Get out your knee-pads."

Jasper rises from the bench. He is headed to the computer, to look at the satellite pictures and draw his own conclusions, when she says, "But we were talking about your insomnia. I have one guess. Daphne."

Jasper decides to go ahead and eat a scone. Okay, half. Apple-cinnamon. Does the apple cancel out the butter?

"I take that for a yes."

"Yes, Loraina. Eating is my form of the affirmative."

"Kit's bound to take you back to that time, so no surprises, right?"

"He's not like his mother, though. I mean, he doesn't remind me of her."

"Of course he does." Loraina frowns at him like a teacher at a lazy pupil.

"It's more like I'm reminded of the responsibility I had for him. And then, weirdly, didn't. How he gradually—not suddenly, which would've been the case if he'd been younger—I mean, he somehow stopped being my responsibility, a weight on my mind the way Rory and Kyle will always be. God, Kyle." Jasper refills his mug. "So it's like I feel guilty about all the years he hasn't weighed on me, and now, kaboom, he does again."

"He's fine, though, right? He's hardly Kyle."

Jasper shakes his head. "He's in a lot better shape than Kyle, sur-facewise. But no job, two kids to support . . . Leave all that aside, though. Loraina, he's come to find out who his father is. Was. His 'natural' father, maybe you'd say."

"Come to you? Why you?" Loraina has moved to a rack of fleece tops. She checks the tags, evens out the space between the hangers. "We need more pink in the small sizes. God, I loathe pink, but it's predictably popular. Especially with the size-zero bottle blondes." She aims an expectant look at Jasper. "So why you?"

"He tried Daphne. No luck." Jasper sighs. "Don't think I ever knew the guy's name—what would it mean to me? He wasn't some hood with a switchblade, but hell, we are talking about an act of adolescent foolishness at a fancy-ass summer camp, forty years ago. Forty-plus. Daphne could've handed the baby over to some fine upstanding childless couple from Topeka, who mighta never even told the boy he was adopted."

"But she didn't," says Loraina. "And you think he shouldn't care? Like there's a shelf life on curiosity about your genes? Your blood-lines, or roots, whatever you want to call it? The possibility of meeting someone who solidifies your you-ness? It's all over the airwaves, in case you have ears. Everywhere from *Oprah* to la-di-da *Fresh Air.*" While talking, she's pulled together a dozen items on hangers. She holds them out to Jasper. "Sale rack?"

"That's your decision. Fine by me."

Loraina carries the items to the counter. "My point is, there's this epidemic of reconnecting with lost links from your past, shaping and pruning your family tree. Genetic memory, ethnic character, cultural identity. Et cetera et cetera. Not that I think much of such notions, but they're everywhere."

"I could take it as an insult, couldn't I? His wanting another family besides the one I gave him. Never mind the one he's got."

"You would, wouldn't you," Loraina says drily.

What Jasper won't say is that she's probably right on the money. He is repeatedly shamed by the way he underestimates Loraina. Maybe he really is a chauvinist throwback, an accusation fired at him by Daphne more than once on the downhill slide.

"Well," he says, "the bottom line here is whether I owe Daphne the total silence I promised on that subject."

Loraina laughs sharply. "Honey. Owe *her*?"

"I happen to think a promise is a promise."

Loraina moves toward him, and he wonders if she might touch him, but not quite. She stops close, facing him, holding two empty hangers in one hand, her coffee in the other. "That's why I do, actually, love you," she says, though she's careful to smile in a way that might (or might not) make it a joke.

He waits until she moves again—not, alas, toward an embrace but toward the stockroom.

"So you say I should tell him whatever I know."

She turns in the doorway and says, "Me? That's what I'd do. But don't ask me to decide for you. Don't put me there. Today, I decide what goes on sale and by what percentage. That is the scope of my authority, hon." She points at the clock. Donning her best southern accent, she drawls, "Y'all do remember, honeypuss, that Iron Man Rod is gracing us with his presence before we open?"

Rodney, the controlling partner in the corporation that runs their side of the mountain (some junior relation to the devil from Atlanta), wants to discuss his new marketing plans. In the recession, ski slopes, even in central Vermont, have to become as territorial as tigers. Or so said Rodney at a staff meeting in August (after which they laid off another half-dozen full-timers). The one thing they've got going for their business is that skiing, however expensive it may be, is as much an addiction for many folks as booze or porn. And you can't replace it with anything else. There's no methadone for skiing, no Alpines Anonymous.

"So." Loraina narrows her eyes at Jasper. "Are we up to speed on our Facebook tutorial, all this woofer, tweeter, blitzkrieg jazz? I'll bet you forgot to read the stuff in that folder I gave you." She shakes her head. "I hate it when I know you like a mom."

"You do the talking when he shows up. Could you?"

"If y'all could treat me to dinner at the inn for my birthday. Which happens to be a week from Tuesday, bluebird."

"You're a very bad Scarlett O'Hara, but you have a deal," says Jasper, relieved. Even if she hasn't solved the biggest family problem he's faced since Kyle last showed up shitfaced and squirreling for money.

On the way home, he picks up a meatball sub. He pulls over just before his driveway to finish it off, spreading the greasy wrapper across his lap. Not that Jim or Kit would give him grief, but he wants to enjoy this particular sin in private. As he eats the sandwich (the whole damn thing), Jasper can hear the deafening complaint of the chain saw. He could turn on the radio, but the only station he likes is the one he thought of as Rayburn's. Turn it on now and he'd be listening to his friend's replacement. No thanks.

When he drives in, he can see that Jim's almost finished off the tree. Kit stands nearby, peering up at the house, looking perplexed. The sun is sinking toward the treetops; Jasper had hoped the three of them could polish off the exterior work and the insulation while there was still light, but they will have to combine the tasks if they are to seal the house before the storm.

"Hey," Jasper greets them. "Snow's on the way."

"Tomorrow. Maybe," says Jim.

"I think your maybe's out of date, my friend."

Jasper goes inside to change into his fix-it clothes. On the kitchen counter, he sees a bowl of meat chunks marinating in oil and herbs. He sniffs: lamb. He feels guiltier than ever. Just lose your broom-up-the-ass sense of honor, he tells himself. "Some VIP coming to dinner?" he shouts as he heads upstairs.

Jim lays aside the chain saw so they can work together on the house. He and Kit take turns on the ladder, hoisting the heavy planks, while Jasper works mostly from the inside, making sure the thick cushions of fiberglass don't pop out of place. It's so different from his collaboration with Loraina, this give and take. Very few full sentences are uttered; think of language as coins and they communicate in plain old dirt-brown pennies.

There.

Hammer.

Gotcha.

Tuck it.

Lower?

That's it.

Left. Up.

Bingo.

Like surgery on a TV show.

Jasper is so absorbed in their efficiency that he doesn't hear the car arrive, the driver approach.

"Oh man, what happened here?"

As Jasper peers through the narrowing gap in the living room wall, the visitor enters his sliver of view.

"House got a trim," says Jasper. "Hello, Kyle." He walks around through the kitchen, outside. It's just dawning on Kyle who the guy on the ladder is.

"That you, Kit? Holy Moses, look at you! What brings you way the hell up here? Do I smell a midlife crisis?"

"Kyle," scolds Jasper.

But Kit laughs. "Yeah. That's the short version. How are you, Kyle?" They embrace, the grown-up boys, the never-quite-brothers.

"I am fine, fine," says Kyle as they separate, quietly taking in the changes.

Jasper's glad he told Kit about Kyle, if only to prepare him for the shock of how Kyle must look after all these years: not just older and more worn than he ought to look, but heavier by fifty, sixty pounds. There are pouches of spent flesh beneath his eyes and chin, and his hair, once thick and dark, is gray and cropped too close, the way a child's hair gets cut for lice. It still makes Jasper wince. That and the several tattoos on his arms, each one the apparent record of an emotional urge better off forgotten. (At least in winter the tattoos are hidden.)

A shameful thing, Jasper knows, to size up a child every time you see him as to whether he might be drunk or stoned. Shameful but prudent. Kyle's clothes and hair look clean enough, his voice and posture steady. Jasper exhales quietly into the prism of early twilight. This time of year, the collective shadow of the pines accelerates the onset of darkness.

"Inside, fellas," says Jasper. "We are done for today. I'll just run the dogs."

Jim gathers up the tools, already difficult to see among the matted leaves and needles underfoot. He carries the chain saw to the shed. Kit, on his own, folds the two large tarps; Jasper is touched by his surprising deftness. (Honestly now, why does he deny the boy his talents? Sins of the mother; is it that crude?)

The dogs jump on the chain-link fence as he approaches. They haven't had a real run in days. "Hey, rogues, let's go," says Jasper, unlatching the gate. They stream past him, Trixie and Yoda first, now that Pluto's gone. Mitchum, Kilroy, and Belle push through together, followed by the rest. Thirteen dogs take the meadow like a battlefield, stealthy as they spread out, gaining distance from one another only to charge back together again. They get their ya-yas out, shake their lush grizzled coats, then, suddenly nonchalant, cruise the perimeter to mark the trees, squat in the shadows. Trixie is the first to return to Jasper.

"One more litter for you, girl? What say to that? Still got the maternal moxie? Yes. Yes, you, dollface." Jasper whispers as he leans over her, rubbing behind her ears, scratching her hackles. She pants, arches her back, answers him with her ice-blue gaze.

So-called dog people talk about measuring their lives in the number of animals they've owned, the number they've outlived. Over the last five decades, Jasper's had too many, an overlapping succession, to make any such calculation. But he knows that if he breeds Trixie, the next generation will be the last he raises. The last whelping. He must be careful to consider all the work it entails, always more than you remember, especially if the litter is large.

Stars begin to pierce the hood of darkness; so much for imminent snow. Loraina's source was overeager. Reflexively, Jasper smells the air, tries to divine just a hint of the metallic aroma that tells you a good storm's approaching. No, but the temperature's falling. His knees and ankles know that for sure. Let it fall just enough, not too much.

Trixie loses interest in his affection, wanders off again. The dogs crisscross the meadow, noses down as they gather the scents absorbed by its dry grasses, quilting it with their own. After watching them for a few more minutes, Jasper claps his hands, and they raise their heads, almost in unison. "Squadron, back to the fort!" He starts for the kennel; they fall in behind him. His dogs are well trained. Loraina used to pester him about taking them out for competitions. "And I'm getting that extra time from what bank?" he'd ask. "The free publicity, numbskull. Just think of it" was her reply. "Showing off's not my thing," he'd say. "Suit your slacker self," Loraina said. Always let women have the last word: Rayburn's advice.

As he walks the dogs back to feed them, he looks through the kitchen window: the three younger men mill around the table, drinking from bottles. His heart beats a little faster, worried for Kyle. He wishes he'd bought some of that counterfeit beer to have on hand. Just in case. His slacker self hadn't bothered.

The minute he walks in the door, his eyes shoot to Kyle. He's peeling potatoes by the sink. Beside him is an open bottle of Mountain Dew. Again, Jasper exhales his relief. Though, Jesus, that stuff tastes like horse piss.

Jim and Kit are over in the living room, conferring quietly. Jasper assumes they are building a fire.

"Thought I'd stick around a couple days," Kyle says. "I could help finish those repairs." He doesn't look up from his task.

"Sounds good," says Jasper. "Everything okay by you?"

"Okay enough," he says. "I think I have a lead on something."

"Yeah?"

"Know the artsy new mall, the one they're building in that old stone warehouse on the river down near Quechee?"

Jasper puts away the breakfast dishes, which Kit must have washed.

"They need an on-site manager, kind of a liaison between the developer and the contractor. Had a good interview yesterday."

"Good for you," says Jasper. "Any strings you need me to pull?"

"No, Dad." Kyle doesn't meet his eye. Did Jasper insult him? Why does talking to his son have to feel like teetering his way along a tightrope?

Jim and Kit are still in the living room. Coward that he is, Jasper wishes they'd return to the kitchen.

"Kit's looking great," says Kyle.

"He is."

"Showed me pictures. Lucky. His kids are good-looking."

"Sandra, too," says Jasper. "He landed a good one." Inside he cringes; sometimes he feels as if every compliment he pays someone else in front of Kyle might be read by Kyle as a reference to something Jasper is sure his own son can't do or will never have.

But Kyle chuckles. "Smokin'."

"Well."

Jasper starts toward the living room just as, abruptly and far too loudly, music throbs out of the stereo speakers. Jasper gasps; he hasn't used the record player in years. "Holy F. Christ, that still works?" he shouts over the onslaught of guitars. Music as a pack of hounds.

"Good as new!" Kit calls back, turning down the volume.

"Let it blast!" says Jim. He begins to dance in front of the sofa. Kit is kneeling by the cupboard that holds the records, pulling them out and sorting them into piles.

Jasper strains to recall the singer's name. Bob Marley. "A lot of those records belong to your mother," he tells Kit. "Welcome to help yourself. I never play them. Take the turntable, too. Give your kids a taste of the past."

Jim has begun to sing along as he dances. He moves oafishly and manically, like a bear that's stepped in a yellow-jacket nest. " 'In this life, in this life, in this *oh sweet life . . .*' "

Jasper stares at him. "Looks like somebody needs a night on the town with his wife."

Jim pauses, laughing. "Jazzman, this is vintage." He waves his beer bottle, as if to toast Bob Marley. "And boy am I hungry."

"There's plenty for everyone," says Kit.

"Oh good," says Jasper. "Got me a frat house now. A frat house with a hole in the wall." The corner of the room is finally closed to the elements, but silvery insulation glints through the gap. The cosmetic interior work comes last. Jasper suspects he'll be alone again by then, all his visitors gone. He pulls firewood from the barrel beside the fireplace. He'd like a beer, but he will abstain, for Kyle's sake. Well, for his own, too.

Once the fire catches, he heads quietly upstairs. He's sheepish about the impulse, but Kyle's discharge counselor at his first rehab told Jasper that precautions are more than wise; they're kind. They're about support, not suspicion. In the bathroom, he scans the shelves inside the medicine chest. He removes the bottle of Percocet left over from the rotator-cuff business he went through last summer and, after a small hesitation, the naproxen he takes on days his hip acts up (most days). He shoves the vials into his pocket and is about to leave when he sees Kit's toiletry case sitting on the tank.

Cursing quietly, he opens the bag and rummages through, half fearful. He's had enough surprises this week. Nothing, thank heaven, but a tiny bottle of Tylenol. "Score one blessing," he hears himself say, Viv's little way of thanking the cosmos for unearned favors.

He flushes the toilet as an afterthought, washes his hands. As if to conceal a crime. In the mirror, the geezer shaking his head looks more

irritated than sad. Which makes him, genuinely, sad. The presence
of Daphne's son is, he realizes, making him miss Vivian more than
he has in a while. The wife who left him without any such intention.

In the morning, the instant Jasper steps outside, here it is at last—
a fragrance crisp and specific as new leather, terse and bitter as steel:
the smell of incoming snow. The sky is gray but still timid: two
hours, he'd wager, till the first flakes arrive. Once again, he leaves
before Kit (or Kyle) wakes—this time because he wants to get his
workday over with early.

He can tell that Loraina is on the phone with their snowboard-
ing vendor. The salesman is a young Turk who'd flirt with a flag-
pole; Loraina's giggling and blushing. Everyone wants to be Shaun
White these days; the boys who board now sport those cocker-spaniel
tresses, wear torn jeans (onto the slopes!) and graffiti'd jackets, vamp
their way to the lifts. Jasper will never get it, but he doesn't have to.
He just has to rake in the dough.

Stu has shown up on time for a change and is making sure (or
pretending to make sure) that all the rental footwear is organized
correctly, by size and binding type, on the shelves in back. He puts
on an obsequious show of greeting Jasper. Jasper tries to play gruff.
At least Stu isn't growing out his hair.

Loraina hangs up.

"The dudester ask you to elope?"

"We're almost there, but he's old-fashioned. He's taking his time.
May come to you for permission, since you're the closest I've got to
a dad."

Their running joke is that since only Jasper has met the salesman
face-to-face, he may well envision Loraina as a husky-voiced babe,
a Scarlett Johansson or young Sigourney Weaver. (The names Bette
Davis and Lauren Bacall, Loraina informed him, would mean squat
to a kid like that. Probably wouldn't know Meryl Streep from Merle
Haggard.)

"I tell you, that boy has a crush on me," she says, smoothing her
dowdy fleece vest against her waist: a very alluring waist when freed
from Polartec and other less-than-sexy fabrics.

Jasper's first job is to update the whiteboard with the latest reservations and any special clinics. Stu maintains the schedule online and prints it out for Jasper every morning. It's also his least favorite job. Leaning against the counter, he lets himself be distracted by the local paper, lying by the register. The lead story is a rhetorical plea for snow—as if you can petition for it. Jasper skims the predictable text about the weather outlook around the state. When his eyes reach the fold of the paper, he lifts it from the counter and snaps it open. Just below the fold, he spots a story that would be secondary to weather only in a state like this one. Not that any of the so-called news in this gimcrack rag would register on anybody's Richter scale. But there are exceptions to every rule. To wit:

SENATOR BURNS HOSPITALIZED.

God, thinks Jasper. Actually, yes, *God:* this sort of coincidence leads you to believe there's got to be one lurking somewhere, and He's the kind of guy who favors fart cushions, pulls quarters from behind His ear, puts cling wrap over your toilet bowl.

"Something of interest?" says Loraina, seeing Jasper's face.

"I thought Burns retired ages ago. Must be as old as this mountain."

"Speak for yourself." Loraina looks at the article over his shoulder. "You know, there were rumors he'd retire, but then there was that scandal with the guy who'd have run for his seat. Remember the business with the Polish exchange-student nanny?"

"Missed that election, I guess. Have to confess I don't always vote."

"Have to confess I don't ever. Register, they nab you for jury duty."

"You are a terrible citizen," says Jasper. "Shame on you."

"I pay my taxes. That's plenty of civic sacrifice, buster."

From the meager paragraphs beneath the tiny picture, Jasper learns that Ezekiel Burns is eighty-three, eleven years older than he is. He is in stable condition after suffering a stroke while playing tennis—indoors at some swanky club, no doubt.

Burns is one of those politicians with a PR shtick that makes him look like an up-from-the-manure success story. While it's true that he grew up on a dairy farm during the Great Depression, the farm was a paradise of more than a thousand acres and half as many cows, Burns's father an agricultural impresario. The guy flew around the country lecturing men in three-piece suits eager to plow their fortunes, purely for profit, into rural land as different from their club-lounge domain as the Sahara Desert. To Burns the Elder, dairy wasn't so much milk and cheese: it was a commodity as imperial in its potential as gold bars in Fort Knox or hotels in Atlantic City, a commodity to protect from the profit-killing effects of local unions and French imports alike.

But that's history, about which Jasper doesn't give a hoot. What Jasper wants to read about is Ezekiel Junior's current family, wife and children. Nothing, of course. It's not an obituary. Not yet.

Jasper eyes Stu, who's helping a customer—a very pretty customer—try on one of those new, featherlight Patagonia jackets. Later, when Loraina goes out to get lunch (Jasper will be sure to send her), he'll ask Stu for a favor—and Stu will jump. The kid may be exasperating, but when it comes to using the Internet (Christ, just keeping track of this new Facebook page that Iron Man Rod regards as some kind of magic bullet), Stu is an ace. Jasper will have him find out if the Other Grandmother is still alive and kicking. That will be step one. Can't do any harm just to know that much.

They had been married for five years when, late one summer night as they lay together in bed, trying to sleep in the humid stillness and the clamor of crickets, Daphne said to Jasper, "Don't you sometimes long to hold a baby again, go back to when your boys were tiny?"

"Never," he said without missing a beat. Not to be cruel but because this was something he'd worried about when he fell for Daphne, something she assured him he needn't fear.

He heard her breathing, felt her shifting toward him, caught the flowery vapor from her body and hair.

"But you do," he said. No point in playing dumb.

"Yes." She touched his naked arm.

Jasper knew, or thought he knew, what was going on. Kit was fourteen; he'd entered the years of willful withholding and casual scorn that child-rearing experts told you were cause for rejoicing. They're finding their independence! Their hormones are surging! They're growing up!

Rory had been entering this zone of defiance just before Vivian died; clearheaded woman that she was, she'd bought a book or two. So now it was Kit's turn to turn aside; and frankly, from what Jasper could tell, he was going about it a good deal more gently than most boys.

"You miss the old Kit, that's what you're feeling," said Jasper as Daphne stroked his arm.

"It's not about Kit."

"Don't think you can be so objective, darlin'. I've seen the looks he gives you—gives us both. I've seen how it hurts you, his pushing you away."

"No," she said. "I mean yes, but this is something different. This is me finally waking up to the realization that being a mother is what I love best. I became a mother too soon, I know that. But because of that—and believe me, I see how ironic this is—because of that, I never fully embraced it."

Damn the tireless, obnoxious insects, thought Jasper. He needed sleep; he did not need *this*. He said, "You're a great mom. Not just to Kit. To my boys. How I got so lucky there, I've still got no idea." Had he ever voiced his gratitude? Was that part of her itching for more?

"I love Rory and Kyle. It took a little time, but I woke up one day to find out I love them *fiercely,* sweetheart. Just in time to send them out into the wild blue yonder." She sighed mournfully.

He had to wait now, see where she was headed.

"So what I find myself thinking," she said, "is that there's room in our family for one more. Just one."

He inhaled sharply. "You're not pregnant."

"No." As an afterthought, she laughed. "But." Her hand moved from his arm to his hip. They lay on top of the sheets, naked, nothing to interfere with the contact between their bodies.

"Daphne." A caution.

"Jasper . . ." A plea.

"Daphne, no more babies. We settled on this."

"Five years ago, Jasper."

"My mind's not changing."

"We didn't know what to expect back then. Now we know how well we work. Together. All of us."

The heat of her body against his felt oppressive. "Five of us is plenty. When we're all here, a full house. A crack poker hand."

"And how rare will *that* be, now that Kyle's off to Burlington?"

"Daphne, darlin', we work well together because it's just right, this family we've got. And no way could we afford to have you quit your job, not with another kid." He resisted pointing out how old he'd be when this hypothetical fourth kid left the nest. Never wise to remind her how much older he was, how *very* much older he'd seem in another twenty years.

She moved away. She said quietly, "Families aren't balance sheets." Beneath the sweet fragrance of her perspiration, Jasper could almost smell her reasoning at work, her powers of persuasion churning to win his agreement.

"I'm sorry," he said. "I'm not going to be changing my mind."

"It's late and we're tired. We'll talk more when we're fully awake."

Had that been the beginning of the end? Jasper wondered when she left. Most certainly the end of the beginning. Or had it been a sign that they were doomed from the start? Not that such niceties mattered.

"Oh my," said Rayburn when Jasper told him about this can of worms. "Don't you know that law of physics?"

"I stopped at biology," said Jasper. "And cheated to pass."

"Second wife's gotta have at least whatever the first one had. If not more. The law of matrimonial equilibrium."

Jasper didn't bother to answer.

"Two kids for Vivian, ergo, two kids for Daphne."

"That is the most cockamamie thing I ever heard," said Jasper. "Vivian got an early death. You think Daphne wants that?"

"Parse my advice till the cows go to Harvard, but you'll see I'm speaking the truth here, boss."

One thing Jasper did not ask Rayburn was whether he thought Jasper should say yes to Daphne. After all, it didn't matter. He was certain, and furthermore, they'd agreed on this before they married.

But what if he *had* said yes? Would they still be together, still happy, more or less? Would he have a daughter, someone to care for him when he, too, lost his mind? Though look at Rayburn's daughter out in Chicago; she came back maybe three times a year.

Rayburn might have said, *Oh just give in. What does a loser like you stand to lose?* Rayburn was full of hot air, mock abuse, callow gener-alizations that often turned out to be true. Is, Jasper has to remind himself. Rayburn still *is*.

———

Within half an hour of the first flakes, Jasper can usually predict the outcome of a snowfall—leave aside the meteorologists' satellite photos, the computer's sparklings and twinklings. This will be a true storm, a humdinger, he knows ten minutes after it begins. The snow falls with a determination at odds with the feathery look of the flakes. It's coming down thick yet dry, dead vertical, swift. No drifting, dallying, gusting. No flirtation. The ground takes none of it in.

He's home, enjoying his usual solitude for the first time in days—or the illusion of solitude. He came back at three to find a note from Kit: gone to the store to "stock up." Kyle's rusty Jeep is still in the driveway. Standing at the bottom of the stairs, Jasper can just detect the sound of light snoring from upstairs. Please, he thinks, let him not be sleeping something *off*.

He remembers the night, not two years ago, when he woke up to the sound of muffled wailing. Realizing it was inside the house, he picked up an old bowling pin he kept under the bed and crept out onto the dark landing. The sound came from the boys' bedroom.

Two scenarios, he knew, and he wasn't sure which he dreaded more: a total stranger in there or Kyle, who should have been in Rutland leading his own life. But there he was on the lower bunk, sobbing into a pillow; the odor of booze was powerful, even from the doorway. Jasper spent that night curled around his son's shaking body in that child's bed, trying in vain to comfort him. The next morning, while Jasper was in the shower after feeding Kyle breakfast, he bolted. Didn't return his father's calls for days.

Jasper can't help looking in the bin where the bottles are thrown.

So far, so good. Mountain Dew galore: piss made potable.

Not that Jasper's history is all that pristine.

The week after Daphne moved out, he kept up his work routine, but every evening, once he'd sloughed off his gear in the mudroom, thrown food at the dogs, he aimed his whole being at the business of drinking like a pirate on shore leave. It wasn't easy, considering he had Kit shuffling sadly about whenever he wasn't in school. Some sort of masochistic guilt made Jasper continue to feed him, even if he did nothing more than shove a frozen dinner in the oven. At times,

Jasper wanted to howl at the boy to get lost, vamoose, good riddance, with his Jezebel of a mother. Every time he caught a glimpse of the unguarded Kit, however, he looked ready to collapse in tears; Jasper almost wished he would.

"Oh Jasper, I was so, so afraid this would happen, and it did. I've fallen in love with someone else, a man who wants to have more babies with me. I fought it as hard as I could these last months, but the heart will have its way." Right along with the pussy and the womb, thought Jasper as she delivered the initial thrust of her bayonet. At least, Rayburn pointed out, she didn't offer up some pathetic fib about "needing space." She just let the guillotine fall.

Jasper wasn't sure whether he was angrier at Daphne for fucking the man-who-wanted-babies or at his own dull-witted self for not guessing. (He assumed Kit hadn't guessed. Too painful, and pointless, to ask.) But the anger, like a four-alarm fire, required a major hosing down. So Jasper started with the random collection of spirits they had kept for guests. He'd pour a glass of gin and curse himself, then a glass of vodka and rip into her. Day four or five, he started on the liqueurs and aperitifs, the so-called *cordials:* her beloved crème de menthe, the giant bottle of Kahlúa a visitor had brought, the bitter Lillet that Daphne had read about in some travel magazine. After Kit was holed up in his room that night (studying or mourning or raging—likely all three), there was Jasper, puking green-and-taupe foam into the kitchen sink.

When Jasper had failed to open the shop for a second day, Rayburn showed up at the house. Jasper was so steeped in bile, so racked with pain of every conceivable sort, that Rayburn had to piece the story together for himself. Not exactly rocket science, what with all the blank spots on walls and shelves.

"If I told you I saw it coming, I wouldn't be lying," he said, "but shit, man. Up and leave on a fuckin' dime? I'd like to nail her prissy, two-timing ass to a tree. Or drop her off the North Ledge. Hope for a catamount to finish the job."

Rayburn poured the last bottles of sweet, syrupy liquor down the drain and took Jasper out for a steak at three in the afternoon. Only at the restaurant did Jasper tell him that Kit had chosen to stay. Rayburn's eyes widened.

"That's fateful," he said, with none of his usual embellishments.

"That's a testament. Just think about it. If you're half smart, you'll take it as a lifeline."

If anyone could predict the future, at least a sorry fraction of the time, that would be Rayburn. Rayburn when he had all his marbles.

Jasper calls the shop to check in with Loraina. Lessons for the next week are stacking up like planes at JFK. The Cocoa Hut is up and running ("Doomsday for my hips"), and all the grooming machinery in the big shed is purring and stuttering to life. Jasper tells Loraina to start e-mailing the A-list instructors, make sure Stu knows he's on all weekend.

"Stu there, as a matter of fact? Put him on."

Stu takes his time getting to the phone. Jasper hears a customer asking if the water bottles are stainless steel. In the background, the bell above the door jingles repeatedly.

"Boss."

"Results?" asks Jasper.

"Not much of a challenge, dude. Ezekiel and Lucinda Burns, Sanctuary Farm," and he rattles off an impersonal-sounding address on some numbered rural route. But Jasper recognizes the name of the town (its stone walls straight, its houses old and proud, its common—flanked by three steeples—the stuff of tourist brochures). "Want the phone number?"

Jasper scrambles in a chaotic kitchen drawer to find a pencil.

"Children? Names of their kids?"

"Yeah. Well, a son named Jonathan who lives, I'm pretty sure it's him, in Berkeley, California, and a daughter, Christina, in Burlington, married name McFarland."

Jasper, high on his success, is tempted to offer Stu a bonus, but he lets the urge pass, not wanting to encourage the boy's smug, lazy attitude on days the snow isn't falling. "Good job," he says. "Thank you."

"No problem. You're the boss," says Stu, his tone implying neither gratitude nor resentment. The general tonelessness of young people's speech mystifies Jasper. Maybe it's all that texting. They don't know how to exercise their vocal cords for social niceties, never hear themselves converse. Talk-deaf.

He takes the sheet of notes to his desk and puts it in the top drawer. He still has a great deal of pondering to do. As he stands at the computer, wondering if he will succumb to the vortex of e-mail (there will be a buttload, weather like this), he sees Kyle standing at the foot of the stairs, watching him.

"Dad," he says, "okay if I hang till the roads are clear?"

"Of course. But prepare to dig in—and then dig out. We're now lookin' at a one-two punch. Two storms ganging up, from the west and the south."

Kyle grins. "Good news for you."

"Careful what you wish for, as is often the case with weather."

Kyle's smile is suspiciously polite, a little too Eddie Haskell. He must be getting up the nerve to ask for something. If it's anything other than money, Jasper will be floored. He lets a moment pass, then says, "Kit take the truck? I don't like the thought of our professor on these roads in his suburban putt-putt."

Kyle nods. Still he hovers.

"Going out to check on the dogs," Jasper says.

Kyle quickly offers to join him.

In the kennel run, the dogs' paws have packed down the snow, but still it sits surprisingly deep. Behind the fence, their masks are dusted in white, as if they've been painted on velvet. Jasper tells Kyle to get the mucking shovel from the shed while he lets them out for a romp. Kyle can make himself useful, too.

The wind pushed east by the second storm has risen and scoured the meadow, sculpting the snow into waves and troughs, trampled brown grass showing through at the low spots. "A quick one, gang!" calls Jasper as the dogs spread out, leaping, sashaying, shaking their voluminous fur.

Kyle is suddenly at his side. "Dad, looks like I might be getting married."

Jasper turns his head, dislodging the hood of his parka. Snowflakes find their way in at once, pricking the back of his neck. "Married?"

Kyle actually blushes. "Sally."

"Sally." Jasper sees Dot starting into the woods. He calls her back.

"She's great, Dad. She really understands me. What I've been through."

"She does." No mistaking the plea in that "Dad," yet still Jasper cannot respond the way a father should to news like this. Good news, for a change—isn't it?

"She's been through a lot herself." Kyle is shivering, his jacket too light for the weather. "Dad? You don't look too pleased."

"I'm stunned, is what. I mean, you're certainly old enough." He stops short, realizing how cruel this must sound; Kyle is forty-six years old. "But I guess, being the duffer I am, I wonder if maybe you don't want to be a little more . . . your feet more solidly planted. This job you mentioned . . ."

"Dad, it's not like I've quite asked her."

"Quite asked her? Then how can you be sure—"

Kyle stamps his feet, horselike. He makes a sound that could be laughter or throat clearing. "We know each other pretty well. What am I saying? *Really* well. We've had more than a few of those what-if conversations." He pauses. "I met her in AA, a couple of years ago. Supposedly it's not kosher to hook up like that, but we were really careful. I mean, took our time. Like I said, she's been through a lot, too. Has a really great daughter. I think we could do a great job of . . . holding each other together."

Jasper wishes he could forget how many setbacks and breakdowns Kyle has had over the past "couple of years." Too often when Kyle is talking or laughing, Jasper fixates on the broken tooth that Kyle doesn't have money to fix; only a small corner snapped off, but Jasper can't forget the binge that led to the breakage, his trip to the emergency room to rescue and try to steady his errant son. What was that—three, four years ago now? Was this Sally around to witness and tolerate all that hysteria? Or, God forbid, was she an accessory? Jasper takes a deep breath of the harsh dry air. "I'm glad you've found someone. I'd be happy to meet her."

"Well, I hope so!" says Kyle. "She'd love to meet you. She asked before now, but I wanted to be more committed about it. Us, I mean."

Didn't want me passing judgment if you failed, thinks Jasper. As indeed he would. Kyle may not be wise for his age, but he does know his father.

"She used to be a competitive skier," Kyle adds. "Way back."

Jasper has to clap his hands to break up a spat between Dot and Trixie. He wonders if Dot is getting close to her heat; he'll have to check the calendar he keeps inside the shed. His neck is now cold and wet; when he pulled up his hood, the snow that had gathered inside it fell onto the back collar of his shirt.

"Sorry I seem so damn speechless," he says. "I should be congratulating you." Is that Kyle's hand on his well-padded back? "Congratulations, Son."

"Dad, you have a thousand reasons to be skeptical."

"I know, Kyle. And I'm going to try to squelch each and every one."

The lights of the truck veer around the side of the house, casting twin beams through the dense snowfall. A door slams. "Hey!" Kit waves at them with both arms. Three of the dogs run toward him, barking, looking for a new playmate. "A big limb's gone down at the bottom of the road!"

Jasper sighs, glad (coward that he is) to have a reprieve from heavy talk with Kyle. He's dismayed at Kit's news, but it's no surprise in a storm like this one.

"I'll go help with groceries," says Kyle, heading toward the truck.

Jasper calls the dogs to the kennel, more loudly than usual; the snow filling the air muffles his whistle and the clapping of his hands. Snow may fall without emitting a noise of its own, but it greedily consumes the sounds of whatever world it fills.

After shedding his wet parka and boots in the mudroom, Jasper digs around in a closet till he finds the crank radio Rayburn gave him for Christmas a few years back. "If limbs are falling already, we'll lose power. Prediction's for a rise in temperature, just enough to make the snow turn wet. Heavy." To Kit, who's unpacking the food, he says, "Want a hot meal, I'd start on it now."

Check e-mail. Call the shop. (Remind Loraina and Stu that cellphone reception is basically null out here.) Haul in extra firewood. Light the woodstove. Build a fire in the hearth. Test flashlights. As he starts in on his mental list, he hears and then smells onions cooking in oil. That boy follows orders fast. He deserves a job, deserves one more than Kyle does. Unfair thought, but true.

First e-mail's from Loraina, already anticipating his troubles. Iron Man Rod is salivating for all the eager customers, the income promised by a storm like this one, but even he knows when to close the hill. Today they'll close even the main run before dark; the rink will close, too, due to driving conditions. Jasper looks out the window: nearly night already. He phones.

"Yee. Hah," Loraina deadpans. "Rod looks like he's on crack."

"Not there now."

"Gone home to celebrate with whatever vice he fancies."

"Body like that, I'd say steroids."

Loraina laughs her ratchety laugh.

"You better go soon," says Jasper.

"Plows are running and I've got chains. To quote Aretha, 'Chain, chain, chain!' I'm makin' Stu stick around another hour, help me get all our ducks in phalanx formation. We'll leave in tandem." She deepens her voice. "'Con-voy.'"

"What are you on, Loraina?"

"The promise of a steady income, bluebird."

"Well, global warming's off our ass for now," says Jasper. "Storm's to go through tomorrow afternoon."

"Rod's gambling it'll taper off by noon. Nobody gilds the lily like weatherfolk. One thing we can all agree on."

"Noon," Jasper ponders aloud.

"He's got his fingers crossed for a solid afternoon, evening, of business."

Jasper hears the oldfangled adding machine Loraina insists on using to tally her numbers.

"Jasper?"

"Still here."

"Don't drive on the roads out by you, all right?"

"Dogs're good to go."

"Yeah, but stay in with your boys. Play Scrabble."

"Old Maid's more like it." The only time he ever played Scrabble was with Daphne; that scab-colored box went to the dump with most of her flotsam two weeks after she moved out. (The robe she left on the back of the bathroom door. A set of cutesy little knives with ceramic flamingo handles. A French jam jar filled with squiggly hairpins, a straw gardening hat, a frayed silk scarf. He was tempted to toss her records but couldn't bear the waste. The tapes she took.)

The house lights go off, then on. The digital clock on his desk flashes noon—or midnight. (What does it say about you, whether you see those fallback numerals telling you it's day or night?) "Gotta go," he says to Loraina.

In the kitchen, Kit's chopping like a samurai. Rice is cooking on the stove. "Chicken and peppers, ten minutes away," he says.

Jasper hears Kyle upstairs. The shower goes on.

Hot water. Right. The sequence of likely failures trickles through Jasper's corroded brain. Come to think of it, at least one winter's gone by without a loss of power; maybe two. In the old days, when his boys were boys, they'd lose electricity two, three, four times a winter. "Some things do improve around here," he says to himself.

He finds a dry down coat, two canvas slings, and heads out to the woodpile. He lugs in the wood and, stopping just inside to catch his breath, fills the barrel by the fireplace. After foraging through various drawers, he marshals miscellaneous batteries, a package of candles, and four flashlights; lays everything out on the coffee table. There are boxed matches and the Coleman lantern on the mantel. Daphne was always after him to buy a generator, something he's continued to resist, especially as the outages have dwindled.

"Ornery, that's your middle name," he says out loud as he tests the flashlights. Another accusation of Daphne's, affectionate in the beginning.

The lights flicker again. Better check e-mail one last time.

Loraina and Stu have closed up shop. Nothing else.

Jasper opens the desk drawer containing Stu's rudimentary detective work. Facing the computer, he's also facing the kitchen. Kit is busy at the stove. Kyle's still upstairs, the shower silent.

jonathan burns berkly cal
DO YOU MEAN Jonathan Burns **Berkeley, California**

"Yes I do, widgets-for-brains," he can't resist muttering.

From the kitchen, Kit glances over at Jasper, smiles and waves. The storm seems to have brought out the cheer in Kit. A boy after all. Grown-ups see the first flakes and think about all possible disasters. Children, if they're normal, see nothing but fun.

There are five Jonathan Burnses linked with Berkeley. One is a professor at the university who teaches gender studies. (Jasper would have finished college if he could've majored in *that*.) Professor Burns has a Web page for his students. At the top is a photograph of a balding, gray-haired, but youthful-looking guy. Helps that he's tanned, posing against a big rock in magaziney hiking clothes.

Is he old enough? He could be midforties or midsixties, the way people work at preserving themselves these days. Jasper cannot enter the site without a user name and a password, but he is free to scrutinize the photo.

The caption beneath it reads *Place of origin: Vermont.*

"Jesus." Jasper is careful to curse in a whisper. "Jesus, Joseph, and Jerry Garcia."

"Food's about ready," calls Kit. "We can eat now or later."

It's not yet six o'clock. Cocktail hour, thinks Jasper. Except.

"Serve it up. After, we'll check out the TV buffet if we still have juice." He abandons the Internet, calls upstairs to Kyle. He volunteers to set the table.

Kit passes him, headed for the living room. "How about some music?"

Digging in a low drawer beside the sink, under pot holders and pizza-parlor menus, Jasper fishes out three rumpled cloth napkins, artifacts of Daphne he missed on the day of his angry purge and never bothered to chuck. Paisley.

Jonathan Burns (purple socks above his hiking boots) looked like a paisley-temperament sort of guy. Jasper sneaks a glance at Kit; he'll have to go back to the professor's site and look for family resemblance. Did Kit get those pale blue eyes, those attractively unremarkable ears, from Burns?

Bob Dylan whines from the speakers. *Lay, lady, lay.* Jasper hasn't heard this song in ages. He likes Dylan, but the guy always sounds like he's singing through a bad cold. Or recent dental work.

Memories like the ones busting through Jasper's dam demand, at the very least, beer. Except. "Crap," Jasper mutters. No wonder his son is a drunk.

And here that son is in the flesh: clean, neatly dressed, as put together as he has looked in a while. "Hey, Dad. Wow, Kit, you're the man." How hard he's trying. And how hard Jasper's resisting, wishing he were immune to disappointment. But this Sally person might be something special, the extra incentive Kyle needs.

"Looks stupendous," Jasper agrees.

"Silver lining of unemployment," says Kit. "I cook."

It's tasty, Kit's beat-the-clock dinner, and he's served it up with glasses of local apple cider. The G-rated kind, fresh, with a nice peppery zing. A boxed pie sits on the counter. ("Tofu?" Jasper inquires. "Low-fat banana cream," says Kit.)

Between large bites, Jasper describes the worst storms he's weathered in this house. Once, in the midseventies—between Vivian and Daphne, he realizes but does not say—the power was out for four days.

Kyle nods. "A doozy, that one. We baked potatoes in foil, in the fireplace. Robot turds, Rory called them. Remember that, Dad? We snowshoed to town in the dark that last day. The plows hadn't made it out this far."

"We couldn't stand it anymore, nobody's company but ours," says Jasper.

"We could've been the last people left on earth. Rory had me convinced of that. I was terrified." Kyle pours himself a third glass of cider.

The phone rings. Jasper answers; it's Rory, who's seen the storm on CNN. "We're thinking of cooking up some robot turds," says Jasper. "If desperate."

Rory is silent for a moment, then laughs. "You remember that?"

"Your brother's here. Your other brother, too."

Rory asks to speak with Kyle, who tells him right off about Sally. Jasper worries that Sally should confirm the engagement first, but who is he, Miss Manners? Kyle carries the phone to the living room, his voice disappearing under the music. Jasper listens for a minute. It occurs to him that Johnny Cash sounds like an old-fart dad, Dylan his petulant teenage son.

Soon Kyle waves at Kit, who goes to the phone. Jasper enjoys the brief delusion that maybe he's forgotten about the paternity stuff, the quest for his "true father." Maybe Jasper, after all, is father enough. And then he remembers how absent he's been, how he made excuses not to go to Kit's college graduation. He couldn't face Daphne with her new-model husband, a baby girl to boot. Selfish fool. He would've survived it.

Jasper takes his plate to the counter. He peers through the plastic dome at the snowy surface of the pie. *Low sugar! Low carb! No saturated fats!* brags the label. What the hell is left after sugar, carbs, and fat are sucked from a dessert? Maybe, like the fleece garments they stock at the shop, the pie's made from recycled soda-pop bottles.

After Kit hangs up, he says he should try calling home before it's too late.

"Rory sounds good," says Kyle. "Haven't seen him in a year, I realized."

"He'll be here for Christmas. You should bring Sally. Her kid, too."

"Thanks, Dad." Kyle's having seconds.

Will there be a real wedding? There ought to be. Should Jasper offer to pay for it, throw a party next summer at the ski lodge? He's not used to planning anything celebratory with Kyle. Or, come to think of it, with anyone. What's the last party he helped host, how long ago was that? He and Loraina, intimate as they've been in the past, never paired up that way, with other people at a table, not unless you count meeting friends at the Loft for a burger and beer.

A beer. Christ! Why is it that having to pass the time with his recovering-alcoholic son makes him want a drink more than ever?

Bob Dylan's first set comes to an end. Kit is laughing in the living room, still on the phone. "You told the teacher what?" he says, incredulous. "Did you get in trouble for that?" He laughs again. "You are one lucky guy."

"I wonder if I could ever be a father," says Kyle.

This startles Jasper. "Well, one thing at a time."

"I know that," says Kyle. "In spades."

"Got my fingers crossed you'll get this job."

Kyle shrugs. "I think I made a good impression. It's out of my hands."

Without the music, the sound of the wind takes over, assaulting the joints of the house: here comes the second storm, the drama queen. Somewhere nearby, a large limb cracks. Jasper thinks of the big pines sheltering—now possibly threatening—the kennel. The yin-yang of living in a forest.

"Sally's still young enough," says Kyle.

"Excuse me?" Jasper turns from the sink.

"To have another kid."

"Oh." This is not a subject he wants to discuss. Not for a blessed minute. He leans toward the nearest window, as if he hears something worrisome. "I better go check on the dogs."

"I could do that."

"No, no. Nice of you, but I think they need my fatherly reassurance." He winces at his reference to parenthood. Why is it all one mogul after another?

At the door, he puts on his coat and boots. Kit's heading back to the kitchen, looking pleased. "Back in two," Jasper tells him. "Dogs."

Wind drives the snow in splinters against his face. He points the flashlight up into the trees. Despite the powerful gusting, snow clings mercilessly to every branch and twig; the creaking strain is audible. He points the light down at the ground. Whatever tracks he and the dogs made earlier are completely erased. The kennel run is empty, sheetlike. Within the enclosure, the beam of the flashlight reveals the dogs, wise creatures, curled against one another in a gray furry mound. Their eyes open in response to the intrusion, but they know it's Jasper and barely stir. "Scouting trip tomorrow, I promise," he tells them.

Exactly as he turns back to the house, the lights go out. Every pane goes black, leaving a mosaic of afterburn on his field of vision. The beam of the flashlight is instantly doubled on the darkened kitchen window, a blinding supernova. Jasper pauses in his tracks for a moment, waiting for his eyes to adjust or for the lights to come back on. They don't.

"Well, folks, the show begins," he announces to no one. From inside the house, he hears Kyle and Kit whooping at the blackout like children.

He wakes in a blaze of antiseptic light, face numb in the frigid air. The fire is down to dry ash; the woodstove must be cold by now as well. It's still snowing, but at a dignified pace. The wind appears to have passed on through.

The boys slept in their rooms, but Jasper pulled out a sleeping bag (which, he realizes now, reeks of mildew) and slept on the living room couch, across from the hearth. His legs cramp as he tries to stretch them. The wall clock in the kitchen, smug in its battery-powered immunity, tells him it's past eight o'clock. "Christ," he groans. "Christ on crutches."

He forces himself out of the sleeping bag, confronting the shock of winter air indoors. Doing a jittery dance to get his thick blood flowing, he lays a fire, lights it, tackles the kitchen woodstove. The three men stayed up late, playing cribbage in front of the hearth, finishing off the gallon of cider—for which Jasper's bowels punished him severely in the depths of night.

He takes coffee and eggs from the fridge, then remembers the electric stove is useless. Cursing, he fills the kettle with water and sets it on the woodstove instead. "Bread," he says out loud. Thank God Kit went shopping.

After peeing, he pulls corduroy trousers and two sweaters over his long johns. Extra socks. Boots. Hat. Touching his nose is the only way to be sure he still has one.

He cranks the radio. A quick bulletin, a cup of instant coffee, and then the dogs. He peers out the window over the sink. He sees a few tails, flags over parapets of snow. Using the top of the fence as his measure, he reckons the snow's at least two feet deep in places.

Power's out across most of four counties. Well, some consolation in all that fellow suffering. Or, really, inconvenience. Sensible folks who live in this state are prepared for such emergencies. The not-so-sensible ones deserve what they get.

Footsteps overhead; the radio has roused the boys. "Rise and get ready to shovel!" Jasper shouts to the upper regions of the house.

He was smart enough to bring a shovel in last night; and this, the heavy snow, is why God created sliding doors. The flat face of snow exposed when he opens the kitchen slider collapses inward. He takes the shovel and begins to carve a path toward the kennel.

So much for the soft, feathery stuff of the first, more feminine storm. That's how Jasper thinks of the snow: the light stuff girlish, desirable, pure seduction; the deadweight of wet snow brutish, unyielding, destructive in excess. Testosterone snow. This is the stuff that fells men his age when they try to move it. How many heart attacks will there be across the state today, how many fatal?

As if channeling his actuarial speculations, Kit is suddenly behind him. "Let me do that! Please!" Knowing he should save his strength for feats he can't foresee, Jasper hands Kit the shovel, goes back in. Kyle is slouched at the table, a blanket over his shoulders, hands gripping his tiny furnace of coffee.

"Glad you stayed?"

"Not sure it's much better in town, Dad." Kyle points at the radio. "State of emergency."

"Oh that. Governors love national attention. Moment in the spotlight."

Kyle laughs, shakes his head. "I know you want people to *think* nothing fazes you."

Jasper considers scrambled eggs on the woodstove. Easier than toast. Warmer than cereal. Better fuel. Maybe he'll treat himself to real eggs, yolks and all; skip that glop in the carton.

Kit's back, huffing in the doorway. "Dogs look okay."

But Jasper still needs to feed them. He walks the waist-high path so efficiently shoveled by Kit. The dogs bark, too excited by the snow to resist.

"Pipe down, hepsters," says Jasper. "No snow day for you."

He goes to the shed for a spade with which to break the ice on their water trough. As he pushes through the drift against the backside of the fencing, he sees the tracks: two sets, beginning with a scuffled spot where they jumped too easily (how tempting is a fence that's suddenly shrunk from six to three feet high?), resuming with a full gallop of paw prints pointing toward the hogback.

"Crap. Crap in a bucket of fish." Jasper surveys the gleeful trajectory of their escape. He knows, without checking, who the culprits are. Mitchum and Zev. Hounds at heart, those two, they'll choose freedom over food any day. Call of the friggin' wild. They'll come back on their own, but the storm isn't over, and the conditions, wet snow laid down over dry, worry Jasper. (Never mind irate landowners with the inability to tell a dog from a coyote and one of the various firearms Vermont so blithely lets everyone carry about like tote bags.) Three years ago there was a small avalanche in the valley on the opposite side of the mountain, the snowpack sledding down a forty-five-degree ledge. No one caught in its path, but a rescue chopper called it in. Avalanches are rare so early in the season, but he will not rest till he gets those dogs back home.

He breaks the ice, pours out food, shovels a swath inside the fence. Takes attendance as the dogs eat in their relentlessly frantic way. He guessed right.

Kyle and Kit have already cooked up the eggs. They left a good portion in the skillet for Jasper. "Dogs okay?" says Kyle through a mouthful of food.

"Two are thinking they're especially okay right about now. The two heading off on a toot."

Kyle, overplaying the sympathy, groans.

"They'll come back, won't they?" asks Kit.

"In their own sweet time. But that's not what I have in mind." Jasper looks out the window; the snowfall's weakening. Iron Man may get his wish: a Saturday afternoon of human gridlock on the slopes. If the humans can get to the slopes.

One of the two boys should go with him, but he can't take both— and one should stay at the house. He knows that if he asks for a volunteer, they'll both speak up, and he'll have to choose. He'd rather leave Kit alone in the house, but he'd rather have him as company, too.

"Kit," he says, before he can think too much, "I'll need you to head up with me on the sled."

"Not taking the snowmobile, Dad?" says Kyle.

"Last one gave out. Haven't replaced it." In fact, Jasper sold it. Part of that decision was Kyle's joyride, with a bar buddy, two years ago. Jasper spent three long hours in a panic-stricken rage.

"Pack us coffee, water bottles, crackers, trail mix, dried fruit if I've got any left. I'll get the gear together," Jasper tells Kit. "Kyle, deal with the cars. Power comes back on, call the shop. Get Jim over here with his plow."

Kyle salutes his father. "Aye-aye." More overkill.

"Take extra clothes from my room," Jasper tells Kit. "Clean thermals in the bottom drawer. I hope clean."

He glances at the comatose computer and feels its dispiriting pull: the sense that if he can't hook up to some satellite—scan the weather from above, know who wants to reach him, see the day's headlines beyond this mother of a storm—the day cannot properly begin.

He thinks of Jonathan Burns's Web page. He has, for the first time, a name. Which means that he has something concrete to withhold; no more claiming he can't remember or doesn't really know. Perhaps he should have asked Kyle, not Kit, to be his companion.

The dogs whine as soon as they hear the door to the bay in the shed where the sleds are stored; they bark when Jasper comes into view with the harnesses looped over his arm. These new, candy-colored harnesses, which Loraina spotted in a catalog last year, even glow in the dark. "Kids, we have a mission!" he says. Carefully, apologizing to those who'll stay behind, he releases only the eight dogs he'll use on this trip.

"*Hi hi hi!*" he shrills, calling them to the sled, to the task they love so much—or do in order to make him happy. In the very best dogs, true motivation is never entirely clear. Perhaps it's all one, pleasing master and self. (Does such a dog even have a self? Do dogs have selves of any semblance? Here's the sort of philosophizing Jasper misses in losing Rayburn to the fog of dementia.)

Without the poor departed Pluto or the delinquent Mitchum, he'll put Yoda and Mojo at the head of the tugline.

Jasper helps Kit match the names on the harnesses to the dogs they fit.

Kit looks bright with anticipation. One thing about a storm and its aftermath: your mind takes a wide detour from the most abstract of all your concerns. For today, Kit is a man with a job, possibly several. Kyle, too. Jasper is grateful to the elements for putting off questions he'd rather not have to answer; even for keeping him away from the shop.

The snow hisses under the runners. Sharp snow, Jasper calls it when it's this wet, this unyielding. The tracks they leave will ice over almost instantly. The return trip may be rough on the team's paws.

The dogs yip and pant as they find a shared rhythm, get a feel for the weight of the two men they're hauling. After a series of veerings and lunges away from the tugline, they settle toward a center. The tracks of the renegade dogs quickly leave the trail, of course. Nothing's that easy. Jasper knows the places they favor, but the sled must follow the meandering track to the top.

Kit crouches before him, under a fleece blanket, holding the front rail.

Jasper concentrates on the trail, trying to see as far ahead as he can. He hates using goggles, but snowflakes sting his eyes. Now and then, heavy clumps of snow fall from high branches, briefly spooking the leaders. This is where Pluto excelled. Nothing much deterred him from forward motion. Mitchum's the same, but his bravado is rash, not a dividend of experience. He started out as a pet, a puppy too headstrong for life as a suburban pooch. (Where the hell is he now, that scoundrel?)

"*Hi hi hi,*" Jasper urges them on. Not necessary, but it's reassuring to hear his voice penetrate the harsh brilliance of their surroundings.

At a place where the track dips into a hollow, "*Ho!*" he shouts once, halting the dogs for a rest. Kit unfolds himself slowly from the sled. Together, they release the dogs, who run in circles, gulping snow, digging, marking random trees. Their noses point toward the sky as they yearn for promising smells. They're like children begging for a story.

Jasper takes a swig of coffee. Kit declines. "I'm remembering everything," he says.

"Everything?" Jasper says, alarmed.

"Everything about this place—the trails, where they go. The hide-outs I had with my friends, to get away from you and Mom."

"Don't tell me things I'd rather not know," says Jasper. "Even in hindsight, ignorance is bliss." He whistles to Yoda, who's wandering. "You must miss your family."

Kit nods.

"Things all right with Sandra?"

Kit looks directly at Jasper, though most of his face is obscured by the knit hat pulled low, the scarf wrapping his chin. "I'd like to say yes. But no is probably the truth. At least my kids miss me."

What the hell is Jasper doing? "Ah well, those periods come and go." With his mittened hand, he makes a hills-and-valleys motion.

"Not counting my mother," says Kit.

"Sandra's not your mother, that I promise you. Not to—"

"Insult Mom? Say what you like. Right now I'm pretty pissed at her. I can't believe I actually came here thinking I could somehow outsmart her."

Jasper says quickly, "I'm glad you came here. That was a good thing. Good for me, too, by the way. Today, especially!"

Kit gazes around at the dogs, laughing. "Until we disappear into the wilderness, never to be heard from again."

"Hey. You're with an elite survivalist guide. I've got certificates to prove it. I'm your next best thing to a bulletproof vest."

"Ski Bum Number One. You think I've forgotten?"

He didn't start mushing until he and Daphne had been married for two or three years. The first time he took her out on a sled, she told him it felt like *Doctor Zhivago:* she was Julie Christie to his Omar Sharif. That, in a crazy way, he misses: a woman to exaggerate the romance of everything, turn up the volume on beauty. You could never say that of Loraina. Loraina's a leveler. Viv, he imagines, would have viewed the team like a harmless fraternity, including the bitches. "You and your dogs," she'd have said, the way other women scoff at a husband's poker crowd, his fellow Sox fans down at the juke joint.

Jasper is the product of one cliché begetting another. He is the man neck deep in dogs because he was denied even one as a child. Why? Because his father was the postal carrier who hated dogs.

Jasper's mother kept a parakeet in the kitchen, caged in the warmth of a sunny window. Its ceaseless chitterings sabotaged all attempts to eavesdrop on conversations between his parents that sounded tense or urgent. Early on, Jasper figured they had to be about money. Later he found out that they were about his mother's cancer, something secret and female that took years to eat her from the inside out, the way termites consume a house, finishing the job when Jasper was ten. His father was a veteran of Belleau Wood who carried with him, as heavy as his mail pouch, a lingering darkness, a weary pessimism. He'd arrived late—reluctantly rather than gratefully, Jasper has guessed—at marriage and fatherhood. He died two months after Jasper married Viv. The one thing Jasper could thank his parents for was raising him near a mountain, letting him seek refuge there—from his father's negative pronouncements on the future of mankind, from (though he didn't know it then) his mother's drawn-out sufferings.

Viv was tender about that distant loss. He claimed not to remember much about his mother's death; there was no ritualized good-bye, no emotional father-son bonding. An aunt had broken the news to

Jasper. Viv told him that all these vaguenesses only deepened the wound. She promised to take care of herself as well as any children they might have. "Don't you worry: I'll outlive you," she said, "even if it's the last thing I want to do."

Oh, promises.

An hour later, still no sign of the escaped inmates. Jasper guessed wrong on three spots where he assumed they might be loitering. The coffee's long gone; the crackers are stale, the dried apricots tough; his fingers feel brittle despite a change of mittens.

Jasper gives the team a second break. This time Kit says very little. He's probably wishing he had been assigned Kyle's post. Probably the power's back on at the house, Kyle sitting on his toasty butt, watching cop-show reruns.

"We'll do a loop round that hill, head back," says Jasper. "We can do chili on the woodstove. Nothing like beans to heat you up from inside out. Furnace food. Just the ticket for today."

Kit merely nods before helping him hitch up the dogs yet again.

The trail that lassos the high foothill before them cleaves to a steep slope on the far side. He will have to maneuver the team tightly for a stretch. But through a break in the trees, they'll have a broad view of the valley. Jasper will broadcast a big *yahoo*. If the dogs are anywhere out there, they should heed his call.

As they make the curve, Jasper spots a cardinal through the trees below. Is it time for cardinals? Shouldn't they be on vacation somewhere down south? Viv knew birds; Jasper knows trees, terrain, skies. That final year, they advertised hikes for birders. Viv led the first of those outings. It was the last one, too.

The bird is some distance downhill, but suddenly it moves in a way that corrects the scale: it's a hell of a lot larger than a cardinal, farther away than his eyes first told him. At the same time, Kit points, and the ersatz cardinal morphs into a person in a red jacket, waving hysterically.

Jasper halts the dogs. They look back at him, whining. Trixie barks.

The red figure begins to climb toward them, clumsy and slow.

"I'll go," says Kit. He waves and calls out.

Jasper wants to be the one to go down, but he should stay. The sled is on the narrowest part of the track.

"Help me!" calls the oversize cardinal. "My boyfriend!"

Backcountry fools. Storm chasers. The sort of people who think it's fun to swim in a riptide, surf in a hurricane, ski in a blizzard, sail across the ocean in a washtub. Idiots who, Jasper thinks privately, deserve whatever fate the elements hold in store. Now Kit is face-to-face with the fool, who gestures spasmodically. All Jasper can hear of their conversation is the helium pitch of the girl's voice.

Kit motions her to stay where she is and climbs back up the slope.

Panting, he tells Jasper, "Campers. The boyfriend's leg is broken. Slipped off a ledge."

"Where the heck is he?"

"Somewhere up ahead. She came toward us when she heard the dogs."

Jasper thinks about the logistical fix they're in. The prospect of chili, more glorious than ever, recedes across a day that's suddenly looking unbearably long.

"She says we'll see the tent if we go farther along the trail."

Jasper takes the first-aid kit from the pack attached to the sled. "Couple aspirin and an Ace bandage in here, that's about it. You go with her. I'll go round, tie the dogs, climb down from there."

The dogs are revved now, as if they know the outing's changed its purpose. Only a minute round the bend, he has to rein them in again when he spots the peak of the tent a couple hundred feet down the slope. Yoda and Trixie bark their objections, and then they're all putting up a ruckus.

Suddenly, out of nowhere, Mitchum and Zev are mingling with their teammates. "Christ all blooming mighty," says Jasper. "Boys, you are in one big fat cauldron of trouble, know that?"

From next to the tent, Kit's waving at Jasper. Now he gets it: the runaway dogs, in their free-agent wanderlust, found the campers. By happenstance, sure, but Jasper can see the local headlines already: Mitchum and Zev elevated to heroes on the order of Balto. Loraina will be pleased: nothing like free publicity.

Leaving the dogs hooked to the tugline, Jasper detaches it from the sled and fastens it around a tree. "Set your furry butts down and stay."

As he starts down the slope, snow up to his groin, Jasper feels the sensation he dreads most, that nerve-twisting click in the joint where thighbone meets pelvis. Because he slept on the couch, not in his room, he forgot to take the naproxen this morning. Even with the pain dulled, moving downhill is torture. He clutches at a sapling. Right now, like it or not, he's going nowhere.

The red girl has disappeared—presumably into the tent. Kit is looking expectantly up at Jasper.

"Can't!" he shouts down. "Fuck," he says quietly. "Sorry, Viv."

Kit pushes up the slope till he's next to Jasper.

"I'm fine," Jasper insists. "Except I'm stuck. Stuck and madder than hell."

"They screwed up, and they know it. But we've got to take the guy out."

"The idiot girlfriend, too."

"You can take both, can't you? You've got the two other dogs now."

Jasper actually remembered to pack the extra harnesses. He feels the pain in his hip settling from a bellow to a mutter. One marvel after another. Still, he hasn't seen the boyfriend to assess whether it's safe to move him.

The girlfriend's joined them. "Oh my God, we were going to die out here, I swear. If it wasn't—" She looks at the dog team, lying together in a hollow they've dug from the snow. "Oh my *God*, are those amazing dogs yours?"

Jasper looks at the young woman's face, her skin a mottled mask of red and bluish white. He unwinds his scarf. "Wrap this around your face." He can't help sounding brusque, but the rage he feels is at his own limitation. He cannot go down to that tent. "Anybody know you're out here, anybody likely to be looking for you?"

She shakes her head. "We figured we had our phones, but it's like we're in a black hole of some kind. . . ."

From Kit's face, Jasper can see that the boy knows how angry he is. Kit says, "Raven and I can pull him up. I think that's what we have to do."

(Raven? This blond matchstick is named Raven?) Jasper nods at Kit. "Can you pull him uphill in a sleeping bag?"

"Wait." Kit goes to the sled and shoves things around. He comes away with the two extra harnesses, the ones Jasper packed for

Mitchum and Zev. He holds one up before him, turning it this way and that.

"You hear me, Kit?"

"I have it figured out, I think. I hope."

Raven's wrapped most of her face in Jasper's scarf. She's a wispy thing, to start with, but now her muscles have probably turned to jelly from the stewed effects of cold and fear. She'll be useless. Useless with a touch of frostbite. Kit tells her to stay with Jasper.

Jasper has managed to pull himself to the trail, using the trees. This is it, he understands: the beginning of his retirement, right here on this side of a not-even-mountain. Here he stands, marooned with this helpless harebrained girl, while his suburban stepson, a professor of *art,* is left to deal with the kind of problem that he, Jasper, is trained to solve.

"I'm coming, Bruno," Kit calls down to the tent.

Raven and *Bruno?*

Kit gallops back down the slope and goes into the tent. The harnessed dogs wait quietly now, having played out the ritual of scolding, inspecting, and forgiving the two scofflaws.

"Climb in the sled and wrap yourself up good in those blankets," Jasper tells Raven, who's crying steadily now.

"I'm sorry," she says.

"You're all right, you're just fine now," he tells her gently, though what she needs is a good dressing-down.

"We came up a few days ago. There was no sign of *this* in the forecast," she says through chattering teeth. "No warning."

"You have a radio?"

"We brought our phones."

"Never enough."

She cranes her neck to see what's going on below. "Oh God."

Not a sound from the tent until Jasper hears an outburst of fury or pain. The tent seems to shudder, and from inside emerges a composite human creature made of Kit and a tall, thin young man. It takes a minute or so for Jasper to see that Kit's used the dog harnesses to strap the two men together at the waist. Kit has one arm clamped around Bruno's back, his opposite hand clenching the harness at the front of Bruno's waist. He is virtually hauling the guy up the slope. Bruno clings to one tree after another as they climb.

Close up, Bruno is disturbingly pale and has no energy to speak. He doesn't even seem to see Jasper; he's attached in every way to his rescuer. Kit has broken out in a sweat and cannot seem to speak, either. "Blanket," he gasps, and Raven climbs out of the sled to surrender the fleece throw in which she's been wrapped. "Ground."

Kit unfastens the harnesses only when he can lower Bruno onto the blanket. He then goes back to the tent. Jasper won't ask any more questions. He feels as if he's being rescued right along with these silly young lovers.

Kit brings the sleeping bags from the tent and makes a nest of them in the front of the sled. He instructs Raven to help him pull Bruno to the sled.

"Can you splint the leg?" Kit asks Jasper. "I assume that's what we have to do."

Still Bruno says nothing. His pleading gaze darts between Kit and Jasper. He is shivering feverishly. "Don't touch," he whispers, his shaky hands shielding his injured leg.

"Got to. Won't be too bad," lies Jasper. Inhaling against his own pain, he gets down on his knees in the snow and, with his knife, slits the boy's jeans and long underwear. He's seen worse breaks. No bone exposed. On the other hand, he doesn't dare guess what shape the boy's feet might be in. Not a good idea to take off the boots.

"The dogs were with us," says Raven. "They kept us warm."

Jasper sets about finding a straight branch. Kit hands him the Ace bandage. Jasper works on Bruno's leg while the boy whimpers and the girl jabbers manically about the dogs saving their lives, about how she tried to light a fire but all the wood was wet, how she tried to find a trail but the snow hid everything, how she couldn't leave Bruno alone because how would she find him again, how the weather came out of nowhere and when did it ever snow this much so soon in the season. . . .

Midway through binding the leg, Jasper stops to stare at her until she stops speaking. "Let's conserve our energy," he says. She reminds him so much of Daphne at her worst, Daphne in a panic over some minor catastrophe or other. They will all get through this alive, maybe minus a few toes, an earlobe or two. Kit and Jasper may have to take turns mushing and walking—depends how supple the snow is on the return—but the sky is clearing, and the sun will be out long enough for them to reach the house before dark. Loraina will be in a very bad mood, holding down the commercial fort. That's fine, but please, thinks Jasper, please let Kyle be sober, just for the rest of this difficult day. His hip rebukes him as he stumbles to his feet, but the dogs are eager and ready to go.

Kyle's not at the house when they make it back, but he left a note: *How's this for lunch? Gone to check on Sally and Myrtle. Back soon with more coffee!* And, the cosmos willing, a case of Mountain Dew.

Sitting on the warm woodstove is a pot of boiled hot dogs and another of canned beans. On the table sits a bowl containing chopped-up lettuce and chunks of carrot. Beside the salad, Paul Newman's at the ready with his jaunty carnivorous smile and famous blue eyes. (Eyes like a husky, come to think of it. That spooky crystalline blue.) Kyle's even put out plates and forks.

It's clear he got the small plow rigged to the front of Jasper's truck and got it down the driveway; a wobbly track leads to the road. Power's still out, but the town rigs are going through; you can hear, from somewhere near enough, the grinding protest of their blades as they strike the potholes in the road. Without the truck, however, they can't get Bruno to the hospital on their own. Kit volunteers to head down and flag the first vehicle pointed toward town. He'll ask the driver to call an ambulance once he gets there. Jasper can't wait to be rid of Bruno and Raven, return them to the world of perpetually generated warmth, electricity, and people paid to deal with the damages wrought by human folly: privileges the pair do not seem to appreciate.

He's sitting with Raven at the kitchen table. Bruno is propped on the couch, wrapped in comforters, triple dosed on Jasper's painkillers, a blazing fire in the hearth. After eating a few bites of hot dog and beans, he dozed off.

Among the too much information Jasper now has about this couple, he knows that Bruno and Raven are "collaborative creative engineers" who teach at the famous art school in Providence. Once it was clear to the girl that her boyfriend would survive, once he fell asleep, her hysteria gave way to hunger. After two large helpings of everything, she's begun to sermonize. She explains how they've compromised their aversion to all things urban in order to be the art-ists they are meant to be. Together, they construct bamboo bridges linking trees together in parks, on college greens, sometimes on pri-vate grounds. The idea is to draw people into dialogue with trees. "So many people don't realize that our survival, our very ability to breathe, will come down to the worldwide fate of trees. It is almost as simple as that!" She seems to think of herself and Bruno as arbo-real missionaries. Every chance they get, they flee the city and find someplace off the beaten track. Nature in the raw is their inspiration.

And just about their demise, thinks Jasper as he listens to Raven yammer on while they wait for the medics to arrive.

"Sometimes we think of doing what we do off the grid. Except that so many people who do that are totally crazy. I mean, I hate to say it, crackpots. And it would defeat our ultimate purpose. The problem with cities is that really, when you get down to it, they are such small places. I mean, all the spaces you inhabit are so confined, the ways of thinking so yoked to that kind of living, living in boxes when you think about it, never mind all the dependencies you develop. We need places like *this* to get ourselves centered again."

She gestures out the window at the snowbound world from which she's just, by the skin of her well-tended teeth, been rescued. "I just love how *big* it is!"

"Quoth the actress to the bishop," mutters Jasper. He's turned away from her, adding wood to the stove.

"Excuse me?" Ah, the sharp ears of youth.

"We all love that, don't we?" he says blithely, turning to face her. "The bigness. It's not called the great outdoors for nothing." He lis-tens for a siren. What he wouldn't give right now for a hot bath and a shot, just one, of Jim Beam.

Kit comes in and tells them help should arrive soon. He stopped a plow, and the driver radioed his boss. Failing to read Jasper's rescue-me expression, he joins Bruno in the living room. After a bit, Jasper hears them talking quietly. Christ, are they talking about the glory of the great outdoors as well?

As Jasper contemplates telling Raven he's got to go check on the dogs (he doesn't; those creatures are out for the count), a minor cacophony of clicks, hums, and groans announces the return of power. He listens for a few minutes, waiting to see if it will hold.

The computer twinkles.

"Snow in the forecast? How's that for breaking news?" says Jasper. He realizes he forgot to power down the computer before the blackout.

As he walks toward his desk, the phone rings.

"Well, now I know we're both alive to face the invasion together," says Loraina.

"How many runs are open?"

"Three. The usual suspects. Power came back a few hours ago."

"You get through the night okay?"

"All digits intact. Thought you'd have been in here by now. Plows have been through, haven't they?"

"Small detour from the daily norm," says Jasper. "Remember those hikers from Rhode Island?"

"Who?"

"Never mind. We stumbled on some backcountry . . ." He almost said *backcountry wankers,* a term used fondly by Kirkus, an Aussie on the ski patrol. But then he remembered that the wankers were both within earshot. "Hikers who lost their way in the storm."

This is when he becomes aware of the siren.

"Have to call you back. Under control over there?"

"Stu made it in on time. I've got Carlos and Ginny lined up to give lessons. Hey. Know what? You'd be redundant."

"Best news I've heard all day," says Jasper.

Flashing lights assault the interior of the house, and the EMTs pour out of the ambulance like a SWAT team in a cheap action movie. Here come the heroes, the ones who can almost always work some kind of small, crucial miracle. Except when they can't.

After the backcountry wankers have been dispatched in the ambulance—based on the demeanor of Raven, it doesn't look like they learned much of a lesson—Jasper goes upstairs to his bedroom. Kit is on the phone with his family.

Despite the repairs on the damaged corner of the house, a miniature drift of snow weaseled its way through the chinks that remain. Now, with the heat rising, it's melting swiftly into the seams between the floorboards. Jasper fetches a towel from the bathroom and throws it over the wet spot.

He wants to lie down, but if he does, he'll fall asleep instantly. He knows he won't make it to the slope: the sky's already edging toward dark, though normally that wouldn't be an excuse. Still, he has things to do before he can let himself collapse. And he's suddenly hungry, having sacrificed most of his lunch to the "creative engineers."

How he craves that bath, or just a good blistering shower, but the water won't be hot enough yet, probably not for an hour. He stands idly in front of his dresser and gazes at the framed photograph of Vivian holding Kyle, one week old, Rory standing beside her, his smile a poor disguise for his confusion.

The last of the day's sunlight, angled toward the picture, shows how dusty it is. Back when Loraina spent the night, she'd tell him how silly it was not to pay for weekly visits from a housekeeper. "Good for the flagging economy, not just your lungs," she said, patting his chest as they lay in bed.

Kit's voice rises through the house: he's telling one of his children about the sensation of driving the dogsled through the deep snow. (Funny how you can always tell from an adult's voice when a child is being addressed.) Jasper and Kit took turns on the way back home, holding the dogs to a moderate pace, partly to minimize the impact on Bruno's leg. There was too much tension for even bare-bones chit-chat, but once it was clear the awkward scheme would work, once the snow had stopped falling for good (and once he took three aspirins from the first-aid kit), Jasper felt the pleasure of deep winter penetrate the chill—January two months early. What this means about the rest of the season to come is anybody's guess. Jasper laughs at the local "sages" who swear, year after year, by the *Farmer's Almanac*. They always have good if convoluted excuses handy when its predictions clash with how the seasons really do play out.

Not that Jasper's short on convoluted excuses of his own.

Kit says good-bye to his son, tells the boy how much he misses him, how he thinks he'll be home within a week. "Take care of your sister," he says. And after the boy's reply, "I know you don't think so, but I promise you she does."

Jasper goes back downstairs. "Everything good at home?"

"They got six inches," says Kit. "Not enough for a snow day, but the kids are thrilled. Enough to go sledding."

"Or take a whack at skis."

Kit laughs.

"I'm going to wear you down before you leave."

"You already have," says Kit. "And now I'm going to cook a real meal, no offense to Kyle."

"He used the resources at hand, and that's our good fortune." He almost said, *And that's a miracle.* This is it, Jasper tells himself: the end of his having so little faith in Kyle. If his faith has been resurrected only to be crushed anew, so be it. Throw the boy a wedding, he thinks—then wonders at this turnabout generosity. Maybe it's the expansive relief he feels at having shed Raven and Bruno.

He is heading to the computer, ready to face the e-blizzard, when the phone rings. Loraina. He forgot to call her back.

"Hey, doll," he answers.

After a pause, he hears, "Hello there, Jasper. It's good to hear your voice."

Not possible. He holds his breath.

"Jasper? I don't mean to give you a scare. How are you?"

"Daphne." Jesus Crooked Christ. "How am I? Snowed in." The easiest answer to hand.

"Us, too," she says. "Was that a perfect storm or what?"

Quoth the breathless bishop to the actress splayed on the fucking sheets.

"Jasper? Are you still there?"

"Here I am. Yup. Right here."

"Okay. I called because I'm trying to reach Kit. Sandra told me he's with you. I hadn't heard from him in weeks, and I just . . ." It's finally hit her, how wrongheaded this conversation is, at the very least how absurd. She says primly, "I'm glad you've stayed in touch, the two of you."

"Matter of fact, we haven't. Let me get him." He carries the phone through the kitchen and into the mudroom, where Kit is poking through the freezer.

"Your mom." When he sees Kit's face, he says, "My guess is no one's died, because she started off talking weather." Kit takes the receiver as if it might burn his hand.

"I'll be visiting the dogs." Jasper goes outside just as Kyle drives up.

"No shortage of excitement around here!" Kyle exclaims as he takes grocery bags from the passenger side of the truck. "You were heroic, Dad."

"Once upon a time, that was part of my job description."

"Hero?"

"More like idiot-finder."

"They were damn lucky."

"They were." Jasper starts toward the kennel, then stops. "How's Sally?"

"Doing great. She's smart enough to have a generator."

"Don't start."

Kyle laughs. "Just saying, Dad!"

"Of all the things on my Santa list, a generator's pretty far down," says Jasper, but Kyle's already maneuvering the groceries through the kitchen door, and Trixie's barking. *What are you waiting for, slowpoke? We've earned two dinners today,* she's telling him, and justifiably so.

Jasper goes up to the fence and says, "I am the decider-in-chief around here, missy. I say what's what." But he'll give them extra kibble, and he'll set aside scraps or drippings from whatever dinner Kit conjures for the humans.

When he goes in, Kit looks up from measuring rice and says, "I didn't tell her why I'm here. I left her to wonder."

Kyle, who's accepted the thankless job of chopping onions, says, "Why *are* you here, Kit?"

The next day at the shop is hell or it's heaven, depending on whether you see it in terms of energy expended or funds gathered. Loraina falls quickly into what Jasper calls her "honey groove," sweet-talking customers fast and deft as an acrobat juggling torches. Stu keeps finding excuses to visit the stockroom and hide from the melee. Jasper can hardly blame him. God but people are whiners these days.

At 11:00 a.m., on the main run, there's a collision resulting in a fractured leg and a concussion (the damage one-sided). By two the

Cocoa Hut runs out of Reddi-wip, and the line at the lift threatens to snake right through the lodge and into the parking lot. (Never mind the money. Is it worth the wait, that rush of the descent?) Complaints come in from the rink that an eight-year-old's birthday guests are hogging the ice.

Looking out at the junior slope, where three instructors are hard at work, Jasper realizes that he's never going to teach another lesson—though he would make an exception if Kit brought those city twins north. The remainder of his days at this place are likely to be spent indoors, checking inventory, answering phones, doing his best to avoid mastering the latest computer wizardry designed to maximize profits. (*Follow us on Twitter,* his sagging ass.)

At five-thirty, by which time darkness has finally put a crimp in business, Loraina says, "Go home, old man."

"Not time yet, darlin'."

"I'm serious."

"Who's ordering who around?"

"Whom."

"Thanks, teach."

"Stu wants overtime. Iron Man won't mind on a day like today. So go."

"I haven't forgotten about your birthday dinner."

"Nor have I, buster."

"Sure you want to be seen on the town with an 'old man'?"

"You know what they say about beggars."

"Thanks a lot."

"Y'all are so welcome, bluebird." She bats her blue lashes.

On the drive home, when he isn't focusing hard on the road, dreading a spinout, he thinks about his welcoming committee: those two boys in their separate forms of limbo. Time to send them home, too.

When he walks in, Kyle is setting the table, Kit putting food on three plates. They're chatting about children. Kyle's bragging about Sally's girl as if she were his own: her good grades, her prowess on the swim team.

"K One and K Two," announces Jasper when he closes the door behind himself. "You're acting like a pair of girlfriends." In another era, he'd have said *a pair of homos,* but time and various female companions have taught him to watch his tongue. Can't help it if his mind won't come to heel.

"Hey, Dad. Right on cue. Loraina gave us the heads-up on your ETA."

"That meat loaf?"

"Turkey," says Kit. "A recipe I found, believe it or not, while waiting for an oil change at the mechanic's. Some food magazine called *Lite* or *Lean*."

"So I can't get a doctor's excuse to kick you out."

Kit and Kyle look at him, then at each other.

"Joking," says Jasper. "Half, anyways. Certainly let's have that meat loaf. Maybe a farewell round of cribbage?"

They are so agreeable that he feels sheepish when, after dinner, he tells them he needs to get back to his routines. "Kyle, I'm sending you back to Sally."

"Tonight?"

"No time like the present. Get up off your duff, down on your knees, and propose. Do it properly, will you? Then get back to me."

Kyle laughs nervously. "Dad?"

"Kit here's going to get up early tomorrow, help me finish the fine restorations"—he gestures at the corner of the living room—"then get his own duff back to New Jersey, before he turns grizzly, immune to civilization."

Jasper must ignore the look on Kit's face: the bookish word *crestfallen* (does anybody ever say that?) comes to mind. "We will talk in the morning," he says, "but for now I'm done. Finito. I am sleepwalking here. You two clean up, I'd be grateful." He wills his old-man hips to let him rise from the couch. "Alley-oop," he says.

"And upward," says Kit. He and Kyle look at each other and laugh.

Before they can make further fun of him, Jasper goes to his room. He hears the two men murmuring below, running water, filling the dishwasher. He is asleep before he can make sure that Kyle's out the door.

Waking, he smells toast. It's not yet seven. "Who beat me to it?" he calls out as he hobbles to the bathroom.

"Only me," Kit calls out. "Kyle says he'll phone tonight."

"Coffee ready?"

"Whenever you are."

No avoiding it now, and really, what is the big deal? Will there be blubbering? Is that his true fear: emotion? What emotion, after all the years, the births, the wrongful deaths (aren't they all?), the disappointments and shamings, the switchbacks in fortune, could be too fearsome for Jasper?

He puts on two layers bottom, three layers top, a pair of thick fleece socks. The house is blessedly warm, but outdoors the air looks so clear, every pine needle in such startling focus, that he has no doubt it's seriously cold, summa cum laude frigid.

Kit's at the stove, making—what, fried tomatoes? And he's found those godawful egg whites, which Jasper thought he'd hidden behind the cold cuts.

He picks up the mug of coffee Kit has poured for him. "Moment of truth," he announces. "I just needed to poke around a little before I could be sure of what I know. Stoke the embers." He taps his forehead. "I mentioned that your mother told me about that fellow's family, how she had a little help from his folks after you were born. For a few years."

Kit turns around. He looks far more frightened than eager.

"I told you that much, didn't I?"

"Help?" says Kit. "They helped?"

"Please don't burn my breakfast," Jasper says.

Kit slides the skillet off the burner, turns the knob. "Just start again. Whatever you know."

"It was the mother who helped, I mean with some money. The Other Grandmother, that's how your mom referred to her. The money went toward your mom's school costs. While she lived with your grandparents—I mean the ones you do know. Did know." Jasper sighs. "I happen to be famished. Can we eat while I try to make sense of this story?"

Kit fumbles in the cupboard for plates, in the drawer for forks. Like a child, Jasper stays at the table and waits to be served. When the food's in front of him, Kit seated across the table, he takes a bite of fried tomato, chews and swallows it before speaking again. "She got to see you a couple of times, when you were a baby. This Other

Grandmother. But according to your mom, at some point she tried to set some conditions that seemed unreasonable."

"What conditions?" Kit hasn't touched his food.

"Oh, Christopher, I don't know those details. Honest to God. By the time I heard all this, your mother saw it as water way the heck under the bridge."

Kit's jaw tightens. "Right. That's how she puts it to me. Water under the fucking bridge."

"Calm down," says Jasper. "And would you please eat something? Or don't. But just listen for a sec. This isn't easy, and when I say this stuff, it sounds absurd. I'll scare myself silent if you don't watch out."

Kit stares at him quietly now. He's back to his essential state of waiting, listening: the cautious child who never took to barreling down the mountain with a war cry of some sort. Suddenly Jasper sees it as sadness, not grace.

"The point I'm getting to is this," he says. "Your mom cut ties with that family when you were still a baby. She did it when she was independent enough to take care of you. No small feat. And she did it, maybe, because it hurt too much that the guy wouldn't be a part of her life and yours—and I swear to you I never knew his name. I think she felt like she couldn't go forward if she didn't do it alone. So for all the sins I will never forgive that mother of yours, don't you start building up unnecessary grudges."

"God, Jasper." Kit breathes heavily, as if the air in the kitchen has grown as cold as the outside promises to be.

"What I'm saying is, you go forward, too. With what I have to tell you."

"You know who that woman was. The grandmother."

Jasper nods, chewing his egg whites. Kit spiced them up a bit: not bad.

"Is there any chance she's still alive?"

"Matter of fact, she is," says Jasper. "But I can't vouch for compos mentis. She'd be in her eighties. She lives up north. Husband's a state senator named Zeke Burns. Your grandfather. Also alive, if maybe barely."

He's probably going about this all wrong. He's no social worker. Kit will have to cope with his clubfooted methods.

Now the boy is practically hyperventilating. "Up north? You mean here, Vermont? I have grandparents here in Vermont? What about my father? What about him? If you know who his parents are—"

"Hold your Holsteins. I have a hunch about him, but I think we're best off starting with the grandmother."

"Should I write her?"

Jasper goes to his desk. "I have it all here: address, phone number, e-mail. These people even have a fax machine." *These people?* Christ.

"I could drive there. I could drive there today."

"Now wait," says Jasper. "You're not giving anybody a heart attack. Drive up to their door, you just might do that. Or they'll peg you for some sponge-brained evangelist."

Kit reaches for the piece of paper Jasper's holding. Jasper thinks about the elderly senator felled by the stroke, his possibly-soon-to-be-widow. "You could call this woman, I suppose—you could do it now, from here—but what if . . ."

"What if she doesn't want to hear from me? Right," Kit says quietly. "After all these years, why would she?"

Jasper has thought this through; Viv would be proud of him. "Well, say that's the case. Which I doubt. Then we go ahead and look for the son. Your father." Go slow, he reminds himself, seeing the wide-eyed, feral expression on Kit's gentle face. Loraina's right: people hunger to know where they came from.

"He never wanted me, did he?"

"We don't know that," says Jasper.

"Of course we do!" And here, finally, are the tears, angry tears, wiped roughly away with a dish towel.

"Kit." Jasper wants to go around the table and touch him, but he figures that might not be wise. "How about I be the one to call her? I can call her right now, hand the phone to you if she gives the word."

Kit struggles to control himself. "I'd better eat something first."

"Tuck in." Jasper takes his own plate, scraped clean, to the sink. "Know what? I'll miss your cooking."

Kit looks up from his food. "I'll be back, Jasper. I promise."

"You better." Jasper decides to wash the skillet; it keeps him at the sink. Best hold his tongue on the subject of promises.

"What's her name?" says Kit, almost inaudibly.

Only a coward would stall with *Whose name?* "Lucinda Burns."

"Lucinda Burns." Long pause. "So my name would have been Burns."

"Well, maybe in a life you should probably be glad you're not living." The emotions are deepening in a way that makes Jasper queasy. The skillet is clean, the sink empty. He *is* a coward. "Hey," he says, forcing himself to return to his place at the table, "like my name hasn't served you just fine?"

"Sorry."

"Oh, don't be a moron. I'm ribbing you."

Kit shakes his head. "Mom's going to kill me, I guess."

"Throw a few punches. Big deal," says Jasper. "You've been a good son to that mother of yours."

"Until now."

"Forty-odd years of being the perfect son? I'd call that plenty. I'd call that boring. How about you take a page from Kyle? Though Christ, could he take a volume from you."

Kit carries his plate to the sink. He's rinsing it when he says, "Kyle's not bad, not anything near bad."

Jasper wants to object—to say *Now did I ever call him bad?*—but he has thought in those terms. He is not always a good father. Who is? And this takes his thoughts to the fellow who might have held up his side of the biological bargain and stuck around for Kit. Or no; for Daphne. For the first time in ages, for a passing moment, he feels the same shielding compassion he felt for her on the night she was brave enough to tell him her story—or what she could bear to tell of it. But Kit is the one who matters now.

"I'd better feed the beasts. Then let's make that call."

"I plan to help finish the work, you know." Kit looks at the corner of the room that needs new paneling.

"Nah," says Jasper. "You're headed home today. I've got Jim signed up for that. No offense intended, but I won't have to babysit the job."

"No offense taken," says Kit.

"I don't think he's worse off than when you last saw him," says Sharon. "Sometimes, though, he gets a little paranoid. The doctor says that's not unusual."

"Who's conspiring against him?"

"Oh, Jasper, stop expecting it to make any sense. That's what I have to keep telling myself."

They are sitting together on a couch in the reception area of the place Jasper has come to think of as Rayburn's new home. More like Rayburn's last home. Sharon's wearing a yellow dress, an obvious effort at cheer; lipstick gives her a much-needed touch of youth. Rayburn may not be worse off than he was three weeks ago, but Sharon looks like she's three years older. Jasper doesn't recall those creases in her throat. She's also become accidentally slim, the kind of slim one should resist complimenting.

"Sharon—"

"Stop. I already hear what you're going to say. 'Sharon, you are . . .' Multiple choice. A saint. An angel. A trouper. A devoted wife." She ticks the options off on her fingers, then pauses before making the sound of a game-show buzzer. "Wrong. Correct answer: none of the above. Want to know what I am, Jasper? A woman with no choice. Simple as that."

Jasper had planned on option A: a saint. Useless chump that he is.

Sharon smiles apologetically. She taps Jasper's knee. "You go see him on your own. Tell him I'll be back for lunch tomorrow. If he asks, which I bet he won't, I'm going home to eat takeout linguini with clams and watch *Roman Holiday*. Netflix is my latest vice."

"Audrey Hepburn."

"No, Jasper. Gregory Peck." She leaves without kissing or hugging him. She's probably sick and tired of all the affection people think will somehow make up for no husband. Worse than no husband: an impostor husband.

Rayburn perches on the edge of his bed, wearing a blue tracksuit. In his former life, Rayburn wouldn't be caught dead in an outfit like this. He'd have called it something like yupster jammies. He needs a haircut and a shave.

The bed is made but mussed up. Two Kinky Friedman mysteries are about to slip off the mattress into the gap at the footboard, along with the local paper. (Yes, speaking of saints, there's the story about Mitchum and Zev, the front-page picture showing the dogs outside the hospital, one posed to either side of City Boy Bruno, who's grinning shamelessly from his wheelchair. After the editor begged—and Loraina told Jasper to get off his high horse—Jim drove the dogs over for their big tabloid moment. How to make heroes out of scoundrels, celebrities out of blockheads.)

"Hail, chief," states Rayburn, saluting Jasper.

"Hail to you, boss." Jasper sits in the armchair near the window. The view is calming: the edge of a woods striped with pink-skinned birches.

"She gone?"

"She has a date with Gregory Peck."

Rayburn looks worried; he seems to consider this. "Maybe in my situation that's the best thing."

"Your situation?" To think he'd begun to relax.

"Whatever you do, you mustn't tell them."

Jasper knows better than to ask what it is he mustn't tell whom. He points at the paper. "See how my two ill-behaved mongrels are suddenly stars? I could charge good money for kids to come over and pet them. About all I'm fit for these days. Run a petting zoo. Every morning I get out of bed, some new joint cries uncle."

Rayburn picks up the paper, stares at the picture of the dogs, but shows no recognition or interest. "Thing is, I couldn't resist her. She was . . ." He drops the paper and groans with longing. "You remember how they are at that age."

Jasper simply nods.

"She was ripe is all I can say. Without getting down to details. She wouldn't like that." He flicks his eyebrows at Jasper. *We looking at a hot dame or what, boss?* Rayburn's expression when they spotted Daphne at the reception after Litch's funeral.

"The bad news is, her parents are going to hunt me down here, and if Sharon finds out, I am cooked. I need some kind of decoy, a way to divert them."

"Sharon won't find out, I'll make sure of that." Jasper can't bear this. "I have a bunch of news, though, news of my own," he blurts out loudly. "Kit came to visit for a few days. Daphne's boy. You remember him."

Jasper watches Rayburn shift gears. The gears are grinding, but he's getting there. At some point, he probably won't be able to do this anymore. His world, says Sharon, will keep on shrinking until it's like a little snow globe of his own making, capable of agitation but never change.

"Christopher," says Rayburn. "The one who stuck by you."

It takes an effort not to praise Rayburn for getting it right. "He's married with twins. Lives in New Jersey now."

"That's old news. I haven't gone totally senile yet."

"Well, we don't always remember these things, do we?" It's hard to hold fast to Rayburn's gaze, not because Rayburn looks distracted but because he looks so intent on connection, as if to string a tight-rope between them. After a moment, it's too hard to sustain; Jasper's eyes wander. He sees the hospital slipper socks on Rayburn's feet, the bag of cookies Sharon must have brought. On the windowsill, not far from the cookies, a plastic pitcher with a cap, a telltale shape. It's for pissing in.

He forces himself to look back at Rayburn, who seems to be wait-ing for him to continue. "The twins are nine years old now, can you believe it? Anyway, he was here for the big storm. He was with me when we found those fool hikers, the ones in the story." He points back at the newspaper.

"He doesn't know about me, does he?"

Jasper hesitates. "No, Rayburn, nobody does. You're safe."

Rayburn shakes his head. "I wish that were so."

"Kyle was around, too. And here's the big news: Kyle's getting married. It's not going to be easy—Kyle never goes for easy—but she's more than nice. She's strong. That's obvious. She's known him for long enough, too."

Rayburn beams. "I've been waiting for that news. You getting married again. About time. About goddamn time. You've mourned too long for Viv. Bite my head off, but it's the truth." He holds out his hand. "Congratulations."

Jasper shakes his head, waves his hands in denial. He laughs, try-ing not to sound nervous. "Kyle. Kyle's the one getting married."

"Kyle owes you money, doesn't he?" says Rayburn. "I hope he appreciates all you've done, all these years. And you know, I don't think his brother's been too helpful there. I don't care if he lives in friggin' Siberia."

Jasper sighs. "Can I have one of Sharon's cookies?"

"Help yourself. Cookies are too fattening for me." He lays a hand across his gut and whispers, "Have to stay as young as possible now, keep my mojo up and running."

Jasper fetches the cookies. The surface of the ziplock bag is fogged, which means they're still warm. When he opens the bag, the scent of chocolate gives him a surge of wayward bliss. In a cruel flash, he imagines marrying Sharon.

"I can't stop seeing her," Rayburn says urgently. "And the fact that she'd go for someone like me—would you be able to resist? It's risky, but . . . life is short, as you well know." He chuckles. "She has a ring in her belly button. Gold. Fourteen-karat gold. Tip of my tongue fits right through it."

"Well!" Yikes. Enough of this. Returning to his chair, Jasper glances at the table beside Rayburn's bed. He sees a list of words written on a piece of paper. The handwriting is a shakier version of Rayburn's normal scrawl.

Rayburn sees that Jasper's spotted the list. "My words," he says. "Words it occurs to me I'm losing. So when I capture them, get them back for a minute, I write them down. That way I can't lose them again. Did you know that writing actually wires stuff directly into your brain?"

"Makes sense to me," says Jasper. Thank God for chocolate-chip cookies. He takes two and puts the bag back on the sill, careful to lay it some distance from the pitcher for pissing.

"Let me read you today's list." Rayburn holds the paper at a distance. "*Wavelength. Scrotum. Downpour. Arboretum. Scrotum* reminded me of that one, so I thought I'd put it down, too. *Meniscus.* Which reminded me of *hibiscus.* Also, *discus.* . . . And how about *hyperbole*?"

Jasper wonders if it's a good thing, or a bad thing, that the words on this list aren't words like *dog* or *shoe* or *pillow.*

"We're all shedding the nouns," says Jasper. "The nouns go first, is what I've been told. Personally, I can live without *arboretum* or *hyperbole.*"

"But not *scrotum*!" Rayburn exclaims with joy. "Not *vulva*!"

Jasper wants desperately to look at his watch. He wants to be with Rayburn at the nearest bar, with music too loud for all this distressing conversation. Some lousy local garage band would do. He could ask Sharon's permission to get his old friend into some authentic clothing and take him out, but Rayburn would probably lose his bearings, might even panic. This room, along with a few others in this big old house, is where he leads his entire life these days.

Rayburn says, "I am so glad you are getting married again. Do I know her? Tell me I know her."

Jasper looks him in the eye and says, "Loraina." If this gets back to Sharon, and he doubts that it will, he'll go from there.

Rayburn looks as if he's straining to remember her. "Whoever she is, I hope she's your ace in the hole."

Jasper smiles. "Quoth the cardinal to the bishop."

Rayburn returns his smile, but with a shadow of confusion. He startles Jasper by calling loudly, "Sharon! Get in here, Sharon!" He waits, listening. "She in the kitchen? Let's share your news."

Jasper sighs. "Forgot to tell you, she's gone out. Shopping. You know what? I'll call her up later and tell her myself."

"She'll like that," says Rayburn. He looks content. He closes his eyes. "I think I'm tired. Nap time. I hear that's good for my . . . Well, lost another word there. Down the rabbit hole."

"Constitution, maybe," offers Jasper. Libido, he thinks.

"*Constitution* is a good one," says Rayburn. "Many meanings there. A legendary ship, for one." He locates his pen and adds it to his list. It seems he can spell just fine. He opens the drawer in his side table, slips the list in. Jasper can see that the drawer is jammed with slips of paper. Lists of lost words.

"I'll invite you to the wedding," says Jasper, "when I've got the date." He stands up, brushing cookie crumbs from his lap onto the linoleum floor.

"Don't tell her, either, okay? If you don't mind. I know it's hard to keep things from your sweetheart, but this is me asking."

"You're the only one who could hold me to that promise," says Jasper. He pats his friend on one shoulder—the prominence of the bone another pulse of heartbreak.

You could think of promises as a series of nets: some hold for a lifetime; others give way, surprisingly flimsy, in no time at all. Promises to keep secrets, those are the trickiest ones—especially when they're secrets you don't even know you've been keeping.

He walks as fast as he can through the lobby, waves at the attendant, welcomes the slap of cold air once he's out. As he crosses the parking lot, he licks melted chocolate from between his fingers. Maybe you could call it the taste of a good marriage, of love expressed in forbidden but wholesome pleasures. Jasper didn't bother to correct Rayburn when he made that remark about mourning Viv too long. But come to think of it, he was on the money. Maybe Daphne never quite took hold on Jasper's heart. Maybe that was part—just part—of why she skipped out. Maybe it's also part of why Jasper felt reluctant to betray her long-outdated trust. Guilt.

He shakes his head vigorously, like a dog, as if unwanted memories and duplicitous emotions could fly from your head like droplets of water.

The sky is both fading and brightening: the crisp daytime blue is changing, simultaneously, to a timid grayish pink at the horizon, to a robust sapphire high overhead. The temperature is expected to rise in a few days; the snow will begin melting, then freeze. Driving will be treacherous, the skiing crummy. He and Loraina will have more time to bicker as customers dwindle. But right now the slope's got to be crowded, the shop's registers consuming money the way an ex-con tucks in meat.

The past few days, after nine, ten hours at the slope, Jasper has returned home, once again, to solitude—not counting the dogs. It feels good in some ways, in others not. He sleeps better than he has in a while, and his hip is giving him a reprieve, as if to reward him for coming to his sorry senses.

S HE WALKED ACROSS THE MEADOW surrounding the Silo, the blond surface of the empty stage reflecting the last vestige of sunlight. She stopped to stare at it, watching for the glow to fade. She imagined not the upcoming concert in which she would play her solo but a concert much further in the future, when she would return to play as a visiting artist, someone the campers would revere and discuss at a Saturday morning breakfast, coveting her dresses, guessing at her love life. In a fantasy stretched further yet, she was married to Malachy. They toured together—and lived in a penthouse near Carnegie Hall. Daphne had been to New York City just once, on a family trip when Andrew turned eighteen. They hadn't gone to any concerts—the trip was her Neanderthal brother's celebration, so a Yankees game was the highlight—but her mother had taken her for a walk along the façade of the legendary concert hall, to browse the posters and linger for a moment under the crimson awning of the Russian Tea Room.

"Dreaming of our glorious debut?"

She gasped and then, defying her nerves, laughed. "I wish you'd stop sneaking up on me."

"You've sneaked up on me just as often, haven't you?" said Malachy. "Isn't that how we met?"

"I think it's hard to take you by surprise," she said.

He wore jeans that looked brand-new and a brown sweater over a pale blue T-shirt. "So, shall we head over early, get front-row seats?"

For the Fourth of July, they had a rare night off. Daphne was surprised; only a minority of their teachers and conductors could claim this holiday as theirs. On the other hand, who didn't love fireworks? Most of the campers had crowded into cars to head for the display in the nearest town, but according to the solfège master, if you went to the strip of beach, or anywhere along the lake, you could watch the fireworks go off in several towns on the opposite shore.

The spot where they had first talked—which Daphne still thought of as hers, still enjoyed alone most afternoons—was empty. Through the woods, she heard a few people talking on their way to the beach. They sounded like adults, not campers.

Malachy had brought along a blanket and a Hershey bar. By the time they settled comfortably, the sky was almost indistinguishable from the water, both a fathomless gemstone blue.

"I want my money back if the show isn't good enough," said Malachy. "But first. Do we save the chocolate or eat it right now?"

"Now," said Daphne.

"I agree. Now is almost always the better choice. You never know about later." He unwrapped the bar and broke it in two. He held out the halves, waved them around a moment, and said, "One promises fame, the other happiness. Be careful which one you choose."

She laughed; he was always making her laugh. "Will you tell me which is which?"

"Of course not. And I'm not sure which one I'd choose."

"Then don't share. Take both."

He shook his head. "Can't have both."

"Can't you?" said Daphne. "So you think Esme McLaughlin is unhappy? I mean, she certainly has the fame."

Malachy gave her a look of mock disbelief. "I am talking about the virtue of sharing. My mother brought me up to share. That is why I can't have both." He bit into one half and handed her the other. "There you go, Miss Indecisive. One way or another, our fates are sealed."

There had been several concerts since opening night, but the girls couldn't stop talking about Esme: was it fair to have so much talent and beauty at once? Talent that was *rewarded*. Because they all knew that being gifted alone promised you nothing—oh no, as their teachers repeatedly warned, not without the work.

"Work, it is zee ox-ee-gen of art," droned Natalya when they wearied of playing the same measures over and over again.

At last it was dark. A number of boats had anchored, also awaiting the show. It began with a starburst of orange to their left, a casual crackling, a muffled boom.

"Ooh," said Malachy. "And aah. And ooh again."

Tentatively, Daphne leaned against him. He did not lean away.

They watched as the fireworks rose, geyserlike, from an unseen source: higher and higher, more varied in color, their reflections projecting farther and farther on the surface of the lake, as if reaching toward the two of them.

"I've never had private fireworks before," said Daphne.

"Then you're a virgin?"

She was stunned. Her arm, against his, felt glued in place.

"I'm sorry," he said. "I'm prone to bad jokes. That's how I am." He put his arm around her shoulder.

"I like how you are." She kept her voice level. When he didn't make another joke, she put a hand on his leg. "Can I just say it? How different you are? From the other guys here? Like you're older. Even if you're not." Of course, maybe it was just that he had finished high school a year early, while Daphne still had a year to go.

"I told you. I'm a weirdo."

"Maybe I'm one, too." *Takes one to know one,* she could have said.

"Not you, Swan."

"Maybe you should stop calling me that."

"I thought you liked it."

"I do. Or I did. But it's like . . ." She wanted to hear him say her name, hear *how* he would say it. Would that tell her how he felt? Her friends at home said that if a guy wanted you, he'd make the moves on you the first chance he found: *jump your bones,* she'd heard her brother say, typically crude. But Malachy was obviously different. Maybe he was courtly. Maybe he was shy: clever but shy. Why did boys have to be the ones to make the moves?

Awkwardly, but with an optimist's determination, she faced him, took hold of his face, and turned it toward hers. (Not as if she hadn't made out before—though never with a boy like this one.)

He kissed her back, but carefully. It felt as if he were studying her lips with his; a few seconds later his mouth opened, just slightly. He groaned, the way boys always did when they realized they had your permission, and he put his arms around her. They lay back on the blanket, laughing briefly at the impact of the rock when their heads met the ground. They kissed for a long time, and at some point the fireworks ceased, the chorus of crickets rose, and the air grew colder around them.

He was the one who stopped. "Daphne."

"You said my name," she whispered.

"Daphne, is this . . ."

"Are you going to ask if this is a good idea? We wouldn't be the only ones. Mei Mei and Craig . . ." Don't talk, she told herself. Listen. Did he have a girlfriend at home? If he did, he had never mentioned her.

Malachy sat up and rubbed his face, looking out at the lake.

She sat up beside him. "I just. I want . . ." She could hear her friend Lucy saying, *Never tell them, never be the first one to say it! It's the kiss of death!*

But Malachy said, "I know. I like you, too. I do. Daphne."

She ran a hand along his back, his knuckled spine. He stroked her shin.

"But this summer," he said.

"I know," she said quickly, before he could continue. "My mom says it's the time of our lives, and we need to focus on our work, I know that. But we're *doing* that, and we won't blow it. We won't stop working as hard as we are."

"I'm not worried about that." He sounded suddenly cold, almost indignant. "I'm just thinking that all this . . . intensity, that how we feel about everything here, everything and everybody, it's so . . ."

She hadn't known him to struggle with words, and it made her feel powerful. "If it gets in the way of work, we'll stop. But it won't."

To her dismay, he stood up. But he took her hand and pulled her to her feet.

"So that song," he said.

"What?"

"It's Erik Satie," he said. "Esme's song. I ran into Esme's piano player on my way over. Aren't you impressed that I remembered to ask after all this time?"

Daphne stared at him, openly confused.

He touched her forehead with one finger. "'Je te veux.' The encore."

How could she have forgotten? She thought of Esme leaning down as her voice plunged into its lowest register. If someone had taken an

EKG of Daphne's heart just then . . . "Erik Satie," she said as lightly as she could. "I don't really know his work. Honestly, not at all."

Malachy led the way through the bushes, back to the path. He held up a branch so that Daphne could pass beneath it. "Always more to learn," he said. "That's the pain and the pleasure."

3

Things I Wish Were True

T HE MEN FROM THE medical equipment company were
exceptionally kind for deliverymen: unrushed, careful to wipe
up the snow they tracked onto the front hall carpet. In the living
room, they offered to move the long damask sofa into the back hallway. Lucinda had already managed, in this reorchestration of furniture, to move the gateleg table from the hallway to a corner of the
den. Passing down the hall will be awkward now—the sofa is much
wider than the table—but Lucinda is the only one who needs to get
to the pantry.

Now, like a tyrant who's pulled off an overnight coup, a hospital
bed commands attention where the sofa has defined the room's commerce for more than forty years. She could have banished Zeke to the
den, but he'll be happier with the view he loves best: the patchwork
of irregular fields, stitched with stonewalls, that represents the last
of his father's once-sprawling farm. By the time Zeke Senior died, he
owned land that straddled the borders of two adjacent towns. Since
this is New England, not Iowa, his green empire included tracts of
judiciously timbered woodland, but his main enterprise, the source
of his pride, was the herd of Jersey cows that grazed the hilly pas-
tureland: a firm stand against the encroaching Holsteins, champion
producers but only in quantity. "Milk as thin and tasteless as wash
water," Zeke's father would say. "Though modern fools care only
about how much, not how good."

A glass case crowded with trophies and ribbons, many won by
her husband and his brothers when they were boys—a few, and this
still amazes her, won by her own sons—serves as a museum to her
father-in-law's standards. When he was alive, the case monopolized

the longest wall of the living room; after his death, Lucinda lob-
bied for it to be moved to the den. The living room wall now dis-
plays four landscapes by an artist who paints the natural beauties of
Vermont.

Jersey herds have gone the way of most independent farms. Nev-
ertheless, when Zeke faced selling off some of his inherited share of
the land—a decision both practical and thrifty—he sold most of it to
idealistic entrepreneurs, typically rich New Yorkers and Bostonians
who wanted to try their hand at growing heirloom kale or fussing
over goats. Zeke once described such ventures as "the number one
New Age hobby-loss line item," but he finds them far preferable to
the housing developments that pour down the picturesque slopes on
the tract of land left to his older brother.

Lucinda did not remove the Chinese rug, though the deliverymen
warned her that the wheels of the bed, when locked, might damage
it. Never mind. She is hopeful the bed won't be here too long. She
will not turn this room into a clinic.

In an hour, her daughter, Christina, will arrive in that profligate
minivan of hers, and they will drive to the rehab center, to bring
Zeke home. If she puts her mind to it, Lucinda can accomplish a lot
in that hour—though all she wants to do is to lie down upstairs, forget it all in sleep for just this last sliver of time alone. Tonight she'll
sleep on the foldout in the den—to be nearer Zeke in case he panics
or becomes disoriented in the middle of the night.

All right then: the flowers. With no time to visit the florist on her
round of errands, she chose the least sorry specimens at the grocery
store: yellow roses that are flawless in form but smell like old ice
cubes. She scans the high shelves in the pantry and chooses a vase of
dark blue glass.

After trimming and arranging the roses, Lucinda takes a package
of boneless chicken breasts out of the freezer. Bake them in tomato
sauce with herbs and capers? Or maybe that's too acidic for Zeke,
after all the bland geriatric food at the center. She worries that she
never heard him complain about those meals; did the stroke rob
him of taste as well as mobility? (Zeke loves eating out and eating
well, loves the richness of French food, the spice of Thai, anything
assertive in flavor. The few seasons she campaigned with him on the
deli/BBQ/doughnut tour—DBD heartburn their name for the usual

payback—they would end each day, alone in their bedroom, by listing the abominable foods they'd had to eat with such gusto. She was relieved to stay home when, after two terms, Zeke's seat was secure.)

Safer, she decides, to sauté the chicken in butter, mix it with pasta—shells, not spaghetti—and peas. Early this morning, she baked a pear pie.

When she opens the refrigerator to check on the ingredients— yes, good, a block of Parmesan—she decides on a glass of white wine; Christina will do all the driving. She pours a glass and sets it aside. First, she'll grate the cheese and put a large pot of water on the stove. Should she set the table? Will Zeke be able to sit at a table yet? Stairs are out of the question for at least a month, the therapist said, but didn't she say he'd be able to get around with a walker? Suddenly, Lucinda is terrified of being home alone with her husband in his abruptly altered state.

Your husband has a stroke: a common fate for women her age, yet it's hardly something you plan for. She imagines an educational seminar at the town's Senior Health Colloquium, called "In the All Too Likely Event" or "Worst-Case Scenarios." More practical than chair caning, holiday crafts, or Pilates (unpleasantly, Lucinda thinks of Pontius every time she sees that mystifying word).

She carries her wine into the living room and stops. Her habitual place on the sofa is gone because, of course, the sofa is gone. She chooses one of the wingback chairs flanking the fireplace—not the one where Zeke always sits but the one that belonged by custom to his father. (At Christmas, her son Mal used to joke that he could see his grandfather's ghost in this chair, warming his bony butt by the fire.) So now she faces the hospital bed, its taut sheets covered with a quilt she brought from upstairs, the one she made for Jonathan when he was ten: red airplanes, appliquéd square after square, on a pale blue sky. When Lucinda ordered the ugly, sinister bed, she knew this moment would come, the past hurtling forward into the present.

Twenty years ago, after her older son's final stay in the hospital— though, since he had survived so many infections by then, beaten so many odds, she did not see it that way—his doctor had suggested renting a bed like this one. She had even helped Lucinda order it. Hours before Mal's discharge, Lucinda directed the men up the steep stairs of the city brownstone to her son's apartment; remarkably, the bed made it all the way up. They were clearly familiar with maneu-vering such a bulky item through narrow spaces.

But Mal refused to sleep in that bed. "I see you've summoned the chariot of Thanatos," he said when he saw it, a jarring addition to his small but stylish living room. "Well, no thank you, Mom. I'll hail a cab when it's time to go. Preferably a Checker."

The insult of the bed was minor compared with the insult of his disease, which long before then had made a mockery of his dignity, his body, even his job at the paper—from which he'd been forced to retire. He was thirty-eight years old when he died. Until the very end, Lucinda wanted to believe that Mal's illness had also stolen his faith, so that saving his soul would be a matter merely of reclaiming it. In his last years, he told her repeatedly that he had never felt that kind of devotion, but she wouldn't believe it, not entirely, not until he chose to end his own life rather than live out the course of God's plan. Who could honestly say there had been no hope of recovery? Now, belatedly, she understands that void all too well, that dark cav-ity widening around the heart, that pitch-black hollow at the bottom of her rib cage.

She was so deeply alone with Mal's death. That he had died of AIDS, a disease barely touching their staid rural community, seemed to embarrass even her best friends, no matter how genuine their condolences. Christina was immersed in raising babies, a task she undertook with the same ferocity she had applied to studying and practicing law. Jonathan, adrift in his own life, flew from Califor-nia to New York and tried, mutely, clumsily—and, in retrospect, fearfully—to help his mother cope with his brother's "affairs" (such a painful word to Lucinda in the context of the disease, which killed Mal before he could find any sort of lasting love). Jonathan did tackle the essential work of packing the most portable contents of his brother's elegant apartment and shipping them to Vermont. For that much, Lucinda was grateful.

Zeke had been preoccupied with a possible run for a seat in Con-gress. Though he took a week's break from all the necessary scheming, he was constantly on the phone. Two months later, almost overnight, he dropped the notion of higher office. Sometimes Lucinda won-ders if all that networking, glad-handing, and calculated stroking of wealthy egos had simply been the best way for Zeke to hold on to his sanity. One of them had to stay sane, and it couldn't have been Lucinda.

Without consulting her, Zeke bought airline tickets to Italy that summer. He had rented a house near Perugia for a week. Lucinda had no desire to go anywhere yet no will to resist. Because she couldn't even think about packing, Christina filled an absurdly large suitcase for her mother with a wide range of outfits. It was featherlight next to the sorrow Lucinda was sure she would carry with her forever: so heavy, so immutably leaden, that she half expected to set off alarms as she and Zeke passed through airport security in Boston.

Italy was a colossal mistake. Everywhere, everywhere—in churches, in museums, even etched into the façades of buildings—Lucinda encountered Mary. Mary receiving the miraculous news. Mary holding her chosen baby son, a golden dinner plate perched on his head. Mary at the foot of the cross; Mary—visibly shattered; forget whatever prophecy some angel had revealed—cradling the beaten, lacerated, bloodied corpse of Jesus. The stigmata painted on his hands and feet were the color of the poppies that bloomed along the Umbrian roads, their petals fluttering in the dusty air stirred by passing trucks and cars.

Zeke did not share Lucinda's faith (though now and then, with an eye on his constituents rather than the Lord, he tagged along to Mass). So he couldn't understand that beyond this tauntingly ubiquitous reminder of losing a son, and to such a cruel death, Lucinda felt keenly the sacrilege of aligning her pain with the Virgin's incomparably holy anguish. All at once she could not accept the inevitability, let alone the celebration, inherent to the Passion; Mary was that boy's *mother*. If God were the least bit merciful, she'd have died first. And where was Joseph when she needed him most? (Perhaps he'd been busy contemplating a run for Congress.)

After their second day of sightseeing, a day of wandering the lofty rose-colored lanes of Assisi—Lucinda waiting outside the basilica while Zeke went in to admire the frescos—she refused to leave the rented house. It was large and magnificently old, though its stone walls sealed inside its rooms a damp, tomblike chill. At Lucinda's insistence, Zeke would go out alone for the day. She would sit under the awning over the patio, sometimes attempting to read a novel but mostly staring out at the neighboring fields, exactly as she'd been doing back at home. The one welcome difference was the privacy. No one came by to take the temperature of her grief. No one asked her if she had been eating or sleeping. No one tempted her to wonder, so uncharitably, if their motives were more prurient than loving. And perhaps because of the privacy, she did not cry so much. She wrote falsely reassuring postcards to Christina and Jonathan, and she thought about a quilt she might make if she could find fabrics in the particular blues, greens, and fleshy pinks of her surroundings.

Each evening, Zeke would return with cartons of restaurant food. He would read aloud from an English-language newspaper sold at a shop that catered to local expats. Lucinda listened almost contentedly to news of political strife and natural disasters, thankful for its irrelevance to her own tragedy. At the end of the week, they returned home, wearier than when they had left, to face the last trickle of condolence letters, from places as distant as Moscow, Rio de Janeiro, and a town in Italy to which they could have driven, from the rented villa, in under an hour.

Mal had traveled to every civilized, highly cultured corner of the world. Mal had been a well-known music critic, an authoritative lover of opera, ballet, and classical music. He had not been a fan of, as he put it, "the let's-all-pretend-we're-tone-deaf-and-bash-on-a-trash-can scene." To the openings of nearly all the events he wrote about, he had worn a tuxedo.

He did live one hell of an amazing life and he knew it!

He packed three lifetimes into one.

Few people who live to be a hundred can look back on a life so richly lived.

Such sentiments filled the notes from Mal's colleagues and friends. Did they really believe that quality trumped quantity? In this case, Lucinda realized she stood firmly in the camp of how much over how good, Holstein over Jersey.

In the growing mansion of her mourning—that's how Lucinda began to think of it within hours of seeing her son's body—another large room had opened when she found out that Mal had disposed of all his classical music recordings. Why on earth had he done such a thing? But stacked in a file drawer were dozens of CDs, sound tracks to Broadway musicals, a kind of music he never reviewed but enjoyed in a casual way. One of the last evenings Lucinda spent with her older son—though, again, she had no idea it was a "last" anything—they sat on his bed and watched *An American in Paris* on TV.

Months went by before she opened the boxes Jonathan had packed, searching for this collection. She lined up the CDs on a shelf in her sewing room. As Mal would have done, she grouped them by composer, anthologies by singers. She bought herself a portable CD player, a cheap thing designed for college students or housepainters. On nights when she stayed awake long past Zeke, working on her quilts, she would put one of Mal's musicals into the machine and play it at a moderate volume.

She liked the intimacy of playing all these jubilant, dramatic songs sotto voce. The sewing machine hummed heedlessly along, white noise behind seductions and street brawls and men throwing fateful dice and kings dancing with commoners. People fell in and out of love, despaired and rhapsodized. Orchestras swelled. Imagined theater curtains, like velvet evening gowns engaged in a waltz, gathered up in curtsied folds, then fell to sweep the surface of the imagined stage.

Mal had inherited Lucinda's tendency toward late-night wakefulness; many nights during his twenties and thirties, she would think of her son during those hours when most people in their time zone were sleeping, and she'd wonder if he, too, was up. How complicitous it felt. They both disliked the word *insomnia* for its implication that sleep would always be preferable. That might often be true, yet Lucinda and Mal were pleased by how productive they could be while everyone around them slept. It was a gift, said Mal, if you were a music critic for a newspaper, overnight deadlines a piece of cake. As for Lucinda, she can still do trapunto at four in the morning, her stitches tight and steady.

She returns the empty wineglass to the kitchen. Twenty minutes remain until her daughter is scheduled to pick her up. Christina is always on time; her punctuality is (and she has said so) a reaction against a childhood whose comings and goings were often dependent on the unpredictable responsibilities of a father in politics.

She thinks of the odd message on the answering machine: someone named Jasper Noonan, his voice kind and polite (setting him apart from the meddlesome reporters): "Mrs. Burns, I have news I think you'll be happy to receive. I promise you I'm not a salesman." She has listened to the message three times. She's not sure she has energy to spare for even the best of surprises.

She might have erased it, but for one tattered hope she's hoarded for decades, one she has wanted to act on so often. Zeke warned her, however, that she would be overstepping her bounds, imposing her selfish desires on someone else's family. She has defied Zeke in the past, but he is probably right about this.

She took down Jasper Noonan's number on the memo pad Zeke keeps beside the phone, every sheet printed with his various phone and fax numbers, under the seal of the state of Vermont. She touches the receiver.

But the last thing she wants is to have Christina walk in on the middle of a momentous, possibly very private conversation. She will call after they get back, once Zeke is settled and Christina's gone home. Lucinda can call from upstairs, a domain that will be hers alone for at least the next month, according to Zoe, Zeke's PT. Zeke should have stayed at the rehab center another week, but he insisted (as best he could) that he would recover more quickly at home. Even if he has to pay extra, he wants the therapists to come to him. Lucinda suspects that he also wants the reporters to tell his constituents that he's gone home, so they'll think he's in better shape than he really is. (Or perhaps it's wishful thinking that he is still capable of even the simplest political scheming.)

And all of a sudden here's Christina, her wheels on the gravel drive, her door slamming, her looming, puffy-coated figure striding through the front door, her sunglasses coming off as her eyes adjust from the snowy glare of the countryside to the dim foyer of the farm-house.

"Okay, Mom," she says without a greeting, "let's hit the road, shall we?"

"Coat and boots, and then I'm ready."

"Well, speak for yourself. But that's you, Mom: ready for anything. I've gotta hand it to you."

Hand what to me? Lucinda thinks crossly. Another citation for community outreach or social betterment? (Is *betterment* even a proper word?)

"I brought you a cocoa, Mom. It's in the car."

Lucinda regrets her spiteful urge toward her daughter. "Thank you, Christina. I'd love a cocoa."

Once the world at large—or the "media," to be more accurate—beatifies you, life is never the same. And because you cannot resist the stoking of your ego, no matter how hard you try, you begin to lose sight of yourself as just another workaday sinner.

Father Tom, whose retirement Lucinda still mourns ten years on, was the only one to hear her voice such thoughts, from behind the lattice in the confessional. One Sunday, when he spoke about the sin of pride through virtue, Lucinda wondered (compounding that sin) if she had inspired the homily.

Lucinda helped found The House at a time when she believed that all three of her children were well on their way toward secure, prosperous lives. Christina was out of law school, working at a prestigious firm in Boston. Mal was in New York—not a practicing musician, as Lucinda once dreamed, but writing about the music he loved. Jonathan was in his junior year at Bowdoin.

The political work Lucinda did in support of Zeke's causes began to feel shallow, a brittle, inadequate mortar to the structure of her life. She also yearned to do work in service of her faith, though she had always been mindful that anything public she chose to do could affect her husband's career. By then, Zeke had been elected majority leader of the state senate. He knew full well, however, not to take anything for granted. "Political winds blow this way and that, always this way when you're thinking that, spinning the compass ad infinitum," he'd say. "If you fail to keep your full weight on both legs, you'll up and blow away." Philosophy straight from Zeke the Elder.

Just as Lucinda began to talk with Father Tom about how she could find a place for herself in the church's outreach program, a small tragedy befell their parish. A sixteen-year-old girl found herself pregnant and, fearful of her parents' wrath, tried to abort the baby herself. She succeeded, but she wound up in a hospital, barely alive, and had to have a hysterectomy. Through Father Tom, her parents asked for donations of blood.

While Lucinda hardly knew the parents, the event seemed like a sign from God, a tap on Lucinda's shoulder. *Yes, you. Yes, this.* Moreover, it seemed like a stroke of symmetry, a reminder, however unwelcome, of her lost grandchild. (Somewhere out there in the world, he was eight years old.) Perhaps Lucinda needed to be reminded that Daphne's decision to have and keep that baby was courageous and, no matter what else she had decided, a blessing.

Lucinda had seen the child as a newborn, a baby, and a toddler, three times only. Each time, Daphne had driven from New Hampshire to meet her at a restaurant in Woodstock. Lucinda had met Christopher—Kit, Daphne called him—as any casual friend of the family might. During that time, she sent a check every six months. She told herself to be patient; there would be years ahead in which to become the freely doting grandmother she longed to be. She also knew that mother and baby lived comfortably, in Daphne's parents' home, though Daphne hadn't felt ready—not yet, she said—for Lucinda to meet her family. About this, too, Lucinda had willed herself to wait; after all, no one in her extended family knew about Christopher, either.

So Daphne's letter, which arrived a month after their last meeting, just shy of Christopher's fourth birthday, assaulted her with the shock of a traumatizing burn. Daphne thanked Lucinda for her support, but she had decided to go forward on her own. She would be moving into an apartment with Kit, and she had a part-time job. He would go to nursery school while she worked. Folded inside the letter was Lucinda's most recent check. Daphne ended by saying that if she changed her mind, she would be in touch again.

Through angry tears, Lucinda thought immediately of lawsuits she'd heard about, estranged grandparents suing for visitation rights. Leaving the claims of biology aside, surely her bank statements would be proof enough of her commitment. But when Zeke saw Daphne's letter, he told Lucinda that they would be crazy to entertain such an idea. Zeke had never been keen on meeting the child to begin with; he'd found the entire situation next to unbearable. At one point, early on, he had literally covered his ears. "Give her money if you like, I'm not opposed to that, but please remember that she's the parent, she's the one who was so determined to raise that child. She never considered our son's feelings; remember that, too." Defending Daphne's harsh decision in the letter, he said, "Maybe she'll find a man to be the kid's father. Maybe she already has, and he wants you out of the picture. That's their right. This letter might be good news, Lucinda. Good news for the child." He refused to say Christopher's name.

Father Tom, her only other confidant, told her to pray for guidance. He wasn't one to offer a mortal opinion on something so thorny, so fraught with human follies. She prayed to the Virgin, that mother of all mothers, but if guidance was sent, it must have gone to the wrong address.

So there she was, a few years later, searching for a mission. She knew, from a letter campaign aimed in part at her husband, that a grassroots group called Liberals for Life had begun lobbying the legislature to allocate funding for "religion-free counseling on options for mother and child." *We are not anti-abortion,* one leaflet read. *We do not adhere to Christian scripture or religious teachings of any kind. We want to see babies born and properly cared for, girls on the threshold of womanhood given the respect and nonbiased counsel to make grown-up decisions.*

Lucinda phoned the founder of this quirky group, a thirty-seven-year-old massage therapist from Middlebury named Pamela who wore Birkenstocks and a baby sling harnessing her fifth child tight against her muscular torso. She declared to Lucinda, over chamomile tea in a Winooski café, "Let's get this straight. I'm a plain-vanilla Episcopalian who happens to believe that all life, from the moment ovum collides with sperm, deserves to be protected. But rosaries, nuns, original sin, the pope . . . all that liturgical crap—and I do mean crap—gives me the heebie-jeebies. No offense, but I see the cross around your neck, and it's gotta give me pause. So if you're cool with that as a starting point, let's talk. And one more thing: we do not demonstrate against anything. Our group is about being *for* something, never against. No antis except on my family tree." She smiled tersely.

Lucinda did not like this blunt young woman, but she was intrigued. Being for, not against: this way of living rang true to Lucinda. The church's prohibitions, all the shalt-nots, sometimes cast a pall over her faith. Driving home from Winooski, she fingered the cross around her neck. Delicate though it was, perhaps it branded her as someone ready to judge and condemn. And she thought of the time she had taken a long bus ride to Washington, with Father Tom and other parishioners, to join in a shouting, sign-wielding rally against military spending, an episode that left her with aching arms, a sore throat, and a queasy, flulike feeling of futility.

This was the beginning of Mother the Mothers, an organization that started with seed money from Lucinda's share of Zeke's well-invested inheritance, along with fund-raising efforts greased by the social contacts of a political wife and, through Pamela, the feminist alumnae network of Bennington College. (Mal, after hearing the story about his mother's first encounter with Pamela, referred to her as Plain Vanilla. "Which, by the way, makes my Catholic upbringing, what, bitter chocolate? Amaretto, perhaps?")

The House itself was a rambling, dilapidated brick residence on the outskirts of Montpelier that the organization bought in foreclosure. They enlisted bakers and bankers and educators to set up training programs. An architect, eager to burnish his civic glow, contributed blueprints for renovating and "repurposing" the building. An attorney took care of the copious paperwork required to secure their nonprofit status. Eventually, they would employ a social worker and a doula.

Finding the pregnant girls to nurture and guide was the easy part. They were sent by Planned Parenthood, school nurses, pediatricians, and priests; by parents lucky enough to be trusted by their terrified children. When a reporter from the *Christian Science Monitor* expressed interest in writing a feature on The House, Plain Vanilla was on bed rest, pregnant with number six. "You go, girl," she told Lucinda. "You take us global. You be our shining face."

Lucinda knew something about being a shining face turned out toward the world. She had smiled and waved at strangers for years, had learned to echo her husband's positions with bumper-sticker brevity. But this—go out in public to represent an initiative that, on the face of it, didn't seem controversial yet somehow, she knew, would cross the sights of a loudmouth crackpot somewhere—this seemed risky. Like it or not, she realized that she was now exposed to those fickle political winds, this time without Zeke at her side.

Zeke, however, was thrilled. He told her he was much happier to see her, not some sandaled vegetarian feminist hippie, become the voice of a cause with which he would be permanently linked, if only through his money. He asked his favorite PR guru to put Lucinda through a mock interview.

And so it began, her beatification. She gave interviews to journalists from *Mother Jones,* the *Boston Globe,* even *Glamour*; they praised her for giving a sane face to the "pro-life agenda." She was called pro-motherhood, pro-sisterhood, pro-family, the "right kind of Catholic." (She still wore her small gold cross.) She declined to discuss abortion.

Minor grumblings arose from adoption advocates, who felt that idealistic girls should not be encouraged to undertake a task for which they couldn't possibly be prepared—and whose undertaking could not be reversed—but no crackpots emerged. Fortified by praise, singled out as she had never been while stumping for Zeke, Lucinda felt younger. She blossomed. She enrolled in social work classes. She took aerobics. She joined a quilting circle that included two gay men (vainly hoping this might bring her closer to Mal). She began to dress in festive clothing and jewelry from shops in Burlington frequented mainly by students. "Mom, you look fantastic, like you've moved to California," said Christina, expressing rare approval. How gratified Lucinda was to win admiration from the child who had chafed most belligerently against the teachings of the church. (When Christina was pregnant with her first child, after three years of marriage and five years' work as a tax attorney, she had calmly told Lucinda that she was grateful to live in a country where she could get the safe, affordable abortion she'd had in law school. "Without which, God knows where I'd be. Not married to Greg, that's for sure." Lucinda had been speechless.)

But saints, like tyrants, fall hard. Saints are merely tyrants in the kingdom of virtue.

"Take it easy, Dad. I know that's not a word in your vocabulary, but *easy.*"

Christina helps her father out of the car while Lucinda wrestles with the walker, unfolding and locking its cheap metal wings. Each of the women holds on to one side while Zeke fumbles for a grip.

Even though she knows he's stooping to keep his balance, acquiesce to this crablike contraption, Zeke seems disturbingly smaller to Lucinda. He dozed on the half-hour drive from the rehab center, and now, still, he says nothing.

Once inside the front door, he glances around. He spots the hospital bed. "Christ, it's come to this," he says. Though it sounds like *Frise, come to fiss.*

Dear God. Mal's contempt and resistance all over again; like son, like father. (Will Lucinda face her own dwindling with so little grace?)

"Zoe will come every day for the first week," she reminds him. "She says if you do the work, you could be climbing stairs by Christmas, even sooner." She sounds like she's talking to a child. "Do you want to lie down? Are you hungry?"

"Calls," he says.

Over Zeke's tilted head, Christina rolls her eyes. "Dad, you're not up to making calls. Everybody's rooting for you, and David's coming by tomorrow to fill you in on what you've missed, but as I said before, you've got to *take it easy.*"

Zeke begins to move on his own, but one of the walker's wheels lodges in a crevice between two of the skewed antique floorboards. Stubbornly, he pushes it forward until it tips and falls, taking him with it.

"Dad!" Christina grabs for an arm while Lucinda cries out incoherently. Tears come to her eyes.

They get Zeke and the walker upright. "Sit, Zeke. I'll get you a snack," says Lucinda.

Once he's seated in his chair by the fireplace, she goes to the kitchen. She leans over the sink and grasps the edges. Where is her strength, for heaven's sake? She longs for the bygone readiness of prayer. She glances at the eggcup on the windowsill, the nest for her rosary. The beads are furry with dust.

Christina is right behind her. "Mom, Greg has a work dinner I can't get out of. I have to leave in fifteen minutes."

"Go, sweetheart. Don't worry about us."

"But I do."

"Well, I give you permission to stop. Zoe comes first thing tomorrow morning. How badly can I mess up in that short a time?"

"I'll get his things out of the car."

Lucinda cannot remember the last time Christina came to visit when she didn't have a pressing engagement to take her away ever so slightly sooner than would be ideal. Even now that Christina's three daughters are grown, one in college, one in law school, one teaching English in India—soccer games, teacher conferences, orthodontist appointments relics of the past—still the obligations come thick and fast. Maybe Christina's profession has conditioned her to guard even her "unbillable" time in units of five or ten minutes.

You are unkind and paranoid, Lucinda tells herself. Your daughter is a busy woman with a rewarding and complicated life. Wasn't that the sort of life Lucinda had until a few years ago, when she stepped away from The House, turning it over to a director who wanted to "diversify" its mission?

She starts to shave slices from the sharp cheddar Zeke loves—then realizes that he's not supposed to eat dairy products in the afternoon, because of some pill he's taking. She puts the cheese back and takes out cured olives and a box of cranberry-studded crackers she found at the gourmet shop.

She hears Zeke calling incoherently from the living room. She answers that she's on her way. She remembers the sound of cows and their calves bellowing back and forth from one barn to another during the weeks of weaning. When the last of the herd was auctioned off, she was glad to be done with that annual source of sadness.

He is still in the chair, pointing toward the phone. "Shejiz," he says.

"Zeke?"

"MEH-shejiz."

"Yes, I'll check the messages," she says. He must have noticed the blinking light. At least he's observant. (She collects these precious positive signs like pearls scattered from a broken necklace: always searching for more, fearing that some may have slipped between floorboards, gone for good.)

She pushes PLAY. David, Zeke's current intern, wants to know when he should come by. Zoe is confirming the first PT appointment. Jonathan wants them to know he's thinking of them and will call tomorrow. He's going out to a dinner party with Cyril as soon as he finishes teaching his last seminar that day. If Lucinda needs to reach him, she can try his cell. (He puts a meaningful stress on *need;* in other words, not if she merely wants to hear her son's voice.)

Is Zeke tipping over or simply leaning toward the machine, to listen? Lucinda is relieved when he asks if there are other messages from before. His speech is still slurred, but she's become a good translator over the past few days.

"That's it. There's mail, but nothing dire. David's dealing with that." She thinks again about Jasper Noonan. That message was specifically for her.

Lucinda returns to the kitchen and pours a glass of orange juice. She carries it to the living room along with the crackers and olives. She puts the food and drink on the small table beside Zeke's chair, pulling it around so that it's right in front of him. His hands quaver badly as he picks up a cracker, but he gets it to his mouth. When he lifts the glass of juice, it's all Lucinda can do to keep from asking if she should hold it for him. A few drops escape, falling on his corduroy jacket. He doesn't notice.

The grandfather clock chimes six times. Lucinda watches Zeke and tries to calm her face. He is looking around the room.

Except when he is reading, Zeke does not care for silence. This is the hour when, if he's home, Lucinda listens to his rundown of the day's feuds and compromises, the absurdities of legislation, the toadying of lobbyists. He always wants her opinion. He always asks about her day, too.

She feels the threat of tears. What will she do with all this unfamiliar silence? How will she fill it, with what kind of small talk? Or is she supposed to let Zeke's brain rest, renew its focus? The problem with all this silence is that it tempts her deep into the catacombs of memory when she has no desire to loiter in the past; she wants to be assured of the future.

Why isn't the phone ringing? Shouldn't colleagues and friends who know Zeke is home be calling to check in, ask what they can do, when they can visit? Of course, they do not have nearly as many friends as they did the last time they faced the sort of crisis that summons casseroles and vows of dedicated prayer. Too many friends have died, many in the last year or two.

"Feez," he says quietly. He's glaring at the wall of paintings.

Help me, thinks Lucinda. "I heard Joe's going to have a new show next month, at a gallery in Boston," she says. "He's offered to have us to his studio before he sends the paintings down. He's been doing watercolors of Lake Champlain."

Zeke frowns. "Towfeez."

"The trophies? They're in the den, you know that." Is she supposed to tell him what he ought to know? "Did you want to look at them?"

He scowls at her. "Yeh, know zhat, Oothinda. Just . . ."

She waits.

"Tha letter. Moozeum." He smirks. "Moo Zeum. Hah."

Yes, the letter: from a dairy museum run by the Cabot people. They wrote a month ago, asking whether Zeke might consider letting them visit to look at family belongings related to the showing of their cattle; the museum is planning an exhibit on the history of agrarian fairs across the state.

"I'm glad you reminded me." Then she does, because she can't help it, start to cry. "Oh, Zeke, I'm glad you're home," she says, though how false she feels when she recalls what she was thinking at the hospital.

She had waited in the lounge where she was directed to wait. Zeke's tennis partner, Mike, who'd been the one to phone Lucinda, had to get back to the capitol as soon as she arrived. By herself, Lucinda had waited another half hour, staring out the window at the parking lot. She noticed how many cars there were in dull, dispiriting shades of slate, green, and gold. Two red cars, a lime-green VW bug—but what had become of orange and purple cars, the many brilliant blues? Hadn't cars been more colorful in the past, and what did this mean about the world she lived in?

Finally, a young doctor opened the door to the lounge. "Mrs. Burns?"

He crossed the room and beckoned her to sit beside him on a stale-smelling couch. He introduced himself and shook her hand. He said, "I have good news, Mrs. Burns. Your husband is going to survive. I need to warn you, though, that we have yet to see the extent of the damage. He's stable and sedated right now. We'll be doing some scans of his brain. Even if we see significant changes, recovery is unpredictable." He paused. "You can visit him briefly, if you like. But maybe you want to call your children first?"

Christina and Jonathan. It hadn't occurred to her, in that suspended hour, to call either one of them.

The doctor smiled. "I've got to tell you, Senator Burns is a vigorous guy for his age. Maybe I shouldn't say this, but I'm feeling pretty optimistic. Hey, I've voted for him every time since I was old enough to vote." He laughs. "Okay. From the look on your face, Mrs. Burns, I can tell you think that was yesterday, but it wasn't. Your husband's in good hands with me, I promise."

She had yet to say a single word. This doctor, however good his hands, however many elections he'd ticked off Zeke's name on the ballot, could tell nothing from the look on her face. He had no idea what had crossed her mind during the few seconds it had taken him to enter and cross the room. In that brief time, Lucinda had recognized a shocking flash of hope that the doctor would tell her Zeke was gone, passed on, dead. It was only a flash, fleeting and terrifying, like a bat swooping through the room (so fast it might have been a mirage, a vague disturbance in peripheral vision), but she will never forget it. Father Tom, endlessly merciful, would have said that what she'd felt was the desire for Zeke's suffering, not his life, to end.

Sometimes she wonders if Father Tom was the supporting beam of her faith, if it began to slump as soon as he retired. But no; Lucinda knows the precise moment her certainty about the cosmos—or, more truthfully, her place in it—cracked and collapsed.

Five years ago, she was in Montpelier, heading to meet Zeke for lunch. An overweight, angry-looking young woman was walking toward her. Lucinda was careful not to meet her eyes—mentally, she had already passed the woman—but as they drew close, the woman stopped and blocked her path. "You."

"Me?" said Lucinda, insipidly.

"Yeah. You. You ruined my life, you know." The woman's expression slid from menace toward contempt. "You and your fucking—oh, wait, your *mother*fucking mission. To fill the world with babies. Jesus. Meddling like that." She pursed her mouth as if to spit. Lucinda flinched, shielding her face.

The woman did not spit. She simply stared for a moment, then smirked dismissively. "You can bet I'm not the only one, either." Then she passed Lucinda, knocking her with a shoulder, setting her off balance. Lucinda stood in the middle of the sidewalk, immobile for several seconds, before navigating the last half block. At the restaurant (Zeke was, as expected, late), she went into the ladies' room and dry-heaved over a toilet, unable to vomit or even cry.

She did not tell Zeke, or anyone else, about the incident; Father Tom was long gone by then. Especially disturbing was her failure to recognize the woman, yet she knew instinctively that the assault was not a case of mistaken identity. At The House, they made every attempt to follow up with the young mothers after they completed whatever tutoring or training programs they'd been guided through. Inevitably, a number of the women moved away or lost touch. In a few cases, Lucinda knew that the children had ended up in foster care. Of course this made her sad. But not until that day had she come face-to-face with a failure of her intentions—a flesh-and-blood failure.

You cannot save every soul, she'd admonished herself. What a grandiose notion! Yet she could not help feeling that something false within her had been unmasked: some naïveté rooted in her safe, relatively easy childhood. Since then, any poorly dressed or hostile-looking youngish woman heading in her direction makes Lucinda's heart race, makes her cross the street or turn aside, pretending to look in a shopwindow or hunt for a phantom object in her purse.

Meddling like that. This is the phrase that crushed her.

When Lucinda was a child, her father was the manager of the local savings bank, entrusted with Zeke's father's accounts. Not many people in northern Vermont, back then, had trust funds for their children before they were even in high school, but Ezekiel Burns Sr. (known as Zeke the Elder, once a junior came along) had a way with investments. Most of his dividends he poured into buying more acreage, enlarging his herd (his fanciest breed stock imported from England), and advocating what businessmen would one day refer to as "branding"—not the kind that left hieroglyphic scars on cowhide. He traveled a lecture circuit down the East Coast and through the Midwest, promoting the premium products that came from Jersey cows, helping farmers form cooperatives. He orchestrated symposia on animal husbandry, everything from quality of feed and barn hygiene to studbook record keeping and show-ring standards. People who liked him called him enlightened; people who didn't called him slick. Lucinda never saw him in what she thought of as farmer's clothing. Milking, plowing, haying, repairing equipment: all such tasks, by the time she first laid eyes on her future father-in-law, were delegated to hired hands and to his sons.

All three Burns boys learned the manual rudiments of farming, down to castration and composting. Even after the lean years of the Depression (during which Zeke the Elder made a point of holding payroll steady), they had chores before and after school. Known collectively around town as the Heirs, they were pleasant-looking, smart, and well mannered. Zeke the Elder intended that all three should go to college, as he had not.

They were older than Lucinda by eight, four, and two years. The one she couldn't take her eyes off was Matthew, the middle, dark-haired son, the one who looked most like his beautiful mother. ("Gypsy beauty," Lucinda's mother called the look of Mrs. Burns: hair true black, eyes a penetrating blue.) When Lucinda was twelve, she told her parents she wanted to join 4-H. Her mother laughed. They lived in town; the only animal they owned was Duke, her father's aging boxer. Lucinda told them she had always wanted to raise rabbits (though she'd just come up with the notion). Her father approved of it as a financial enterprise, a lesson in business—so he and Lucinda's older brother, Patrick, built a hutch in the backyard. With babysitting money, she bought herself a pair of Harlequins. They wasted no time in living up to their reproductive reputation.

As Lucinda had learned from an interview in the town paper, Zeke the Elder excused Matthew from milking duties in exchange for his attending the 4-H meetings in the town-hall basement to help the youngest members with their projects. ("Contributions to one's community are an essential part of any sound business," stated Zeke the Elder.)

At Lucinda's first meeting, she stood quietly against a wall and listened to Matthew chat with a third-grade boy about "converting feed to flavor," whether you were talking milk or meat; about how you could guess a cow's diet by looking at her hide. Just before he left the meeting, she asked if the feed-to-flavor principle applied to rabbits. "I'm sure it would," he told her, "but I've got to confess, I don't know rabbits from raccoons. I'll nose around, though." He came to the next meeting with pamphlets from the co-op where his father bought the grain that kept his cows' hides so glossy, made them gleam in the sun as they grazed his carefully seeded pastures.

Matthew gave Lucinda no more attention than he gave the other kids. She wasn't foolish, and she certainly hoped she wasn't vain; she knew she was too young to hope for more than a friendly hand, but a few years might change all that. The next summer, when she was thirteen, he volunteered to help her build a second hutch to house the kits she planned to sell. (Which ones became stew and which became pets, she didn't like to know.) Her brother teased her relentlessly. Patrick was on the high-school baseball team with Zeke the Younger; he threatened to expose her crush. She didn't care. If Patrick said anything to Zeke, how could it hurt? Zeke was just the little brother.

The following spring, Matthew helped her start a vegetable garden from seed, but over the summer she had to miss 4-H. When her father's secretary left to have a baby, he decided that Lucinda could fill in for a month or two. He was a "modern" father, he maintained; Lucinda should go to college, aim to earn a living—though of course she'd want a family, too.

Confined to the stuffy bank—the window fans doing little more than move the hot, syrupy air in a vortex—Lucinda saw Mr. Burns at least once a week, when he came to withdraw pay for the farmhands. She listened hard to his casual conversations with her father or the teller, but she heard nothing new about Matthew. She couldn't wait for the fall, when she would start high school. There, she'd see him in the halls; she would know if he had a girlfriend.

Matthew was a senior. He smiled or waved whenever they passed between classes, and if she timed it right, she could walk out right behind him at the end of the day. He and Zeke sometimes had one of the farm's trucks, and they'd give her a lift into town.

Their older brother, Aaron, was up in Burlington, halfway through college. The village hummed that fall with news of his engagement to Dora Keene, whose father ran the Keene Canteen, the sandwich and provisions shop. While waiting for Aaron to return with his degree, Dora waited on her father's customers: on Aaron and Matthew's father, on Lucinda's father, on teenagers who colonized the counter on Saturdays, drinking shakes made with the foamy, sun-colored milk from Aaron's family's well-nourished cows.

The Japanese bombed Pearl Harbor that December. Aaron, almost the minute he arrived home for Christmas, enlisted in the army. Matthew vowed that at the end of the school year he would sign up, too. Zeke swore he'd join them the minute he turned eighteen—if his brothers and their friends hadn't won the war already.

June was a time of sudden exodus: it seemed as if all the boys fresh out of high school were being spirited away en masse. Later that summer, Lucinda ran into Matthew's mother at the Canteen. Summoning every ounce of courage, she asked Mrs. Burns if she might have Matthew's mailing address. She wondered if Mrs. Burns looked down on her because she was Catholic, though theirs was a community where how hard you worked mattered much more than where you worshipped. Mrs. Burns told her Matt had written home to say that training was tough. Never having been away from the farm for more than a few days, he was pretty homesick. "I'd say the postmark alone will cheer him up," she told Lucinda as she wrote the address on the back of a coupon.

Address in hand, Lucinda walked straight to Saint Joseph's to pray for the safe return of both Burns boys and to confess her less-than-chaste feelings toward the one whose heart she was determined to secure. She wrote to him that evening; within two weeks, she had a reply. He asked about her rabbits, her parents, the weather. Was his little brother, that chowderhead, keeping up with the haying? What he'd give to have been there for the Fourth of July parade! (He would have driven the tractor pulling the wagon with the 4-H float; Zeke had taken his place.) Had Lucinda saved a program from the concert on the green? Could she send it along?

Her heart felt as if it had rocketed to heaven, then drifted back to reside in her chest. She went to the backyard and hugged her rabbits. She would show two of them at the fair in August. If she won a ribbon, she'd send it to Matthew. What if she bought him a Saint Christopher medal; would that be too bold?

She wondered if he would have to fight. Older girls bragged about what heroes they knew their boyfriends would be. They'd mow down the Nips and the Huns as sure as they knew how to mow down corn and hay. Lucinda didn't care if Matthew came back a hero. She just wanted him to come back alive. Was it insolent to ask this of God? *Matthew Burns, Matthew Burns, Matthew Burns,* she murmured in private, the syllables like beads on a rosary, the name a prayer in itself. Matthew Elijah Burns would come home from war, go to college, then come home again and marry Lucinda Margaret James. Where they lived was of no importance; let Aaron and Dora take over Sanctuary Farm. She and Matthew could have their own farm; a house in town; a hut by the river. Lucinda would never love anyone, she swore, as much as she loved Matthew Burns.

She wakes with a sore neck, her left arm numb. It took hours for her to fall asleep, the bars of the sofa bed's frame palpable through the skimpy mattress; she will never subject another guest (another welcome guest) to a night like that. She gets up and uses the washroom off the kitchen that was once used by the hired hands before the midday meals that Zeke's mother cooked for a dozen men.

She'll get the coffee going, then check on Zeke. The percolator parts are still in the dishwasher. She will have to devise a new routine, make as many preparations as possible in advance. Everything will take more time.

Jasper Noonan, she thinks. Speaking of time, she must somehow carve out enough of it to call him today. She'll call while David is here. (If she were Zeke, she would ask David to Google Jasper Noonan before returning the call.)

When Lucinda goes into the living room, she sees Zeke lying on the rug next to the hospital bed. "Oh God!" she cries out and kneels beside him. "Zeke!"

He opens his eyes and stares at her blankly for a moment.

"Are you all right? Did you fall?" The bed's guardrail is down.

He frowns at Lucinda. "Washleep."

"I see that now, but you gave me a heart attack. Did you try to get up by yourself? I left you the bell, to call me."

"Shridiculish." He turns slowly until he's lying flat on his back, staring at the ceiling. "Whole thing ushurd."

"I know it is, Zeke. But, please, can we get you up here, just to the chair? If you let me lift your shoulders . . ."

He winces and crosses one leg over the other. That's when she notices that his pajama bottoms are wet.

The phone rings. Struggling to rise, she thinks, I am way too old for this.

"Mom? Did I wake you? I have a superlong day and I wanted to catch you. Between classes and office hours, I am totally unreachable today."

"No, Jonathan, we're awake."

"Is everything okay? Is he okay?"

"He's lying in the middle of the living room floor right now, staring at the ceiling. But he's fine." She knows that her telling this to Jonathan will annoy Zeke and get him to move. Or so she desperately hopes.

"I wanted to tell you I'm coming out a few days early."

"What's that, sweetheart?"

"A colleague will cover the lecture I'd miss. I've got papers coming in from my seminar students, but they get turned in by e-mail these days, so I can read them just as easily out there. So here's the plan: Cyril and I will do all the cooking. Are Teeny's girls coming? Maybe we should do the meal at her house? We're totally flexible, Mom. You call the shots."

Lucinda carries the phone into the living room, where she can keep an eye on Zeke. Unkindly, she thinks of the urine sinking into the Chinese carpet. She will have to look for that pet deodorizer spray they used when Jethro was old and arthritic, too weary to bother with going outside. (Zeke loves being greeted by a dog when he comes home, but thank heaven they hadn't replaced Jethro yet. Debilitated husband plus puppy: imagine!)

Zeke's eyes are closed, arms at his side. But for the regular movements of his chest, he looks like a corpse.

"Jonathan, Thanksgiving was the furthest thing from my mind."

"Mom, it's in less than two weeks, and no way are we going to skip it. How about you leave it all to us? I made a reservation for me and Cyril at that great B and B. Let us be your slaves. You can kick us out whenever you need to."

"That's so generous, sweetheart. But please stay here. I always like having you here."

"Are you okay, Mom? I mean, are you managing?"

"Honey, I have enough help for the time being. This place is going to be like a hive today. It will be good to see you whenever you can come."

"Next Saturday," he says. "I'll be your slave for a solid week. How's that? Cyril can make it on Tuesday. He's going on to Boston for a Hawthorne symposium, so it works out perfectly."

Jonathan and Cyril—the man she is now accustomed to thinking of as her second son-in-law—are tenured professors at Berkeley, Jonathan in gender studies, Cyril in American literature. (Their two most recent books—Jonathan's *Sexual Identity in Firstborn Children* and Cyril's *The Fine Hammered Steel of Woe: Ecclesiastes and Melville's Ambivalent Soul*—sit on her bedside table, beneath others she is far more likely to read.)

Zeke is now struggling to rise. "Raaaahg!" he bellows, walruslike.

"Is that *Dad*?" Jonathan sounds horrified.

"I have to go. I'll call you later—tomorrow. We're doing fine, sweetheart. I love you." She hangs up.

Lucinda drags one of the armchairs over to help Zeke pull himself up. She braces the walker against the chair. "We have to get you to the bathroom, get you dressed. And I know you don't like it, but you've got to let me help."

"Pished onnarug like a dog."

"Well, yes," says Lucinda. "You did." She hopes he'll laugh. She hasn't seen him laugh once since the stroke. Zeke is a man with a hearty, charming, persuasive laugh. (Can a stroke knock out the specific zone in your brain that generates laughter?) He doesn't even smile. All right, he's in a rage. The doctor warned her that this would be a normal reaction for a man accustomed to Zeke's level of activity and control.

With the help of the walker, she guides him to the larger bathroom for guests, off the front hall, but there isn't enough space for both of them and the walker. She leaves him there so she can go upstairs and get him clothes. At the rehab center, Zoe made Lucinda practice undressing and redressing her husband. Zeke made Zoe leave the room. They worked in embarrassed silence, Zeke refusing to let her take off his undershorts.

When she returns, Zeke has locked the door and won't let her in.

"Zeke, I have your clothes. You're going to freeze."

The door opens a few inches. One hand, shaky, clawlike, emerges: an image from a horror movie. "Giff me clojsh."

She hands him his boxers, then his trousers, then a shirt. She says, "You're going to need my help, especially with the buttons," but the door closes.

Through the tall windows flanking the front door, Lucinda sees an unfamiliar car pull up. It's already nine-thirty, and she's still in her nightgown.

Zoe approaches the house and, catching sight of Lucinda inside, waves.

When Zoe comes in, she wipes her feet with the same enthusiasm she applies to her difficult work. She hangs her yellow down jacket on the coat rack, looks Lucinda over, and shakes her head. "Rough morning."

Zoe is small and wiry, astonishingly strong; Lucinda has seen her lift Zeke from a fall, supporting his entire weight. Her hair is dyed albino blond, a color defiantly incongruous with her dark eyebrows and cinnamon-colored skin. Lucinda imagines her growing up as the lone little sister to a pack of brothers who brought her up scrappy and resilient but confident, too. She radiates the contagious calm of someone who's well and widely loved.

"He's in the bathroom," says Lucinda. "He won't let me dress him."

"That's your husband all right." Zoe calls out, "Hey, Zig, it's me—Zag. Holler if you need me. We got our work cut out for us today!" She turns back to Lucinda. "You go get dressed—no hurry. Have breakfast in peace. Read the paper or just chill. Chillax, as my ten-year-old loves to say."

Lucinda, unlike Zeke, is happy right now to have someone order her around. Chillax, she thinks. She will do her best. But first, she'll dress herself.

The things we take for granted, she muses sadly as she hooks her bra behind her back, a daily act she hasn't consciously registered for years. What if she, too, were to have a stroke, lose the ability to do so much as button a blouse? She thinks of their collective fate in the hands of their two surviving children, Christina and Jonathan. How long before she and Zeke are both consigned to a nursing home, however deluxe?

For the past few days, the morning light in the bedroom has startled Lucinda, as it does every year when snow arrives. The deep drifts left by the unexpectedly early blizzard still cover the fields, their milky radiance filling the upper rooms of the house, lending the white walls a pristine eggshell luster. Beautiful light, beautiful views—but waiting for the plow to get her out had been unnerving. At least the phone lines had held through the storm. She was able to call Zeke at the center, assure him she was fine.

From the window in her dressing room—the room where Zeke's mother kept all three of her sons as newborns—Lucinda has a head-on view of the long lane connecting the house to the road. When she was a young bride, she drove the length of it several times a week, visiting her in-laws for dinners, attending church fund-raisers. Dutch elms, planted in two perfect colonnades, enclosed the lane, their suppliant branches interlacing overhead. By late June, the glossy foliage formed a tunnel of cool moist air; to the younger Lucinda, entering that tunnel stirred up restive, conflicting emotions.

All the elms—all fifty-eight, though no one had bothered to count them before—died of beetle blight in the early sixties, soon after she moved into the house. From this window, she saw them wither and succumb. No amount of money or horticultural expertise could save them. Removing the stumps cost a fortune. The lane remained barren, the timothied meadows lapping thirstily along its bermed edges, until a few years ago, when Zeke decided to plant rows of a specially grafted disease-resistant maple (for now the maples are threatened by yet another blight). The new trees are still tentative and spindly, but last summer they leaped in height, and a month ago they blushed dramatically, the leaves on their young limbs flushing a regal, violet shade of crimson.

She wishes she could go for a long walk; it's time to get out her snowshoes. Walking a good distance, alone, always cheers her up, sets her right. But solitary luxuries must wait.

A delivery van turns down the lane. Not until it steers onto the loop in front of the porch does Lucinda recognize the logo of the village florist. "Fiddle." She sighs. Bring on the parade of floral tributes. Zeke will rage at this, too.

As Lucinda rushes downstairs, hoping to reach the door before the bell rings, she catches sight of Zeke, now dressed, in the living room with Zoe. She's brought her "toys": the massive rubber ball, the thick elastic bands, the Gumby-like gizmos that strengthen hands and feet.

Lucinda signs for the flowers quickly, making no small talk. Gladiolas, the funeral flower. *To our champion and friend: We pray daily for your speedy recovery!!! With affection and blessings, Father Jess and the staff of St. J's.*

Lucinda laughs. Ecumenically tolerant though he may be in public, in private Zeke rails openly against the backward teachings of the Catholic Church and the harm it has done to the world's poorest peoples (that plural an irritation to Lucinda, a sign that he's a politician down to the marrow, even in his kitchen, alone with his wife).

Sadly, his accusations were reaffirmed by the selection of the latest pope. Benedict's views mirror those of Father Jess, who succeeded Father Tom with what some of the most vocal parishioners praised as an invigorating return to "more solid values." To them, Father Tom was a good, hardworking man, but he'd been tarnished by achieving priesthood in the age of Father Drinan and the Beatles. Lucinda wonders if that is precisely what she loved about him, that tarnish. You might have defined it as a wider latitude of forgiveness. Not long before Mal died, Father Tom assured her that God had made her son the way he was, that Mal would be blessed and welcomed to the kingdom of heaven so long as he fully embraced Jesus Christ as his Savior.

Which, Lucinda knew in her heart even then, he probably never had, perhaps not even as the small child who always seemed to have his own opinions, often lofty or contrarian, about the world around him. Mal had been her easiest baby: he seemed to "catch on" to everything, from nursing to turning over to sleeping through the night, with an almost condescending ease. Yet once he learned how to express his thoughts (early, of course), he became the kind of child who exhausts his parents with every possible iteration of *why, but, not so, isn't true!* He questioned the absurd delights of nursery rhymes, the happy endings to fairy tales. And Lucinda, in struggling to respect his challenges and doubts, came to feel far closer to him than she had to Christina or, later, to Jonathan. He was, she secretly felt, the child she could most confidently call *hers*.

After Mal died, she wished that she could gather up and possess his entire life. She had a hard time parting with any of his belongings. She had the impulse to claim even his pet parrot, Felicity, whose exotic aloofness and dark stare had always made her uneasy. But Felicity had already been in the care of Fenno McLeod, the friend who had so charmed Lucinda and then been the one to help Mal end his own life. It took her months to forgive Fenno, to stop seeing his complicity as a betrayal, to realize that Fenno might have been, at the end, the closest thing her older son ever had to a spouse. He had been, quite literally, a helpmeet. She has lost touch with Fenno, and now, all of a sudden, she feels sad and rueful about that, too.

Lucinda invited David for lunch, not realizing that this would subject Zeke to having his junior assistant witness how infuriatingly infantile his eating habits have become. She set the kitchen table for the two of them, hoping to leave them alone together—but what was she thinking?

And soup: what a cruel food to serve Zeke. She puts the bowls back in the cupboard. Sandwiches don't seem like enough to offer, however. Cut vegetables? On two plates, she arranges slices of cucumber, halved cherry tomatoes, carrot sticks. She spoons hummus into two small dishes.

After cutting Zeke's turkey sandwich in quarters, she decides she had better do the same with David's. Maybe she should just go ahead and arrange the vegetables into smiley faces.

A bowl of chips. She now buys the kind made from sweet potatoes, though she doubts they're much healthier than the usual (and far less expensive) type. The packaging on food has come to resemble political advertising. (She long ago stopped commenting on the alarmist radio spots and glossy postcards cooked up by Zeke's so-called troubleshooting team.)

The doorbell chimes exactly at twelve-thirty. David's comings and goings are as prompt and cheerful as birdsong. His ambition ripples off his perfectly pressed shirts like heat off the tarmac in August.

Lucinda starts toward the front door and then sees Zeke heading there with his walker. (Another pearl for the broken necklace.) She retreats quickly, pours iced tea into two thin, lightweight glasses (graspable in one uncertain hand?).

Zeke enters the kitchen first, so slowly that Lucinda has a hard time just standing there, waiting, as if it's perfectly normal to take twenty seconds in crossing the room. "Good to see you, David," she says.

Right behind Zeke, his towering height now exaggerated by his boss's shrimplike posture, David beams at Lucinda. He's carrying an armload of folders, so he doesn't shake her hand. "Great to see *you*, Mrs. Burns. The senator's doing fantastically, don't you think?"

"Rubbish," says Zeke, this word coming out clear as a bell. "No shickophantijm round ear."

David tries to laugh lightly. He casts a fleeting *oops* sort of smile at Lucinda. He's someone too reliant on his charms, but he's good at what he's supposed to do, and that's what matters. Especially now. She doesn't want to think about what will happen to Zeke if he can't keep up with his work. Even the optimistic young doctor wouldn't give a prognosis on that. She thinks of Father Jess's most ardent supporters and how, flowers and prayers for swift recovery aside, they would love to see Zeke's seat not only vacant but filled by some bushy-tailed young Republican. Vermont has more than its fair share of Sarah Palin clones just waiting to boast about the state's permissive gun laws. If retirement would cripple Zeke, *that* would kill him. Look what happened in Massachusetts when Senator Kennedy died.

This latest intern in a decades-long parade is the most handsome one since Leo, the intern Zeke had back in the late eighties, who stayed nearly four years, far longer than any before or since. Leo was working for Zeke when Mal died, twenty years ago now. Because Zeke worked from home so much that terrible spring, Lucinda saw a great deal of Leo. She saw up close what Zeke's interns did for him: the stupefyingly boring tasks outnumbering the ones that gave them any sense of political know-how. She concluded that politics itself, even at the highest level, involves a staggering amount of exhausting, mind-sapping, tedious work. Not unlike, it occurred to her then, the work of getting back to living your life after losing a child.

She stands by, like a maid, until she sees that Zeke will be able to manage (if barely) with the meal. David takes a few bites of his sandwich, then shoves it aside to make room for work. He's looking down now, not watching Zeke as he slowly raises a chip to his mouth.

"Well then," she says, "I'll leave you two to your own important devices."

"Aye-aye, Mrs. B," says David.

Lucinda is tempted to take the stairs at a run, so happy is she to be free of her husband's trembling hands and obsequious intern. She goes straight to the back room that serves as her sewing room and study (Zeke's bedroom when he was a boy). Laid across a card table are the wax-paper templates for the quilt she's making Jonathan and Cyril: a traditional wedding quilt, white on white, all grapevines, the leaves and fruit in relief (though logically—she hopes!—two men in their fifties hardly need their union blessed with a symbol of fertility). She aims to finish it by their first anniversary, next July.

She takes the sheet of notepaper with Jasper Noonan's number out of her pocket. She looks at the telephone; this one still has a receiver joined to its base by a corkscrewed cord. She refused to let Zeke replace it; the connections are always clearer than on the cordless phones. Some new things do not improve on their older models.

The phone at the other end of the line begins to ring. Lucinda leans on the table, weight on her elbows, feet secured in the rungs of the chair: a defensive fetal position, she recalls from her training in body language, one of many courses she took when she started her work at The House.

After several rings a man answers, "Dad's place," out of breath.

"Jasper Noonan?"

"Hang on." Not far from the phone, he bellows, "Dad!"

She hears clumping; muttered words; a door closing.

"No, not Loraina!" calls out the man who answered.

And then, "Noonan here." He, too, is out of breath. Already she hears his age in his voice. It's a well-used voice, saturated with woodsmoke.

"Jasper Noonan, this is Lucinda Burns. You left me a message a few days ago." At first, she hears only harsh breathing.

"The senator's wife, yes?"

Oh no. He's a reporter after all. Of course he is. "I'm sorry," she says, "but Senator Burns isn't doing interviews. He's home, he'll be fine, but he's very busy. If you'd like to reach his office, I can give you that number."

"Whoa. No, ma'am. It's you I'm looking for, and I hope you'll bear with me if I'm clumsy with the news I have. I'm guessing you'll want to hear it. If not, I'm going to owe you an apology."

She hears him sigh, as if he's changing his mind. "Please go on."

"Mrs. Burns, would you remember Daphne Browning? Her son, Christopher? Would you have a connection there?"

The sound that escapes from Lucinda's mouth is shrill. "Yes," she manages, worried that if she says nothing, the man will hang up. That mustn't happen. She winds the cord more tightly around her fingers.

"Are you all right, Mrs. Burns?"

"Dear God."

"Is that a yes? I'm sorry to shock you like this."

"Just please go on, would you please?" Tears stream over her cheeks. What if Christopher is dead? (In a spiteful reflex, she wonders whether she would care if Daphne is dead.) "He's my grandson. Or he . . . was. He is, if he's—is he all right?" She did not know her voice could rise to such a pitch.

"Should I worry if you're alone?" Jasper Noonan asks her.

"I'm not," she says quickly. "I mean, I'm alone in this room. It doesn't— I'm fine. Talk about Christopher."

"Well, just as you say he 'was' your grandson, he was my stepson."

"Was? Was?"

"Wait up there! I mean to say, technically, he still is. Even if his mother's not married to me anymore." Behind him, Lucinda hears the sound of hammering. Also a radio or a record: jazz, a lovelorn trumpet.

"Mr. Noonan, please just let me know if Christopher is alive and well."

"Good Lord, sorry! Yes. Yes, both. He's just, he's decided . . . he's looking to find out about the man who was his . . . *biological father*'s the correct term, I'm told. And forgive me if I'm busting a confidence here, because Daphne kept the whole thing a secret, even from me in a way, but by some fluke I remembered—which amazes me— remembered that you're a grandmother to Kit."

"Yes. I am. His grandmother." She looks around desperately for something with which to blow her nose. She takes a strip of orange poplin from the basket where she keeps her smallest scraps. "Excuse me. Please wait." She disentangles her hand from the cord, lays the receiver down on the quilting templates, and blows her nose, though now she is crying ceaselessly.

She picks up the receiver. "Mr. Noonan. Mr. Noonan?" Her ears are clogged, from blowing her nose too violently. "Just talk, Mr. Noonan. I'm fine, even if I don't sound fine."

He curses under his breath. He yells at his son to stop hammering and take a break. And would he turn down the damn radio?

"I'm going to walk upstairs with this phone, Mrs. Burns. This is not a conversation I rehearsed."

"How could you!" She finds herself falling in love with this stranger. "Just say whatever. Whatever you can."

"So I hate to do this sort of snooping, but I needed to know some things. So I went on the Internet and found out about your son. I saw his Web page, the one he's got for his students. And I thought I would just e-mail or call him, but I didn't know whether . . . Look, all I could remember from Daphne had to do with you, how you helped her with Kit in the beginning."

"I guess until she met you."

"No, no, I came along later. It was just her wanting to be . . . independent. Daphne was always like that. To a point. But never mind her."

"Is she . . . did she die?"

Jasper Noonan sighs. "She jumped ship, is how I put it. Kit stayed with me another year, till college. She's got her own life, Daphne, she's fine, but let's just . . . I'm just making this call for Kit. It's Kit who . . ."

Like one of those science filmstrips of a blooming rose or a sinking sun, Lucinda begins to picture a rapidly aging little boy, college already sped by, so that he's . . . how old now? Her hands are shaking almost as badly as Zeke's, and her mind won't make the calculations, though it's done so at various idle moments before now. He's . . . is he forty? More? He cannot be that old—yet, equally implausible, she is more than twice that age. How can she have lost all those years?

But her mind is rushing ahead like a fool toward an unseen cliff.

What if Kit wants just to *know* about his "biological father"? He wants only the knowledge, the genealogical facts, not the complications of meeting anyone new. His search might be a matter not of desire but of delicate urgency: a child in need of bone marrow, a spare kidney. What if that's why Jasper Noonan is the one calling her? After all, he mentioned Jonathan.

"Mr. Noonan?"

"Yes, Mrs. Burns."

"Call me Lucinda, Mr. Noonan. And please just tell me what Kit needs."

"Needs?" He pauses. "To know his . . . 'roots,' I guess. Used to be, people hid this kind of thing, right? Kept it under the rug." Again he pauses. "Christ, listen to me. I'm supposed to be the messenger here, not the philosopher."

Caution begins to enfold her heart like a fog. Who exactly *is* this man with whom she's having this intimate conversation?

"Are you still there . . . Lucinda?"

"I'm here, and I'm falling apart a little."

"Falling apart's okay. I'd fall apart big time, news like this on top of what you're going through with your husband."

She thinks for a moment. "Did you ever meet him—Zeke?"

"No. But I saw the paper. I hope he's recovering all right."

"Thank you," she says. "Is Kit there? Would he speak with me?"

"I left that message while he was here, but he's gone home. Only reason I was the one to call is I worried what might happen if, in case . . ."

"In case I didn't want the connection."

"That's the thing."

From downstairs in her own house, Lucinda hears the scraping of furniture. No outcries, no indications of a fall. Is David leaving already?

"Mrs. . . . Lucinda?"

"Yes?"

"I didn't tell him about Jonathan. Just told him I knew about you. I asked him to wait till I spoke to you. He did call me this morning. . . ."

"I'm sorry, Mr. Noonan, that I didn't try you sooner. My husband's been . . . I've been—" Again, the instinctive caution of the politician's wife censors her. As if the entire state doesn't know about Zeke's stroke. Probably, by now, about his urinating on the Chinese rug.

Why does he keep mentioning Jonathan? Never mind. Be direct, she tells herself. She has dealt with strangers' emotions; she was trained to do it.

Into the pause seeps distant music: country this time, no longer jazz. "Should I call him? Call Kit?" she asks.

"Yes!" he says. "If you would. He . . . it may sound absurd after all these years, but I think he's waiting. Not to rush you."

"All I want to do, first, is talk to my husband." Which wouldn't have been easy even in better circumstances.

"And·maybe Jonathan," he says.

"Jonathan?" She finally gets it. "Mr. Noonan, Jonathan isn't Kit's father. No. My other son. Malachy. Who's gone. He died."

Jasper Noonan's sigh is so long and heartfelt that Lucinda feels ashamed she told him so much, so bluntly.

"My dear woman. I am so sorry."

"A long time ago now." Though all that "long time" has done is move the pain to a more distant room. When she enters that room, though she does so less often, the pain still blinds her with its keen, diamondlike brilliance.

"I'm sure it makes little difference. Time," he says. "I've got two sons."

"I would tell you to take good care of them, but I imagine they're old enough that they have to take care of themselves," she says.

"Mostly you're right. Mostly."

The protracted silence separates yet joins them. In the farther reaches of Jasper Noonan's house, Lucinda can just make out the words of a song. Some twangy-voiced singer wails about the virtues of his long-dead father. Good God.

"That was your son—who answered the phone?"

"Number two," he says, oddly brusque. Is he impatient to get off the phone? Lucinda finds herself desperate not to sever the thread of their fragile connection, peculiar though it is.

"Nice to have them at home sometimes, isn't it?" Where is she going?

But he reels her back in. "Lucinda. I think now's where I give you

Kit's number. I'll call him just to say we spoke—that you'll call. He says you should call after nine o'clock at night—if you would. He says to tell you he's always up till eleven. That work for you?"

"Fine!" To make this call, though she can't yet imagine how to do it, she would stay up till all hours of the night—which, in any case, she often does.

"Bear with me while I go downstairs again. Number's on my desk."

As Jasper Noonan goes downstairs in his remote house (though according to their shared area code, it's not all that remote), as the music grows louder, someone downstairs in Lucinda's house picks up the phone, taps in a number.

"Hello? Someone there?" David's voice (unguarded, impatient).

"David, it's me. Is everything all right?"

"Oh yes, Mrs. B. Sorry to interrupt you. My cell's acting up, but—"

"Lucinda?" Jasper.

"Hang on," says Lucinda. "David, I'll let you know when the line's free."

"Sure thing." He hangs up.

Lucinda's heart beats so hard that she cannot believe its palpitations aren't visible through her blouse. She apologizes for the interruption.

And then she has it: the telephone number of her long-lost grandson.

"You'll call him tonight?"

"Or tomorrow," she says. "I want to tell Zeke."

"Naturally."

She's pushing herself to say good-bye when Jasper says quietly, "Do you want me to tell him about . . . I'm sorry, what was your other son's name?"

"Tell him the story about his father is complicated. Tell him he needs to ask me and I'll tell him everything." Selfishly, she wants this for herself—not that she wants to inflict pain, but the details have to come from her.

"Sounds best that way," says Jasper. "And hang on to my number, would you? Call me for any reason. I know Kit. Or I used to know him, and now I know him again. A stroke of luck I owe to you, in a roundabout way. For which I thank you."

"No, Mr. Noonan. I'm the grateful one here."

"Jasper," he says. "Please."

"Jasper," says Lucinda. "Tell Kit I'll call him by tomorrow night."

The sun is on its way down, the snow warming toward a buttery pink. If she watches for long enough, can she actually perceive the lengthening of the shadow cast by the enormous, empty barn? Of the original outbuildings, it's the only one Zeke left standing after he sold the last of the herd, after Mal and Jonathan complained that they'd had enough of showing cows. (As sixteen-year-old Mal announced, "We've put in our time on the family legacy.")

The barn is important to Zeke as a symbol of his father's achievement—which he extols as the groundwork for his own. He spares no expense to keep it painted (pure white from the ground to its red-shingle roof) and properly buttressed, even if it's nothing now but a city of swallows. During the time Lucinda sits facing the view, the sun sinks just enough to shine directly in the window. On the table before her, it sets alight a porcelain dish filled with straight pins, dispersing splinters of phosphorescence all over the walls and ceiling of the room, across the front of her blouse. She is shivering.

"Mrs. B?" David's calling up the stairs.

"Oh, I'm sorry! The phone's free now," she calls back. She feels permanently fastened to her chair.

"I think I'm headed out, if it's okay by you." He's waiting.

She puts both treasured phone numbers, written on the same sheet of paper, back in her pocket. Somehow she's able to rise and go to the stairs. The look David gives her from below is a new one, an ever-so-covert smile.

"How's Zeke? How was it, going over the things he's been missing?" she says when she joins David near the front door.

"He'll be up to speed in no time, Mrs. B."

This is such an absurd speculation, such a fatuous lie, that she nearly laughs in David's face. "He's still in the kitchen?" she asks.

"Going over a few things I've left him to sign." He lowers his voice. "Maybe you'd help him with the actual signing. Just steady his hand a little."

Lucinda takes David's coat off the rack and hands it to him. Suddenly, she wants him gone. "Drive safely. There's black ice where you get back on the road. I'll need to get it sanded."

After he leaves, she goes to the kitchen. Zeke, his back to her, is hunched over the table, a pile of documents before him. Lucinda says loudly, "Well, your young intern thinks I'm having an affair." But when she rounds the table, to wash the dishes left by the sink, she realizes that Zeke is sound asleep in his chair.

She forgot to ask Zoe about when to wake him and when to let him sleep. She wants, more than anything, to pick up the phone at the stroke of nine, but she needs to figure out how to tell Zeke what she's found out—and she needs to wait till he's rested. She voices a silent apology to Kit, but one more day can't hurt.

As she rouses Zeke and guides him to the living room, Lucinda cannot resist the vain thought that Kit owes his very life to her as much as to his mother—and the corresponding shame at the way in which she betrayed her husband. It was a necessary betrayal; that conviction will never falter. The uneasy question is how it changed Mal's life, altered his path. If he were still alive, he would be fifty-nine years old.

How proud they were when Mal was accepted to that famous music camp. To prepare for auditions, he had worked with his flute teacher four afternoons a week for two months. Only then, as she eavesdropped on these lessons from the kitchen, did Lucinda realize that her son had real talent.

Because the camp was in Vermont, most of the young musicians came from New England and New York, but a few came from farther away, even from Europe. Some were prodigies who, not even finished with high school, had already left conventional schooling behind. Zeke would never have allowed Mal to take that risk; to him, Mal was just a boy who loved to play his flute and, having played it with such dedication for nearly ten years, had forged his own talent, a source of pleasure and self-discipline more than a "gift" pointing him toward a predestined profession. But Lucinda, as she mingled with some of the other parents and mentors at the camp's orientation, began to envision her son on the stages of concert halls in cities all over the world.

Mal was barely sixteen, but because he had skipped sixth grade, he had already graduated from high school. A common refrain on his report cards was how "old" he seemed for his age. At his flute teacher's urging, he had applied to conservatories as well as nearby colleges, and halfway through that summer he was offered a place at Juilliard. Lucinda was elated. But to her surprise, Mal wrote her a letter to say that he had decided to take a year off. One of his instructors at the camp knew a New York record producer who had a satellite studio in Burlington; the man agreed to hire Mal as an office assistant. Lucinda was even more surprised when Zeke approved. "Any business experience is money in the bank of pragmatic living," he said. "Especially if my son's going to make a bid for Carnegie Hall!" Later, Mal would say that he never believed he had what it took to be a marquee performer, but Lucinda had to wonder if she and Zeke were to blame for letting themselves believe all the flattering nonsense about their son's exceptional maturity. It is still unbearable to imagine how Mal must have felt when he learned just how badly he had let them down.

Not that Lucinda knew a thing about what happened at the camp until the letter she received in October: this completely unknown girl writing to tell Lucinda that she was pregnant with Mal's baby. *Dear Mrs. Burns, What I have to tell you will come as a shock, and I apologize for that. . . .* Had there been a second Malachy at the camp? She took out the programs she had saved from the two concerts she and Zeke had attended. . . . Yes, there *she* was, this *Daphne Browning, Violincello,* but that did not mean . . .

Should she call Mal, at his job in Burlington? She pictured him in an office filled with strangers, answering the phone for someone else. But first Zeke should hear about the letter—the preposterous claim. ("Mrs. Burns, he's in a legislative session that might last the rest of the day; is this an emergency?" Of course it was an emergency. But no, she told the secretary. And what had she planned to do—read the girl's assertions of love and devotion over the phone to Zeke?)

All afternoon, as Lucinda waited for him, the letter lay open on the kitchen table, indigo cursive on cream-colored paper folded twice, top and bottom reaching up like pleading arms. The letter dared her to disbelieve it, dared her to flee the house and pray it would vanish in her absence.

Zeke arrived home at nearly eight o'clock. She handed him his old-fashioned and sent Jonathan upstairs to do his homework. No TV that night; because she said so. She led Zeke into the den and closed the door.

He sighed. "Jonathan in some kind of fix at school?"

She simply handed it to him. He read it quickly, still standing, letter in one hand, drink in the other. "Lord Almighty."

Lucinda could do little more than stare into space, her arms folded tightly against her chest. She couldn't even scold Zeke for his language.

"There is so much we cannot take at face value here," he said. "Just what the hell went on at that place?"

"You can't forget those amazing concerts, Zeke. They had to be playing music most of the time, wouldn't you say?"

"Did we meet this girl? Did we know he had a girlfriend there? Christ, has he *ever* had a girlfriend? He didn't even go to the prom!"

Lucinda tried to remember whom they had met. At the two concerts they attended, the young musicians had huddled together, mostly aloof from the adults. The parents had talked politely among themselves, sharing a sense of elite satisfaction that their talented children were mature enough not to follow the Pied Piper movement toward rock and roll—and all the other bad behavior that went along with music like that.

Zeke drained his drink. "You haven't called Mal."

"No." She realized that this was what had to happen right then. She thought of Mal as more her son than Zeke's, yet she had no idea how to broach a subject like this.

Zeke asked her to get him another drink and to leave him alone in the den. "I cannot have this conversation with you listening, I'm sorry." But she didn't want to listen.

Half an hour later, Zeke emerged and demanded a third drink. "One to get the news, one to confirm it, and one to tell you where we go from here."

Lucinda went upstairs to make sure Jonathan had turned out his light. She looked in at him, still reading under the quilt with the red planes, and she wished that she could keep this one, the last one, a child forever. She made him promise to put the book down at the end of the chapter. She closed his door.

She found Zeke in the kitchen, eating a brownie he had cut from a tray on the counter. "Those are for the parish bake sale, Zeke."

"Most of them are," he said. "Unless I decide otherwise. At the moment, my cause is more urgent."

"It's true?"

Zeke took a sip of his third drink and winced at the clash of flavors. "He's known about this for a couple of weeks. The girl called him. He says he's been 'paralyzed.' He swears it was just once, just the one time. A mistake, which he regrets."

Lucinda, though she had been a "good girl," a virgin when she married, knew full well that this wasn't likely to be something you did just once, not if you gave in. She knew the times they were living in. It also dawned on her that the very thing these parents assumed had kept their children "safe"—their intense focus on complex beautiful music, their prodigious hours of rehearsal—might in fact have left them wishing for greater release, wilder abandon, in the spaces between their precociously brilliant work.

"A mistake with consequences," she said, deciding it was pointless to argue with Mal's version. "He does understand that, doesn't he?"

"He is not going to be a father," Zeke said. "Not this young, he's not."

Lucinda laughed bitterly. "Well, it looks like he *is*. Biology has a big say in this matter. Did he miss that class when he skipped ahead?"

Zeke's expression was one of pure sadness. She thought he would reprimand her for being sarcastic. He said quietly, "Arrangements can always be made."

She thought about this for a moment. "Adoption."

Zeke shook his head. "I shouldn't speak with you about this, but it's not as if I would hide it from you, either." He told her about the grown daughter of a colleague, her visit to a clinic in Montreal.

"Zeke."

"Lucinda, this is your son's life. And though right now I couldn't give a hoot about her, some girl's life, too."

"No, it's the life of their son. Or daughter." That's when it struck her that this girl's pregnancy was destined to produce her first grandchild. "Oh, Zeke."

"The bottom line, Lucinda, is that the person who makes whatever decisions there are to be made has ultimately got to be this . . . what's her name?"

"Daphne." Whose letter now seemed to Lucinda not insolent but brave.

"We must have met her parents. I'm betting they're educated people."

"Zeke, please don't try—"

"I am going to handle this fairly. I am not going to threaten or pressure—"

"But you're going to offer money! Is that what you're going to do?"

He stood up from the kitchen table and put a hand on her shoulder, intended to calm her. "I didn't say that."

"But that's what you're going to do, isn't it? Try to buy this poor girl off?"

"This 'poor girl,' from what I understand, is no less responsible than Mal."

"Neither of them is old enough to be 'responsible' for anything!"

"Lucinda, that's my point."

"This is in God's hands, Zeke."

"According to your faith, my soul is lost already, so let's leave God out of this for now."

"God doesn't step out of the room, Zeke, like some jury that isn't supposed to hear the lawyers' sidebar."

"Am I actually going to hear a sermon now?" said Zeke. "Really?"

They talked in circles for another half hour, until Zeke declared they should go to bed, "sleep on it" (*he* might sleep!), and he would handle everything in the morning. He went upstairs first. When she heard water running, Lucinda took the letter, including the envelope with the return address, carried it up to her sewing room, and tucked it deep in her scraps basket. She cut and ironed pieces for a quilt until the first intimations of dawn.

A few hours later, when she got up, Zeke was searching the den and the kitchen for the letter. She told him she'd find it while he was at work; he mustn't be late.

As soon as his car turned from the lane onto the road, she called directory assistance and obtained the number of the girl's home in New Hampshire.

An end run, Zeke and his partners would have called it. Once she knew she had secured the trust of the girl—who wanted that baby; who wasn't looking for a "procedure" of some kind, thank heaven—Lucinda wrote a long, impassioned letter to Mal. She drove straight from the post office to Saint Joseph's. In the false anonymity of the confessional, she asked forgiveness for defying her husband's wishes and quite possibly her son's. God's eternal imperatives, however, dwarfed those wishes. They were incontestable.

By the time Zeke came home from work that night, she had set a plan in motion. "This isn't my decision or yours," she said. "It's hers."

"And God's, I'll bet. Right? Is that what you told her? You brandished the damnation card?"

Lucinda walked out of the kitchen.

"You will regret this," Zeke called after her.

She walked the fields for two hours. When she came in, Zeke was eating canned soup and talking business on the phone. She waited for him to hang up.

"I won't ever regret this," she said. "And someday you will thank me."

"Will Malachy thank you?" His voice was so quiet, she was chilled. The conversation was over.

If there was one thing Zeke knew from both farming and practicing law, it was how to cut his losses. For weeks, she would sometimes catch him looking at her as if she were a foreigner, an alien being who'd beamed right into his house from outer space. He did not go to Mass with Lucinda until many months later, when she finally insisted. She was going to pray for the happiness of the new mother and baby. "This is your grandchild," she reminded Zeke, and though he shook his head, she had to believe that in some corner of his soul he, too, rejoiced.

"Leg shkilling me."

"Hang on, Zeke." Lucinda puts her book aside and turns on another lamp. It's nine-fifteen.

She pushes the button that magically jackknifes the mattress, allowing Zeke to sit up. She massages his cramped leg.

"Shleeping in clohjz," he mutters.

"David wore you out. But he was pleased with how much you accomplished. Why don't I get your pajamas?"

He nods. He leans back and closes his eyes. "Dreamed brother."

She turns around. "You dreamed about your brother?" She sits down again. She doesn't ask which one.

"Zjuh," he utters. "Brother-zjuh."

"Both of them."

"Haying. Shree of us. Rainj coming and Mashew'j goofing off. Won't lishen to Aaron. Aaron waj alwayj bosh."

"I remember," says Lucinda. "I mean, I remember your stories."

He stares at Lucinda gravely. She hates how watery his eyes have become. He says, with contemptuous precision, *"Don't treat me like an old man."*

"We're both old," she says, "though we can do our best to act otherwise. I was thinking today about what would happen if I had a stroke, too. Or fell down the stairs. What Christina and Jonathan would do."

This earns her a grudging smile. "Chrishtina'd take me. Jonathan you."

"I'd have more fun," she says. "I'd get to see San Francisco, go to dinner parties with artists and intellectuals; what does Cyril call them, the culture queens? The velvet mafia? You'd be stuck with the lawyers and eco-freaks. I'd have a garden with climbing jasmine and palm trees. You'd be cooped up indoors half the year." She thinks of the plantings she saw as she walked around Jonathan and Cyril's Berkeley neighborhood, the climatically illogical mix of jasmine and cactus with tulips and roses. The air was ethereal in its variegated sweetness.

"No," says Zeke. "You'd be shtuck in bed like jish. Maybe *view* of palm treejh." He closes his eyes.

Lucinda asks if he wants dinner. He seems to consider the effort it will take, and then he says he wouldn't mind another sandwich.

On the way upstairs to get clean pajamas for Zeke, she sees the four flower arrangements she banished to the long bench by the front door; they look like patients waiting to see a doctor. She will take them to the church tomorrow, even the gladiolas sent by Father Jess (or by his latest secretary; Lucinda no longer visits the parish house often enough to remember her name). She thinks of the countless flower arrangements that have come up that farm lane following news of a dozen deaths. Weddings, too. *Matthew,* she thinks, then veers away. She mustn't forget Zeke's evening pills.

After she helps him into his pajamas, she makes sure he goes to the bathroom. In the kitchen, she moves the documents Zeke has to sign from the table to what they call the later-box, on the back counter. Zeke is silent while she makes them grilled ham-and-tomato sandwiches. The sound of sizzling butter fills the kitchen in its comforting way. She finds a jar of watermelon pickles.

Lucinda waits until they're seated, relishing the smell of their hot sandwiches, before she pulls the sheet of paper from her pocket and lays it down between their plates—the one with the phone numbers.

"Zeke, I have some amazing news."

By the end of the war, their village had lost eight boys. Aaron Burns was the first, killed almost exactly a year after Pearl Harbor. Mrs. Arnold, a client at the bank, guessed before anyone knew; she was on her way to make a deposit when she found herself stuck behind an unfamiliar car that moved slowly, hesitantly, along the road toward town, finally stopping at the entrance to Sanctuary Farm. As she passed the car, it turned down the lane. The driver wore a uniform. "I have a hunch he was the bearer of sad news," she told the teller who took her deposit.

Arriving home from school, Lucinda heard it from her mother, who'd heard it from her father when he came home for lunch.

Zeke was out of school for close to a week. Just as abruptly, Dora wasn't at the Canteen. Other girls, the ones who had boasted what heroes their boyfriends would be, looked tearful and worried. The war was now a *real* war: a hastening of death, not just a temporary absence of loved ones or a cause for compulsory thrift. Even farm equipment was rationed. At Saint Joseph's, a Mass was dedicated to Aaron Burns; on the board in the vestry, parishioners tacked up prayer cards wishing his family solace and blessings, dropping their nickels and dimes in the box. That the Burnses weren't Catholic didn't matter.

Lucinda was a sophomore. As far as most people knew, she was a serious student with her mind on work, not boys, but in the bottom left drawer of her desk she kept her letters from Matthew Burns. They weren't love letters, but she saw the slowly accruing stack as evidence of a solidifying friendship that, like a sapling, would imperceptibly grow into something stronger. You turn around one day and, presto, the sapling's become a tree. Those letters were like the widening rings in the trunk that represent the necessary seasons of growth.

She sent him packages of socks, candy, and small souvenirs: a brazen maple leaf pressed in wax paper, a scalloped coaster from the Canteen, a program from the glee club's Autumnfest concert, a pennant from the Thanksgiving football game (played that year by an ever-so-slightly-greener-than-usual crop of boys). Matthew was somewhere in Europe: he had described the countryside and local farms, the weather and the way people dressed. He told her about his two best friends and a stray dog their unit had adopted; they named it Ajax, after the great warrior. (When he stopped mentioning the dog, Lucinda didn't ask why.)

Matthew was granted a furlough of two weeks, through Christmas. His homecoming was anticipated with mixed emotion; it would be anything but a triumphant return. He would be suffering along with his parents and Zeke, through a holiday normally filled with joy. He would also be reminded of a fate that could just as easily have been his—and might still.

But Lucinda's emotions were hardly mixed. From the day she knew he was back (someone in the bank confirmed seeing him in his father's car), she waited for his call. It would come later; for now, his family would be a closed circle. She imagined his kind, beautiful mother, crying her eyes out. Lucinda had already sent Mrs. Burns a note, saying how sorry she was, how they were all in her prayers.

On the third day of his leave, Matthew was spotted by some of the kids on their way home from school, but no one approached him, because he was sharing a bench on the town green—never mind that it was freezing cold, inches of snow on the ground—with Dora Keene. She was crying into her mittens. He had an arm around her shoulders. This report came in the following morning, as everyone shed boots and coats at their lockers, rushing to make their first classes.

Poor Dora. Were people writing notes to her as well? How awful to be receiving letters of condolence along with Christmas cards.

On the fifth day, a Saturday, Lucinda carried her father's lunch to the bank. He had called to say he was too busy to come home. Waiting outside her father's office, along with Zeke the Elder, was Matthew. His severe haircut revealed ears that were larger and fleshier than those she remembered; they looked sunburned, odd in the middle of winter. He was also thinner in a way that made him look taller—and there, catching sight of her as she walked into the bank, were his same blue eyes. Those hadn't been changed by the war.

"Lucinda James, my best pen pal!" he exclaimed. Matthew's father gave her a smile she recognized as the one grown-ups lavish on children they find adorable or entertaining.

Matthew leaned toward Lucinda and kissed her on one cheek; perhaps he'd have hugged her if she hadn't been carrying her father's tin lunch box. Through the open door to his office, Lucinda saw him talking on the phone.

He hung up and waved them all in. She watched him enclose the right hand of each man between both of his, first the father, then the son. "We are all so shattered at the news," he said. "I'm sure you're tired of hearing people say that Aaron will be remembered for his sacrifice, even if it's true. Whatever I can do to make things easier, please put me to work."

Lucinda had managed to utter nothing more than a stuttered hello to Matthew. Except to glimpse his father's patronizing smile, she had ignored Mr. Burns altogether. She had behaved like the child he thought she was.

As the three men sat down, she handed her father his lunch. While he leaned down to set it under his desk, Matthew turned toward Lucinda and asked her how her rabbits were.

"Huddled up against the cold," she said. "Sometimes I envy them those thick fur coats." Did that make sense? Had she contradicted herself?

But Matthew nodded and said, "Amen to that. This place makes Europe look balmy. If I get a chance, I might come over for an inspection. How about it?"

"Sure," she said. "That would be swell." Had she really said *swell*? Now her father was smiling expectantly at her. She was like the odd player out in a game of musical chairs.

"Tell your mother I'll be home by three, all right, Lu?"

"Glad I got to see you," said Matthew. "And can I tell you, those blue socks in your last package? They're my new favorites. Really warm."

Rushing from the bank, Lucinda felt as if her face were one massive bee sting. She practically ran the few blocks to her house.

The next day, so many people poured into the Congregational church—Catholics, Episcopalians, and Lutherans defecting from their respective sanctuaries for this one solemn day—that some people had to stand outside. Hymnals and prayer books were passed back through the open doors, each one shared by six or seven people.

Lucinda had been in this church before, but still she was puzzled by its bleakness: the plain pine cross; the unadorned altar; most of all, the transparent windows. They made Lucinda feel weirdly embarrassed, as if the church were a woman caught naked in public. In place of saints and angels, a view of the mortal world. Saint Joseph's, with its stained glass and gilt trim, its carved wooden figures gazing toward heaven from their alcoves in the wall, made her feel cocooned by God's Word, the deeds of the apostles.

The minister talked about war and sacrifice and the healing effects of a community binding its wounds and the consolations that springtime on a farm would bring to this family a few months hence: new calves, new shoots from the ground, flowers blooming, peas and beans twisting up trellises in the sun. He said very little about Aaron as a real person, and there wasn't much talk involving God—who, as Lucinda saw it, had determined this wretched course of events, from Japan's attack on the navy down through proclamations made by Roosevelt and Churchill, all the way down to the death of Lieutenant Burns on a hot beach in Africa. Lucinda's father had explained to her that the battle in which Aaron died was only a strategic prelude to the "ultimate showdown" that would be fought in Europe. Would Matthew fight there? She hoped not—and when the minister asked them to bow their heads (but not to kneel), she prayed for exactly that: *Mother Mary, full of grace, please spare Matthew Burns from the evil of war. Please give him tasks to help the Allies that don't mean fighting or killing. Please don't make his mother lose another son.* She knew she was praying that others be chosen to die instead. Those others, as it turned out, would very nearly include her brother Patrick, who fought in the Pacific and, after a month in a Hawaiian hospital, came home wasted by a tropical fever and missing his right leg. Matthew would return from France with a thick scar on his right hand from a gash inflicted by the jagged edge of a large can of tomatoes opened with a farm tool. Zeke the Younger, though he wanted to enlist, was compelled by his parents to take a farm labor deferral.

After the service, Lucinda waited with her parents for an hour in the reception line at the church hall. One by one, friends, well-wishers, and voyeurs shook the hands of the Burnses and thanked them for their son's life. When Lucinda shook Matthew's hand, he leaned down and kissed her on the cheek again, so close to her mouth that she thought she might faint. But immediately after, she had to shake his mother's hand. Even through a thick layer of powder, Mrs. Burns's face looked ruddy and tender, but for that day, at least, she had stopped crying. (So many years later, Lucinda would wonder how.)

"Hello, Lucinda. Thank you for helping us say good-bye to Aaron. Thank you for being a friend to Matthew." And then she released Lucinda's hand and reached for her mother's. Lucinda would never remember shaking the hand of her future husband. Probably he ignored her, reaching out instead to Patrick, shortstop passing the ball to second base—someone he knew outside the ruthless rituals of mourning. She was just the little sister of his teammate.

In 1944, within a month of returning home and laying aside his uniform, before Lucinda even saw him, Matthew was engaged to Dora Keene. He married her in the exuberant heat of August following the end of the war: a ceremony in the big plain-windowed church with two hundred guests long starved for a true celebration. That night, the two families hosted a dance party in a pasture mowed, just for the occasion, by Matthew and the two Zekes.

Lucinda was out of high school; in September, she would go to college in Middlebury. At the party, she tried not to watch Matthew dancing with Dora. The hem of Dora's white dress was stained bright green from the newly cut clover. She looked too happy to care; had she so easily forgotten Aaron, buried less than a mile up the road? Were the brothers so interchangeable to her?

"Hey, Pat's little sister, why the long churchy face?"

Startled, she turned to answer Zeke the Younger. What could she say? "Just thinking about going away in a few weeks."

"Don't worry. You'll come back," he said lightly, "your head stuffed to the rafters with knowledge. You won't pay much heed to us farmers then. But for now . . . dance?"

His request was so sudden, she didn't have time to say no; the brothers were not interchangeable to *her*. As they moved among the other couples, she became conscious of dancing with one of the only able-bodied young men in town who had never even gone to boot camp. He had worked hard on the farm, of course—extra hard. He'd been indispensable to his father, who had lost his best hands to the army. No one looked down on Zeke Jr.—they knew he would have gone to war in a flash if his service hadn't been needed at home—but he didn't have the swagger of the boys returning from foreign perils. (Who cared if all they had done was load supply trucks or work a transmitter at an air-force base? They'd been *over there*.) Even Patrick, with three bony limbs and one artificial leg, found a way to stride down the street like a hero, not a cripple.

Lucinda did go to college that fall, and in a strange twist—she pictured the Möbius strip that her algebra teacher had made from a simple bit of paper—Zeke began to write her letters. The pile of envelopes in her dormitory desk grew far faster than the pile of letters she had gathered from Matthew Burns. But there was no comparison to be made except in memory: bitterly, Lucinda had discarded Matthew's letters after hearing about his engagement to Dora.

At Lucinda and Zeke's rehearsal dinner, in a toast he must have thought sweet and funny, Matthew raised his glass and said, "To Lucinda, who may have had a schoolgirl crush on me but found the right brother in the end . . . and to my baby brother, Zeke, who kept the home fires burning bright while the rest of us skipped town. He kept those damn cows milked, the fields mowed, the tractors running—and our girls safe from the threat of invading Huns. Though maybe not safe from his charms!"

Perhaps she had found the right brother after all, she thought as she absorbed the unintended slights of that clumsy toast; yet for years to follow, whenever she saw Matthew dancing with or simply leaning close to Dora, she felt a vestigial yearning. Almost worse, she sensed—from looks that lingered a beat too long, from the occasional wink—that Matthew saw her yearning. At least he and Dora had moved away, settling in western Massachusetts, so she didn't have to endure this awkwardness too often. And then, fifteen years ago, Matthew sold his half of the farm to a developer. He was tired of leasing the land from afar. Besides, with their grown offspring scattered across the country, he and Dora had decided to move even farther away, to a beach house in Florida. Zeke spent hours on the phone trying to change his brother's mind about the fate of the land. For once, his persuasive powers failed him.

Lucinda hasn't seen Matthew since then, not since he came up to close the deal in the very office where her father once worked (the bank now an insignificant link in a national chain, little more than a teller's window, a pair of plywood cubicles, and a vestibule with an ATM). Five years ago, Dora died of colon cancer. Lucinda sent the requisite donation to the cancer foundation named in the death notice and wrote a short letter to Matthew. *I will never forget that beautiful wedding in the southeast field. Dora was the happiest bride I'd ever seen. I'm sure she believed you saved her life, and probably you did.* The reply she got, thanking her for her "kind gesture," was from Matthew's oldest daughter. She wondered, sadly, what it might have been like to get a letter from Matthew Burns himself so many decades after the last ones he had sent her. She can remember his handwriting—larger and more legible than his brother's, though Zeke, even before law school, was always more eloquent. She still has the letters of courtship and love he wrote to her when she was in college. Christina and Jonathan can read them one day, after she's gone, and know that whatever else they've wondered, their parents married out of love. For Lucinda, was it displaced love? Sometimes she worries that it was, but really, what did she know—what did either of them know—back then?

Zeke has been home for a week and a half, though Lucinda could swear it's been a month—and still she cannot tell if he's improving. One day he seems sure-footed, the walker obsolete; next day it will take her ten minutes just to help him out of bed. It's too soon to expect dramatic results, says Zoe, who came this morning, followed by the speech therapist. They won't come again for close to a week, because of the holiday weekend. This will be a test for Lucinda, even with visitors to help in a crisis. She has yet to spend a night upstairs in the bedroom, and her back is killing her from sleeping on the sofa bed. When she happens to mention this to Jonathan, who is reading student papers on his laptop at the kitchen table, he looks up at her, eyes wide, and snaps the computer shut. "There is no reason not to fix that problem now, Mom!"

He sprints upstairs and back down, returning with his iPhone. Peering into its genielike screen, tapping and stroking it furiously, he murmurs, "Yes . . . yes . . . oh good . . . huh. All righty . . ." Without looking up, he says, "Mom, don't you guys have a Sleepy's in some mall around here? Yes! Okay. Here we go." Lucinda doesn't follow him into the den; she hears him opening the sofa, talking to someone on his phone.

He returns to the kitchen and announces, "New and much better mattress will arrive today between noon and five. How's that?" With a flourish, he slides his phone into his shirt pocket, sits at the table, and opens his computer.

"Sweetheart, I can't thank you enough," says Lucinda.

"You are welcome. And now, *eh bien,* back to Simone and J-Paul, the ever-dynamic duo. Let me know when Dad wakes up. I'm going to get him to play chess. Zoe told me it's good for his brain *and* his hands."

In the two full days since Jonathan's arrival, his effusive energy and nearly manic helpfulness put Lucinda in mind of a dervish, though she isn't quite sure what a dervish is. Yesterday he got up at seven, spoke with his sister on the phone and made a long list, after which he drove to the monstrously overstocked grocery store (the one whose parking lot and checkout lines Lucinda cannot endure) and the gourmet shop and the wine store. He insisted on going alone, and when he returned, he ferried what looked like dozens of bags from the car and put everything away on his own.

"And these are for you," he said, presenting his mother with four gaudy, durable cloth sacks emblazoned with the logo of the monster grocery store. "Save a few maple trees, Mom." She thanked him, even though she already owns dozens of these eco-friendly bags. No senator's wife, least of all a Vermont senator's wife, should be caught wasting resources of any kind. (Forget that the fuel bills for the monster store negate, to a laughable degree, any do-gooding efforts at conserving grocery bags.)

Now Lucinda hardly dares open her own refrigerator, for fear of dislodging a torrent of vegetables, fruits, breads, boxes of pastry, artisanal goat cheeses, and bottles of champagne. Hunkered down beneath all this bounty is the carcass of a formerly free-roaming, organically fed, never-drugged turkey that Jonathan ordered online while back in California and picked up in person at a farm half an hour away.

Lucinda likes to orchestrate and shop for Thanksgiving herself, but under the circumstances (including treacherously icy roads) she is relieved to let someone take over. Until a few years ago, Jonathan would have been the least likely candidate for this role. She's pretty sure the catalyst is Cyril, who will arrive tonight. Jonathan says that he and Cyril will spend tomorrow making a "royal feast" and that no one else will be allowed in the kitchen all day.

Jonathan has found domestic happiness on the late side, in his fifties. Perhaps, having found it so late, he's making up for lost time. That's the only way she can explain the startling changes in her son. He has lived in California for close to thirty years now, giving Lucinda only the rarest glimpses into his adult life. During most of that time, he did not mention attachments of any kind. And then, five years ago, he met Cyril. Two years after that, Lucinda and Zeke made a trip out to see the house they bought together (which Zeke thought a risky arrangement, just from a legal perspective). Still, when Lucinda found herself giving advice about their wedding last summer, what felt unnatural to her was not that her son would be marrying a man but that he would be settling down in any conventional sense.

This visit is the first time she's seen Jonathan since then, and it's clear that he's added muscle and a healthy bit of flesh to his bony frame. His clothes—just the jeans and striped shirts he wears around the house, the colorful socks in which he pads to and fro like a playful cat—look as if they've been more consciously chosen; and is his hair actually styled? It's wonderful, the apparent contagion of Cyril's confidence and flair, but it worries her just a little, too.

Jonathan has a fine academic reputation of his own (she heard this, time and again, from the university colleagues she met at the wedding), but sometimes it looks to Lucinda as if her son has blissfully donned the mantle of cheerleader wife. He is constantly telling her about Cyril's glowing book reviews, his never-ending honors, his keynote addresses to conferences in luxurious locales. Last year, according to Jonathan, Harvard tried to "poach" Cyril from Berkeley with a tempting offer that included the loan of a historic house on Brattle Street where Longfellow and Hawthorne frequently dined as guests. Lucinda felt a pang at the thought of her son moving so much closer to her; if Harvard had offered a position for Jonathan as well, would they have moved?

Christina e-mails her mother to say that she will bring a cranberry cheesecake and her traditional sweet potatoes (mashed with too much butter and maple syrup). She and Greg will drive down Thursday morning with their youngest daughter, Madison. Courtney is still in India, and Hannah is going to her boyfriend's parents' house in Albany.

Lucinda wishes they were coming sooner. She has decided that she will tell Jonathan and Christina the extraordinary news about their forty-two-year-old nephew once they are all together. Zeke seems to have agreed with this plan, though once Lucinda told him about Kit's desire to be in touch with them, he had surprisingly little to say. Perhaps he was too tired to react properly to something so cataclysmic—perhaps she shouldn't have told him at night—but it was clear that he understood right away what she was talking about when she described her conversation with Jasper.

She called Kit's number at nine-thirty the following night, sitting alone in the den. As she had expected, her hands shook and she was short of breath. As she had forgotten to expect, a woman answered.

"May I speak with Christopher?" Lucinda asked.

"Who's calling?"

"Lucinda Burns. Do I have the right number?"

"Yes! You do! Just—yes. Hang on, please."

Lucinda shivered as she waited.

"Lucinda Burns?" The voice was loud, tense. "This is Kit. Christopher."

"Kit." She paused. Which one of them was supposed to ask questions first? Her voice trembled when she said, "I spoke to Mr. Noonan. Well, you know that, don't you?"

"He says you're my grandmother." Obviously trying to put her at ease, he forced a laugh. "Are you?"

"I guess I am. Or no, I'm *sure* I am." But was she? Should she, like the credit card people, ask him to state his birthday, the last four numbers of his social? Of course not.

"I can't believe this," he said. "I'm, I have to . . ."

She could tell he had covered the mouthpiece. Returning, he apologized. He laughed again, this time the sort of laughter that acts as a reminder to breathe. "I asked my wife—Sandra—to let me talk to you alone. This is so—"

"Strange," said Lucinda. "I'm too nervous. I wish we could just— see each other. I'm counting on that. I mean, hoping." Was this too forward of her?

"I am, too," he said. "Hoping we'll meet."

Do not cry, she reminded herself. She took a deep breath. "I know the person you're hoping to meet is your father."

"Yes. If I can. If he would. I know it's a lot to ask."

"Kit, my son Malachy was your father, and I wish you could meet him. I'm sure he'd have wanted that." Did it matter if this was a lie? Was it? She had no idea. "I'm sure you'd have met him already if he were alive."

She had expected silence, but almost right away Kit spoke. "My mother told me he died. That's all she told me. I didn't believe her."

Had Daphne known about Mal's death? Or had she simply claimed he was dead from the moment Kit could ask? One thing Lucinda knew she mustn't do was to make Kit any angrier at his mother than he might be already.

"Your mother was telling the truth. I think you'll see why she had a hard time telling you more. Mal was gay, and he died from AIDS. Twenty years ago. I can talk about it, so don't think you can't ask me anything you want. I want you to." *I want to have a new reason to talk about him*, she could have said. *No one wants to hear about him anymore. Not from me.*

After a moment, she said, "I'm sorry if I was too blunt."

"It's me who's sorry," he said. "Sorry for you. That's so awful."

"Yes. It is. But you know what? You have an aunt and an uncle— Mal's sister and brother. I know they'll be dying to meet you."

"They know about me?"

"No!" she said. "Not yet. But how could they not? Want to meet you."

Though what if everything Kit had to absorb now—gay father, dead of AIDS—made him change his mind about meeting even Lucinda? "Please forgive me if I assume too much," she said.

"Wow." He sighed loudly. "There's no book on how to do this, is there?"

"Probably there is. But if there isn't, I won't be the one to write it." Why was she making a joke of something so serious?

He was quiet for a few seconds. "I need to tell you that my mother doesn't know I'm doing this. Finding you. She's never wanted that."

"You know what?" said Lucinda. "I'm yours to find. I always have been." She resisted the urge to say that a part of her has been waiting, wishing, to be found. Is that why she's outlived so many of her friends?

He whispered something she didn't catch.

"Your mother will understand, Kit. I remember her. She'll be all right. She's—if she's the girl I remember, she adapts to things. She couldn't have raised you otherwise." That part was true. But as for what Daphne wanted or would understand, that didn't matter anymore. Lucinda felt a surge of a fierce, mean emotion: triumph.

"I don't know, but here we are, right?"

"Yes, here we are."

"So where do we go?"

"Toward knowing each other. I hope. If that's what you still want."

"Of course I do," said Kit.

"So you," said Lucinda. "You live in New Jersey. You're married."

"We have two children. Twins."

Lucinda felt her triumph give way to wonder. "Twins!" she exclaimed.

So many Thanksgivings in Lucinda's life are entwined with momentous events or revelations. She and Zeke announced their engagement over a just-carved turkey in this very house, during her senior year of college; a year later, they announced her first pregnancy. (Dora had two children by then.)

Eight Novembers passed without incident until the year in which Zeke the Elder died of a stroke the week before Thanksgiving. The meal at the farmhouse was canceled; it fell to Lucinda and Zeke, with three young children underfoot, to fit everyone into their modest house in town. Subdued but still hungry, people ate off their laps in three rooms; on one arm of her old sofa, now upstairs in the boys' bedroom, she can still make out gravy stains where Matthew's son upended his plate.

The next Thanksgiving was the first one Lucinda hosted at the farm. Zeke's mother lasted alone in the house for three months before she confessed that she felt frightened living alone. The den became her bedroom.

Over yet another Thanksgiving, his first visit home from his first year of college, Mal came out to Lucinda. The two of them were washing dishes while everyone else slept off the excess food and drink. (That expression, "coming out," was as foreign and irrelevant to her then as Tunisia had been before Aaron Burns died on a beach in that country.)

Mal had not gone to Juilliard. Because he hardly spoke to Lucinda during the year he worked for the record producer in Burlington, she was never able to talk to him about his decision to go to the University of Vermont instead. Zeke had told him about Lucinda's support of Daphne, her promise to help with the baby however she could. It was hard, after that, for Lucinda not to see Mal's turning away from his music as revenge, the dashing of her fantasies. This was absurd, she knew, yet the resentment Mal felt toward his mother was real.

"He might never lay eyes on that kid," Zeke said to Lucinda after she received news of Christopher's birth, "and still it will change his whole life."

"He's too young to see it clearly yet," she said.

"See what clearly? That his mother wants to make sure he understands the consequences of giving in to human temptation? What he's not too young to do, Lucinda, is cut you off from his life."

"Sounds as if you wouldn't care."

"Frankly, I'm staying out of it. What goes on between you and Mal is beyond my powers of negotiation." Zeke's sarcasm silenced her.

The only sympathetic man in her life was Father Tom, who told her to exercise humility in the face of her son's withdrawal. "God isn't the only one who works in mysterious ways," he said, smiling at the truth become cliché. "Our children do as well. Mal is a talented young man, and he will find his path. Perhaps he'll teach music. Perhaps he simply knows that he's not mature enough yet for life in a big city. New York—well, New York! When I go there myself, I feel like an ant. Which, I admit, is a useful perspective."

Was that it? Had Mal simply wanted to stay near home? Lucinda would never know. When he finally spoke to her about something meaningful, the news he shared toppled anything so trivial as where he had chosen to go to college.

They stood side by side at the sink, the usual wash-and-dry assembly line. She asked him about a class he was taking in European cultural history, which he'd brought up over dinner in a conversation about French movies with Zeke. Silent at first—had he heard her question over the running water?—he finished drying one of the fragile, gold-rimmed wineglasses and set it aside with its mates. He put down the towel and faced her. "Mom, I don't want to talk about European history. I'm behind on the paper I'm writing about Vienna, so I'd rather not go there anyway."

"To Vienna?" she joked nervously.

"Funny."

"What should we talk about?" She didn't care what they talked about. After months of ignoring her letters, of calling home to speak only with his father, her son was finally, freely speaking with *her*. She had been prepared for him to dry the dishes without a word, then go upstairs to bed.

"I want to talk about my homosexuality. Or I need to. I don't mean to shock you, but there's no other way to do this. I'm not going to give you a bunch of wink-wink hints. Dad knows already. I talked to him Tuesday, when he picked me up. Moms are supposed to be easier—most guys start with their moms, or that's what I hear—but not everybody's mom is . . . religious the way you are. I know you're thinking I'm damned to hell. If that's what you believe, I can't change it. If you want to talk about God, you're wasting your time. Sorry."

She wasn't thinking about the fate of Mal's soul—not yet. She was thinking that he had told Zeke two days before he told her. More upsetting, Zeke had said nothing to her, had not even seemed out of sorts the past two days (though she had not been alone with him at bedtime those two nights, staying up in the kitchen to cook).

She said, "Mal, sweetheart, I'm glad you can talk to me about this." She knew she sounded anything but glad. She was thinking, or this was the gist of the storm occupying the space where her brain had been, *You presume a lot, speaking to me so harshly after breaking my heart for so long with your silence.*

She sat down at the kitchen table. "Please sit, Mal. I need you to sit down, honey."

For once, her most obstinate child obeyed her. "I asked Dad how he thought you'd take this. He took it better than I thought he would. Though maybe that's politics. I mean, he has to accept a lot of people for what they are, people other people would avoid. It's their opinions he wants to change."

Lucinda assumed Mal wanted her to laugh, so she did.

He didn't even smile. He said, "I realized I needed to tell you this, now, for a couple of reasons."

"You're in love with someone?"

"No. I'm not getting ready to bring someone home to introduce to the family, if that's what you're thinking."

She pictured him walking through the door of the farmhouse with another young man. How could she face that? Had Zeke, who took the news so calmly, imagined such a scene?

"Did you just realize this?" she said.

"No." He looked directly at her, and she had to struggle to meet his gaze, which had steered clear of hers for so long. Her son's gaze, when serious, was almost foreboding. "How long I've known isn't important. Part of why I took the year off was to try to . . . get clear about it before . . . well, whatever comes next."

"But Daphne—" Immediately, Lucinda knew she'd said the wrong thing.

Mal frowned. "That was a mistake. A mistake in every way. I am never going to be a father, and I made that exponentially clear to her. So by involving yourself . . ." When he sighed, he sounded so heartbreakingly boyish. Lucinda thought of Father Tom's advice: to accept Mal's anger with humility.

He slumped in his chair and teased at the fringe of a woven placemat. "I wasn't going to talk about this. Even though, I guess, this is one of the reasons I needed to tell you. The fantasies you probably have." He sat up straight and pressed his long hands—hands God had made to play a musical instrument, Lucinda was sure of it—flat against both sides of his long face. He squeezed his eyes shut and mussed his hair, as if waking himself up. He made a sound of muted desperation. When he finally looked at her, he said, "I'm not making as much sense as I planned to. Well, does one ever? And come to think of it, not much of the past year has made any sense to *me*."

"But you are," she said. "Making sense." She wanted only to keep him talking.

"I thought I would never forgive you for what you did, but I love you, Mom, so not forgiving you isn't an option. Life is too complicated right now, or maybe too simple. I'd have crashed and burned at Juilliard—or anywhere I had to go on doing nothing but drilling myself mad trying to be a Great Musician."

But you are, you could be, she wanted to argue.

"I need to be selfish now, and I need to be honest, too. Steer clear of bullshit. But now you know what it is I'm concentrating on."

"Life," said Lucinda, and when she said it, she was filled with admiration. She realized her son was more valiant than foolish, whatever he was doing with the gifts he had, even if he set them aside for a time, hid them under the proverbial bushel.

"Well, Mom, you could put it that way," he said. "That's one way to put it." He smiled at her, with genuine if cautious warmth. It felt to Lucinda as if they were meeting each other on a narrow bridge across a wide river or canyon that had divided them far longer than the year of wounded feelings. "Let's finish doing the wineglasses," he said, "and let's go to bed. And let's actually get some sleep. No quilting allowed. I'll be listening for the machine."

"No quilting," she said. "I promise."

Cyril's arrival, late on Tuesday night, seems to intensify Jonathan's joie de vivre. Lucinda is already in the sofa bed (with its wonderfully dense new mattress) when she hears the two men enter the house, Jonathan making more noise shushing Cyril than Cyril might have made had he been talking.

She puts on her robe and goes to greet them. She hugs Cyril in the dim front hall. She says quietly, "It would take an airstrike to wake Zeke. Come into the kitchen and have a cup of tea. A glass of wine?"

She sees Cyril hesitate but decide to accept, perhaps out of courtesy.

"It's only nine-thirty back in Berkeley," he says once they've shut the kitchen door. "I'm still wide awake. So wine would be fantastic, thanks."

"Aren't you exhausted by that ghastly security nonsense you went through in Boston?" says Jonathan, pulling his chair close to Cyril's. Lucinda pours them each a glass of red wine. Jonathan pushes his glass away, but Cyril takes a sip and nods with pleasure.

"Hey, they didn't lose my luggage. That's always something."

"That's cause for *rejoicing*," says Jonathan. "These days, I think the airlines want you to feel grateful just for arriving at your destination *alive*."

Cyril laughs quietly but looks at Lucinda. "How's he doing?"

"Making progress. I think. He's discouraged about how hard it is to express himself. But it's looking like he's all there—his mind—as if he just has to push his way out of a stuffy, windowless room."

"To have his faculties intact—that's a real blessing."

Lucinda feels genuinely liked by Cyril—she likes him, too—but sometimes she has the sense that he cannot stop thinking of her as "religious" and taking care not to offend her. When the two men called, on speakerphone, to announce that they were going to get married, Zeke pointed out that same-sex marriage had been legal in California but not anymore; did they realize that?

"Dad, I think we know the laws of our own state," said Jonathan, "especially as they relate to biases that affect us directly. Biases we refuse to condone. We know that the *state* would see what we're doing as a commitment ceremony, but to us it will be a real wedding. Your wedding to Mom in the church? That was just as 'symbolic' to the state of Vermont as this one will be to California."

"It's not symbolic if you believe it's a sacrament," Cyril said at once. And then it sounded as if he was leaning closer to the phone. "Lucinda, I just want to say that I respect your Catholic views on this matter. I know you're pretty liberal, which I love about you, but I don't want you to be uncomfortable. There's this one priest—I guess he's an outlaw of sorts, but he holds Mass in the Castro—well, I was thinking that maybe we'd have him be part of the ceremony."

"I don't want you doing that for my sake," said Lucinda. "It's your day, and I'll happily play whatever role you like."

"Mother of the groom," chimed in Jonathan. "That's a no-brainer. The orchid corsage, the great hat, the usual."

"Mother of *a* groom," said Cyril.

"Of the older groom," said Jonathan. "The one who was almost an old maid."

"Oh, stop," said Cyril, who was five years younger. "We're both getting long in the tooth, and the point is, Zeke and Lucinda, that's something we want to continue to do together."

The wedding took place last July, on a grassy hillside with a dizzying view of San Francisco Bay, Jonathan and Cyril wearing white suits. Lucinda liked Cyril's parents. His mother was English, with the muted accent of someone who had lived in the States for most of her life; the father was an architect. At the rehearsal dinner, Lucinda sensed that the fathers of the two grooms were watching each other, quietly competing, convinced that many of the guests wondered how they honestly felt about watching their sons marry other men. Each gave a toast that was almost embarrassing in its self-conscious balance of humor and liberal-minded bravado.

Even when Lucinda had asked Zeke, in their suite at the Claremont Hotel that morning, how he honestly *did* feel about the wedding, he had smiled tersely and said, "With all we've been through, like it or not, we were catapulted long, long ago into a world no one could have pictured back in our 4-H days."

Was he referring to Mal, going through the hell-on-earth of AIDS, the disease itself and then the political fallout (for her personal; for Zeke professional, too), or was that her imagination? Was it pathetic that nearly every intense emotion she had experienced over the past two decades circled back to the life and death of her older son? He was dead by the time Jonathan came out to her—Mal's death spurred his confession—and as Lucinda lurched through the days of her horribly altered life, she would sometimes stop to wish that the greatest challenge of her life, and of Zeke's, had been facing up to having two gay sons, but two gay sons who would outlive them. That—oh that would have been easy!

Zeke is sitting on the edge of the sofa bed, his walker beside him.

"Honey? Are you all right?" Lucinda sits up.

"Ruckish in air," he says, but he gives her the one-sided smile she's beginning to accept as a version of normal.

How she slept through it, while Zeke did not, is a wonder to Lucinda. Maybe because, finally, she's sleeping on a comfortable mattress. Zeke is right: there's quite a ruckus coming from the kitchen. Laughing, singing, the repeated roar of a blender. It's seven o'clock in the morning.

With painstaking care, Zeke pulls his legs onto the mattress and lies down beside Lucinda. He sighs. His hands lie limp on the front of his thighs. His eyes are closed, so she stares at him briefly. Zeke is an old man, his throat a rumple of flesh, his face dappled with nutmeg age spots. Were they so prominent before now, or is it just that he's pale from lack of sun?

He will have to retire. She's suddenly certain of this; is he? Less than a month ago, one reporter called him an "inspiringly vigorous octogenarian."

That Zeke's mind may be as sharp as ever isn't entirely good news; he is lucid enough to be despondent about his diminished prospects. When the doctor agreed to discharge Zeke earlier than he would have liked, he warned Lucinda about patients who set impossibly high standards for themselves. "The all-or-nothing patients are the hard ones," he said. "Sometimes, if they can't return to what they see as 'one hundred percent,' they give up, and then they go into a downward spiral. You have to help him be realistic."

Lucinda pats Zeke on one knee. "I'll be right back. Sleep if you want."

When she enters the kitchen, she says to Jonathan, "I know I said your father sleeps soundly, but not this soundly."

He and Cyril turn toward her from the long wooden counter where they are chopping vegetables, grating cheese, and filling bowls. The oven is on, and a dozen serving platters are out on the table. "Mom, we got carried away."

"We're so sorry, Lucinda," says Cyril.

"Never mind. Zeke's in the den now."

"Can we play music?" asks Jonathan. "We love cooking to music. And I found that great collection in your sewing room."

Lucinda sees the stack of CDs, along with her player, by the bread box. She never brings them downstairs. "They were Mal's."

"I know." Jonathan looks confused; she realizes she's frowning.

"It's fine, fine," she says. "Use what you need, play whatever you like."

At least they made coffee. She pours herself a mug and returns to the den. Zeke's eyes are closed, so she moves quietly, setting her coffee on the desk. She should go upstairs and dress, find a space in the kitchen to make breakfast.

"We tell jhem today."

"Tell them, Zeke?"

"Kit."

"No, Zeke, tomorrow. When Christina's here."

"Tomorrow."

"Thanksgiving."

"I know," he says impatiently. "Thought shwaz today."

"You'd think so from the level of chaos. But I guess I've always started the food this early, too. I feel redundant, though, and I hate it."

"Think you do." He makes the guttural sound she recognizes as a tattered remnant of his hearty laugh.

"So now there are two of us."

"Kit," he says.

"Zeke, I can't believe it—that we'll see him after all these years. You—you for the first time." She wonders if he's up for it; she should consult his doctor, but she doesn't want to hear that this encounter might be stressful. And Christmas is still a month away. "It's all right with you, isn't it? That he's coming to meet us. Here."

Zeke nods, his eyes still closed. "Handshum boy."

Is he thinking about Mal now, or Jonathan? Jonathan's in good shape, but he's never been as good-looking as his siblings. His face cannot quite reconcile his mother's delicate chin with his father's jutting brow. Or maybe Zeke's thoughts have drifted to Cyril, with his thick blond hair and Devonshire-cream complexion. ("When I first saw him, I thought I'd fallen down a wormhole into *Chariots of Fire*," Lucinda has heard her son say more than once.)

"I'm glad Cyril was able to come," says Lucinda. "I just wish Christina's older girls could make it, too. I wonder if Hannah and that boyfriend are thinking about getting married."

"Kidj take time now," says Zeke. "More careful."

Lucinda thinks inadvertently of Daphne and Mal, how very uncareful they were. "Should *we* have been more careful?" she teases.

Zeke opens his eyes. "War shped thingj up. Carpe diem et shetera."

"We did everything sooner. As if we had no time to lose." After losing so much else. And yet, if she thinks back to the war years, she does not remember any greater awareness of her own mortality, only the worry that her ongoing life might be changed unpredictably. As one of her classmates put it in French class, "If the Germans win, will we have to learn German instead? Will we eat things like bratwurst and cabbage?" Even when Lucinda's brother shipped out, she didn't think much about the possibility that he might die. Only decades later did she understand her mother's wanderings through the downstairs rooms so late at night. Patrick had survived, of course, only to die of skin cancer in his sixties (all that Pacific sun, or so reasoned the doctor who failed to cure him). At least their parents were gone by then.

Lucinda hears a heavy metallic object hit the floor in the kitchen. Much laughter, alongside the overture to *South Pacific,* the movie version. Mal's collection includes the Broadway version, too. She knows them both by heart.

"Let me get breakfast. I'll bring it in here," she says. "I don't think we're safe in there. Sounds like a combat zone."

"Eggjh. Thank you." Zeke closes his eyes again.

The chefs give Lucinda permission to cook breakfast in "their" kitchen; Cyril clears a miserly swatch of countertop. Jonathan is singing "Some Enchanted Evening," exaggerating Giorgio Tozzi's Italianate ardor. This is not the son she remembers from his teenage years, the child who earned Bs in nearly every subject, played no sports, hung out with girls, and spent much of his spare time reading biographies and organizing a stamp collection in tiny wax-paper packets. She had worried about him for so long.

Nowadays, with all the information thrown at parents (at least in the liberal Northeast), she might have guessed that he was gay. But Jonathan, unlike his brother, made efforts to keep his parents in the dark. He brought young women home from college, never claiming romantic involvement yet acting, around these charming girls, in ways that left Lucinda relieved and hopeful. "I went through a whole barbershop of beards," he joked in his wedding toast to Cyril.

Once he moved to California, in his late twenties, he rarely came back to Vermont. The first time Lucinda and Zeke saw him out there, he looked as if he was leading a contentedly solitary life. Lucinda can remember thinking that if she had raised him fully in the faith, without the dilution of his father's indifference, he might have become a priest.

He did not tell them the truth about his life until the week after Mal's funeral. He was thirty-five years old.

They were in the car, just the two of them, returning from grocery shopping. The last mourners had drifted away; the refrigerator was empty. Jonathan was to fly back west the following night. They had ridden in silence for the entire ten minutes, Lucinda dumbfounded and sedated by grief, glad of one thing only: that she was done having to talk with strangers who had apparently been close to Mal. (Why had she never met them before?) When Jonathan pulled up to the house and turned the engine off, she was inert. All that spring and summer, there were times when she felt as if she had no joints or muscles, no physical means with which to move about the world. She could lie in a bed or sit on a chair unable to recall what it felt like to rise and hold herself upright on her feet. It was like paralysis, she imagined—or no, maybe the opposite, since paralyzed people could remember standing, balancing, moving forward, with an exquisite sense of longing. She was indifferent to motion.

Jonathan turned to her and said, "So before I go back, I have to tell you something. The timing is terrible, but it's now or never."

She didn't even look at him when she said, "If it's bad news, sweetheart, you'll have to put it on hold."

He said, "It's just that I finally have to tell you that I'm gay. Too. There wasn't ever a good time, and now there couldn't ever be."

Lucinda's first emotion was anger. Out of her mouth came a sound of irrepressible disgust. She was no longer so naïve as to think this was something he hadn't known for years—years during which Jonathan could surely see that his brother's coming out hadn't changed him in his parents' eyes. Jonathan had no reason to be fearful.

"I know how this must hit you, Mom, especially now," he said, gripping the steering wheel of Zeke's old Volvo.

"Mal knew this?" she heard herself say. Which was really to say, had Mal withheld this from her? Because of course he must have known.

"I think he suspected. But I figured you and Dad couldn't take it—two of us, both of us . . . you know. I didn't want Mal to bear that burden."

"He *didn't* know?" But if Jonathan hadn't told Mal . . . "Do you mean to tell me that all these years, the years your brother was sick and dying *because* he was gay, you hid that from him? How could you?"

"Mom, I didn't 'hide' anything. Look, I live on the other side of the country, and we were never close. But to tell you the truth, it only got harder to tell him once he told us he was sick. You have every right to yell at me. You think I'm coldhearted. But here's the thing: I'm negative. I don't think that would have helped him at all. I think he'd only have felt more alone."

"You, a pessimist? And what kind of an excuse is that?"

Jonathan looked baffled. Then he said, "Negative—Mom—what I meant was that I don't have the virus. I'm not sick. I tested negative."

Lucinda was stunned. Here is the bad news, here the good. Except that she could not absorb the good news in any way signaling relief. She understood now—perhaps—why Mal had often referred to his brother with a tone of dismissal or even scorn. She knew they hadn't been close, but maybe now she knew precisely why. Mal was too smart not to have guessed.

"And I wasn't as brave as Mal, okay? Neither as talented nor as brave." It was Jonathan's turn to sound angry.

"I would never compare you," she said. "Certainly not now."

"Well." He laughed coldly. "If I were you, I'd be comparing like crazy. The son you lost versus the one you're left with. Raw deal."

"Oh, Jonathan." How could she be enduring this conversation? "I cannot take this in right now. Or take it in graciously."

"I must seem incredibly cruel. All I can say is I'm sorry. It's just, if I didn't do this, I think I might never be able to come home again. I'd suffocate. From my own cowardice." Jonathan looked as if he might cry. The car, sitting in the sun, had grown uncomfortably hot. Lucinda could smell the large slab of salmon they had bought to grill for dinner.

"I haven't told Dad yet. I wanted to tell you first. How you feel matters most to me." Then he did cry. And still, God smite her vain indignation, she couldn't stifle her fury. Never mind the brute irony: that *this* son came to her first, before telling his father. She got out, took two bags of groceries from the backseat, and carried them into the house. Jonathan followed a few minutes later, his composure restored.

As they put the food away, Lucinda said, "I hope you have someone loving in your life. And I hope you'll introduce him to us if you do. I don't think Mal ever had that. A real partner."

"He had so many good friends, though."

"Not the same thing, sweetheart. I hope you know that."

"Of course I do," Jonathan said coldly, and they let it rest there.

That was so long ago, years before he met Cyril.

Lucinda eats two pieces of toast while she scrambles eggs for Zeke. She spoons the eggs onto a plate, then slices a banana into a small bowl and scoops vanilla yogurt on top.

Jonathan and Cyril appear to be cooking far too much food, but Lucinda keeps this thought to herself. She will try to behave as if she is the guest and they are the hosts. Really, she's lucky they are doing all the work.

Her son comes over and puts an arm around her shoulders. "I see your sidelong glances, Ma. Let me reassure you, we'll have this place cleaned up by the end of the day. Table set and everything. We want tomorrow to be totally relaxed. Totally! All we'll have to do is stuff and roast the turkey and bake the bread pudding. So try to ignore the pandemonium."

"Thank you for doing all this," she says.

"We are *thrilled* to be doing all this," insists Jonathan. "Your kitchen is twice the size of ours, so we're having fun with it. Nothing like a big old farm kitchen, designed to turn out meals for dozens of hardworking men!"

"He's right," says Cyril. "We are envious."

Lucinda looks around at the scarred wooden counters and dull blue linoleum, the outdated appliances, the rusting can opener screwed to the broom-closet door. "Well," she says. "It has served a lot of feasts in its day."

She arranges Zeke's breakfast on a tray and takes it into the den. He's pulled himself up to a sitting position on the sofa bed, but she wonders if he can manage eating off his lap. "Do you want to go into the dining room?"

"Here," he says. "And no huffering. You get dreshed."

Upstairs, Lucinda puts on corduroy pants and takes out a turtleneck sweater. If she's to be banned from her kitchen, maybe she can go out on her snowshoes. Or maybe, it occurs to her, she could drive Zeke to the movies. Unless he doesn't want to risk conversation with people who will no doubt recognize them. For the second time in a week, she puts on her bra with such acute consciousness of her own dexterity that her fingers fumble at matching the tiny hooks with their respective apertures. Is there a synapse of the brain that handles this specific task? What does it handle for a man—loading a gun in the dark?

The syrupy crescendo of "Younger Than Springtime" rises from below.

"Don't I wish," she tells her mirrored self. In the calendar of her life span, she is just about exactly where she finds herself this month: in late autumn, surprised by a sudden storm, a storm that only seems untimely. Is she facing her own metaphorical Thanksgiving? The gratitude before the last decline, the toss of the calendar into the recycling bin. What a maudlin train of thought!

When she returns to the kitchen, Jonathan is standing in the center of the room, wearing a flowered apron that belonged to Zeke's mother, arms outstretched, eyes closed, singing "This Nearly Was Mine."

"'*So clear and deep are my fancies of things I wish were true—*'" He opens his eyes and sees her. "Mom!"

Cyril turns from the sink. "He thinks he's Carreras. I'm putting on something less obnoxious when this ends. Definitely less sing-along-able. Do you have any Gregorian chant, Lucinda?"

Jonathan sashays toward Cyril, holding out the corners of the apron. "Gayer than laughter, what can I say?"

Lucinda picks up the case. "This is my favorite song in the show."

Though it wouldn't have been when she was much younger. It's an old person's song, a song with a panoramic view of the past.

"I don't think I've ever heard it before," says Jonathan.

"And you're not going to hear it again. Not if I'm around," says Cyril.

"Are you finding everything?" Lucinda asks. After Cyril assures her that they are perfectly self-sufficient, she tells them she is hoping to get Zeke out of the house for a few hours. The energetic repartee of the two younger men is not only wearying to her but oddly worrisome. Perhaps their sprightliness, especially here in her house, merely reminds her how old both she and Zeke have grown, but still she feels as if Jonathan, however happy, just isn't himself. Can persistent happiness change someone, fundamentally? Well, why not?

Persistent unhappiness changes you, this she knows—but not as much as it does your sense of purpose. She thinks of the contemptuous young woman on the street in Montpelier. *Meddling like that.* She hastens back to Zeke.

Why does it feel as if she *begrudges* Jonathan his obvious happiness? This terrible thought did not occur to her until she watched Jonathan and Cyril proceed (radiant with glee, nearly romping) back up the aisle after their wedding vows. Zeke squeezed her arm. She felt the profound relief of a mother seeing her child engulfed by joy, but she understood, too, exactly why she couldn't quite join in. She wished that it were Malachy's wedding. She wished that Mal could have been the one standing there in the field with his true love: Mal in the white suit, Mal against the white sky and the sunstruck surface of the bay, Mal in the blanching flashes of camera after camera sealing the moment to hold it far into the future. Even if he'd still had to die so young, she wished she had been able to witness a moment like this in his life.

There must have been two hundred wedding guests on that hill, so happy for Jonathan and Cyril that they cheered, as if the two men had won an athletic competition, not solemnly promised to be together forever. Lucinda felt as if all these strangers loved her son more than she did. What was the matter with her?

After Mal's death, numerous friends and fellow parishioners told Lucinda that she must learn to "let him go." They might mean that she should let him go to God, let him be released from his pain, or relinquish her possessive grief. What it meant to her, however, was that beyond accepting his death, she had to understand that from then on he would belong as much to others as he did to her. She had loved him too much, perhaps, more the way she ought to have loved his father. And God forgive her if, in helping all those girls have those unexpected babies, learn to be mothers far younger than they should have, she had been trying to undo that death.

"Can you finally, after all these years, stop calling me that?" Christina is extracting herself from Jonathan's embrace.

"Oh, Teeny, lighten up," says Jonathan. "I love how you grew so completely *out* of that nickname."

Greg is hanging up coats, Madison is carrying bags to the kitchen, and Christina's two Labs are thrashing their bargelike bodies against the furniture. They act like bumper cars, as if their objective is to make a contact sport of being indoors. Lucinda finds it amusing that in the midst of her daughter's admirably disciplined life, she cannot seem to make her dogs behave, but she is not so amused by her worry that one of them may knock Zeke off his feet.

Christina catches Lucinda's look. "I know, Mom. But by the time I realized we should put them at the kennel, it was—*down*, Ferris! No!" She follows the dog into the living room. "Dad, hey, you look great. I said *down*, Ferris!"

"Dog's fine," says Zeke. Ferris, his front paws up on Zeke's thighs, is avidly licking his face. Zeke is petting him.

"That is so disgusting, Mom. Don't let him do that. Yuck," says Madison, returning from the kitchen. Cyril comes in behind her, and for a moment, all of them stand awkwardly around Zeke, who finally says, "Could use a little dog shlobber, lighten shings up round here."

Relieved laughter. But now the second dog, Jimbo, is careening in circles around the room.

"Stop NOW!" shouts Greg in an artificially deep voice, spreading his arms wide, like a scarecrow. Jimbo instantly responds, crouching by the fireplace.

After an awkward freeze-frame, Lucinda says, "Well. Happy Thanksgiving, everybody. I'm so glad we're together."

Jonathan, too soon in Lucinda's opinion, takes drink orders. Cyril, carrying a large tray of hors d'oeuvres, pauses near the coffee table with a glance at the dogs.

"Christina," says Lucinda, "could you please put those beasts in the den?"

"Mom, they'll be fine. They're just working off all that cramped-up car time. Greg's got them trained not to eat off tables."

Cyril, obviously more trusting than Lucinda, sets the tray down on the coffee table. Instantly, the dogs crowd in, but they merely sniff, whiskers grazing the cheese. Greg commands them to follow him to the front hall, where he makes them lie down after an absurd amount of menacing talk. He sounds as if he's doing a bad imitation of Arnold Schwarzenegger, minus the Austrian accent.

Jonathan and Cyril moved Zeke's bed against the front windows and brought the sofa back from exile, but now the furniture is all much closer together, like a group of people who don't know how to keep a proper distance while having a conversation.

A champagne cork fires off in the kitchen. A dog barks in response. "Qui-ET!" booms Greg. The bark shrivels to a whine.

Lucinda catches sight of Madison, sitting on the bench in the front hall, fingering her phone. She's wearing a pretty blouse, but she's also wearing blue jeans that show every curve of her slim yet feminine form and ballet flats without socks. (Is that a tattoo on her granddaughter's ankle?) Lucinda remembers the crinolined dresses she bribed Christina into wearing to all holiday occasions when this house belonged to Zeke's parents. She feels ominously behind the times; would she, at the height of working with those young mothers at The House, have thought twice about what *this* young woman is wearing? She thinks of Kit's nine-year-old daughter, whom she will meet (she hopes) at Christmastime. Kit has e-mailed her pictures of his family, including Frances—Fanny (how fine and old-fashioned a nickname)—and already Lucinda has imagined how Fanny will look up to her three grown cousins. Perhaps Madison will take her skiing or shopping (or, God forbid, to get her first tattoo).

Lucinda calls her in. "Madison, sweetheart, please join us. I know it's tedious, but I need to hear how your year is going."

Madison smiles at her grandmother, tucks her phone in a pocket. As she crosses the room, Jonathan hands her a glass of champagne.

She looks surprised but pleased. "Twenty was way over legal in my day," her uncle tells her.

Forget about "legal." It's barely noon. Lucinda has never offered liquor before midafternoon. *I am a guest*, she tells herself for the tenth time today. She sits on the couch next to Greg and Cyril.

Christina is in the kitchen with her brother. Madison (whose tattoo reveals itself to be a tiny mermaid, not so egregious) has taken the wing chair nearest to Zeke and is making an effort—obvious, but so it goes—to tell him about her studies, her vacillation between majors, and what she sees as the inevitable decision about whether to follow the "family imperative" toward law school. "Looks like Courtney's the only one to escape," she's saying. "But she had to go halfway around the world to do it! India's too crazy-far for me, I'm sorry."

Zeke, also making an effort—just to hold himself still without trembling—laughs quietly. "Law shkool leadj many places."

"Oh, I know that," says Madison. "Like look at Dad. Or you, of course. You can do useful things, not just sue people. I do realize that."

Lucinda makes herself focus on the conversation beside her. Greg and Cyril have met only once before—at Cyril and Jonathan's wedding. Greg is an environmental consultant; he helps people with large tracts of undeveloped land figure out ways to preserve it without compromising too much on potential income. He comes at it from the law side, not the nature side, which means that engaging him in small talk about his work elicits digressions on subjects like eminent domain and conservation easements—often abetted by Zeke. Greg is the kind of man people refer to as "brilliant" in a defensive tone, because even though he's almost terrifyingly smart, he's socially tone-deaf, rarely able to discuss matters too far from his professional concerns. After an evening in his company, Lucinda often has the shameful reflex of reminding herself what a steady husband he is to Christina and how game he's been about raising nothing but daughters. Visiting their home, Lucinda has witnessed Greg, alone in the room they call the man cave, cheering on a sports team, while Madison, Hannah, and Courtney perch at the kitchen counter trading magazines or vials of nail polish. The girls played sports in high school, but only Hannah continued her soccer in college.

Cyril, accommodating to the opposite degree, has drawn Greg into talking about the ruthless cuts in state funding to California's parks. Cyril looks riveted as Greg lays out, in numbing detail, the plan that the governor *ought* to follow.

Turning her attention to the hors d'oeuvres on the silver tray (a trophy for best-in-show heifer at the 1947 state fair), Lucinda spreads an unfamiliar cheese on a paper-thin cracker. She is counting the minutes until the meal is served, but the cheese tastes exquisite. Now she tries a few of the tiny grapes. Also exquisite. Jonathan does know how to shop for food.

Christina calls from the kitchen, "Mom, can I get you in here for a sec?"

Lucinda wipes her fingers on a napkin and excuses herself.

Joining her children, she is pleasantly surprised to find that, as promised, order has overcome chaos. Along one counter, stacks of bowls and plates wait to fulfill their purpose; along another, covered dishes sweat and steam.

"Just about ready," says Jonathan as he unties the flowered apron. "But how do you want to manage things for Dad? Teeny says he'll be insulted if we cut up his food in advance. I mean, we're serving bisque first, but for later . . ."

"He hates anything resembling condescension. You know that," says Christina.

A week ago, Lucinda would have agonized over this decision. Today, all she can think about is Kit, the news she plans to spring on her family. (The phrase *tidings of great joy* has sprung to mind several times this morning, as if some evangelist is perched on her shoulder.)

Her children face her, expectant.

"Oh, I don't know," she says. "I don't think he'll notice if you just go ahead and make the food easier for him to eat. Everyone will be talking. It's no big deal." Everyone will indeed be talking.

"Exactly what I was saying," says Jonathan. "Soup bowls, Teeny? Mom, you go back to being a guest. Just please tell Cyril it's time to light the candles."

Zeke will have to be helped to his chair in the dining room; he told Lucinda that he would not use the walker and insisted she take it upstairs for the day. He doesn't want anyone even to see it. "*I* don't want to shee it," he stressed.

So Lucinda and Greg escort Zeke to the dining room while Madison is sent to take the dogs for a quick run out back. The swinging door to the kitchen is propped open, bowls of soup and baskets of bread ferried through by Cyril and Christina. Jonathan is fussing with the CD player in the living room. He chooses Handel, something rich and imperious with trumpets.

Lucinda and Zeke occupy their customary ends of the table. Cyril and Greg sit to either side of Lucinda, Madison and Christina flanking Zeke. Jonathan, who is filling everyone's champagne glass (and this time Lucinda accepts), has a place between Madison and her father.

"I think," Jonathan says once he's seated, "that we need to start with a toast to Dad." He waits for the others to raise their glasses. "One word. Indomitable."

This isn't the usual ritual, but nothing is as usual today. So much for the blessing; silently, Lucinda recites it, out of habit more than devotion.

The soup is a lovely shade of pink, with a spiral of green in the center. She's sure the pilgrims never ate lobster bisque with cilantro coulis, but they never drank champagne, either. Or sat around a coffee table making small talk—or, she notes with dismay as her gaze rests on her granddaughter, texted underneath the table.

She glances at Christina, wondering if she will admonish her daughter—but from a faint glow on the buttons of Christina's blouse, Lucinda can tell that she, too, is checking on her connections to the world beyond this table.

"Let's all be in the here and now," Lucinda says. She sounds shrill.

"Absolutely!" says Jonathan. "So here and now, because I just can't stand keeping it a secret, let me share our news, something *we're* really thankful for this year. Cyril and I are going to become dads!"

"Not really dads," says Cyril, though he's grinning. "Not technically."

"Well, effectively!" Jonathan scolds.

"I'm finally going to be an aunt?" says Christina. "Wow. Better late than never!"

Lucinda is stunned. She cannot find traction in the moment—the "here and now" she wanted them all to occupy—nor can she summon the proper expression of joy or congratulation. Zeke looks confused or skeptical; the stroke has distorted his face in ways that make it so much harder to read.

"You're adopting?" says Christina.

"Now *this* calls for a toast," says Greg.

"Okay, okay." Cyril waves one hand in the air. "Let's back up. Jonathan and I have been approved as *prospective* foster parents. We'd be taking in a teenager, a boy in high school."

"Which is going to be a challenge," says Jonathan.

"Which is going to change your lives like you can't begin to imagine," says Christina.

"Please, Teeny, as if we haven't been through endless counseling and psychological profiles here. What we're going to be doing is providing a stable home for a kid who's come out as gay with no solid support, who's had it rough and needs genuine empathy. God knows Cyril and I have been there."

Zeke startles everyone by speaking. "Rough? You had it rough . . . in shkool, here?"

"Well, not here, no. I didn't come out here. You couldn't, back then. That would've been crazy. But it's rough spending so much energy hiding who you are, not even really knowing if you're normal. Or sane. I only realized just how rough it was years and years later. Not *your* fault," he says to his father.

So he knew he was gay all the way back in high school. Lucinda says, "Do you know when this boy will move in?"

"It's not definite yet, not completely, but we're getting ready for it to happen in January," says Cyril.

"What about all your traveling?"

"That will have to change. Obviously," Cyril tells her. "I don't have to go to so many conferences."

"Mom, he doesn't have to *prove* himself anymore. His department chair would die before she'd let Cyril go. We can now become the homebodies we've always longed to be."

As Lucinda understands it, travel is what they enjoy more than anything else. But things change, of course, and so do the ways in which people see themselves. "Does he have a name, this boy?"

"Technically, we can't discuss it, or him, till the arrangement is definite," says Cyril. "Jonathan's jumping the gun. But it's great to tell you in person. It's not like any of you are going to call up the child services people in Oakland."

Lucinda checks on Zeke; he's carefully, slowly ferrying soup to his mouth, breathing noisily between spoonfuls, as if he's climbing a steep hill. He has often said that nothing anyone does or says can surprise him anymore. And why should this news surprise Lucinda? Jonathan has, after all, been brought up by parents who "give back," as it's fashionable to say.

"Cool," says Madison belatedly. She appears to have put away her phone. "I won't be the youngest anymore at these family things."

"Be careful what you wish for," says Christina.

"What's that supposed to mean?" Jonathan says.

"Nothing, little brother. And maybe we could use a little shaking up."

Jonathan glances pointedly at their father. "I'd say we've had plenty to shake us up lately."

Zeke answers Jonathan's gaze. "You've thought about shish."

Cyril leans in and says, "It's something we've been exploring for a while. We could be getting in over our heads. We know that. But the rest of our life runs like a Swiss watch these days. We're spoiled rotten. We look around us and notice how smug everyone's getting. The people we spend all our time with. It's like we've accidentally joined some privileged club and don't even realize it. The International Smug Club."

Jonathan doesn't look happy to have Cyril speak for both of them, but he waits for his husband to finish. "Dad," he says forcefully, "this isn't some rash decision. The thing Cyril's not telling you is that I'm the one who had to come up to speed. And I'm not ashamed to say that it's helped me find the right therapist. And, I'll just come right out with it, the right meds. I have a much better grasp on the world these days. I know you and Mom used to worry about me. That I was some kind of malcontent or wouldn't find my purpose or—Mom, don't try to deny it. It's okay. We're okay. More than okay."

Had she even opened her mouth? Lucinda feels profoundly speechless. In fact, it looks as if all conversation has been permanently thwarted until Christina says, "Wow. Good for you guys. And that Smug Club? Greg and I are probably charter members."

Greg laughs nervously. Madison smirks. Cyril says, "Not to get trivial, but who's ready for turkey?"

Zeke has finally finished his soup. Jonathan is clearing the bowls.

So Jonathan is on an antidepressant. Lucinda should have guessed. From Ambien to Zoloft, crack to weed, her days at The House taught her plenty about drugs of all kinds: pharmaceuticals, recreationals, street names, detox. ("Time to talk pharm and rec," one counselor joked whenever they met to discuss the girls' habits and needs.) There is no reason this should disappoint her or make her feel even a splinter of blame, yet when she hears Jonathan imply that he didn't have a proper "grasp" on the world, isn't that part of a mother's job—making sure a child can hold securely to things, so he won't fall down too much?

Out comes the turkey on the Blue Willow platter that belonged to Lucinda's mother, carried by Jonathan; out come the side dishes, carried by Christina, Madison, and Greg: a parade. Cyril, the grand marshal, waits at the sideboard with the carving utensils.

Greg pours red wine into a new set of glasses. Cyril takes orders for light or dark meat, gravy or none. Jonathan brings the laden plates to the table. Almost in unison, the three men sit down. But then Jonathan says, "Teeny, can you please fetch the condiments?"

She is standing, rolling her eyes at the nickname she cannot shed, when Zeke says, "Shildren, stop." Everyone stares at him; his voice is harsh.

Seeing their fear, he softens his tone. "Your mother. Hass newj for you, too. Shake you up more," he says, looking at Jonathan. "Lishen to her." He turns to his daughter. "Sit."

Lucinda did not expect this: that Zeke would make it easier. Even before the stroke, it was her job to make things easier for him. She looks plaintively at her husband; perhaps now isn't the time after all. But even in his skewed face, she recognizes his determination. *Do this, and do it now.*

Full plates steam at every place on the table. Christina does not get up to fetch the condiments. Madison and her father put down their forks.

Lucinda begins, though not in the way she planned. "Christina, the news I have *will* make you an aunt, and Maddie, sweetheart, you *do* have cousins younger than you . . . and one who's older. You just haven't met them."

Everyone stares at her. She struggles with what to say next. "We always, at this table, at all occasions like this, we always remember Malachy. Which we haven't done today. Not yet."

Cyril fingers the stem of his wineglass, anticipating a toast.

"But this time . . ." She swore she would not choke up. "I have to tell you something that your father and I have known for years but never . . . we could never tell you, for so many complicated reasons, but now . . . now we can." She looks to Zeke; can he make it easier, again? But all he offers her is a slightly lopsided gaze, as if he, too, wonders what on earth she will say next.

"Mal had a son. His name is Christopher—he's called Kit. He's forty-two."

Lucinda expected an audible reaction; Christina's gasp is the most dramatic. Maddie utters a quiet expletive. Her mother glares at her.

Lucinda holds up her hands to ward off interruptions. "This is a very long story, which you will all hear in good time, but let me get right to the good part. A few days ago, I spoke to Kit for the first time, and he is eager to meet all of you. He's married, and he has twins; they're just nine years old. They live in New Jersey. They'll come here—I think they'll come here at Christmas. After Christmas. Jonathan, I know you and Cyril probably have plans at home, but maybe you could come back. We'll happily pay for your tickets."

"How could Mal have had a *child*?" says Jonathan. "Who's, what did you say? Forty . . . two years old? Forty-two? That would mean—" His gaze is directed at the ceiling as he adds and subtracts, makes calculations along the family timeline as if it were an abacus, each of their lives a finite row of beads.

"He was seventeen," Lucinda says. "It was an accident. He was never really with the girl. The mother. Kit's mother."

Zeke startles her by speaking. "Not his wish. Not in the leasht."

"Well, I'm guessing he was *with* her," says Jonathan.

"Can we ask who she was?" says Christina, and Lucinda can tell that she is pushing beads to and fro on the timeline of her own life, thinking of girls she knew at the high school. She and Mal were only fourteen months apart in age, though the friends they chose could not have been more different.

"No one you ever met. That's the truth, Christina." Here is the hard part, unless she chooses to hide more than she should. "I did meet her, and I met the baby, Christopher—Kit—after he was born. For a few years I tried to help out, with money, that's all she'd let me offer, but then she—"

"Mom," says Christina, "was she at The House? Wait a sec, because if—"

"Stop," says Zeke. "Lesher mother speak."

Lucinda sighs. "I thought that if I was patient, if I waited just a few years, I could somehow bring her and the baby into our family, even though Mal was so unhappy about it. It wasn't—obviously it wasn't a situation Mal wanted, but I thought we could make the best of it, that once he was older and settled in his own life, he could make room for a child." Hearing herself tell her other children that she had been willing to defy their brother's wishes, even in support of so vital a cause, she is struck by how selfish she sounds.

How selfish she was.

Jonathan lets out a whistle. He is shaking his head vehemently. "Mom. Christ, Mom." He looks at Cyril, whose expression is opaque. He is utterly still, focused only on Lucinda. "Everybody figures their parents have secrets, but Jesus—sorry, Mom. I don't know how to wrap my head around this one."

"Nothing went the way I expected. I was naïve." No one rescues her from this confession. No Hail Marys are assigned. "Well." She picks up her fork. "Let's all please eat. I didn't mean to starve everyone with so much drama. I'm sorry."

"Sorry?" Christina exclaims. "This is beyond amazing. I am totally going to be here at Christmas to meet him. I am going to make sure all the girls are here. This is going to be . . . wild. Momentous. Maddie, are you taking this in?"

"Wild. That is one word for it." Jonathan shakes his head and looks at his plate. "Well, I am not letting this food go to waste." He takes a bite. He winces. "Okay, I know this is *rude,* but I am taking my plate into the kitchen to nuke it. Anybody else want their food warmed up?"

"Jonathan, these plates don't go in the microwave," says Christina. "Who cares if it's not piping hot? We're not at Chez Panisse. And by the way, Cyril, your stuffing is out of this world. I would eat it ice cold for breakfast."

"Candied chestnuts," says Cyril. "Soaked in Armagnac. Imported from France to California and then, wrapped in my socks, from California to here. The largest carbon footprint ever left by a handful of nuts."

"What's the green stuff?" asks Madison.

"Watercress purée," Jonathan tells her. "It's half cream. You'll love it. You're young enough not to care about your arteries."

In the silence that follows, they hear a dog whining in the den. "God knows what mischief they're up to," says Christina. Both dogs, as if they'd been waiting for their cue, begin barking.

"Qui-ET!" Greg bellows. After only a brief pause, they start up again. Greg stands. "I'm sorry. They may need to go out. I'll make it quick."

Lucinda thinks how glad he must be to get away from this awkward, perilous conversation, the rich food that's gone tepid because of it.

"Look. Mom, this is—you know what? It's like an earthquake." Jonathan seems to have changed his mind about reheating the food. "I don't even know what to ask you. Like . . . all these *years*. He's been out there, and you knew it, and you said nothing to any of us. Nothing? I'm always telling Cyril about what it means to grow up Catholic, all the superstition, the stoicism, the guilt, the—"

"I lost touch with her. With Kit's mother," Lucinda says sharply. "That's really what it comes down to, Jonathan."

"Lost touch? How would that happen?"

Lucinda says, "It was her decision. To . . . go it alone. Cut ties."

"But you had rights!"

Lucinda looks to Zeke. He is concentrating on food, no help to her now.

"Times are different. Secrets are made to be exposed. It wasn't always like that, Jonathan. And please don't blame it on the church."

Jonathan frowns at her. "This wasn't just about you, Mom. This was about all of us, don't you think?"

"Those are your California values talking," says Christina. "Frankly, this was more about Mal than anybody else. Poor Mal. He must have thought about that child all the time. I'm still trying to process that."

Jonathan turns his disapproval on his sister. "I'm proud of what you call my 'California' values. Better California than tax-averse Republican right."

She snorts. "I am not a Republican. Can we leave politics out of it?"

"Fine," says Jonathan. "Sorry. But doesn't this upset you at all? Mom, I can't help looking at you and Dad differently."

"Can't you appreciate how complicated this is?" says Christina. "Or is this your old fear about being upstaged by Mal? Could you let that go by now?"

How foolish Lucinda was to imagine a feel-good round of toasts, of memories honoring Mal and excitement about meeting Kit. "I never stopped thinking about this boy—or his mother," she says. "And I prayed. I know you all scoff at such things, but I do feel as if my prayers were finally answered. Last week I found out that Kit was looking for his father."

"Who's long gone," says Jonathan. "Didn't he know that?"

"No," says Lucinda. "No. Mal was not in touch with them, either. He never was. That was his choice from the very beginning."

No one, now, has anything to say. They eat. They hear Greg coming in the back door with the dogs, the jingling of tags, the *good boy good boy good BOY* litany, the door to the den closing. When he enters the dining room, he stands still for a moment. What a glum tableau they are, Norman Rockwell in a slump. "Everything okay?" Greg says.

"Sit down," says Lucinda. "We're fine here, we really are."

Jonathan gets up. "Me, I'm having seconds. Anyone else?"

Madison holds up her plate. "Sweet potatoes? Turkey?"

"*Please,*" prompts her mother.

"Please," Madison repeats.

Jonathan takes her plate.

"I didn't mean to bury your news, sweetheart," says Lucinda. "I'm proud of you, taking a risk like that, to help a lost boy."

"Thanks." Jonathan hands Madison her plate, then carries his own to his place. "I've been so focused on that, and I was looking forward to telling you. Cyril was right that we should have waited."

Cyril says nothing. Lucinda is thinking about what Christina said a few minutes ago. She ought to have considered Jonathan's ego, fragile as ever. Of her three children, Malachy was the one with a "gift," and the others knew it. Nothing is ever equal among siblings.

Lucinda hears Greg say quietly to Christina, "What did I miss?"

Jonathan raises his hands in a touchdown gesture. "All right, everybody, reboot!" he exclaims. "Me especially."

Madison can't help laughing.

Christina's cell phone rings under the table. Greg frowns at her as she answers it. "Sweetheart! Oh, honey, same to you!" she cries. "Everybody, it's Courtney, calling us from India! . . . No, sweetie, your timing is perfect. You're missing a knockout meal, courtesy of your sophisticated uncles. Here; speak to your grandmother." Christina hands the phone down to Lucinda.

"Hello, precious," Lucinda says to her granddaughter. "Tell us what you're doing there while we eat turkey here. We miss you so much."

They eat dessert in the living room. Ferris and Jimbo, becalmed by food, are out on parole. They settle near the fire, next to Zeke's chair. After Cyril removes the plates, Zeke dozes off, though he tries not to, while Lucinda tells her children everything she's learned about Kit. Greg and Cyril wash dishes in the kitchen. Madison, now shameless in her yearning to be elsewhere, stares reverently into her tiny screen.

After they finish the cleanup, Greg and Cyril offer to set up Zeke's bed in the living room. "Leave that till tomorrow. Just open the bed in the den," says Lucinda. "I'll sleep upstairs." Let Zeke sleep in his shirt and trousers; he wouldn't be happy to have his children (never mind their husbands) put him in his pajamas, and she is too tired to try it on her own.

Like the dogs, the humans begin to doze, sedated by their feast. When the clock chimes eight, Christina insists that it really is time to get on the road. Lucinda cannot persuade her to stay for the night. She takes Zeke's barn coat from the hook where it's hung, unworn, since last spring, and puts it on to walk her daughter outside.

When Greg claps his hands, the dogs vault into the back of the car. Madison sits inside already, possessed by her gadget, her smooth young face opalescent in the dark. Lucinda thinks of the paintings she saw in Italy: the Madonna glancing down, demure, receiving news of one kind or another.

Christina hugs her mother tightly. "So much to think about. I'll call you tomorrow. Do you think it's good for Dad, all this drama?"

"It's something to look forward to. Also, to untangle."

"It's knotty all right."

"I thought it would be easier."

"Easy? What's that? Nothing's easy in this family. Probably in any family. Mom, stop fretting. You're doing that Catholic thing and finding a way to take the blame. Sorry. But it's true, you know?"

Greg has the car running, headlights on, radio voices tuned in to keep him alert. Lucinda wishes Christina would say more—even her iconoclastic thoughts are welcome now—but it's clear she wants to get into the warm car. "Good night, sweetheart. Careful on the roads, they'll be icy."

"Night, Mom. We love you."

Lucinda watches them drive down the lane between the rows of young trees. The night sky is busy, stitched everywhere with stars.

Avoiding the frozen puddles, guided by the chore light, she follows the driveway back to the barn, slides open the door, and flicks the switch. She's almost surprised that the light still works; when was anyone last in this place after dark?

Two feral cats dash across the concrete floor and up the stairs to the loft.

The water troughs and hayracks still run the length of the barn on both sides. The iron stanchions, rusted long ago, still mark a clear space for each cow. Uncracked, swept clean, the concrete floor slopes toward the drains. Overhead, the rafters look sound.

Zeke kept a herd of fifty head until both boys were in high school—trophy cows, the last of the best breeding lines. He insisted that Mal and Jonathan join 4-H in grade school; each boy chose a heifer to raise and exhibit on his own. Unlike his father, however, Zeke never forced his sons to hay the fields or oil machinery. He hired local men whose fathers had done the same tasks for his father. "They should grow up seeing that life, where they come from," Zeke said to Lucinda when the children were small. "But I'll be perfectly fine if they grow up to choose something other than farming. Sad to say, I'll be relieved."

When Lucinda asked him why, he told her that farming as he'd known it was no longer a viable living. "Not here," he said. He welcomed the thought of his children heading out to a world much wider than the one he and Lucinda had known—the one they would never leave.

They auctioned off the cows and most of the machinery—keeping the Oliver and the combine, since Zeke had no intention of selling the fields they still hayed—the same summer Mal went to that music camp. What a fateful summer that turned out to be.

Matthew came up from Massachusetts for the auction, alone. It might have been Lucinda's imagination, but she thought she saw a gloating look on his face more than once, as if the sale of the livestock, the tractors and wagons—nearly everything that defined the farm as a true farm—was a sign of surrender or defeat. Lucinda knew that wasn't true; Zeke was simply ready to devote himself to the law, and to politics, and he had satisfied himself that his children were headed elsewhere, too. If anything, what he wanted was to help preserve traditions like the one he was personally setting aside. That's what he told the people who gathered to hear him when he first ran for office.

After the cows were trailered and driven away, after a catered supper for local friends and out-of-town bidders, Lucinda came out to this barn to see it empty for the first evening since it had been built. She stood, just as she stands now, marveling at how big a place it was, how quietly grand, even palatial.

She thought she was alone until she heard a voice, from just behind her.

"End of an empire."

She turned around and clamped a hand to her chest. "You nearly gave me a heart attack, Matthew."

He laid an arm across her shoulders. "It'll be quite the operation, taking this place down. Someone will want to salvage the boards and those beams. Antique hunters will pay a small ransom. Don't forget about that."

"Zeke won't take it down."

"Sure he will."

"I don't think so."

"We'll see."

They stood side by side for a few minutes in the faltering light from the open door, the air stippled with tiny insects. He was the one who broke the volatile silence. "I do sometimes wonder what it might have been like."

"If you'd been the one to take over the farm?"

"No. Oh no," he said. "If I'd been the one to marry you."

She became aware, longingly and fearfully, of his bare forearm against the skin along her shoulders, the prickly chill of sunburn. She had chosen an almost-strapless dress that morning, knowing she'd be out all day in the persistent heat (shaking hands, pouring iced tea, making sure the visitors' children were entertained and out of the way).

Matthew was taller and heavier than Zeke: no longer as trim as the younger brother but still the one who could turn women's heads, who flirted by instinct. "Don't be silly. You fell in love with Dora," she said. Why didn't she say, *And I fell in love with Zeke?*

"I don't know," he said. "I came home from France, and there she was, as if she didn't know she was supposed to stop waiting for Aaron. As if she was an actual widow."

"I was there, too," said Lucinda. "Waiting."

"Sure, but you were a girl. Just a girl. Though not for long. So maybe I'm the one who should have waited. But I was ready for the next thing. Raring to be a grown-up. I wasn't the only one."

"You're not sorry you married Dora," she said, careful not to make it a question. Matthew's arm had slipped down, across her shoulder blades. His wide palm supported her rib cage just above her waist.

"Of course I'm not," he said. "Dumb luck, you could say. But that doesn't mean . . ." Abruptly but easily, he used his strong arm to turn Lucinda toward him. He kissed her, without a bit of doubt or hesitation. She let him take her head between his hands, push his fingers deep into her hair. She let him feel that this was still something she dreamed of; she couldn't help it. Only when he began to guide her toward the stairs to the loft did she pull away and tell him no.

His hands dropped to her shoulders, and he looked into her face, at first without speaking. "Dora wouldn't know," he finally said, "but he would, wouldn't he? You're not good at pretending. You never were."

Lucinda raised her hands to his elbows, so that she could hold him and yet, at the same time, hold him away. "You told me I married the right brother—remember the dinner, before the wedding? And I did."

"You certainly did. It shows, too." He looked her up and down, admiring her in a way that made her almost wish she could change her mind. He laughed self-consciously and stepped gracefully away from her touch. "Just a passing bout of nostalgia, shall we chalk it up to that?"

"Yes," she said. She left the barn before he did. She made sure that they were never alone together after that. Not once. Now she suspects she will never see him again, not unless Zeke dies first.

She hears the cats moving overhead in the hayloft. The tiniest rustlings echo loudly in the barn's cavernous void. Even the loft is empty; these days, the hay is trucked away as soon as it's baled. She has disturbed the cats' nocturnal routine, probably scaring whatever mice they could have caught back into the knotholes of the desiccated boards that hold up the roof—the boards for which some salvage hunter would pay a good sum these days.

In that first conversation with Kit—which had lasted nearly an hour, until the battery in Kit's phone gave out—they exchanged details about their lives as if they were prospective roommates. Lucinda told him that she couldn't wait to meet his family—her *great-grandchildren*—but that night she wanted to hear about him. Just him. Between his telling her about his passion for northern art and his confessing to her that he had lost his teaching job, there was an awkward pause. It was during this pause that she realized something shocking, though it was logical: Lucinda *knew* the voice on the other end of the line. She hadn't heard it in twenty years, because it was Mal's voice. Gentler, less edgy, with none of her son's urban irony, but Mal's voice all the same.

Lucinda cried as quietly as she could for the next several minutes, making sure that Kit kept talking. When she regained control of herself, she told him about the farm: what it had been like before Mal was born, then during his childhood, and since Zeke's decision to enter politics.

"Jasper told me about his stroke," said Kit.

"He's doing very well."

"I just wish . . ."

"I know what you wish. That you'd looked for us—for Mal—sooner."

Kit sighed. "Yeah."

"But here we are," she said. "Let's just take it from here."

"The phone is a terrible meeting place," he said. That's when his phone began to beep, as if it were personally offended. "Oh God, I cannot believe this."

"You know what?" said Lucinda. "Let's say good-bye, just for now, and let's send each other pictures." Quickly, she took down his mailing address. Lucinda had no photographs of Mal on her computer; really, the only photos she had in this form were those her children sent to her, as attachments to their e-mails. She went straight to her sewing room and chose three pictures of Mal that normally she would have been heartbroken to surrender. She folded them into a piece of stationery and sealed it in an envelope. She wrote DO NOT BEND on both sides of the envelope and inscribed it with the name and address of her grandson.

Jonathan and Cyril are still awake upstairs. They are talking, and their conversation, though she can't hear the words, sounds tense.

She returns Zeke's coat to its allotted hook and goes through the living room, turning off lamps. She opens the door to the den as quietly as she can.

But Zeke is fully awake, sitting up on the mattress against the back of the sofa. He is still dressed, and he is holding a large envelope in his lap.

"Something tell you," he says.

"Oh, Zeke, it's been such a long day. You need sleep, and so do I."

"Tell you now."

"Please," she says, "no more bombshells."

His expression, yet again, confounds her. Does he mean to look so serious, as if he is about to break terrible news to her?

"Zeke, you're scaring me."

He hands her the envelope. "Open it."

Lucinda holds the envelope in her lap and closes her eyes briefly. She feels the warmth of Zeke's thigh against hers. Her hands are cold from her time in the barn; there were no gloves in the pockets of the coat.

"All right then." It's one of those interoffice messenger envelopes, printed with columns of lines on which to write the names of the serial recipients, closed with a red string that winds around a small cardboard disk. She hasn't laid eyes on one of these objects in ages. Does anyone use them anymore?

She pulls out a sheaf of photographs, some in color, some black and white. A young boy on a sports field, wearing a baseball glove. The same boy, a bit older—thirteen? fourteen?—eating ice cream with another boy, in a playground. And then, again, wearing a black robe and mortarboard, mingling with other young graduates under a tree.

The boy is never quite facing the photographer, never quite close enough to the camera to see all that clearly, but by the fifth and final photo, Lucinda knows who he is, because she's recently seen pictures of him, on her computer, as an older but still-youthful man.

"When did these come?" she asks Zeke. "I don't understand. Did David pick these up with the mail when he came by yesterday? I asked him to leave the mail on the front table."

"Not David. Not mail."

"I don't understand."

Zeke seems to be inspecting his hands, which he holds in his lap. She can tell that he is trying hard to keep them still. He says, very slowly, to get each word right, "I paid a detective. I paid to know. Back when."

Lucinda continues to look at the photograph of Kit the high-school graduate. "Zeke."

"For Mal."

"What do you mean, 'for Mal'? What are you talking about, Zeke?"

"Mal wanted to know."

"He never told me that!"

Zeke's expression is unmistakably sad. "When he got sick. Was when."

Lucinda picks up the envelope and the photographs and tosses them back in her husband's lap. She gets off the mattress and stands. "What are you telling me? That you and Mal, behind my back, tracked down this boy, photographed him, kept some sort of . . . dossier? A secret file?"

"Yes." Zeke watches her, one of his eyes nearly closed, the muscles too tired to hold the lid open. Lucinda thinks that if he hadn't had a stroke, if she'd found this out and he were well, she might have hit him. She has never hit him.

"For Mal," he says. "Not for you."

Lucinda begins to cry. "This is the worst Thanksgiving of my life." She turns away from Zeke. But she doesn't want to go upstairs; she is afraid of running into Jonathan when she feels so undone, so betrayed.

"Not, it is not," Zeke says forcefully. "Bullshit." That word comes out clearly.

Lucinda faces him again.

"You are being shelfish. *Sel*-fish," he corrects himself, spitting as he nails down the consonant. "*Saint* Lucinda. Don't like you thish way."

"Don't hurt me more than you have," she says.

"Lishen to me," says Zeke. "Mal wanted to know. Know the child was well. Alive. Cared for. You undershtand me? Under *stand*?"

"Of course I under*stand*. Does that mean I'm supposed to feel just fine about this?"

She cannot look at him. She looks instead at the rows of trophies in the case that was moved from the living room decades ago. Some of the trophies are old enough to have been won by Aaron. Why do they still display them? They should have been put in the attic a long time ago; sold as novelties; melted down.

"You think," says Zeke, "you failed as a mother. Wrong about that. Wrong. And wrong that you should have . . . know . . . everyshing. *Thing*."

She realizes that the anger she hears in Zeke is directed mostly at himself, not at her: at the frustration of not being able to speak freely and clearly. It occurs to her that he is the one most unsettled by having to live with these long silences. How do you peacefully contain a self with opinions that cannot simply tumble forth? Words for Zeke have never required exertion. She sits down beside him again and rests a hand on his nearest leg. "Stop talking for a minute," she says. "Just relax for a minute."

"Keep talking if I want."

"I know what you're going to tell me, and please spare yourself the energy. Mal is gone, and Jonathan is here. Christina, too, of course." She sighs.

Something else occurs to her then. Christina is the child who has kept the fewest secrets from her—who has told her more than Lucinda thought she wanted to know. She wishes above all that she did not know about Christina's abortion—yet if a mother thinks she somehow deserves to know everything, then she will have to know things that keep her up at night, won't she? Jonathan, her youngest child, moved the farthest away and, for the longest time, kept his life a cipher. Now here he is, making sure she knows about the things that matter most to him. The people who matter most.

"Allowed, you *allowed* to be angry at Mal," says Zeke. "Don't at me."

"But you're my husband," she says. And what does she mean by this? That he is the one who deserves her anger? That it's his job to tell her everything he knows about their children? Is it?

She thinks of the last months of Mal's life, when he was weak, so thin it was an agony just to look at him. She remembers how manic she became with forced optimism, determined faith, exuberant wit. Each night, she fell into bed exhausted from maintaining the bright, energetic façade necessary to endure every minute of every day. By then, Mal had no job, fewer and fewer of his friends came to visit, and he rarely left his apartment—oh, that beautiful apartment, the home of someone who had seen the world and knew exactly what he liked, what memories he wanted to behold every day in the objects and patterns and books around him. That winter, Lucinda moved to New York and found a separate place to live. She saw herself as her son's handmaiden, his final confidant. This was a delusion, and his last act toward her was a ruse.

To give himself the time to take his life, without fear of her barging in, he arranged for a good friend—Fenno McLeod, the man who really did take care of Mal at the end, who *was* his final confidant—to escort Lucinda to an elegant party, a fund-raiser of some kind, dinner and dancing. Her son, who claimed he was sending them in his place, knew how much she loved dancing.

If Mal had thought her capable of forgiveness, of letting him go, he might have told her the truth, given her a chance to say good-bye. But he was right: she would never have given in. She would have guarded him against himself, fiercely. She would have thrown away all his pills, planted herself at the door of his bedroom, stayed awake for days on end, anything to keep him alive: to keep him. She would have claimed it was about honoring God's will; that, too, would have been a ruse. It would have been about honoring her will, her earthly possessiveness.

"I am a terrible mother," she says to Zeke.

"Moments we all fail," he says. "All us. Fall short."

She remembers her first formal date with Zeke, when he drove to Middlebury to pick her up at her dorm and take her out for dinner. It was during the spring of her freshman year. Over bowls of Indian pudding, he asked her what she thought about his never having gone to war; if she thought he was, to any degree, a coward. He asked her to be completely honest.

The question came out of nowhere, with a blunt, awkward urgency. They had been discussing something suitably bland for a first date—her classes, the gossip from their town, his father's success at business—so she was shocked. Later, she realized it was a frighteningly intimate question. But what she said that night was "You did your duty by staying on the farm. Someone had to do that, and you were the one. I hope nobody tries to make you feel ashamed of it, because that's the person who'd be a coward." She was relieved to have kept her composure, but did she really believe this?

He told her she hadn't answered his question. Did she wish he'd been tested by war? Wouldn't it have made him seem braver? Didn't women feel safer with a man who'd had to fight for his life?

"Maybe that's true. A little," she said. "But I'm glad you've never killed anyone. That would scare me some, to think about that." This was true.

When he drove away, after seeing her back to her dorm, she didn't know if she would hear from him again.

She says now, "I'm cold. Let's get under the blankets here. No, stay where you are." She fusses with the quilt pinned under Zeke's weakened legs, pulling it out from beneath his feet, up and over them both.

"Jamas?" he asks her.

"You want to change? I'm too tired. Way, way too tired."

"Shleep like this," he says.

She reaches over and turns off the lamp on the desk. (Is that where Zeke kept the photographs? Were they there all along? Did he sometimes take them out and look at them; wish, in his secular fashion, for the same things she prayed for when she knelt between the pews at Saint Joseph's?)

"Cyril leaves tomorrow night, but Jonathan will stay for a couple of days." She thought of the outburst upstairs. "I hope."

"Thinks I like playing chess. Makes me."

"You don't?"

"Don't."

"Zoe thinks it's good for your mind."

"Mind's fine. God shake."

True, thinks Lucinda. His mind is fine. She says, "So maybe the three of us can have an adventure. If Jonathan drives, we could go to Montreal for lunch. Have some really good French food. Is that too ambitious?"

"Wanted to take you to Italy again. Idea I had . . . for shish."

"Yes, before this," she says on his behalf. "But you know what? I wouldn't want to go back. I'd rather we go somewhere we haven't been before. And we will. You know where we've actually never been and should definitely go? Niagara Falls. Everybody has to go to Niagara Falls. Once at least."

When Zeke doesn't answer, she turns to look at him. Just like that, he's already asleep.

A S SLOWLY AS THE first weeks had passed, that was how quickly the summer began to burn away once the time of their initiation loomed close. They coaxed and bullied their sonatas, concerti, cantatas, and fugues to a more acute state of perfection than they had ever pushed the most important recital piece. If they had once been sculptors, now they were diamond cutters.

On her best days, Daphne felt as if the cello were her Siamese twin, joined to her body at her left ear, where its neck thrummed under the dictate of her fingers, and at the tenderest part of her thigh, where its voice rose from the hollow of its belly. When Natalya finally escorted them to the Silo, to rehearse in the open air, Daphne discovered how much more care and diligence she had to lavish on strings and bow, which sagged in complaint at the humidity.

That final week, they hammered down every segue in *Carnival of the Animals* until it resembled the perfectly rotating carousel that Natalya had asked them to envision, each creature passing before the listener with equal pageantry. Thursday, she released them at ten-thirty. She instructed them to leave their instruments in the studio— no overnight obsessing allowed—and to sleep late in the morning. She would arrange for breakfast to be delivered there exactly twelve hours hence. They would play the piece through only one more time.

Daphne touched Malachy's shoulder as they walked out into the soft, sweltering darkness. Except when a thunderstorm scoured the air, nearly every night was hot now, the heat as thick as custard, clamorous with insects and saturated with the pungence of mown grass, pinesap, and the minerals exuded by the evaporating lake. Lightning pulsed silently, in all directions, along the seam fastening the sky to the horizon.

"Swim?" she said.

Others had the same idea—especially with the promised luxury of sleeping in. They started toward the dorms to change.

"That does make sense," he said.

"But our place?" she said, lowering her voice. "Let's just go. Now."

When they lagged behind the main group, Seth turned back and slowed as if to wait, but then he leered at them and mimed a big smooch, waved them off with a laugh.

As always, it was empty, as if the only purpose of the place was to wait for them and no one else all the long hours they worked, ate, and slept. The surface of the lake seemed to quaver with expectation.

But they had never gone swimming here, not together. Even in late July, the water was bracing, though Daphne didn't mind; she was used to similar lakes near her home in New Hampshire. "Have you been in at all this summer?" she asked him. "I've never seen you go in."

"By myself. At dawn sometimes, when I wake up too early. Farm boy that I am." He sat on a rock. Would she have to go in first?

They had no suits, of course. Daphne hadn't forgotten this detail. In the second or third week, she had gone skinny-dipping with the night owls—the fast crowd, mostly the campers from New York City—but there had been drinking, too, and the last thing she wanted was to get herself sent home. She had never joined them again.

What she had in mind now, however, would take more fearlessness than breaking any of the rules. Just don't think about it, she told herself. She stripped to her bra and panties and, without turning to look at Malachy, leaned down at the edge and pushed herself off in a shallow dive. Several long strokes away, she turned around, treading water.

Malachy's arms enfolded his knees. She couldn't see his expression, but she knew he was watching her. "You're a graceful swimmer," he said.

"I love the water. It's beautiful tonight. It's warmed up a lot this week."

"So you say."

"Come in. Come *on*."

He stood slowly. He turned his back to her, and at first she was afraid he would leave. But then, taking his time, he removed his shirt and trousers, draping them over the rock. His white boxers gleamed against the woods behind him. He came to the edge and dove, more vertically than she had dared.

Just as she worried that he ought to have surfaced already, she felt a surge of colder water against her legs. He came up beside her. She cried out.

"Keeping the upper hand," he said. He swam away, staying parallel to the shore. She followed him until he stopped. Their arms brushed underwater.

"You know what you are?" he said.

"What am I?"

"You're dangerous," he said cheerfully. He bobbed up and down as his arms milled the water around him, requiring her to keep a small distance between them. "You are a beautiful danger, Daphne. You scare me sometimes."

"How am I dangerous?" Though what she wanted to hear was how he found her beautiful.

"You just are." His voice obeyed the rise and fall of his breathing. His shoulders broke the surface now and then. "I've written a limerick for you."

"Oh no."

"Not to worry," he said. "It's respectful."

She waited.

I once knew this cellist, Miss Browning,
A swan with whom I enjoyed clowning.
But at night when she bloomed
I felt blissfully doomed.
Far from shore, in peril of drowning.

Daphne faced him. They were still treading water, growing winded. She said, "That's respectful?"

"Well, not of me."

"Let's forget about being respectful, okay?" Abruptly, she swam for shore. She pulled herself up on the rock, realizing they had no towels. Now the air felt cold, and she shivered. "Come back," she called out, "before you *do* drown!"

When he emerged, she saw how the summery cotton of his underwear clung to his penis and hipbones. His chest was narrow and hairless, his rib cage deeply furrowed, his nipples large and startlingly dark.

She said, "You're the beautiful one." She couldn't help it.

She felt him resist, just briefly, before he kissed her. But then, to her relief, it seemed easy, even instinctive, this much of their skin meeting, the sensation of water streaming from their hair and finding its way along the contours of their nearly naked bodies. Finally, she thought. Finally, finally this. After all the talking, the practicing, the teasing, the almost-this, now and finally *this*. She had no idea what would happen next—or rather, she did; she simply had no idea how.

When they came apart to breathe, she said, "I'm so in love with you," though she hadn't meant to. "I am so in love with you, I can't not tell you, I don't care if I'm the first one to say it."

He held her gaze. He wasn't smiling, but smiling would have seemed trivial to her. "You are amazing, Daphne. Sometimes I think I won't know what to do without you when we leave this place. Sometimes I can't believe we've ever been anywhere but this place." He sighed. "It's so strange, isn't it? This whole summer. Good strange, but . . . weird strange, too." He sounded alarmingly sincere, the habitual irony drained from his voice.

"Of course it's strange," she said. "But that has nothing to do with me and you, how I feel about you. That—I mean us—we'd feel this way anywhere."

"Would we? Can you really tell what's real here and what's not?"

She squeezed his shoulders, hard. "*This* is real." She didn't care if she sounded angry.

He ran his hands up and down her arms. "Daphne, I take things slowly."

"You? Slow?" She thought of the way he played the most relentless passages of the Bach sonata, how his flute cast notes into the air like a furious scattering of seeds; or what about his quick-witted irreverence? He was anything but slow—or, for that matter, modest. And then it dawned on her: he was a virgin, too. He felt the same fear she did, except that for a boy the fear was doubled.

For the first time, he was the one to kiss her, the kiss more insolent than tender. As she had wished, respect was off the table. He spread his hands across her buttocks and pulled her against him.

"Lie down," she whispered.

"No," he whispered back. He held her, not roughly but with an authority, a knowingness, she wouldn't have guessed. When she started to grasp at the elastic of his shorts, he stopped her. He took her left hand and pressed it, instead, against the right side of his chest. His nipple rose against the center of her palm.

He kept her pulled tight against him, so that it felt as if they were dancing, the tempo slow yet fraught. She broke away from his mouth and breathed into his ear, "I want you." *Inside me,* she wanted to say.

He had barely gasped, "You *have* me" before he uttered a fierce, indecipherable word and pushed against her harder, over and over. Gradually, without releasing each other, they became motionless. She knew they were equally stunned, afraid to look at each other's faces. Her bent arm was hot and numb, pinned between their bodies; she didn't dare pull it free.

He was the one who stepped back. Without meeting her eyes, he turned toward the water, still wearing his boxers, and dove in.

"Wait," she said. All she could do was follow.

He swam straight out, not swiftly but with a clear determination for distance.

"Where are you going?" she called out.

He stopped, but still he faced the opposite shore.

"China," he said. "Or maybe just upstate New York."

She caught up and reached clumsily for his shoulder. "Are you running away from me?"

"I'm always running away. From too many things." He gave her a sidelong glance, half smile, half grimace.

What was she to say? Would he never return her honest feelings? And yet what had she fallen for? If she had wanted earnest or gushing or even possessive, there were other boys with those qualities.

He swam close to her, kissed her on the mouth, and said, "Time to go. Tomorrow is our big day." He swam back to shore. By the time she caught up with him, he was dressed, his shirt soaked through, his sneakers dangling from the fingers of a hand.

Friday night—their Friday night—arrived, and here they were: the boys in their dark suits, many of them bought for this purpose alone (too late, Daphne noticed the price tag dangling from the armpit of Oboe David's jacket) and the girls in demure funereal dresses, their prescribed modesty a trial in the heat. Natalya's gown was also black—but strapless. With her glossy hair surging from her face like a mane, she formed a fierce silhouette against the glare of the klieg lights above and, below, the mosaic of the spectators' faces: a full house and, despite the rumor of a storm, the meadow crowded, too.

Near the front of the stage, the two pianists faced each other across the lacquered expanse of their twin instruments, the arabesque of one tucked neatly into the other. In the brief silence after Natalya switched on the lectern light and before she raised her hands, Daphne glanced furtively backward: there he was (of course he was), aligning his fingers with the polished keys, flexing his lips against the aperture.

But once Daphne raised her bow, his presence was immaterial. She swam in the music much the way she had swum in the lake the night before: diving, surfacing, finding a rhythm to suit the currents, at times treading water. Natalya had promised they would play perfectly, and they did (or sensed they did). No one, however, could have anticipated the rumblings of thunder, the recurrent fissures of lightning, faraway yet bright. The wind blew skirts and unfastened tresses of bobby-pinned hair. Their music was clamped to their stands, which in turn were held in place by miniature sandbags.

Only when they finished playing, as they stood and bowed to the applause (and the shameless cheers of their parents), did Daphne wonder if anyone had ever been struck by lightning here—up on the stage or out in the wide exposed meadow. Antony Carpenter-Rhodes had assured them he would suspend the concert if the storm showed signs of heading directly their way. For now, it lingered over an adjacent valley, pinned there by unseen pressures.

Single file, they receded from the stage and took their seats in the audience. Daphne glanced across to the parents' section; her mother and father, who had seen her only briefly before the concert, beamed and waved. Her mother, wiping her eyes, blew Daphne a kiss.

The rain, when it arrived, was sudden and punishingly loud. It arrived in the middle of a guitar piece, a flamenco-tinted duet that seemed like a brazen taunt to the hovering storm. Except for the technicians—captains of the foundering ship—everyone fled: as the rain intensified, they scattered fast, some for the nearest practice studios—screen doors slamming again and again—others running for the pillared gate and their cars in the lot beyond.

Daphne lost sight of Malachy, whose seat had been two rows behind hers. And then, in the dim, wet pandemonium of bodies hell-bent on seeking shelter, she found herself pulled into her mother's embrace. Her mother was soaked to the skin and smelled of her special-occasion Chanel. Daphne's father kissed her tenderly on the cheek.

"You were a star!" he said, shouting to compete with the rain.

"No, you were *the* star," said her mother. "Oh, honey, that solo."

Daphne wanted to feel touched by their praise, by their presence after more than a month's separation. But all she could feel was that they didn't belong here; she was ashamed of herself, but it was true. This place was hers. "You'd better go," she said. "The roads." Unlike parents who had taken trains or even planes to be there, hers would drive the few hours it took to return home. They were not the type to splurge on one of the nearby country inns.

She saw them to the gate; she hugged them again as quickly as she dared. She promised to call the next day.

And then she ran, through the undiminishing rain, to the main house, where she knew they would all be gathered, her new friends, celebrating. She paused, as briefly as she could, to pull off her shoes and lift her sodden skirt. The grass was deliciously silken against her stockinged feet.

She woke from a dream in which Natalya was announcing that Daphne's brother, Andrew, had been killed. And this time Malachy was there with the others to hear the news. He leaned against the pool table, aloof, without expression, while everyone else embraced her, keening in sympathy. (*But none of them know Andrew!* Daphne was thinking as she struggled toward consciousness, breathing hard.)

Chilled to the bone by her waterlogged dress and nylons, Daphne had gone to bed that night wearing a thick, baggy sweater of

Andrew's (a favorite of his, gleefully pilfered), retreating deep beneath her covers, desperate for the sheets to warm. Now—soaked in perspiration, chilled all over again—she willed herself fully awake, pushing back the urgent fear of the dream.

The rain continued to fall, less torrentially but with an alert steadiness. She could hear the wind, still bullying tree limbs against the walls of the house. Her roommates slept, their steady breathing audible, too.

There had been no celebration after the performance that night. As Daphne had expected, most of the campers were gathered in the games lounge at HQ. Natalya stood before the grand fireplace with its still life of perfectly stacked, never-ignited birch logs. Slipping in among her fellow musicians, Daphne was hungry to hear what would surely be praise for all their hard work.

"Listen, my friends. Listen," said Natalya. She did not have to raise her voice to be heard; she called them many things but never her *friends*. "There was sad news for Carl tonight. His brother who is a soldier has been killed." *Kilt,* she said; maybe she meant something other than actually *killed*. "Probably Carl will not return to us."

No one had spoken for several seconds. Carl's brother was a soldier? But where? Vietnam would be the obvious answer. Daphne hadn't known this; had anybody known? Impossible to tell when she scanned the room. The crying was instinctual, neither heartfelt nor phony, like singing along to an irresistible melody. And Malachy, where was he? Why hadn't he joined the others? Daphne had felt more dismay at this trivial discovery than at the news. That's how selfish she was. She hadn't even been able to summon tears.

So what now, now that she was wide awake? She got up and went down the hall to pee. She did not turn on the bathroom light, and before returning to her room, she stared out the rain-spattered window into the swaying trees. She stood there until the toilet tank filled again, sighed into silence. Back in her room, she looked at the glowing face of her alarm clock. Three-thirty, the no-man's-land of neither night nor morning. She felt a surge of mournful desire. In three weeks they would all leave this place. How could she imagine returning to her high school, much less to that excuse for an orchestra? How could she return to the company of boys like the ones she used to date (only halfheartedly, she knew now), their insistent bodies, their presumptuous hands and tongues?

She went downstairs and stood on the stoop outside the door to the girls' house, beneath the small protective awning. Water rushed from the downspout, carving a furrow in the fragrant pine needles hemming the path. Along one side of the house, she noticed a flourishing colony of ferns. Even in the dark, their green was incandescent. She leaned down and picked the tallest one, using both hands to sever its tough stalk.

"Just go," she whispered.

She followed the path, half running, pine needles clinging to her feet. She clutched the fern in one hand, holding her brother's sweater close to her body with the other. At the Shed, she stopped. She stared at the latch to the barn door. Like most doors at this privileged place, it was unlocked, implying welcome—or daring her to violate its trust.

Crazy. But everything that night was crazy; why not this? Why not her?

She lifted the latch. She pulled the door open by millimeters. Perhaps because of all the rain, nothing creaked or clicked. The sound of water falling on a dozen different surfaces masked any noise she might have made. She felt invisible, canceled by the elements.

The girls slept in a dorm that had once been a dairyman's house; its rooms were small, the amenities few—but it was luxurious compared with the boys' quarters. The Shed was a barely converted barn: rows of narrow curtained stalls partitioned in plywood. Each occupant slept in his own tiny room—little more than a cubicle—but together they shared a single bathroom in the adjoining pump house, the place where the milk had been stored. ("Someone needs to tell them about these people called architects," Malachy had said the one time he showed Daphne around.)

His stall, she remembered, was the first one in on the right. She walked through the opening—he hadn't bothered to close the curtain—and knelt on the rug beside the cot.

He slept on his side, his back to the flimsy wall that separated his space from the one where Trombone David slept. Malachy's mouth was closed, his long hands joined, fingers to palm, at the edge of his pillow. The sheet covered him up to his chest, secured by an elbow.

He slept soundly. She could just stay there and stare at him for as long as she liked, then leave, no one the wiser. Carefully, hindered by the wet nightgown clinging to her knees, she settled into a cross-legged position. Her face was level with his shoulder.

She held the fern to her nose as she waited for her eyes to adjust to the dusty dark of the barn interior. The fern smelled like good, fertile dirt, like her mother's flower beds in the spring.

His eyes opened. He remained silent, but he looked frightened.

"It's me," she whispered.

"Daphne?"

She reached out and touched his mouth.

She rose to her knees and tucked the fern beneath the pillow.

He said nothing, and he didn't move. She stood, as quickly as she could, and wrenched off her brother's sweater, her cold encumbering nightgown. She climbed under the sheet beside him, pushing him back to make space for herself.

His elbow struck the wall, a brief knock, and he started to speak, but she kissed him. She felt, simultaneously, that he was trying to pull away from her and also that he was completely naked, and shaking, under the sheet.

"Oh," he said, speaking into her lips as she pressed her hand flat against his penis, which had been hard from the moment it touched her legs.

How did this work? She began to shake, too. But Malachy's arms folded her close. He pulled his face away from hers and whispered, "This isn't safe."

"Yes, it is," she whispered. "I promise."

"But you" was all he could say before she pressed one leg over his and somehow rolled herself beneath his body.

For ages and ages, this had been happening; everybody knew that. Without diagrams or books or the gym teacher's drawings on the blackboard in the stuffy còaching office behind the locker room. Daphne's period had come the week before. Ten days: that was the margin, she'd read.

It was, and wasn't, what she had imagined. At first it was difficult, the fitting together: clumsy, but not painful. Almost by accident, she found herself turning him, against the wall, forcing him beneath her. He came quickly, the way he had by the lake, and again he kept her against him. This time he went back to kissing her, determined and unceasing as the rain, which clattered so loudly on the roof that Daphne was certain no one could hear them. He pushed a hand between her legs, searching. She almost wanted him to stop, but then she realized that he was hardening all over again, and this part—this was what surprised her completely.

They said nothing, even when their faces were parted, and now it did hurt, though she did not protest. He stayed on top of her, taking his turn as the one who moved constantly, pinning her down with a weight that seemed far greater than his own. It felt as if he were telling her something essential with every part of him except his words (the part of him that had won her over to begin with). This, she thought, was the opposite of poetry.

When they were done, both of them finally still, Daphne felt a twist of anxiety. But their shared warmth was reassuring, and Malachy's sinuous arm, lightly balanced in the niche of her waist, gave a logic to the way she was shaped. His eyes were closed, though she knew this only by feel, her fingers appraising his face. There was no telling what time it was.

"I have to go," she whispered.

Her palm against his cheek, she felt him nod.

"I love you," she whispered.

She waited. He answered, "Daphne, you're too perfect for me."

She wondered why her shoulder felt so scratchy—until she pushed herself up from the cot and felt, beneath her hand, the flattened fern. She left it there for him to find in the light. As if he might forget.

She did not see Malachy until Monday morning, at breakfast; by then, she was desperate with angry confusion. She had been incapable of asking anyone where he was before then. Furtively, she had searched the other boys' faces for mocking recognition of her trespass. She saw nothing—but still, she could not have uttered his name without emotion.

After chamber rehearsal—now they dove full force into Debussy's "Faun," Saint-Saëns a thing of the past, a book closed, a journey all but forgotten—Malachy sat at another table for lunch. During the afternoon break, he was nowhere to be found; at dinner, he was absent.

But as if nothing were different, she ate a large piece of Boston cream pie and walked with Michael to the studio where Viktor Vassily, a visiting member of some Bach society, was tutoring Malachy on the flute sonata. All the campers worked in smaller ensembles as well as in the two chamber groups; Daphne couldn't believe her luck when she was assigned to this trio.

Malachy's instrument was the melodic backbone of the sonata; he would be the star. Michael's harpsichord and Daphne's cello were mere courtiers, sycophants to the flute, though their roles were challenging, too. Under Viktor Vassily's nearly disdainful guidance, they practiced together that night without any humorous asides, with an almost dull-witted focus on the mechanics that could make Bach's music merely workmanlike if the performers were too unsure of themselves (or too unmoved by the music itself).

At nine, when Vassily dismissed them, Daphne was tempted to pack up hastily and bolt to her room. But after thanking their tutor and saying good night to Michael, she stood on the spongy lawn, under the showy stars of a storm-washed sky, and she waited for Malachy, who had lingered in the studio to clean his flute.

"There you are," he said when he emerged, as if he weren't the one who had vanished for the past two days.

She willed herself to say nothing, to let him stay or go, as he wished. She would not appear to have trapped him.

He started along the path that led toward the Silo, but then he turned back, obviously expecting her to follow. When she didn't, he said, "Daphne, we should talk."

"Don't say it was a mistake." Damn her voice for trembling. "Don't you dare tell me that." But she gave in and joined him.

He resumed walking. He held his flute case in one hand, his music folder in the other. "You need to understand something, Daphne. I'm selfish. I guess I was so selfish that I didn't—"

"So we're all selfish!" she said. She stopped, resting her case on the bricks. She hated how unfairly burdensome her cello was, compared with Malachy's flute in its trim, complacent little box. You could flee with a flute. "I'm selfish and, so what, I still love you!" She realized how angry she sounded. "I love you partly because I *am* selfish."

He was forced to turn around and face her. He was clearly uncertain—no, unhappy—clearly thinking hard about how to answer, and suddenly she was furious that he *had* to think about an answer.

"How about a limerick?" she said. "Can you maybe just give me a goddamn limerick?"

His eyes narrowed. "You know, I could, Daphne. I actually could. But what I can't give you is what you really want from me. If you don't believe me, I understand. Or if you hate me. You should hate me."

She wanted to hate him. She wanted to accuse him of using her, but how absurd would that be? "What's it meant to you, Malachy? All this time we—all this—the nights and the . . . how can you deny that we . . ." *Are meant for each other,* she longed to say, but she wasn't so stupid. They weren't actors in a movie. They were a pair of spoiled brats at a hothouse for talented students of music, most of whom would never be famous or successful at what they believed set them apart, made them special. She could not persuade Malachy Burns to *love her* any more than she could persuade Antony Carpenter-Rhodes to give her a solo with the London Philharmonic.

"Daphne, you're my favorite person here," he said. "My only friend. Though I guess I blew the friendship, didn't I? I care so much for you, and the minute I say those words, I know I'm hurting you, and you can call me cruel, because objectively it's true. But it's true by accident, Daphne."

"Accident?" she said. She saw Craig and the two Davids heading toward them on the path. She picked up her case and turned around, stumbling as she tried to run, aiming for the quickest way back to the dorm.

He stopped her at the studio and steered her inside. He turned the lights on again. They blinked in the raw fluorescent glare. Daphne covered her eyes.

"We're an accident? That's what we are?" she cried out.

"No," he said. "That came out wrong. We're . . . a collision. Like a physics collision, not a car crash."

"What are you *talking* about?" she said, though she had to feel hope at the sight of his crooked smile.

"Atoms, I mean." He sat at the harpsichord, on Michael's bench. He was looking at the keyboard as he said, "Someday, Daphne, I'll be at your wedding, and I'll say, 'See? See how it all turned out the way it was supposed to be?'"

There was room for her on the bench, but she stood resolutely behind him. "And what about your wedding, Malachy? I won't *be* at your wedding. I promise you that."

Malachy touched the harpsichord's gold and red keys, his fingers only brushing their scuffed finish, making not a single sound. "Everybody says you can't predict the future, but I won't be having a wedding, believe me."

Suddenly Daphne felt limp, boneless with exhaustion, worn down by the futility of their talk. He was always vacillating, always taking back something he had given—wasn't he? She had to stop pretending that would change; but how could she, feeling the way she did? She gave up on her resolve not to cry, but her tears were invisible to him.

"Did you really want a limerick?" he said.

When she failed to answer, he played a few tinny random notes on the harpsichord and then, as if addressing the instrument, said:

Behold the rich farm boy Malachy Burns
Who plays his pipe among the churns.
He's a coward, he's benighted,
He makes everyone feel slighted,
And all things but music he spurns.

When Daphne sobbed, he turned around on the bench.

"That isn't funny," she said. "And it's stupid and mean. You *are* cruel. You are a coward. Making it rhyme doesn't excuse you."

"You're right. I only wish I could make you see how sorry I am."

"Apologies are cheap and easy." She told him to go to hell. She hoisted her case and left him there. She went to her room and pushed her instrument roughly into the closet.

Mei Mei was sitting on the floor, the Debussy spread open before her. "Hey," she said quietly, and the look she gave Daphne said not only that she understood what had probably happened but that she knew better than to ask.

Daphne was just in time for a late swim, Mei Mei told her. Exactly what the doctor ordered, Daphne answered. Along with her three roommates, Craig, Trombone David, Oboe David, and several campers from Chamber Two whom she hadn't spoken with much before then—how stupid she was; how nice they all were—Daphne went to the lake beach to drink beer, strip, and dive into the water, shocked by the plunge in temperature brought about by all that rain.

4

The Bright Blessed Day

T HE BEAUTIFUL STONES, they *shall* be collected," says Walter in what he calls his lady-of-the-manor voice. He sits cross-legged beneath a striped umbrella, wearing a curtained panama hat that makes him look like Lawrence of Arabia as Monty Python might have portrayed him.

While Kit swims laps parallel to the shore, Fenno and Walter are watching his children play by the ruffled edge of the surf—not that Herring Cove offers any genuine "surf." It's a placid haven for tanners, readers, and retirees. (Walter, who ought to be a father and sometimes wishes he were, insists that he doesn't feel safe taking children to the ocean beaches, where the waves are roisterous and the undertow cunning.)

The boy, Will, trudges in and out of the water, dragging one of those foam boards on a leash. Without real waves, he can't get any momentum, but he seems determined to make it work. His sister meanders along the rubble of the tide line, selecting favored stones and dropping them into a plastic cup from Wired Puppy that Walter fished from the depths of his beach bag. She's amassed a small pile, like an offering, on the edge of Walter's towel. She is drawn not to the smooth quartz orbs or the rough dotted pebbles but to the wafer-like specimens that come in a range of chalky colors from white to charcoal gray.

"The beautiful stones," Fenno says to Walter, "are technically illegal to remove from many beaches nowadays. Possibly including this one."

"Oh, nonsense."

"The hot-stone-massage practitioners are apparently endangering parts of the coastline where beach stones play an essential role in thwarting erosion."

"Thanks, Archimedes, but that's the most ridiculous thing I've ever heard," says Walter, who comes up with random classical names whenever he finds Fenno too eloquent or high-minded. "After all, *if* the ocean level is rising thanks to all those melting glaciers, then if enough stones are *removed* from the water, it will compensate. I don't have a college degree for nothing!"

"I wasn't aware you took geology."

"I took advanced placement Common Sense while you were studying the poems of those poor guys killed in the trenches of World War One."

After too much arguing about the subject—first at home and then in a therapist's office—Fenno and Walter agreed to a "vacation moratorium" on discussing the circumstances surrounding this weekend until it's behind them. Which means that for the past week they've found themselves making elaborate small talk on everything from the current cut in men's swim attire to the wearisome craze among Walter's fellow restaurateurs for putting pork belly in every course from gazpacho to artisanal sorbet. And now: the role of beach stones in the fate of the human race?

Kit drove from New Jersey with his children, arriving late last night; Kit's mother and Mal's mother will arrive, separately, this evening. Though six months have passed since Kit's first letter, Fenno still finds it extremely hard to think of this man as Mal's son—or of Lucinda, whose presence he longs for yet also dreads, as Kit's grandmother. But he has only just met Kit, only just begun to convince himself that this is the flesh-and-blood grown-up version of the boy in the pictures that Fenno discovered under Mal's bed on the day he died.

It's as if this part of Fenno's past—the part that sometimes threatens the life he shares with Walter—had been, for so long, a perfect origami construction (perhaps one of those cranes that Fenno associates, queasily and unavoidably, with the bomb dropped on Hiroshima), and then some blithe stranger came along and decided to unfold it and spread it out flat. But the folds are indelible, so now it's a crazed square of colored paper, its formerly hidden planes jarringly bright, revealing the color of the paper when it was new. And will it ever be folded back into that elegant expression of flight? Doubtful. Unlikely.

Obviously not.

And it's this—the future lying in wait beyond the long-planned gathering of virtual strangers united by inscrutable genes—that worries Fenno more than how the weekend itself will play out. He's sure they will all behave politely, lovingly, telling stories about Mal that summon grateful tears to one another's eyes, his among them.

But here it is, finally, after all the tense quarreling and all the negotiations. Here is Walter, wearing not just his Saharan headgear but oversize sunglasses, a long-sleeved shirt, and a pair of white cotton trousers. Fenno is amused by Walter's love of the beach despite his perpetual fear of the sun. ("Melanoma is a dark and greedy goddess," he recites when browsing the sunscreen aisle at Duane Reade.) Fenno can take or leave the beach, but having spent his childhood summers in sun-sparse Scotland, he cannot resist basking in the exuberant light of an all-American August day. He sits, therefore, just outside the umbrella's elliptical shadow, sections of Friday's *Times* splayed across his sandy legs. It's impossible to read a newspaper at the beach, yet in his own form of illogical behavior, he persists in bringing it along.

Fenno realizes that he and Walter, indolent on their towels, surrounded by a surfeit of paraphernalia, must look to passersby like the prototypical pair of old Provincetown queens, rusty barges among the sleek, high-hulled yachts—except that they are not regulars here.

Walter and Fenno have lived together in New York for almost a decade, though they knew each other in passing (literal passing) for years before that. On the same side of the same city block—a shady stretch of Jamesian row houses on Bank Street—they maintained its only two commercial ventures. Walter's Place was (and still is) a counterintuitively hip meat-and-potatoes restaurant that has spawned a satellite bistro across town and, for the past year, a pair of roving food trucks. The Bull peddles three versions of a ten-dollar roast-beef sandwich ("grass fed, drug free, gently weaned, yada yada yada," as Walter puts it), while The Dog specializes in a trendsetting throwback, the pig-in-a-blanket: pure-beef hot dogs offered in three types of pastry. The Dog is frantically followed, generally via smartphone app, by droves of readers who saw the *Times* review praising the pig-in-a-brioche as "positively Proustian." ("Just what the dick-ens does that mean?" Walter said. "It makes you want to go back to bed for the rest of your life and reminisce about Milanos?")

Fenno's shop, Plume, was a bookstore. Was. Walter's business, now a modest empire, is thriving. Fenno's, as of April, is not—its failure less a matter of shriveling commerce (though commerce did shrivel) than of avaricious landlords. When Fenno's lease came to an end, the new rent proposed—demanded—was the old one multiplied by four. (For a delusional fifteen minutes, Fenno assumed there was a typo in the e-mail.) With insulting alacrity, in his old domain sprouted the fifth Marc Jacobs boutique within a four-block radius, compounding the sense of real-estate déjà vu in a neighborhood where stretches of once-quite-idiosyncratic merchants have been replaced by a prolific redundancy of glossy, mirrored spaces and miniskirted mannequins, each new establishment about as distinctive as a slab of brie from Trader Joe's.

Fenno knows he is over the hill according to the customs and aes-thetics of the place where he continues to live, never mind that he's always been a bit of a codger, even back in his twenties. Now that he's approaching sixty, he has already warned Walter (for whom enter-taining is another form of breathing) that he must resist all urges to throw a party. Not because Fenno will mind turning sixty—the gay men they know would hardly dare admit that they see such an age as anything other than a glorious gift—but simply because he likes his celebrations small. Were they ever to contemplate marriage, they'd be divorced before the engagement party that Walter would have taken such meticulous delight in planning.

Unlikely a match as they are, Fenno and Walter have been called, to their faces, exemplars of post-queer culture: committed compan-ions and citizens who, between them, have seen and been a part of it all—the protests, the epidemic, the pride parades, the uproar against the persecution of gay teens, the fight for equal marriage rights—yet persevere in leading unembittered, fully integrated lives.

"We won't make the gay Mount Rushmore," Walter says, "but, honey, we are the wind beneath those wings."

Whether they are indeed post-, pre-, proto-, or peri-anything, they are spending the second half of their tenth shared summer at the very theme park of Queer, where queer is a language, a dress code, an etiquette, an inescapably florid pungence: in short, the norm. Provincetown was Walter's idea. He believes in fresh air of the metaphorical kind, so every year they travel somewhere new, whether for Thanksgiving, the Fourth of July, or a week to break the long stranglehold of winter. To take a whole month is unprecedented, and Fenno knows that Walter is trying hard to distract him from his accidental retirement.

"A month in Gomorrah?" Fenno balked when Walter mentioned the plan back in April—for apparently it was a plan, not merely a notion.

"Here's the deal," said Walter. "And let me tell you, *we* get the hands-down bargain." One of his regular clients wanted Walter's Place, the entire restaurant, for his son's rehearsal dinner on a Saturday in June. In exchange, he offered the use of his Ptown house for the month of August; he and his wife would be traveling through Europe. "Signed, sealed, delivered," Walter quoted himself as replying. He showed Fenno the pictures online: a white antique clapboard house in the West End, inland side of Commercial, behind a privet hedge. "Are you fool enough to say no?" Walter dared him.

"After-dinner mints, why thank you!" Walter says to Fanny. "I'll take this greenish one if you don't mind." He promptly inserts the stone in his mouth and pretends to chew.

"Noooo!" cries Fanny in a spasm of laughter. "You'll break your teeth, silly!"

"That is so totally gross," says Will as Walter spits the stone delicately into his palm.

"But it tasted like avocado. I swear!"

Through his sunglasses, Fenno watches Kit watching his children watch this man they've only just met. Kit looks tired—he and Fenno stayed up till three in the morning—but he is smiling as if relieved, as if he has finished an exhausting task. Right now Fenno is grateful to Walter, who's in his element wherever people need help feeling at home in their skin.

Among the countless attractive young people who move to New York in hopes of becoming an actor, Walter is one of the lucky ones. He didn't make it much past dog-food commercials and bit parts in World War II movies with five-line roles for tall, blond, big-jawed men with credible German accents—"graduates of the '*Schnell, Schnell!*' Acting Academy," says Walter—but he found a way to make a living as the director and ringleader of a colorful, multisensual production designed to send people home feeling sated, happy, and fortunate. Unlike many others in his profession, Walter loves being conspicuously present at his restaurants. (He has even threatened to ride around on those trendy trucks.) He isn't a master chef; he's a master host.

How differently Fenno conducted the work he chose. His customary station was a desk in a back corner, where he tended happily to the monkish chores of stocking and selling the ineluctably desirable objects known as books (which might also, like a good meal, make people feel sated, happy, and fortunate—even wise). Most of the time, he spoke with his customers only when spoken to. He had employees who answered the phone, roamed the aisles to offer assistance, and ran the readings. Once or twice a year, he endured the intense camaraderie—and, of late, commiserating—at booksellers' conventions.

Walter may be right that Fenno was too passive, even defeatist, but no amount of glad-handing would have kept his rent affordable, and moving was inconceivable; Fenno is someone who believes that souls cannot migrate from one solid entity to another. Plume, with its bonny back garden, its buckled plank floors, its tree-tinted light, was indisputably a place with a soul.

"Can I pick up some food at that supermarket we passed on the way out?" asks Kit. "I'd like to contribute to the weekend somehow. I can also cook."

"You can cook?" interrupts Walter. "Honey, you are on. And don't call me cheeky," he says to Fenno. "I've had enough of your bee-bee-cue chicken with the sesame seeds."

"I ordered posh salads from that make-believe farm stand you love so much," says Fenno. "Since we're not sure who'll get here when."

"I love family reunions," Walter says to Kit, lying through his teeth. "I guess because mine wasn't much of a union to begin with. Forget the *re*." When Fenno told him the plan—to offer this borrowed house as a place for Fenno to meet Kit and bring together his newly extended family (all of them connected only through Mal)—he gave

Walter no more choice than Walter had given him about taking the house. Walter said, "You are packing a keg of dynamite, sweetheart." Aye, and don't I know it, Fenno thought. But it was, undeniably, the right thing to do.

Malachy Burns has been a source of resentment and retrospective jealousy for years, even though (or perhaps because) he was never Fenno's lover and even though he was long dead before Walter so much as shook Fenno's hand. (They had nodded to each other for months on the short stretch of sidewalk between restaurant and bookshop. It took the casual kinship of their dogs—now long dead as well—to force an introduction.)

Walter turns to Fanny and Will. "Ready to head back? I bought a *sack* of lemons for real lemonade. And grenadine to make it pink." The twins brighten. "Speaking of pink? Time for the sunburn test." He presses a forefinger into Fanny's cheekbone. "You're done. Maybe a little rare, but that's how we like our roasted human." He looks at Will and says, "I know. Totally gross."

Fenno and Kit shake out the mats and towels. Walter closes the umbrella, retrieves stray flip-flops, corrals the scattered newspaper sections that Fenno will never get around to reading. Fenno checks his mobile—how he hates yet depends on the thing—to make sure neither of the women have left messages about their arrival. He is always relieved when the miserly screen ("No one could ever call that phone smart," says Walter) shows him nothing more than the same snapshot of Felicity sunning herself, in all her avian splendor, on the back of a chair in the garden behind the shop where customers now casually spend on a single handbag the same sum of money they apparently thought unreasonable to spend on a dozen brand-new hardcover books.

Felicity put up an insolent, deafening fuss when Kit and the twins arrived last night. She was dozing on top of her cage, so when she woke to the invasion of visitors, she raised her wings and puffed up her scarlet feathers, threatening flight.

The boy hid behind Kit, who raised an arm in front of his face.

"Not to worry!" Fenno reassured them. He forced the parrot onto his sleeve. "You're an evil sorceress, you know that?" he said as he stroked her. Once she had muttered her final complaints, Fenno put her back on the cage.

The girl walked cautiously toward the bird. "Can I touch her?"

"Fanny, introduce yourself, please," said Kit.

She blushed and held her hand out to Fenno. Walter took Fanny's suitcase and said, "She's a cranky old biddy, that bird, and it's past her bedtime, but we'll make sure you get acquainted tomorrow. Come upstairs and see your digs, which are pretty amazing. You too, bro," he said to Will. "You're in the hideaway. There's a rumor it was used in the Underground Railroad. I'd sleep there if I could fit."

"We studied that last year! That's cool!" exclaimed Fanny, and without another glance at their father, the children followed Walter. My very own Pied Piper, thought Fenno, who had fallen for Walter much the way children did: here was someone you simply *knew* you could trust, who might nag or infuriate or sulk, but whose greatest charm lay in the most durable of virtues: loyalty.

Left alone together in the kitchen, Fenno and Kit did everything not to stare at each other. Whatever anxieties they had harbored about this meeting, their curiosity would finally have its way.

"She's stunning," said Kit.

"She is." Fenno stroked Felicity's neck.

"She belonged to my father?"

"For a couple of years, until he became ill and couldn't keep her. His doctor said there were . . . issues of immunity." Felicity watched the newcomer closely but let herself be lulled by Fenno's affection. "I lived across the street; my shop sold bird-watching gear as well as books. He took a gamble that I might be willing to adopt her."

"I remember. She's the reason you met." Kit reached a hand slowly toward the bird, but she scuttled to the peak of her cage.

In the one letter Fenno had written to Kit, he'd told the story: how the Audubon prints in the store had given Mal an avenue on which to approach Fenno for an outlandish favor; how taking on Felicity had brought Mal into his life and then, inadvertently, lured Fenno deep into Mal's, just as it began to falter and dwindle.

Kit hovered by the table, glancing around. "This house is seriously old."

"The front portion was built in the late seventeen hundreds."

"Not so old if you're British, I guess."

"Old enough," said Fenno. "Older than the house I grew up in. We're not all lairds of drafty castles with parapets and moats."

"I love all the rafters. The beams."

"Wait till you go upstairs. Walter has to bend down to pass through the bedroom door." He paused. "But it's not ours, this house."

"Yes. You explained."

More slowly than usual, to give himself time, Fenno moved Felicity inside her cage to settle her for the night. He changed her water, emptied and rinsed her food cup, scratched her ruff one last time, and adjusted the cover. "Let me get you something," he said to Kit. "Tea or coffee? Wine, whiskey?"

"I should see about the kids."

"If you don't mind, Walter loves playing godfather. Down to making certain they floss."

They heard Fanny's laughter from upstairs.

"He'll be reading to them," said Fenno. "I realize they're not so wee, but Walter's been known to force fairy tales down the gullets of adolescents. He's a lapsed actor. Needs his daily dose of stage time."

Kit laughed uncertainly. He held on to the back of a chair with both hands, as if he were on a boat or train and might otherwise lose his footing.

Fenno would have liked nothing better than to join Walter in the sleigh bed beneath the slanted ceiling and drift into sleep against the nocturnal shrieks and murmurings of strollers on the other side of the privet: young bucks and partygoers ebullient in the town's warm, salt-steeped air and frothy permissiveness. As much as Fenno had tried to protest Walter's plan, after a fortnight in this place, its paradoxically ingenuous cheer had softened his prudish resistance.

But Fenno suspected that Kit wanted a chance to be alone with him, ask certain questions before the women arrived. Walter was the one who had suggested that if the children would let him usher them to bed, he could discreetly follow suit. ("I do not," he said, "need to stay up till all hours hearing about the lives of the saints.")

Kit asked, "Did Walter know my father?"

So, thought Fenno, now it begins.

"By neighborhood reputation. But that was before Walter knew me. Mal made an impression. As he meant to—something like Felicity here. Me, I was more of a . . . bystander." Fenno paused. Did it sound as if he pitied himself?

"You know what? I'll say yes to whiskey. That's a rare choice for me."

"Rare choice for a rare occasion." Fenno went to the cupboard where Walter had stocked up on liquor.

Kit's laughter came more easily now. "I guess you don't do this every day. God, I hope not, for your sake."

"If I did, I'd be doing a better job of it than this." Fenno went to the cupboard for a glass—two. Whiskey was a rare choice for him as well.

He led Kit to the screened porch behind the kitchen. Up front, the living room had no true ceiling; one could see pinstripes of light passing between the floorboards of the master bedroom above. From the bedroom, conversely, one could hear every sigh, every mote of punctuation, threading the conversation below. In a way, the house wasn't terribly conducive to guests.

They sat down facing each other, but at first their attention was on their drinks. They sipped delicately, almost in unison. Fenno listened to the intermittent tattoo of insects colliding with the screen. Kit spoke first. "It is so bizarre to be here. To state the obvious. You've been so kind to me when I'm probably intruding on your life. Lucinda insisted that you would be glad to hear from me, meet me, but I want you to know I take nothing for granted. . . . More and more that's the case."

"Lucinda's right. I was glad to hear from you. You should know whatever you can about Mal. Your father." Something else occurred to him. "Your children's grandfather."

"They still don't know the story, exactly why we're here. I hope Walter—"

"Not to worry. Walter has the tact of a butler in situations like this." Crikey, thought Fenno, *what* situations like this?

"I'm afraid to ask the wrong things," said Kit. "I did look up his reviews. The *Times* has everything archived now. Lucinda sent me pictures."

"There are no wrong things to ask. If you mean about how he died, how sick he was for so long, you can ask me all about that. Better me than Lucinda."

"I don't want to hear about his illness. I didn't even get to know him then, never mind when he was healthy. The worst thing is knowing that I could have. Known him before he was sick, I mean. But just to have known him at all . . ."

Fenno tried to imagine Mal meeting Kit while he was still healthy—which was, of course, before Fenno knew Mal. Kit would have been a teenager then. But that was immaterial. The Mal whom Fenno had known wouldn't have been able to bear meeting Kit; he wouldn't have volunteered to face his own guilt. While Mal was alive, Fenno hadn't the faintest hint that—as Fenno's dog-breeder mother and even Mal himself would have put it—he had "sired a child."

"Mal was an incomparably clever man," said Fenno. "But lest you wonder what you missed, he wasn't cut from fatherly cloth."

"I guess that's obvious," Kit said sharply.

Yes. Of course there would be anger. After a moment Fenno said, "Plenty of gay men become fathers. Or surrogate fathers." He thought of Walter's stories, both comic and catastrophic, about the time he had invited his teenage punk-rocker nephew to share his flat and work at the restaurant. Thank God Walter had exorcised the fatherhood fantasy before they came together.

"I'm not talking about his being gay," said Kit, "though maybe that's part of why my mother didn't want me to know who he was. I just mean—I mean there are a lot of fathers who take on the job, or even a tiny bit of it, or maybe not very successfully, but they do it because whether they like it or not, they *are* fathers. My mother refuses to see it that way—she's one of those nurture-over-nature people. Maybe I'm a literalist, but I'm sorry: make a kid and you're a father. Biology doesn't lie. Lucinda told me he *knew* that I existed out there in the world, right from the start."

This was not a declaration Fenno wanted to hear, but why should the conversation conform to his wishes? To Kit, he was a conduit, an opportunity; Christ, he was a bloody priest.

"I'm sorry. You're right," he said. "But part of what made Mal so successful was . . ." Fenno hadn't known how dodgy it would feel to risk saying the wrong things—nor how insidious this conversation would be to the way in which he remembered Mal. He had known Mal in life for only a few years; as a memory, Mal had been with him for twenty.

"Mal was the sort of man people described as ambitious, determined—if they didn't like him, as arrogant, tactless. Cheeky. It wasn't just that he pushed hard at what he did or that he was a perfectionist. I think—and I only understood this after he died—that he cleared a wide track before him. He didn't want to face the unpleasant surprise around the next corner." Or maybe this became true only after he had stumbled onto the worst surprise of all. Maybe Mal, before knowing Fenno, had been more spontaneous, more open. "Anyway, to do that, he had to eliminate all obstacles."

That wasn't the right way to put it; he knew this from the look on Kit's face. Fenno had just painted a portrait of someone you might call ruthless.

"Acknowledging that he had a son out there somewhere, yeah, well, that would have been a pretty serious obstacle," said Kit.

Fenno took a gulp of his whiskey. "I'm not doing a very good job here."

Kit sighed. "Please don't see it as a *job*. And I have to tell you, I'm not where I was when I spoke to you a few months ago."

"You're angry now. Is that the difference?"

"Sorry." Kit shrugged. "Weird how dime-store psychology turns out to be true, whether we like it or not."

Fenno would have laughed if he had known this man better.

"I should probably crash," said Kit. "The traffic was horrendous. And I was mad that Sandra decided, at the last minute, she couldn't come along. It's not that she didn't want to meet you. She has a deadline she's worried about."

How unlike Mal Kit seemed, in his apologies and modest desires. Why *shouldn't* he be in a roaring rage over Mal's refusal to face his existence? Had Fenno deserved to know, too? Or would Fenno's knowing about the son have been just another "obstacle" to Mal's plans? He thought of Lucinda, whom he had come to know and like through the last months of Mal's life (through his protracted death, to put it bluntly), and only now did it dawn on him that Kit was a secret Lucinda had carried *for* her son, all those years. Fenno had known Mal to be self-centered, even self-righteous, but now he saw these qualities as less ambiguous, not so easily forgiven. Mal may have died a terrible, unjustly early death, but that misfortune did not absolve him. Now Fenno, too, was angry at Mal.

"Listen," he said, "I'm not sitting here thinking that my memories of your dead father are like some shrine you should be visiting with reverence, some hallowed place of worship. But now I'm afraid you'll get up tomorrow, pack those children in your car, and hightail it home. That I don't want." What did Fenno want, honestly? To sit around spouting stories about a chap he'd known only while he waited for death to outwit him (hard as it had been to outwit Mal)?

Kit stared at him as if chastised. Their glasses were empty.

Fenno nearly told Kit that while he had never been Mal's lover, he ought to have been. Not in a reckless, suicidal way but with all the tenderness that Fenno had been too frightened to show toward Mal. The worst thing was that even though Mal had never mentioned it, he knew. He trusted Fenno to help him die precisely because he knew Fenno was in love with him and didn't want to lose him. To refuse Mal's wishes would have meant to lose him for certain: to lose his regard. To honor them had left a paradoxical glimmer of hope: the hope of failure or a sudden change of heart.

"I am refilling our glasses," said Fenno. "You stay here."

In the kitchen, he listened. No voices or creaking of floorboards. He walked quietly to the living room and looked up: no seepage of light through the planks. Walter wasn't waiting up. This was good; and then again it wasn't.

When he handed Kit his glass, Fenno said, "I should confess that I've been terrified at the prospect of bringing you all together here. For a while, I wondered what the deuce I'd been thinking. But I will always feel I owe something to Lucinda, a debt I can't fulfill."

He told Kit the story of Mal's end: how Mal had sent Fenno and Lucinda in his place to an evening of feasting and dancing in a far-flung corner of the city, a scheme to detour his mother away from his bedside long enough that he could take his exit in private. Countless times over the years since, especially on the always bleak, chilly anniversary in March, Fenno has marveled at how well he played his part that night and, more still, the next morning: how he let himself into Mal's apartment, knowing that he was supposed to hope that he would find Mal good and dead, the pills and vodka deft in their collaboration.

Yet Fenno unlocked the door that morning hoping that Mal had failed, if just this once. Because how could a man so adept at so many things, so formidably sharp in his wit, his intellect, his perception of where each person stood in the orbit of his life, be anything other than somehow immortal? Surely Mal was destined to be one of those wizened, quick-tongued, stylish-to-the-bitter-end ninety-year-old urban sages. Fenno had done what was asked of him, followed his directions perfectly (another instrument of Mal's powerful will), yet even so, against all logic, he was crushed when what he found in Mal's bed was indeed the corpse that Mal had wanted him to find.

But he left these sorry self-aggrandizing details out of the story he told Kit. Kit drank his whiskey and looked not at Fenno but out through the screen into the dull void of shrubbery and woods behind the house.

When Fenno had finished, it was hard to tell if Kit had been paying attention. A long silence drifted between them.

"That is so awful and so sad," said Kit, "but what's really awful is how it feels so completely unconnected to me."

"Because it was. You didn't know him." Fenno felt strangely unconnected to the story as well; he had told it so many times over the years that the words had come to feel like distant cousins to the memories themselves.

"He chose not to know me. That's what I keep reminding myself. But I didn't know that for most of my life. When you don't have a father—or no; when your mother withholds from you who that father is—then one thing you have to imagine is that he doesn't know you exist. She kept it from *him*, too, and that's not his fault! How could he know any better? But you figure he's got to find out—or one day, when you're grown up, you'll find him. You'll know how."

"As you did."

"Except"—Kit laughed mockingly—"except that I might never have done it if I hadn't been pushed."

By Sandra. Fenno knew this part of Kit's story. Sandra whose work kept her from something as important as this weekend. Something else, Fenno feared, was going on here. But it wasn't his place to ask.

"You're talking," said Fenno, "to someone who's had to be pushed toward every important decision he's ever made. If no one had pushed me, I'd still be sitting on the window seat halfway up the big stairwell in my parents' house, wearing trousers far too small for me, reading another book." Except that now his brother David—with his wife and children—lived in that house. He laughed briefly at the image of himself, a grizzle-headed gimpy-jointed man, sitting cross-legged on that tapestried cushion (porcupined with years of hair shed by his mother's collies), and would his reading have matured despite his never leaving that spot? Or would he never have moved past adolescence, advancing through time only according to how the childhood classics continued to eclipse one another? By now he'd be long through Lemony Snicket and *Harry Potter*. He'd have devoured already the *Hunger Games* trilogy, some of the last books displayed in the window of Plume.

"I'm constantly in need of pushing," Kit said mournfully.

"Let's stop being maudlin, shall we?" Fenno said. "You've met Lucinda."

Kit smiled. "At Christmas. She's wonderful. And you know, I do have her. And Zeke—though I wish I'd met him before his stroke. My children don't quite understand who those old people are— Sandra says we can't rush it. Ironic, coming from Sandra. But we've told them a half-truth—that they're new relatives we discovered. They don't know enough about genealogy to ask the right questions. Though I think, any minute, Fanny will get there."

"Lucinda told you we were friends for a while."

"Were?" Kit paused. "She said you are friends. That's why she could put me in touch with you, she said."

"Are. Well. I'm glad she said that."

"You don't agree?"

"I did something—I condoned something—no, I actually *encouraged* something that appalled her. I don't know how much you know about Lucinda, the work she did for years."

"Unwed mothers. Single mothers: I guess that's the politically correct term now for girls like my mother." Kit leaned backward into the palm-patterned couch. He laughed. "You think she wouldn't mention that to *me*?"

"Did she tell you I worked for her after Mal died? For a while, she had a place for girls in the East Village. It's gone now, thanks to Al Qaeda's bloody hatchet job on the city's social-welfare budget, but she charmed me into working there a few years. Training programs. One of the girls worked at my shop."

"That part she didn't tell me. Wow."

She wouldn't have, thought Fenno. She wouldn't want to remember the argument they'd had when Oneeka, already mother to a six-year-old girl, just beginning to find a measure of independence, enjoying her job at the bookshop, got pregnant again. The argument took place after Fenno paid for the abortion. Foolishly, he told Lucinda. Foolishly, after the brusque end to their phone conversation (*I'm sorry, but it's too late now anyway. . . . So you never considered asking me, never considered the life of that baby, not just a child but a sibling?*), he never wrote to salvage their friendship—in part because anything that distanced him further from Mal could only make life more harmonious with Walter.

"The Catholic thing—I can't imagine growing up with that," said Kit. "Lucinda doesn't talk about religion. I guess she respects that my mother raised me without church. Or maybe she's just biding her time."

"No," said Fenno. "You'll never catch her soliciting souls for the Vatican. She's one of those Catholics who's privately ashamed of the pope, the way you might be ashamed of a father who has a violent hobby. It's just that she saw me as somebody loyal to her mission. Most of the time I was. Or I was when it looked easy. I don't know. Maybe you just can't stay friends with someone you feel has good reason not to forgive you."

Once again, their glasses were empty. Fenno had drunk too much and said too much, and already he knew his punishment: no matter how much water he drank, he was destined to wake with a searing headache.

"I should take you to your room. I didn't even ask if you were hungry. Walter bought some special cheese and sausages."

"Food was the last thing on my mind. The scotch—that was essential."

They took their glasses to the kitchen. Fenno had turned out all the lights except the one above the cooker. He was shocked at the hour displayed on the clock. He whispered, "Sleep in, please."

"Oh, but the children won't. It's fine. I need all the waking time I can get with you—and Lucinda, when she gets here."

"And your mother."

"My mother," said Kit. "Well, that's something else. She's been very unhappy about all this, but she's trying to accept it. I'd better tell you now that I more or less bullied her into coming."

Kit's mother would be the girl pictured, with Mal, on the newsletter from that music camp, which Fenno had found with the photos of Kit as a boy; with the letters he had exerted all his willpower not to read. They remained in the box he had hidden away in the commotion after Mal's death. He told himself that to give the box to Lucinda could only cause her further pain. In a way, it contained only clues, not hard evidence, but looking at them, anyone but the most willfully daft would have surmised that the boy was Mal's son and that Mal's mother had played a part in whatever drama surrounded his birth. Other, collaborative clues emerged when Fenno remembered oblique remarks that Mal had made about parenthood, about the perils of first love. To this day, that box sits beneath another of comparable size which contains a pair of dress shoes Fenno hardly ever wears.

He led Kit upstairs. On the way to the guest room, he pointed at the alcove just under the peak of the roof, at the top of a short ladder. "Your children are up there."

"That was part of the Underground Railroad?"

"Oh, I rather doubt it. Walter makes up fanciful things he considers entertaining but harmless."

They laughed, quietly. Fenno went into the bedroom up front, where Walter slept on his side of the mattress, smaller than the one they shared at home. Voices still echoed down on Commercial—happy voices, ribald voices; whispering, yodeling: visitors to the town who, like Kit, wanted to stay awake for as much of their time here as they possibly could. It was time outside of time.

Walter spoons the salads into their hosts' colorful Italian dishes. "Praise be! You remembered to buy some genuine meat this time," he teases Fenno as he fans out slices of gingered pork loin on a platter. Walter maintains that most people eat greens and vegetables only as a bargain with themselves for eating real meat (poultry a distant consolation prize). "And most normal people will choose steak over chocolate any day. Though I can testify with confidence that the ones who order steak just about always order chocolate to follow." He maintains that the fundamentally carnivorous nature of mankind is the number one reason that his restaurant has flourished, outlasting every food fad of the past twenty years. ("Do you remember the cilantro epidemic? The blackened catfish era? Blackened *everything*? Egad.")

Kit and his children are on the lawn. Kit and Will toss a football back and forth; Fanny is counting and classifying her beach stones on a chaise longue.

"Set the table for everyone," says Walter. "Heard from the ladies yet?"

"Lucinda's on the half-six ferry from Boston. I'll meet her at the pier."

"Do not even think of taking the car through that tsunami of tourists."

"I'm not daft."

"Jury's out on that till Monday, buster."

Felicity clings to Fenno's shoulder as he shuttles plates and cutlery to the table against the kitchen window; the house is too small for a dedicated dining room. He feels the prick of her talons on his skin through his shirt. As soon as he comes to a standstill, surveying the table to see what he's missed, she begins grooming herself, stropping her wing feathers one by one through her beak.

"Shall we discuss the forecast?" Walter says.

"I'm afraid to ask. Are we doomed to indoor fun?"

"We might be doomed to basement fun. Though all we've got here is a dirt crawl space filled with spiders. A monster storm is due to wallop us tomorrow night. Unless it doesn't. It's one of those will-she-won't-she tropical divas. Either way, rain and more rain. Worst case, Cape Cod becomes the next Atlantis."

Fenno looks at Walter. "You're having me on."

Walter shrugs. "You know what drama queens the weatherpeople are. But no, sweetie, I am not making this up. Want me to show you on my laptop?"

"No, I don't." To Fenno's secret delight, there is no television in this house, and though there's Wi-Fi, he refused to bring his own computer. Walter, a neophyte devotee of Facebook, would probably rather have left Fenno behind than forsake his brand-new MacBook.

"It's one of those fast-moving storms, so it might be violent but brief." Walter yanks the cork from a bottle of wine. "Like sex with a few scoundrels I knew in the olden days."

Fenno gives Walter a sour glance. "Please mind the visiting children. And grandmothers. A great-grandmother, if my genealogical skills are accurate."

"Have I ever embarrassed you, Mrs. Vanderbilt? Don't answer that."

Fanny careens through the kitchen door. "Didi's here!"

"Didi?" says Walter. "Didi LaVida? How did she find us!"

Didi LaVida, formerly Donald LaPlante, is one of the most conspicuous regulars at Walter's Place. Walter would be able to recite her favorite dishes and describe her most recent escort.

"My Didi." Fanny looks at him, for the first time, with less than adoration.

"Would that be your dad's mom?"

Walter is restored to his pedestal. "Come outside! You have to tell her about the Underground Railroad!"

"I'm getting dinner ready, sweetheart. Fenno?" Walter raises his eyebrows at Fenno as Fanny runs back the way she came.

A third car is wedged into the scattering of peastone beside the lawn. Seated on the chaise with her back to the house, a woman is examining Fanny's stone collection, the girl kneeling on the ground, handing select specimens to her grandmother. Kit and Will stand behind Fanny, watching.

The woman turns her head at the sound of the screen door clapping shut. She looks almost too young to have been a grandmother for nearly a decade. But that, as Shakespeare would say, is the rub. The crux of the matter. The knot in the cord. Her smile is quizzical, uncommitted. It startles Fenno to see in her expression that she has thought about him and that she wishes him to see this.

"Daphne. I'm glad you came." He offers his hand.

She stands and takes it. "Kit is stubborn when determined."

Like his father. Though stubbornness is hardly a rare quality, especially in men. Fenno offers to fetch her baggage.

She leads him to her car. She is the kind of slim called willowy. Her long hair, still half blond, is shot through with micalike glints of gray and springs haphazardly free from a plait that's been crushed against a car seat for hours. Her dress, clingy but long, is the color of blackberries.

Fenno tries to see her through Mal's eyes—but how many years ago was that? He stops himself from doing the sums, calculating everyone's shocking age.

"I've always wondered about this place," she says as she opens the car door.

"Let me." Fenno reaches past her for the small suitcase.

She pulls out a posh shopping bag tufted with tissue and curlicued ribbon. He takes it as well. It's large but light: not the customary vessels of wine or jam.

Kit joins them, reaching for the suitcase. Fenno gives in. "All right then. I hope you don't mind that we've assigned your mum to the other bed in your room. Quarters are a bit tight. Lucinda can have the foldaway in the den, downstairs. Though we could juggle it up, put the women together and—"

"No," Daphne says. "I'm happy to bunk with my son. We shared a room until he was five."

Kit frowns slightly at this disclosure. He takes the suitcase into the house and up the steep colonial stairs. The children follow, eager to show off their allegedly historic lair. "Come see where they hid the slaves!" says Fanny.

In the kitchen, Walter is arranging hors d'oeuvres on yet another platter. "Reality-TV-show contestant number two? How's it looking so far? Keeping up with the Kardashians yet?"

"You will wear me out before they do."

Walter laughs his stage laugh. "Wearing you out is not a challenge these days, let me tell you that."

"Any chance we could prattle about the weather again?"

In fact, Walter's beloved laptop sits beside the microwave; taking Fenno seriously, he hits the touch pad and presto, the dark screen becomes a multicolored, enigmatically patterned map of the country, the meteorologist's MRI. Walter points to the telltale spiral of a hurricane off the mid-Atlantic coast. Walter twirls his finger in imitation of its conjectured path. He does his well-practiced rendition of the theme to *Jaws.*

"Sounds like you're hoping it will hit us."

Walter shuts the laptop. "Of course not. But we need to make like Scouts and be prepared. So I went out this morning for batteries, extra flashlights, and jugs of water. Proud of me?"

"Wouldn't we just get in our cars and leave?"

"As if we'd be the only ones. We'd end up being blown off the Sagamore Bridge, along with the rest of the lemmings stuck in traffic."

Fenno wonders if Walter is hoping to sabotage this gathering, despite his promise in the therapist's office that he would take none of it personally, that he would see himself as Fenno's rock-solid present, at which he would never have arrived without the igneous past inextricably stratified throughout.

"The past is never really past," said Julian, the therapist Walter insisted they see. "Which is why psychotherapy exists in the first place. Do you know that song, 'What a Wonderful World'? You do, I'm sure," he said when Fenno looked willfully blank. "Louis Armstrong? We hear it so often that it's become about as moving as a beer jingle. But it's beautiful. Have you ever listened to the lyrics, closely? The list of things that prove how wonderful the world really is? I'm taken every time by this: 'the bright blessed day and the dark sacred night.'"

The therapist paused for their reaction. After a beat, Walter said, "Well, I am definitely the day, and boy is he ever the night."

Julian laughed with what sounded to Fenno like calculated warmth. "That's funny, Walter, and we should revisit that thought. But what I mean is that the past is like the night: dark yet sacred. It's the time when most of us sleep, so we think of the day as the time we really live, the only time that *matters,* because the stuff we do by day somehow makes us who we are. We feel the same way about the present. We say, *Let bygones be bygones* . . . water under the bridge. But there is no day without night, no wakefulness without sleep, no present without past. They are constantly somersaulting over each other."

After that homily, Fenno nearly freed himself from the overly plushy couch and the overly Buddhafied office. Julian's bony yet lustrously tanned physique (his clothing almost entirely white) put Fenno in mind of some desert cult leader—yet Fenno also knew, too well, his own phobias surrounding the confessional culture of his adopted country. Now several months into this ritual, he has come to accept that the weekly sessions with Julian give Walter a better place and time to vent his frustrations than their apartment at an hour far too late for sane, coherent discourse.

Fenno hears the murmur of Kit and Daphne talking in the guest room above the kitchen. At least there's a real ceiling here, in the newer part of the house; Fenno prefers to do his eavesdropping on purpose. He also hears the percussion of the children's bare feet on the front stairs. They appear almost instantly in the doorway.

"Are we allowed to be hungry yet?" asks Fanny.

"Hungry? Hungry is what makes my world go round," says Walter. He hands her a plate of biscuits, cheese, and sliced pear, all surrounding a bowl of chocolate-covered almonds. "Take it outside, and do not feed the wildlife—by which I mean all those boys dressed as girls on the sidewalk. They bite."

Will giggles.

Felicity, from her post on top of her cage, chuckles in response.

After the children leave, Walter says, "Don't look at me like that. I mean, do you think their dad gave them the PG-rated spiel on Ptown? This week of *all* weeks. Just think how many Cinderellas, Ariels, Jasmines, and Briar Roses, right this very minute, are teasing out their wigs at the Crown and Anchor. No hurricane's going to put *those* crinolines out of commission." It so happens that this is the weekend leading up to Carnival Week; the theme is Classic Disney.

Fenno laughs. Walter's wit has been described as indefatigable. It has also been described as tyrannical and tedious. But his gentle side is worth all the bluff and buffoonery. Walter is emotive, at times volcanic, but Walter is also wise.

Fenno looks at the clock. "Oh, crikey." It's twenty past six. He runs out the front door and across the lawn; on foot, it will take him fifteen minutes to reach the ferry slip—and that doesn't account for the painful weaving through crowds (worse yet, crowds in costume).

Walter was right: the Disney princesses are already out in minor force. The sky is assertively blue, as is the bay beneath it: hard to believe that the weather could betray them anytime soon. Two men dressed as generic Prince Charmings are strolling too slowly in front of him, eating ice-cream cones, their polyester capes swishing capaciously from side to side. "Pardon me," says Fenno, sidling around them. He does hate this particular stretch of Commercial, where the hedgerows surrender to an enervating succession of taffy and tackle shops, the entire district a farrago of trivial, disposable merchandise, crystal paperweights alongside flip-flops, scented candles shelved beneath kites. How cruel a cosmos where *these* places survive yet a bookstore founders.

A fudge shop, he thinks as he skirts a line of people extending nearly half a block down from the door of a confectionery. That's what he should open: a bloody fudge shop. Though Walter would warn him about the meat-versus-chocolate equation. How about a brickle-and-bacon shop, then? Maybe he ought to have sold bacon and brickle alongside the books. Brickle 'n' Bacon 'n' Books! Baco-BrickoBookshop!

Fenno is working himself into a sweaty funk, not a good state of mind in which to greet Lucinda Burns, whom he has not seen in seven years. When they spoke on the phone about Kit, they were focused on a subject so emotionally momentous that to discuss their falling-out would have been counterproductive, retrograde—yet here it is in the front of his mind, the past somersaulting into the present, night intruding on day. Is it better or worse that he will greet her alone?

He realizes that he didn't ask whether she could walk for any distance. How has she aged? She is . . . is she eighty years old yet? He can no longer remember her age. Could he get a pedicab to take them back? He begins to perspire more heavily from nerves than from exertion.

Walter was right: he is off his trolley to have arranged this weekend. Well, maybe he can keep company entirely with the nippers. He's had the requisite heart-to-heart with Kit, whose nature—to his relief and to his chagrin—reminded him very little of Mal's. Kit is a kinder or at least humbler man than his father; is that because he *is* a father? Whatever men acted as Mal's stand-ins for Kit, it would appear they did a decent job. Or maybe being raised by a mother alone was the best fate possible. Fenno tries to imagine having been raised only by his mum, whom some people saw as more devoted to her rigorously trained collies than to her three sons. But they turned out fine. Fine enough.

Arriving at the crowded pier, Fenno sees that the ferry came in on schedule. "Bollocks," he mutters. He zigzags through the phalanx of passengers lugging their bulky belongings toward the town.

He is nearly at the end of the pier when he sees her, standing patiently beside her rolling case. She doesn't look so different. Her once-reddish hair is now thoroughly gray, pinned back rather than loose, but she looks fit, not the least bit stooped. She wears a gauzy lavender skirt and ruffled white blouse, still one of those rare women who do not look silly in clothing designed for a younger generation. He waves, but she is busy reading a pamphlet.

Not until he stands before her does she look up. She makes it easy by throwing her arms around him and holding him close. She smells like roses. When they separate, he sees that she is tearful.

"Are you all right?" he asks. The pamphlet she's holding advertises the whale watch tours; what, other than the prices, could have made her cry?

"I'm fine. It's just—all these young men . . ."

Fenno smiles sympathetically. "All these gay young men."

"They look so healthy." She wipes at her eyes. "Is that a terrible thing to notice? Because it's so much better than if . . . I didn't mean—"

"I know," says Fenno. "I know exactly what you mean." Though in truth, the gay community here tends toward amnesia. This place is not about conscience; here, the past belongs to another dimension. In the context of something like Carnival, the AIDS epidemic feels as necessarily distant as the era when polio took its toll. Even in New York, there is a growing if unspoken sentiment that those who've survived—many becoming arthritic, contemplating lifted chins—deserve a time to be carefree, to go back to acting like they just might be immortal. All right, so they're alive! Still, they were cheated. Shouldn't they be immune to every iteration of cancer, to diabetes and heart attacks, even the freak accident involving the crazy cabdriver who texts while running a light? Don't they get a do-over on the callow youth they never quite got to enjoy?

Lucinda tells Fenno how glad she is to see him, and clearly she means it. He wants to tell her he's just as glad, but he asks her how mobile she is, and she says, "March me wherever you like. Walking sharpens my mind."

He wants to tell her that he's sorry they let their quarrel estrange them, but he asks if she'd like a bottle of water. At a souvenir shop (condoms next to seashell key rings?) Fenno pays six dollars for two bottles of water whose labeling implies that it comes from the South Pacific. He opens one and hands it to her.

"Nice and cold," she says. As they sip their water, Fenno takes the suitcase and wheels it along. She does her best to stay beside him as they join the burgeoning fantasia on Commercial.

He asks her about Zeke. His speech has improved a lot, Lucinda says, but he's had to face retirement—for good. He's focusing all his ambitions on physical therapy, and she dreads the day when he will have made as much progress as he can. "He can do stairs now, but he can't even walk to the end of the driveway."

Fenno remembers the straight pebbled lane leading from the country road to that dowager of a farmhouse, plainspoken in its lack of adornment: its tall unshuttered windows and narrow skirting of porch. He remembers the austere antiques, the vitrines containing dozens of trophies veined with intransigent tarnish. Behind the house, that mammoth barn, vacant but lovingly preserved, and the undulation of flowering fields. Mal once showed him a picture of the farm during his childhood, when the fields were grazed by dairy cows and the barn was one of four. Fenno was there just once, for the so-called celebration of Mal's life, the dispersal of Mal's ashes on Lake Champlain. It was ghastly for Fenno, not the least bit celebratory or cathartic. He felt hopeless, woebegone, his heart fissured and thorny, like the stone tossed away to shrivel and crack after the fruit is consumed. And when he looked closely at Lucinda that day, he could tell that behind her mask of gratitude she felt the very same way.

"Zeke doesn't like slowing down, not one bit," she says, "but we can still go out with friends, enjoy ourselves in a private way. He just has to make peace with surrendering the public."

"That must be so hard." Fenno is probably little more than twenty years younger than Zeke, Walter just a few years behind. He pictures Walter as a much older man in the wake of a stroke: he would sooner die than "surrender the public."

"I have to confess, this break is welcome," she says. "Oh, will you—" She lifts her hand to point and then quickly lowers it, laughing.

"Point all you like. They *aim* to be noticed," says Fenno. Performing an impromptu tap dance in the street are two men dressed as Bambi and Flower.

He explains Carnival Week to Lucinda, but her interest is polite at best.

"Kit's here already, right? With the twins?" she asks.

"Fanny and Will are making themselves at home. Which is good," he adds. "Walter loves entertaining children."

For a stretch, they have to walk single file. Another five minutes and they reach the leafy neighborhood of compact but coveted houses at the fork where Commercial veers toward the coiled end of the Cape.

Walter and the twins are seated at the picnic table husking corn.

"Just please don't tell me," Walter's saying, "that you are one of those white-food-only vegetarians. Because that is but a subterfuge. Actually, that's cheating. That's called being a carb hound."

Fanny laughs. "What's a subtafoodge?"

"A strategy to cover up not liking sprouts and beetroots, that's what he means," says Fenno as he crosses the lawn. "Corn?" he says to Walter. "We don't have enough food already?"

"I bought it yesterday and forgot. Can't let it get any older."

"I like Brussels sprouts," Fanny says. "I even like cabbage, the red kind, in coleslaw. Butternut squash. And zucchini if it's not like all slimy."

"An ecumenical vegetarian. Excellent," says Walter. "You know, I have this idea that I ought to open a vegetarian alter ego to my restaurant. Every yin needs a yang. Karma insurance. So, Fanny, maybe you'd like to help me design that menu. I need to warn you that I draw the line at seaweed."

"Seaweed? Ick." Fanny shudders dramatically.

"Walter?" Fenno says. "Lucinda's here."

Lucinda's been hanging back in the shade of the privet, just watching the children, savoring the sight of them.

"Ha! Where are my manners? Heck, where are my *glasses*?" Walter jumps to his feet and moves toward Lucinda, holding out his arms. "Look at you. Unchanged in every way."

Fenno glances toward the house. Through the screen door, he catches a glimpse of motion back in the kitchen. "Will, could you please go tell your dad that Mrs. Burns is here?"

Fanny shakes Lucinda's hand. "It's nice to see you again," she says in a rehearsed way.

"And a very great pleasure to see you, too. May I help with the corn?" Lucinda takes over for Walter.

From the kitchen, Felicity calls loudly.

Lucinda looks up. "Felicity's here?"

"Yes, she continues to hold court wherever she goes," says Fenno. "I think she's feeling neglected." As he heads inside, Walter whispers in his ear:

"You ready, Barnum? The show begins"—he looks at his watch—"oh, in about two minutes."

Malachy Burns lived on Bank Street across from the restaurant and the bookshop, an occasional customer at both. When Fenno met him, twenty-five years ago, he was at the height of his career: chief music critic for the *New York Times*. Sometimes, as Fenno closed the shop, he would spot Mal, dressed in formal evening wear, rushing to claim a taxi. He was also at the beginning of his physical decline. They began as awkward acquaintances, united by Fenno's adoption of Felicity, but became, almost grudgingly, respectful if not soul-struck friends. And then one day Fenno found himself agreeing, despite his squeamish fears, to act as Mal's "health proxy" and (perhaps Mal's intention all along) the enabler of his death. By then, Fenno had come to know this caustic yet shrewd, moody yet unflinching man all too painfully well.

When Fenno and Walter fell in love, in the calamitous fall of 2001, Mal had been dead for nearly twelve years. To Walter, he was little more than a distant, necessarily vague memory, just one among so many neighbors, colleagues, and friends who had happened into the crosshairs at the intersection of a certain kind of sexual liberation and a cunning, impersonal virus. Walter knew that Fenno's life had been entwined with Mal's—but only because of Felicity. Everyone who had known Mal knew how his beautiful, temperamental bird had become a mascot for the bookshop. After Mal died, some of his friends continued to visit the shop just to see her. Within a few years, their visits stopped.

Brokering a friendship between Walter and Felicity was no easy feat. Walter saw parrots as kin to poultry and waterfowl, which featured prominently on his menu. Felicity saw Walter, once he encroached on her home turf and then on her beloved's physical affections, as a rival. She would agree, disdainfully, to perch on Walter's forearm and then, as soon as he began to relax and turn his attention elsewhere, she'd lean down and, in a flash, nip his hand. *Who, me?* her look said once she resettled on her cage after Walter shrieked and flung her off. "Foie gras de Felicity, how would that taste? I just might find out!" Walter bellowed the first time it happened. Next time, he threatened to have a tiny Hannibal Lecter mask fashioned to cover her treacherous beak.

A month after Fenno gave Walter the task of cutting up her fruit and feeding her, they achieved a truce. At about the same time, Fenno's former partner in the bookshop, an older man who owned the brownstone comprising the shop and three flats above it (one of them Fenno's), decided to cash in. He was done with the peril of icy pavements, done with the grit of city life. He had moved to Sarasota with the lover who he swore would see him to his palm-shaded grave. He promised Fenno to sell the building only with a conditional lease for the bookshop (much bargaining ensued over how long and for how low a rent), but residents of a building containing just three flats could not be protected from a landlord's greed. So, for a time, the shop was saved—but Fenno knew the rent on his flat would soar.

Less than a week after hearing the news, Walter announced, "So I'm tying up my common sense and locking him in a cellar. Gagging him, too. Why don't you move into my place? I'll even take that tarted-out pigeon of yours."

Fenno's furnishings—old on the cusp of ancestral—clashed with Walter's chrome and leather, so he donated most of them to charity. He was content to trade his passive mimicry of the rural house where he grew up (Balmoral Lite, Walter dubbed it) for life in a flat kept spotlessly scrubbed and refreshingly uncluttered. The one piece of furniture he refused to surrender was a primitive antique chair that had belonged to Mal. It featured a removable seat and two fist-worn spindles on its curved, worm-channeled frame: it was, Mal had told him, a chair designed for childbirth. Walter was predictably horrified but allowed it to occupy a corner of their bedroom, where it served as a repository for clothing abandoned at the end of a tiring day, a station en route to the laundry bin.

It never occurred to Fenno that Walter would come to resent Mal more than his parrot or his peculiar chair. They had been living together for two years, even speculating what they would do if New York's legislators summoned the nerve to let people like them tie the knot, when they attended their friend Erik's sixtieth birthday party. Erik was one of the men Fenno quietly thought of as the almost-ghosts.

After the worst of the plague years were over, a true end plausibly in sight, many of the so-called survivors (peers of Fenno and Walter who dodged the virus because they were safely paired off, avoided "risky behaviors," or had T cells apparently coated with Kevlar) let down the guard of their angry grieving, discreetly shredding their ACT UP T-shirts for rags with which to polish the silver they had lived long enough to inherit from their mothers. No longer feeling so threatened, they entered a period resembling a communal honeymoon, cherishing and lauding the ghosts of the men who ought to have remained among them—like Mal. They were, in effect, curators of lost lives. At any occasion entailing sentiment, they might compare their ghosts as they'd have compared favorite books or movies: not merely mentioning their lost compatriots' names but reconstituting their jokes, talents, and proclivities, eulogizing their truncated promise. More than once, Fenno thought of the poem "In Flanders Fields." At some indistinct moment, however—perhaps in the shadow of 9/11, which redefined *before and after* for citizens of Lower Manhattan—it began to seem awkward or passé whenever a spark of memory tempted the survivors to bring their ghosts back into the light. Their habitual guilt felt stale, outmoded, shopworn from its years of confessional ebullience.

People like Erik—those who had dodged death by a whisker, held on long enough to take the right drugs—sometimes amplified that weariness, and the dirty secret was that some of the survivors couldn't quite forgive them.

Erik's party, a crowd scene on the roof terrace of a wealthy friend, was splendid. Erik had just prevailed through another health scare;

once again, his gaunt face had filled out, his skin regained its burnish. He wore sleek new attire that flaunted his slim but not *too* slim physique. (You couldn't help looking him over every time you saw him, alert for signs of relapse.) When the cake emerged, the guests gathered in a semicircle and watched Erik draw a single profound breath with which he heartily dispatched all sixty candles—plus, as he joked, "one to grow on."

As expected, Erik gave a speech about the miraculous gift of reaching this age: how he relished every new issue of the magazine from AARP, rejoiced at the wrinkles gathering on his face, gleefully compared notes with his mother on hearing loss and osteoporosis. Then he raised his champagne flute and said that he wanted to remember all the friends whom he had been certain, twenty years before, he would shortly follow into what he called "the Lincoln Tunnel that doesn't end in Jersey." The guests laughed softly, fondly, waiting for Erik to change the tone to bawdiness or encourage them all to party on. But instead, quite solemnly, he removed a sheet of paper from his pocket, unfolded it, and read a list of two or three dozen names. Fenno gasped when he heard Malachy's name; he hadn't known they were acquainted.

At the end of the recitation, Erik refolded the list, returned it to his pocket, and thanked everyone for "sticking around—to eat cake, I mean!" And, like a one-man bridal couple, he cut a piece of his cake and raised it to his own mouth for a wolfish, delirious, life-loving bite.

A few guests laughed; a few exchanged brief grimaces. The applause got off to a wobbly start, though it quickly rose to cheering. But no one made any toasts. Fenno wasn't the toasting type, but he knew that Walter had prepared a tribute, and it was obvious, from rolled papers stuffed back into pockets, that several of Erik's friends had intended to speak—but changed their minds. They had been silenced, as if scolded, by all those names.

"For Pete's sake," said Walter as they walked home that night, "can I state the obvious, however mean it sounds? Can we move *on* a little here? If I want to visit the Quilt, I'll get on a plane to San Francisco. Or D.C. Wherever it is."

"You've seen the posters and the tote bags," Fenno said. "AIDS isn't over." He meant to lighten the conversation, but Walter had an agenda.

"Nobody's saying that! Did I say that? I gave to *three* of those African funds last year! And to the Trevor Project! What I'm saying is that we have to stop being stuck in the past. Did you see how everybody was paralyzed when he read that list? We *know* how lucky we are. Does he think we need reminding?"

Fenno said that he admired Erik's gesture, even if it came across as awkward. After all, it was his birthday, his moment to say what getting old meant to him. Walter said he couldn't help thinking that Erik wanted to remind everyone that *he* was still afflicted, knew something dire that most of them didn't.

"You're saying," said Fenno, "that he believes his illness makes him superior? That's a jolly malicious thought."

"I am saying no such thing," Walter said fervently. "How could you even think I would? You really think I'm that small-minded."

They walked the rest of the way home in silence.

As they undressed, tossing their clothes on the chair, Walter stared pointedly at it for a moment. He sat on the foot of the bed in his underpants and said, "Were you really never lovers? I find that hard to believe."

His back was to Fenno, who sat beneath the covers, a book in his lap. "Pardon me?"

"Don't play dumb," said Walter. "I heard your reaction when Erik said Mal's name tonight. I saw your tears."

"They were tears of shock. You know that whole story, beginning to end."

"To the bitter and tragic end, oh I certainly do." Walter twisted around, sitting cross-legged on the counterpane. He was shirtless, the blond hair on his chest glistening in the lamplight. "But I'm wondering now if I know all of the middle."

"What is your point?"

"My *point* is that I sometimes get the creepy sensation I'm living with a widower. That you lost more than a friend. That you lost—okay, I shouldn't say this, but it's not going away—like you lost the love of your life. Like you're wearing one of those Victorian armbands on your impeccably ironed sleeve."

Fenno's hands lay together, flat across the face of his book. "You think I've hidden something from you. About Mal."

Walter sighed. "Well, yes, forgive me, but I do. I have for a long time. I know you have those 'special souvenirs' in your bottom drawer: the program from his memorial, his passport, that gaudy bedspread—"

"I shouldn't have keepsakes from a friendship?"

"Oh come *on*. His passport?" Walter groaned. "And that relationship you have with his mother—"

"I work for her, Walter. Not even very much these days. I hardly ever speak with her. It has nothing to do with Mal."

"Don't give me that. I met the dude. I saw the swath he cut—wider than the BQE. The Noël Coward of Bank Street! Feared critic and musical genius! I didn't know you then, but I can only imagine what a perfect match he made for you. *Intellectually*." Walter pronounced the word slowly, almost spitefully.

Fenno decided not to lie. "He might have been. But it doesn't matter, because I was too much of a coward." He should have said, *But it doesn't matter, because then I met you.*

"Oh. So you were a coward because he was sick?" Walter crossed his arms over his bare chest. "Like you never got the bulletins on safe sex?"

"Walter, that was so long ago, I can't even reconstitute what happened and what didn't. I'm knackered. Can't we just go to sleep? You're cheesed off because you didn't get to toast Erik. And I know you worked hard on that toast."

"Erik? What does this have to do with Erik?"

"Walter, this is beyond lunacy. We both drank too much of that posh champagne—"

"Did not," said Walter. "I am sober, and I am being honest with you. I am not a coward. Not about things like this."

"Things like what? Bloody hell." Fenno tossed his book on the side table. "Tony was at that party. You never complain about Tony."

"Oh, Tony." Walter rolled his eyes. "I can keep an eye on him. He's very much around—and very dismissible in my opinion."

Tony was the man who had, in fact, been Fenno's lover—rather disastrously—while Fenno was caring for Mal. "Bloody, bloody hell," said Fenno. He got out of bed.

"Running away?" said Walter.

"Taking a piss and getting myself a glass of water. Apparently, my skills on the witness stand are to be tested. My veracity."

Walter stood and embraced Fenno roughly. He was taller and broader than Fenno, and there were times when the sense of being overpowered was deeply exciting—or comforting. At other times, it made Fenno feel claustrophobic.

"Forget it, Cicero. Let's just forget it. Jury, please disregard that testimony. Cross-examination is not what I had in mind for tonight."

But the memory of that exchange could not be struck from the record so easily, and over the next few years, whenever Mal's name arose in conversation, Walter tightened his lips, assuming the look of a once-betrayed spouse. Or he'd mutter, "Ah yes, the man not taken." When Fenno sparred with Lucinda over Oneeka's abortion, he was almost relieved to part ways with her. And then, last winter, she rang. "Fenno, I'm going to tell you something you never knew about Malachy, and I'm going to ask you a huge favor," she said in a rush, as if fearing he might hang up on her. "Mal had a son."

Cravenly, Fenno pretended surprise. This might have been the time to tell her about the box of photos, the conclusions he had drawn, but wouldn't she be angry that he had concealed it from her? And he needed to know why she had chosen to tell him now, call him out of the blue. As he wrapped his mind around meeting the boy—the way-beyond-boy—he wondered how happy he should be about this news. He gave little thought to just how unhappy Walter would be.

"Thank you, Fenno," says Lucinda, raising her glass, her voice thick with impending tears. "This weekend is such a gift."

Daphne cradles her glass in her lap. "And this place is—well, I get why it's so unique, and I'm not talking about all the Las Vegasy costumes."

They sit on the deck of the Red Inn, tucked inside the scorpion's tail at the town's terminus, the end of the Cape itself. Fenno and Kit balance on the railing, backs to the sheltered, shimmering bay and the spit of sand that curls toward the beacon of the lighthouse. Fenno wonders if he should have stayed behind at the house, even joined Walter and the children on their separate expedition. How easily he could have sent Kit and the two mothers off on their own—but Kit insisted that he act as their guide. He senses now that what Kit actually wanted was a chaperone, a shield.

Dinner was an hour of careful banter, because of the children's presence. Daphne talked about her teaching job at the high school, which led to talk about her own years in high school—the tension felt by all the boys about the Vietnam War, the early flirtation with smoking pot, the longing to flee to the anonymous abandon of San Francisco or Greenwich Village. Lucinda chimed in about how, when she was in high school, World War II had the boys tumbling over one another to enlist—how she sometimes felt that her husband's political career was, indirectly, his way of compensating for having stayed home, "failing" to serve his country.

Lucinda asked the children about their interests. When Fanny talked about playing the flute, Daphne interrupted to talk about the music program at her high school. Through the entire meal, Kit was virtually silent. Fenno saw him watching his mother and his rediscovered grandmother sidestep any subject that brought them too close to Mal. Once, when Lucinda hinted at her long-ago acquaintance with Daphne ("I was so worried you'd give up your cello"), Kit spoke up quickly, warningly, about how the music gene had skipped him. The children, however, were far more interested in the food—especially the two pies lurking on the counter—than in the adults' conversation.

Finally, when their forks were poised over plates piled with both kinds of pie, and two flavors of ice cream, Walter pointed at each of them and said, "Hold on. Are you saving space for fudge? Because that is a must when you're in Ptown, my friends. And after dinner is when the sights are truly worth seeing. We have a tour that starts in about fifteen minutes."

Keeping up his part of the pact with a grace that impressed Fenno (and was clearly meant to do so), Walter enlisted the children to help him load the dishwasher, then herded them out the door. "I promise not to sell them to the first buyer," he said to Kit while Will and Fanny went in search of sweaters. "They're awfully cute and will fetch a high price, so I'll be choosy." Nervously, Kit laughed.

The shallow chitchat continued as the four remaining adults

walked west, peeking through hedgerows to admire other houses en route to the inn.

But now they are seated, no children to eavesdrop, and though the deck is crowded, strangers shoulder to shoulder, there is an unsettling privacy within the tight square they compose. Fenno looks up and notes (also unsettling) that the stars are not on display; clouds have moved in, lowering the sky. The air is cool yet dense. An occasional gust of wind carries a napkin or a cocktail straw onto the sand between the deck and the lapping tongue of the bay.

"Daphne, I need to say a few things right now, before I lose my nerve." Lucinda's voice quavers. "Thank you for coming. I know this isn't easy. You did such an astonishing job of raising this boy—excuse me, Kit, if I can't quite grasp that you're a man. A father, too. Which Malachy couldn't face. He . . . fell down on that. Daphne, that was hardest on you, I know. I prayed for you every day."

"Please," says Daphne. "That's all so far behind us. Let's leave it there. I'm here for Kit. This is what he seems to want."

Fenno notes the chill of that *seems*. He can see that Kit notes it, too.

"Mom, I get why you didn't tell me, didn't want to tell me, and I'm sorry that I pushed you. Except that I'm not sorry I know about Mal. Made the connection to his family." The look Kit gives Lucinda reminds Fenno that they have met before now.

"How I wish you could have known him," Lucinda says.

Daphne gazes fixedly between the two men, out at the water.

Fenno says to Kit, "He would have been fascinated by your study of Eskimo art. He'd have been keen to grill you about it if he were with us now."

"But you realize," Daphne says, "if he could actually be here, with us—if he'd lived that long, maybe hadn't been ill in the first place—you'd probably never have known him, Fenno. From what I understand."

"Maybe he would have looked for me, long before now," says Kit.

"Maybe," says Daphne, "but I doubt it. He'd have had to find me first, which would have meant forgiving me." She looks directly at Fenno, as if she expects him to back her up, to affirm that Mal was unforgiving—and she unforgivable.

Because the two women are sitting side by side, held firmly parallel in a pair of weighty Adirondack chairs, it's easy for them to avoid looking at each other, to look only at the men—or past the men toward the postcard view of dark water collared by the lights along the shoreline.

"If Mal had to forgive anyone, Daphne, it was me," Lucinda says.

"Hey." Kit raises his hand like a schoolchild. "Can we please not talk about me as if I'm some misdemeanor for which anybody needs to be forgiven? I'm about to face having a pair of teenagers who I'm sure will hold plenty against me! Crimes I don't even know I've committed."

"Those children are wonderful," says Lucinda. "I'm so thankful you brought them up to us at Christmas. Trusted us like that."

"Next time," says Kit, "I'd like all of us to get together—Bart too, Mom. Maybe June and her family. I was thinking about Thanksgiving."

"We love hosting Thanksgiving," says Lucinda. "Why don't we—"

"Oh no," says Daphne. "No. I couldn't let you do that."

By now, Fenno feels like a genuine intruder. He looks around the deck and promptly regrets his wandering gaze when it steers him to a man with whom he had a disastrous entanglement in the city before he was with Walter. Worse yet, the man is someone he met at Mal's New York memorial service, someone who worked with Mal at the *Times*. Fenno tries to angle his body away from that side of the deck, which means that he's pressing a knee against Kit's thigh. He shifts again, torquing his body in two directions.

"My son Jonathan cooked a spectacular meal for all of us last November," says Lucinda. "I have a feeling he'd jump at the chance to do it again. And there's so much I'd like to show Will and Fanny."

Daphne stares pointedly at her son.

"Well," he says, "I'm still not certain how to explain to the twins exactly how we're connected. Not yet. But I want them to spend time with you and Zeke—and the cousins they don't know are their cousins."

"I didn't mean showing them things to do with Mal," says Lucinda. "I didn't mean rushing anything."

"I do wonder what they think," says Daphne. "What they thought about that visit. Fanny is a very bright little girl. With very astute little ears."

"She also asks questions," says Kit. "It's Will who keeps what he knows close to the vest. If Fanny guesses something's up, she'll say so."

"All I'm suggesting, sweetheart, is that I think you should be careful not to rock their world."

"I have no desire to confuse them. I'm so glad just to know them," says Lucinda. "But Kit, it's you we're the happiest to know. It's you we're so grateful to—have back." Fenno detects that she is struggling to steady her voice, not to panic in the face of Daphne's tangible resistance.

Wishing heartily that he were somewhere else, Fenno cannot help glancing over his shoulder. Disastrous Entanglement is looking straight at him. The man nods, his bland smile unaltered, then turns back to his companions, exaggerating his amusement at a joke, resting a hand on his neighbor's thigh.

Fenno wonders if Walter is asleep by now—or lying awake, bargaining with his lonely resentment. "I think I might head back, if you don't mind. You'll find your way, won't you? It's a straight shot down Commercial."

"Please don't leave," says Lucinda. "I'm sorry if we seem to be holding you hostage to all this touchy-feely stuff, but I'm so glad to see you again, too. I feel Mal's just that much nearer."

She's right: he does feel like a hostage. But no one's torturing Fenno or demanding hard answers of him. The shameless therapist isn't here to ask, *How do* you *feel about that observation?* or *Is it just too hard to speak about the emotions surrounding that loss?* Of course it's too hard; for bloody whom would it be easy? Sometimes he wants to say, *Didn't you see the place on the questionnaire where I checked the waterboarding option?*

A waiter insinuates himself between knots of people all along the deck, filling a tray with abandoned glasses. Do they want another round? "No, we're fine," Daphne says before anyone else can answer.

Lucinda points across the bay, toward the lighthouse. "Can you walk out there? Or is that an island?"

"You can, but it's not for the faint of constitution." Fenno points to the right, the horizon a necklace of lights muted by fog. "That's a stone jetty—a breakwater leading to a beach and the lighthouse."

"You've been?"

"I keep telling myself I'll do it on the next day that's not too beastly hot. There's a curious memorial there, at the roundabout. A park with stone pavers carved in memory of . . . loved ones lost." What is he thinking, mentioning what amounts to an AIDS memorial? "What's curious," he says quickly, "is that even pets appear to be commemorated. It's a hodgepodge of sorts."

Lucinda nods. "I'm up to try it if the weather clears on Sunday. From what I hear, we won't be going to the beach tomorrow."

Fenno is grateful that she's pulled them away from the quagmire. But in fact, all the conversations around them do seem related to the incoming weather. No one is disputing that it will be severe; many are bragging about staying put, absurdly proud that they haven't turned tail and fled.

Fenno realizes that his guests are looking at him, expectant.

"Well, Walter's seen to it that we have plenty of provisions— knowing him, scuba gear and torches designed for underwater use. He may have procured an inflatable ark." His laughter sounds phony (it is). "On a more pragmatic level, he found the cupboard containing the games."

"The question is," Kit says, "are we a Monopoly crowd or a Scrabble crowd?"

"I always liked the Game of Life," says Daphne. "The orange car was mine, and I loved spinning that clackety wheel. I'd fill the car with those teensy pegs representing children. Oh, how little I knew!"

When they started seeing Julian, possibly the only couples therapist in Lower Manhattan who did not frequent Walter's Place (what vegan would?), Fenno assumed they would spend their sessions doing little beyond haggling out Walter's anxieties about Mal's role in Fenno's past—and of course about the "Kit caboodle," as Walter dubbed the incursion of Kit's paternity search on their lives. To lean glibly on modern psycho-parlance, Fenno expected that they would work through this "issue" within half a dozen hours of talking, arguing, and mediating. Julian would put out the small fires, prevent them from coalescing into a conflagration. But Fenno was naïve to the osmotic ways of therapy, its tentacled reach into every crevice of a life—more complicated still, a pair of lives merged after decades apart, unprepared for their eventual conjoining.

Walter, however, was no stranger to the process (yet another well-minted term of the era). He began their second meeting with Julian by reflecting broadly on how his having been raised by a grandmother, in the wake of his parents' reckless death in a drunken car wreck, meant that at times he couldn't help resenting how Fenno took for granted the "full monty of a nuclear family," the cozy constellation in which *he* had been raised: mother and father contentedly married, living to ripe old ages, dying of natural causes; two sane, liberal-minded brothers who grew up to form their own happy families. (Walter was anything but close to his one sibling, a sultan of finance who lived in Marin County and deified Ronald Reagan. At least, Fenno liked to point out, his brother had been decent enough to vote against Proposition 8.)

Fenno knew the full history of Walter's signal traumas, and he admired Walter for the ways in which he had struggled to achieve independence, prosperity, and joy. But he knew it all by heart. So in the midst of Walter's narrative, nestled helplessly in Julian's bottom-numbing couch, Fenno found himself examining the various Asian artifacts fastidiously arrayed on every surface and wall of the therapist's office, wondering if the ulterior motive behind the display was to prove to his patients that he had rubbed shoulders with enough Buddhists to claim enlightenment—or that he was good enough at his job to pay for numerous trips halfway around the world, with money to burn on buying art. One man's midlife crisis was another man's Hiroshige block print.

Suddenly Fenno realized that here was Walter, describing *Fenno's* family in detail—loving yet irritatingly all-knowing detail—not only as if Fenno were mute but as if Walter were on intimate terms with every skeleton in every musty cupboard of the rambling house in which Fenno had been raised.

"I was pretty nervous the first time I met them," Walter said. "It's our second Christmas together, and we fly to Scotland. A holiday, a foreign country, staying in the family manse with the in-laws: recipe for disaster soufflé. Or at least a Lawrence Kasdan film. But you know what? It's fabulous. His brothers are like the brothers I *wish* I had: one's a country vet, surrounded by a squadron of dogs, the smart pretty wife, the well-mannered kids. That's David. And the other one's a *chef*—he has a restaurant in *France* and this stylish French wife and these four beautiful bilingual daughters! I'm an instant uncle—'Oncle Vol-taire' in French. And we have this perfect week. Perfect.

"Until I'm in the kitchen with Frère Chef and he asks me if I knew Mal. And I say, 'Not really; did you?' And on he goes about what a 'super chap' Malachy Burns was, how tragic his death, what a *shattering loss* for Fenno. And it turns out Mal *visited* there—at the manor house—at least twice."

Julian raised his hand. "Hang on a sec, Walter. Fenno, let's hear from you. I feel at times as if we're losing you."

"You are," Fenno said tartly. "Because yes, Mal did visit Scotland with me. Twice, yes. One time he was in London for Christmas and simply came north to join me."

"'Simply came north'?" repeated Walter, mimicking the burr. Then, seeing the expression on Julian's face: "Sorry. I just hate how a disclosure like that—which seems to me major—is like some . . . passing tumbleweed to him."

"Mal was my *friend*. And more than that, all right, when he was in very bad shape, I felt I needed to keep an eye on him."

"Dragging him overseas?"

"I didn't 'drag' him anywhere."

"This Mal," said Julian. "I take it he was a figure of extraordinary color and intelligence."

"And style. And worldliness. And superiority to the rest of mankind. Oh, and did I forget *sexiness*?" Walter glared at Fenno. "So it bothered me—okay, it hurt me—that after all your protests, I get to find out from your brother how important he really was to you."

Fenno said quietly, "You knew he was important. You know that. You also know he's been dead for decades. Decades." Fenno looked at Julian, as if to a court of appeal. (Bugger, was he beginning to care what this stranger thought?)

Walter sighed. "The bottom line is this: spouses have no secrets from each other. I have no secrets from you!"

"Mal's having met my family wasn't a secret."

"Walter," said Julian, "just what is a secret to you?"

Walter paused. "Anything Fenno knows I'd want to know."

The three of them were quiet.

"Sometimes I have this feeling," Walter said, "that he operates on the philosophy that 'what Walter doesn't know won't hurt him.' And he knows how I feel about Malachy Burns.

"Whether it's rational or not, okay?" he said when he saw Fenno's expression. "That man's gloomy shadow hangs over us at times, and I'm sorry, but it gives me the creeps. So now this business with his secret kid? The fact that it's suddenly Fenno's deal, too? Talk about a bombshell."

"The 'bombshell' you refer to is not falling on us," Fenno said.

"Well, we are in the path of some major shrapnel," Walter retorted. "And that's why we are here."

Fenno glanced at Julian and saw a spark of amusement before he said, "Then that's our work. But I'm afraid our time is up."

In the dead of night, Fenno and Walter are awakened simultaneously by the sound of the first raindrops striking the roof, less than two feet above their heads. Fenno hears Walter sigh, then whisper, "Here we go. Bring on—what's the silly name they've given her? Honoria? Hepsebah? Though I think she's been downgraded. I think we're due for an anonymous hissy fit."

"How worried do we have to be?" asks Fenno, knowing that Walter will have consulted every online weather maven, every satellite photo of the aerial maelstrom approaching.

"The backshore will get the worst of it, but first thing tomorrow we should close the shutters up here."

They listen for a few seconds. The wind is competing with the rain.

"How are you weathering the human storm?" whispers Fenno.

"I'm an oak tree," says Walter. "Creaky, but standing. Or maybe the eye is passing over. Maybe I should be bracing myself."

Something metallic careens loudly down the street: the lid to a dustbin; a hubcap. Once it's passed, Fenno can discern the sound of waves breaking at the rim of the bay, behind the houses on the water side of Commercial.

"I'm having a hard time keeping track of who's related to whom and how," says Walter.

"Five people, four generations. Not easy."

"Insane."

"I'll be relieved when they're gone," says Fenno.

Walter shifts onto his side, facing Fenno on the snug mattress. "Och, ye're not keen on the instant rellies, lad?" Apparently he can whisper even with a burr.

Fenno suppresses a laugh.

"Or maybe you'd prefer them à la carte," Walter says.

"The notion was bringing them together."

"A good pair of kids. You're the surrogate grandfather, aren't you?"

"I'd say you've poached that role, and please run with it," says Fenno, "but I don't think we should be discussing this, even in a whisper, even in the middle of the night. This house is all ears."

"All cracks and crevices, you mean."

The same thought occurs to both of them.

"Have you spotted buckets anywhere?" says Walter.

"If nothing else, we have a multitude of beach towels."

"And a dryer."

"If the power holds."

Walter rests a hand on Fenno's chest. "Well, at least it's not our house, if it blows away."

When Fenno wakes again, he can hear at once that everybody else is up. Walter must have closed and latched all the inside shutters on the second story; this is why Fenno slept late. The bedroom, lit only by chinks of light between the slats, is gloomy. Trees groan, the rain sounds as if it's roaring through a sluice rather than falling from the sky, and thunder resounds in the distance.

Downstairs, Daphne calls out, "Right foot, red! . . . Left hand, blue! . . . Right foot, red—no, a different red!" The children hoot and giggle.

Fenno sits on the edge of the bed, bending forward so as not to strike his head on the dormered ceiling. He snaps on a lamp. It's half nine, and they are, without a doubt, being pounded by a tempest. Whether or not it merits a given name hardly seems germane.

Walter comes into the room. "Don't scold me. I let you sleep in.

Those children—did I call them charming? They were bouncing around at six o'clock, so I made French toast. Rain blew under the back door, but I have it dammed, and Felicity was singing her scales like we're looking at the End of Days. I think she sang herself hoarse."

"Walter, don't make me give you a medal."

"Oh, sweetheart, the chits are piling up, believe you me."

Now the children are calling Walter.

"Save me. They want me to play Twister." But he calls out that he's coming and hastens back downstairs.

Fenno dresses quickly; it must be thirty degrees cooler than yesterday. Maybe they'll use the hearth, though they haven't tried it yet, and the last thing he wants to do is burn the place down.

In the living room, Kit and Lucinda are reading yesterday's *New York Times*. When they look up and smile, he has a glimpse of their literal kinship.

"Quite a stooshie out there," says Fenno.

"At least we know this house has stood for a couple hundred years," says Kit. "That's reassuring."

"Well, until the day it doesn't." Daphne's come into the room, holding the cardboard spinner against her chest. "The children need more players."

"Tell you what, Mom. You play, I'll spin."

"Don't be ridiculous, Kit. Have a little respect for your elders and their joints."

"Can we talk them into a word game?" says Lucinda.

"Fanny packed Bananagrams," Kit says. He goes in search of his daughter, leaving Fenno with the two women.

"Do you fancy a fire?" he asks, regretting the offer at once. He will have to decipher the elaborate note describing how to work the antique damper. Before anyone can answer, he is saved by Walter, who calls his name from the back of the house. His voice sounds quietly urgent.

In the kitchen, the radio is tuned to WOMR, the announcer listing flooded roads and the locations of emergency shelters for the Outer Cape. Walter has already begun to assemble lunch makings on the counter. But now he stands at the entrance to the screened porch, looking out. "Get over here," he whispers.

Fenno joins him. A towering tree in the neighbor's backyard has bowed to a forty-five-degree angle, quite possibly aimed at the front corner of the house in which Fenno and Walter are standing. It might miss the house, but it will not miss a power line that runs from the street to the house. The tree remains poised at that angle, as if time has stalled—though the wind continues to gust, flailing sheets of rain every which way. The porch furniture is soaked.

"Holy moly," says Walter. "What if it goes?"

"Oh, 'twill go," Fenno says. "Its path is the only thing in question."

"Terrific!" says Walter. "Four generations of one family crushed by tree of terror! Two middle-aged queens smooshed as well!"

"I'd say we're fine if we stay at the back of the house," says Fenno.

"Oh my God, are we going to end up sleeping on the floor of some high-school gym? 'Refugee' is not in my repertoire."

"Anyone up for Bananagrams?" Fanny's come into the kitchen carrying a small yellow sack shaped like a floppy banana. "Dad's going to teach Mrs. Burns. Didi's reading. She says her book's too good to put down."

Walter goes into the living room and declares that everyone needs to gather in the kitchen. "I'm baking brownies," he says, "so it's going to be the warmest place to hang—and the place to lick the beaters and bowl."

The game is an each-to-his-own variation on Scrabble, and the kitchen grows quiet as the five players begin. Walter studies the box of brownie mix. Daphne sits at the far end of the window seat and resumes reading her novel.

Fenno asked Walter to turn the radio off, so as not to alarm the children. From what he heard, no one's been killed, and nothing major's been swept out to sea—not yet—but the storm sounds almost worse as background to the newscasters than it does beyond the confines of the house. The dune shacks have been evacuated, and "advisory warnings"—quaint redundancy—to stay off the roads and bridges are broadcast repeatedly for the benefit of citizens too daft to reach this obvious conclusion on their own. Otherwise (but for the threatening tree) it might as well be just another rained-out Saturday in Ptown.

Briefly, Fenno imagines cliques of men dressed as princes, dwarves, and wicked queens stewing in their motel rooms along Route 6. What games will they be playing? Walter would find a good vulgar joke alluding to Bananagrams. In the midst of pottering about with his assigned letters, Fenno stops to watch Walter at the counter as he stirs together the brownie batter. Fenno knows that he will endure their meetings with Julian made indefinitely if that's what it takes to make himself show this man how flat life would feel without him.

The storm remains fierce through the afternoon. Walter and Fenno take turns glancing, furtively, at the neighbor's tree. Miraculously, it remains in its death-defying stance, apparently reluctant to complete its fall. Also miraculously, they have not lost power. Yet looking out the window so often, Fenno has the ominous feeling that they are the only inhabitants within shouting range. The four houses he can see from this one show no signs of activity.

Felicity, who has a habit of singing scales when it rains (sounding like one of those trannies on Commercial trying desperately to channel Barbra Streisand), has mercifully quit. The children have lost interest in the bird, largely because she does not speak, so she sulks on her cage, plumage fluffed, uttering the occasional halfhearted squawk. Fenno puts her on his shoulder when they sit at the table to play games.

They play SpongeBob Uno, gin rummy, and the amusingly anti-quated Careers. At Walter's instigation, they attempt a round of Fictionary; Will complains that he does not enjoy the game or consider it "fair," because it favors his sister's talents. They eat countless sandwiches and a whole batch of brownies. At five, Walter proclaims that the weather calls for sherry. He digs into their host's stash of liquor, finds a bottle of Harveys, and dusts it off.

"Time to build a fire," he says to Fenno, "and you get the job. I've had it with cowering in the kitchen." He hands Fenno the directions on using the flue.

Walter has given over his laptop to the children, who are hunting down bloopers from some movie they recently saw. Every few seconds, they shriek with laughter, and Felicity, back on her cage, provides an echo.

Kit goes upstairs to take a nap; he's volunteered to make pasta primavera for dinner. Walter goes upstairs as well. "Remember: cremation," he whispers to Fenno. "In case that tree gives in."

Lucinda and Daphne, however, remain in the living room, each absorbed in her book. Fenno kneels at the hearth and goes through the directions, step by step. Once he gets a small blaze kindled, he lingers long enough to make sure the smoke is headed up the flue.

"Heavenly," says Daphne.

"Thank you," says Lucinda.

Fenno goes to the kitchen. Huddled at the screen, mesmerized, Will and Fanny look as if they're warming at a hearth all their own. They do not look up when Fenno passes them to check the leaning tree: no, not an inch. Its smaller branches fret in the wind, but the trunk remains staunch in its arrested fall.

He wants to join Walter upstairs, but his upbringing tells him that one of them should be awake to look after the guests—and the fire in the hearth. He offers to make the children cocoa, and at this suggestion they finally notice his presence. "That would be awesome!" says Fanny.

"Thank you," Will says pointedly, poking his sister.

Gratitude, thinks Fenno: how often has he expected gratitude and been disappointed? The greatest favors he's done for the people he loves have by no means made them closer. And why should they? He does want something in return, though; he can't help it. He should be ashamed of himself, but there it is. He doesn't believe that sinners will be punished or that saints will find some otherworldly reward, so why should he expect any sort of quid pro quo? (How uncomfortable he had felt when, working for Lucinda in New York, he saw her lead the girls in prayer. He felt oddly indignant; what right did she have to impose her assumptions about divine justice on those tender young women who had no idea how many forms of injustice awaited them once they had their babies? Much as Lucinda wanted to even the scales, she had no such power. Who did?)

As he stirs the milk, he hears Lucinda's voice, raised just enough that he can catch her words: "That isn't accurate, Daphne. I did nothing to keep you apart. You may not know this, but for a while my son turned his back on me."

"I was the one he turned his back on," Daphne replies. "For good. All those *years* he could have relented, just a letter, a phone call . . . nothing."

"It was your decision to cut ties."

"By then I knew I'd never hear from him. And you were the one who told me . . ." Daphne's voice dips to a murmur.

Fenno glances at the children. They remain hypnotized by the screen.

Should he close the sliding door to the living room, let the women have it out, bury their grudges? He stands at the threshold, out of the women's sight lines.

"All right," Lucinda is saying, "then let me accept the blame. He was so young, and maybe I ought to have been more forceful."

"You couldn't have forced him to do anything. He'd have been miserable. Well. I guess I'd have been miserable, too—wouldn't I?"

If Lucinda answers, Fenno doesn't hear her.

"We can't talk about this now," Daphne says quietly. "And you know what? We shouldn't talk about it at all. I have no desire to talk about it, none. I thought I'd reached the point where I'd never have to. A long time ago. Sorry. I think we have to be honest with each other."

Fenno hears a sudden hissing.

"The stove!" Fanny calls out. "The cocoa!"

The milk is boiling over.

Fenno grabs the handle of the pot and yanks it off the heat. What a bloody mess. The milk has run down between the coils of the electric burner. It continues to sizzle, emitting the stench of charcoal mixed with sour milk.

"There's more milk," he says. "Not to worry about that."

Lucinda and Daphne stand in the doorway, their shoulders almost but deliberately not touching. "Well, here we all are," says Daphne. "Stuck on a sandbar in the middle of a hurricane—and starting a fire, from the smell of it."

"As I said, not to worry." Fenno sponges the top of the cooker, determined to stay calm.

"I'm going to follow Walter's lead and take a nap," says Daphne. "Doing nothing all day is wearing me out."

Lucinda sits at the table with the children, watching them with hungry affection. Fenno feels sorry for her, to see the fulfillment of one yearning lead her on to yet another.

"What do you say to corn chowder?" he says. "All those uneaten ears from yesterday."

"Let me help," offers Lucinda.

"That would be super."

He puts her to work stripping kernels from the cobs while he heats a new batch of milk, giving the task his full attention.

"I'm very glad," she says as she works, "that circumstances have brought us back together. You and I."

"I should have written you ages ago, to apologize."

"No, no. I meddled with something that was none of my business."

"Your convictions are your business. I disappointed you by ignoring them." He spoons cocoa powder into a pair of mugs boasting sponsorship of two different environmentally chivalrous organizations. "But really, what happened was Oneeka's decision, not ours. We were hardly her parents."

"When I ran The House, my worst critics accused me of having a parent complex, of wanting to mother half the world." Lucinda's smile is hard, almost a grimace. "I thought, And so? Who would call that a sin? That was back before the very notion of sinning began to confuse me. Or before I could admit that it did."

Fenno carries the hot mugs to the table and tells the children that they must close the computer while they drink their cocoa.

As he puts the pan in the sink, Lucinda says quietly, "I'm letting go of so much these days. I feel a lot lighter for it."

"Nothing like almost losing your spouse to put things in perspective." Fenno winces at what he's said. Losing a spouse, at least so late in life, is surely nothing next to losing a child.

But she says, firmly, "You're right about that."

Fenno walks casually to the back door. No change. (Is there any law of physics which would allow the tree to stand up again, regain its root-bound status in the earth?)

"The corn's all set," says Lucinda. "And you know what? I'm just going to forge ahead and make the chowder myself. Will? Fanny? You're going to be my sous-chefs." She turns to Fenno, who's quickly moved away from the door. "You. Go amuse yourself. Find a good book, enjoy the fire. Or go take a nap. What do you Brits call it? A kip? That's what this weather was made for: reading and kipping. Heading off to other, sunnier worlds."

Fenno could have kept the bookstore alive if he had been willing to move it to a different neighborhood (possibly a different borough) or to conjure a scheme combining his business with another. The last standing children's bookstore in Manhattan assured its longevity by joining forces with a cupcake vendor. (In fact, mused Fenno, how shrewd to raise children who might henceforth affiliate literature with chocolate sponge and sprinkles. Red velvet Robinson Crusoe. Sword in the strawberry-shortcake stone. Onward and upward to Ivanhoe iced with coconut custard, lemon meringue Lolita.)

But Fenno was incapable of such adaptations. So the mourning process began within a few stunned minutes of hanging up the phone once the landlord informed him that no, the new rent in the e-mail was not the mere slip of a digit.

For one week, he said nothing to his two full-time employees: Dru, a stocky poet whose Technicolor tattoos of teeth-baring, sword-swinging samurai clashed with his gentle, courteous nature, and Oneeka, a tall, flirtatiously cheeky young woman whose afro was dyed the same reddish brown as her amply exposed skin (no tattoos needed). A dozen years before, Oneeka had been a woefully pregnant teenager just canny enough to find Lucinda's haven in the East Village. Through a series of circumstances that baffle him still, Fenno signed on as Oneeka's birth coach—or, rather, as the uptight middle-aged poofter whose quietly panicked presence confused but charmed the entire maternity staff of a major hospital. He cannot remember doing any actual "coaching." What he remembers best is how masterfully he resisted fainting.

Furtively, Fenno devoted all his spare time that week to investigating how he might help Dru and Oneeka find alternative jobs. He made calls; he sent e-mails. He wandered the neighborhood in search of new shops that were not a part of the sartoriocracy which threatened to turn the West Village into one big Barneys window display.

But bearing down on Fenno more heavily than the death sentence on his shop or the prospect of turning out his employees was his innate resistance to telling Walter. His dodgy excuse was that Walter would feel overwhelmed. Already, there had been the letter from Kit—upheaval enough—and then, following Fenno's reply, Kit's call (which Walter had been there to answer).

Rubbish. It was, no mystery, Fenno who felt overwhelmed, Fenno for whom change and risk were terrifying prospects.

The problem with keeping the news from Oneeka and Dru was that the landlord began to request appointments for prospective tenants with far deeper pockets: an indignity Fenno had failed to anticipate. So when a Swedish woman representing a chain of spas offering sea-salt therapies showed up with her entourage one morning, Dru and Oneeka stood by together, alert and still as a pair of deer scenting nearby hunters, while she exclaimed with delight over the wee garden and then clucked in dismay at the substandard plumbing. Her visit lasted all of ten minutes, but the jig was decidedly up.

"Dude?" said Oneeka to Fenno when the woman left. "No chance that bitch runs a book club."

Fenno had long ago given up on mitigating Oneeka's language. Too often, her bluntness was apt.

He told them.

"Oh man," said Dru. "Man, that is a royal bummer."

"Well, fuck that shit," said Oneeka. "Excuse me, but that just supersucks. For you most of all." She meant Fenno. "You, Dru, you'll float."

"Oneeka, I promise to help you find something else," said Fenno.

"So guess what, dude? You got no exclusive on the news around here." She told him that her mother, with whom she shared a flat in Inwood, had decided to move down south—not south as in Bay Ridge or Bed-Stuy, but south as in Raleigh, North Carolina. It was a hotbed of relatives; Oneeka and her daughter would be smart to tag along.

"You want to go?" Fenno asked. "To Raleigh?"

"Hell, yeah. Not because it's with Mom—I could lose her attitude—but I am done with what it costs to live here." No hard feelings, she said, but if she ever wanted to move out of her mother's place, the wages she made at the shop would never permit that. And she wanted Topaz in a decent public school.

Despondently, Dru listened to their exchange. "Can you go to, like, housing court? Appeal this thing? It's robbery."

Fenno stared at Dru, silenced. He didn't want to think about himself, what he would do next. Far easier to think about Dru and Oneeka. He was ashamed, for a moment, that he had imagined himself in charge of their destinies.

"You really just planning to lie down and take it?" said Oneeka.

Hands on their hips, Fenno's young employees regarded him as if he'd gone round the bend. He'd never felt so pathetically old.

"As I understand it, I have no recourse."

Oneeka laughed and shook her head. "'No recourse.' Dude, you know lawyers. Lawyers walk in this place every day, buy their John Grishams, their Scott Turows. Work it!"

He told Walter that night, pretending he had received the news that day.

"Liar," Walter said calmly. "You big fat liar." It was after nine, and they stood together in the kitchen, waiting for the pot roast that Walter had brought from the restaurant to finish warming in the oven.

"Pardon me?"

"Oh yes, as a matter of fact, I *will* pardon you. If you'd held out much longer, I'm not so sure. What is *with* you? Did you honestly think I wouldn't hear about that evil overlord's plan to jack up the rent so we can have another trust-fund hair salon or gourmet olive oil purveyor? Do you think there's any shelter news within ten blocks that I don't hear before anyone else? Ben—hello? He's the one, I promise you, who dug up the skinny on where bin Laden was hiding." Ben was the longtime bartender at Walter's Place; he might have been the city's top psychotherapist if he didn't make twice that money in tips.

"Why didn't you tell me you knew?"

"Why? Because I know you. Because I wanted to see how long it would take you to 'fess up. I wanted to catch you red-handed. This, buster, *this* is why we need therapy. We begin next week, no caveats or codicils."

But softhearted Walter had also spoken to several lawyers who were addicted to his chef's Tournedos Toledo and Osso Buco Chicago. "No way to get around this one," said Walter. "Unless you want to sit tight till they evict you. Which doesn't suit your standards of dignity. For which I love you."

Walter was certain that they'd find another location for Plume. For once, he was wrong: or, to be truthful, when Fenno looked at his options, he couldn't bear the thought of what he would lose—or of spending the money to relocate only to see the shop's revenues continue to shrink.

When they moved some of the final inventory onto sale tables on the pavement, people would stop and say, "Are you moving? Please say you're not closing. Why are you closing?"

Fenno managed not to say, "Because people like you don't bother to buy books anymore—not for yourself, not even as gifts, not even to pile up on coffee tables or stand on in order to reach a high shelf." Sometimes he would go through the tedious tale about the rent, giving rise to much empathic outrage, but when he was too tired to face the scripted exchange on capitalist pigs, he would say, "I'm retiring to Brazil" or "I'm thinking of opening a yoga studio in Fort Greene" or any number of remarks that would move people swiftly along.

The books that wouldn't sell, not even for a dollar, were dumped for pennies at a stalwart used-bookstore on Carmine Street. Fenno sold the bookcases and homely furnishings to NYU students, the vitrines to a woman opening a craft store on Perry. She offered part-time work to Dru, but he had already landed a job as a barista at an independent ethically supplied coffee parlor called Fairgrounds.

Oneeka helped Fenno sweep and vacuum the emptied store. Across the wooden floor, long rectangular swaths of varnish eulogized row after row of vanished books. After a last look at the garden, she said, "You forgot the planters. Real stone. They gotta be worth something."

"They were here when I came," he said. They had belonged to a handsome baker named Armand, who had died during the plague years: one of those lost young men whom it had become so exhausting to remember. Suddenly, Fenno remembered the pavement sale of Armand's equipment, the café tables and chairs. Yes indeed, he thought, what goes around comes around—and tends to wallop you in the face when it does so.

"Dude, you are so friggin' honest, it gives me a migraine, know that?"

Yes, he might have answered, *but honesty comes in so many different shades.*

The rain fades away an hour or so after dinner. Without the muffling effect of all that water, the wind sounds as if it's been amplified, though Walter's favorite weather site assures them that it's slowed a good deal. The half-fallen tree continues to mock gravity.

Not long before dark, Walter puts on a pair of Wellies and announces that he's heading across the street to have a look at the harbor. "Just to see if the Cape's changed its shape. Or if there are major shipwrecks."

Kit has found a book called *Tall Tales of the Deep South,* which he is reading aloud to his children by a rekindled fire. Lucinda is listening, too. Daphne and Fenno are in the kitchen, washing up, Garrison Keillor their sound track. Fenno gives Felicity a shaved corncob to pick at. Even the children seem talked out, gamed out, benumbed by the anxious inertia of waiting for the storm to end.

Walter returns, stamping his feet on the doormat. "Brrrrr-acuda!" he exclaims. "The sky may not be raining, but the trees still are! The waves are *monstrous.* A few dinghies tossed up on the beach, but no oil tankers, no pirate ships, no luxury yachts to plunder." He stands in the doorway to the kitchen.

"What'll it be like tomorrow?" says Daphne. "I want to get home before dark."

"Sunny but still windy, that's the current notion."

From the living room, Kit says, "Mom, you can't stay till Monday?"

"Sweetheart, I have to practice. I have a rehearsal on Monday."

Lucinda joins Walter. "What are you playing?"

"Oh, it's a smorgasbord of baroque. The usual suspects. Designed to please the masses."

Then Kit is standing behind Lucinda. "Mom, I thought . . ."

"Kitten," she says, "plans get complicated."

If one of them must leave, thinks Fenno, Daphne is the one he'd vote for. He wants to believe she would be more congenial under different circumstances, though he doubts he'll ever know. After Walter, Kit, and Lucinda retreat to the living room, she says to Fenno, "So you're the one who knew Malachy best. When he was older."

"I wasn't his best friend, if that's what you mean."

"Did he have one?"

"I don't really know." And that's half true; Fenno wasn't a part of Mal's broader social life—or what remained of it in his last few years. But at the New York memorial service, and again in Vermont, when the closest friends joined Mal's family to scatter his ashes on the lake, Fenno noticed one woman who seemed especially stricken. She had been a fellow writer at the *Times*, and Mal's brother, Jonathan, sat with her at both ceremonies. He would hold her hand or put an arm around her shoulders whenever she succumbed to weeping.

Fenno remembers her name—Judith—but something tells him Daphne would be hurt to learn that Mal's best friend might have been a woman.

"Before I knew him, he liked to entertain," Fenno says. "Big dinner parties in his small flat. I'm not sure anyone got to know him terribly well. Intimately."

"Not to be blunt, but it's obvious he had an intimate life of some kind."

Fenno dries the pot that held the chowder, saying nothing.

"I'm sorry. That came out wrong. I didn't mean to sound cruel."

"But you're right," he says. "I came along rather late to know the details." Though that, too, borders on a lie. There had been the beautiful Armand, whose bakery, vacated after his death, turned into Fenno's bookshop.

"I wish I'd met him just once, as an adult. Just to know whether he was someone I'd still have fallen for. We thought we were so grown-up when we knew each other. Or I did. But that's how you become a grown-up, right? By acting it out first, trying it on. Practice makes perfect. Except when it doesn't."

"Some of us feel as if we're still just acting it out," says Fenno. Immediately, he wishes he hadn't said something so trite.

"He composed limericks," says Daphne, ignoring his jest.

"Limericks?"

"I guess it was an affectation. A kind of seduction, maybe."

"I doubt that," says Fenno. "He always struck me as the kind of man who wanted to be the one seduced. Not the seducer."

"*Did* he," she says, decidedly not a question. "Some things stay the same about a person, and some change." She turns toward the radio. "But listen. It's Guy Noir. I love how he pronounces it *Na-wahr*." She turns up the volume. "The sound effects are my favorite part."

By nine o'clock everyone has gone to bed except for Kit, who said he wanted to catch up on his e-mail and talk to Sandra. Fenno and Walter sit in bed, side by side. Fenno reads a book of Stanley Kunitz poems; Walter, laptop balanced on his thighs, monitors the latest meteorological developments and browses a blog about cheeses from Vermont. Even Walter is talked out.

When they turn off their lamps, Walter falls asleep fast. Fenno envies him his knack for nodding off at will nearly anywhere; he takes cat naps on buses, beaches, even the subway. Most nights, Fenno lies awake for half an hour or more, his mind, hawklike, circling and recircling his life from above. Tonight the incessant wind adds to his customary restlessness—and from the living room below, lamplight leaks faintly through the floorboards of the darkened bedroom.

Walter is snoring gently when Fenno hears someone go downstairs.

"Mom?" Kit, who must be seated on the couch, directly below the bed.

"Sweetheart. I thought I'd make a cup of tea. Or just . . . find the paper."

"Can't sleep?"

"I never sleep well away from home anymore. I'm getting too old for other people's pillows." She must be sitting now, by the fireplace.

"I wish you wouldn't leave so soon. You don't really have a rehearsal, do you?"

"Things come up, sweetheart. Coming here . . ."

"Was a mistake? Well, you told me that before."

"No. I was going to say the timing wasn't good."

A long pause. "She wishes, you know, that she could somehow, I don't know . . ."

"What, make it up to me? Be my friend? Do grandmotherly things with my grandchildren?"

Another pause. "Why do you have to be so possessive about them?"

"Kit, this whole . . . discovery . . . it's yours. I know you wish it could be mine, too, but it's not. My conscience is clear about the things I didn't tell you. I've told you before, I hate the way privacy is so underrated these days."

"I don't want to have this argument again."

"Well, sweetheart, I certainly didn't come down here to have it."

Daphne's mention of conscience (never mind privacy) makes Fenno feel queasy. Should he drop his book on the floor? Clear his throat? He could find an excuse to go downstairs himself, make it clear that others are still awake, too.

"Can I ask you one thing, Mom?"

"You'll ask me anyway, won't you?"

"Did you honestly know he was dead, or did you just say that so I wouldn't think he'd abandoned me, to spare my feelings?"

Fenno surrenders to eavesdropping full on. Is there anything here he *shouldn't* know? Walter lets out a peal of a snore; that should alert mother and son to the intimate nature of the quarters they're sharing. But no.

"I wish I were angry enough about all this not to answer you," Daphne says. "But I'm more worn out than anything else. So the answer is that by the time I told you he was dead, it was true. And I did know it. Would I have told you that anyway?" She laughs quietly. "Well, maybe."

"How did you know?"

"Oh, you can thank your stepfather, I guess. You know how resistant I am to everything high-tech, but back when the school got Internet access, he convinced me that we had to have it at home, too. He told me I'd learn to love it as a 'research tool' for my classes—that it would even let me buy cheaper sheet music for chorus and band. He showed me how I could find handy-dandy bios of all the composers, print them out instead of making photocopies at the library. . . . And now your sister is getting me hooked on Facebook. It's the only way I get to see photos of the baby."

"But my father—"

"Yes, Kit," she says drily. "Yes, I'm getting to that. Because, you know, from about the time I married Jasper . . . about then, I learned that Malachy wrote for the *New York Times.* I saw his byline. Someone always left the big, fat Sunday *Times* in the teachers' lounge. It got so I'd look for his articles. After a while, I didn't find them anymore. I was relieved to stop looking.

"Anyway, there I am, years later, Bart showing me how I can find out about anyone and anything on the computer in our own house. It felt like having my own personal satellite for spying on the world."

Or a personal insomniac listening through the floorboards.

Another pause, until Kit says, "You Googled him."

"Of course I did. I even saw a picture of him at a party somewhere. A society party at Lincoln Center, somewhere like that. Which was spooky. Because a minute later I read his obituary. It was old by then. So the answer is yes, Kit, I told you the *truth*."

"I'm sorry."

"Aren't we all sorry? Isn't that what everybody keeps saying all the time, now that we're a newly united family?"

"Mom."

"Well, now I really am tired, Kit." Her voice moves slightly. She must have stood. "Listen, sweetheart, I respect you for doing what you had to do. I really do. And I tried to be a part of it, this reunion. Maybe if I were a more selfless mother, I'd embrace it all—Lucinda, her family, Malachy's siblings. But can I imagine meeting these people? Being looked over as the girl who might have trapped him into a shotgun marriage?"

"But you didn't! And nobody'd be looking at you like that! I've met Christina and Jonathan and *their* families, and Mom, you'd like them. . . . And they'd like you. They would."

"That's a sweet thought. I appreciate it."

"Oh, Mom."

"Let me go home and give it all time. You know how I am, Kit. I work things out in my own good time. It's like rehearsing a piece. Takes me a while to get it right. A lot of that work I have to do alone."

Her voice is at the foot of the stairs when she says, "Good night, Kitten."

"Night, Mom."

Fenno hears Daphne climb the stairs, run water in the bathroom, and then he hears the creaking of the ladder to the alcove where the children are sleeping.

Sun floods the house, adamantly, staking a claim. This time, Fenno is the first one up. He goes straight to the kitchen and, before filling the kettle, looks outside. The tree hasn't budged, though the wind continues to agitate its boughs. Fenno will call the police department; something must be done to avert its inevitable fall. But first, tea. And, for the others, coffee.

He uncovers Felicity's cage and ferries her to his shoulder. She nudges his neck with her beak, mutters in his ear what Walter calls her cranky nothings.

After emptying the dishwasher, he lines up cereal boxes, counts out bowls and spoons. Or did Walter promise pancakes? He is checking on ingredients when Lucinda's greeting startles him. Felicity utters a sharp scold.

"Hello, you empress, you," Lucinda says to the parrot, but her hands are at her sides. She hasn't asked to hold or even touch her son's bird; no doubt she remembers the rivalrous nips Felicity gave to anyone venturing too close to Mal.

"Heavens, you're looking snappy," says Fenno. While he's thrown a feed bag of a jumper over flannel bottoms, Lucinda is dressed for the outside world, in a cotton dress with sandals. She wears lipstick and pearl earrings.

"Can I ask you," she says, "if there's a Catholic church in town?"

"Goodness." Certainly he's seen churches, but, heathen that he is, Fenno hasn't noticed their denominational flavors. "Consult the telephone book?"

"Never mind. There are whole weeks these days when I go without Mass. I just wondered. Habit." She sits at the table. "Speaking of which, I'd love a cup of that tea."

While he's filling a second mug, she says, "You'll be glad when this weekend's over."

He carries their tea to the table. "Mostly I'm glad the storm is over."

"Walter tells me you've closed your shop. I'm so sorry. It was such a wonderful place . . . just to be. So tranquil."

"Yes," he says. " 'Twas." He recalls the many times he and Lucinda sat together like this, over tea, in Mal's kitchen while Mal slept in his bedroom. There was a period of two or three months, at the very end, when Lucinda and Fenno overlapped a good deal—and Mal slept a good deal. They would speak surprisingly little about Mal, less about his illness. Fenno remembers how easy it was, after a time, to be silent along with Lucinda, as they are now. They sip carefully, faces down, letting the steam penetrate their skin.

He appreciates, too, that she doesn't ask him if he'll be "all right." (What if he said, to the many people who make such inquiries, that he just might not?) She doesn't make him spume forth a righteous indictment of Amazon or rehash the benighted state of book publishing or bemoan the growing disliteracy of humankind. And that's the silver lining of closing the shop: he doesn't have to natter on about such dismaying topics, day after day, with the customers who do still care about saving books or those who simply don't want the world as they know it to change in any way.

He's lucky. Walter, who claims to be wallowing in "a windfall of high-cholesterol-saturated cash and we are not talking the *good* kind," has lately insisted on paying their entire rent (which, he points out, he paid on his own before Fenno moved in). Even if they were to split up, Fenno's inheritance—invested with minimal risk—will keep him afloat, if he's frugal, for another two decades. In a pinch, he could return to Scotland. (He has imagined becoming a bookseller in Dumfries, his hometown. The thought is not inspiring.)

"I think I'll do a little exploring," Lucinda says, startling him. "Head downtown and see what I find. Maybe I'll come back with something rich and naughty. A coffee cake?"

"Well, no one here will object to that. But just so you know, nothing's likely to open for another hour or so."

She nods. "Though I already spoke to Zeke. He's returned to his habit of waking at dawn. I think he's proud of that. He says he sometimes wakes up dreaming that he's left the cows waiting too long. He hasn't milked a cow in over forty years. Fifty. He jokes that it's time to start a new herd. Just a few heifers. Now that he's retired from politics for good." Seeing Fenno's concerned look, she smiles and says, "I'm just thankful he's all here." She touches her right fore-finger to her temple. "I never stopped to think how fast that could go. If he has another stroke . . ."

"Don't think about that."

"Why not, Fenno? I wasn't the least bit prepared when this hap-pened. I just want . . . well, I don't know. I got my wish, about Kit. And it's funny that that's how I think about it. A wish granted. Not a prayer answered. What does that say about me?"

"That you have a complicated relationship with God." What he won't venture is that perhaps she sees God for the phantom that He is.

"You can say that again."

"Say what again?" Kit joins them. "Are my children really still in bed?"

"Unless they've run away," says Fenno.

Lucinda gazes happily at Kit, as if they are lovers who just spent their first night together. "The sea air will do that to children."

"Make them run away?" says Kit. He sits beside her.

She puts a hand on his. "Make them sleep the sleep of the enchanted."

"Me," says Kit, "it just makes me hungry."

She goes to the refrigerator and pulls out a loaf of bread. "Toast? I'm going to have a little something and go for a walk before every-one else is up."

"Absolutely," says Kit. "Toast for me."

Fenno says that he's going to lie down again, that all the talk of sea air and sleep has him wondering why on earth he's not still in bed. He wants, of course, to leave them alone with each other. The smell of toast, as he leaves the kitchen, makes him hungry, but once he's upstairs, the prospect of their host's deluxe sheets, warmed by Walter's body on this brilliant, chilly August morning, makes him glad that things, however imperfect, are exactly as they are: the house and the town still standing; the children sound asleep; Lucinda in the kitchen with the human form of her wish fulfilled; Walter, face creased, lips chapped, hair damp, making space for Fenno in their borrowed bed.

An hour later, Fenno and Walter wake together, to the sounds, directly beneath them, of children exulting while adults try vainly to quiet them down. What makes Fenno sit up is the sound of a car door closing in front of the house.

"Uh-oh," says Walter. "Here comes the surprise contestant in our reality show, *Look Who's Coming to Carnival*. It's Kit's long-lost trans-gendered twin, stolen from the maternity ward by a Mormon missionary who converted to Islam. She's dressed as the Angela Lansbury teapot in *Beauty and the Beast*."

"Stop. Please," Fenno says. Looking out the window, he sees Daphne standing beside her car with Kit.

He hurries into his clothes and goes downstairs. Daphne and Kit are coming in the front door.

"You're not leaving us just yet?" he says.

"Not without saying good-bye—and thank you," says Daphne. "I was just organizing the car. I wouldn't miss Kit's blueberry pancakes."

"Did I hear the word *blueberry* followed by the sacred password *pancakes*?" Walter, calling down from the bedroom.

Kit is at the cooker. It seems to Fenno as if they've done little other than eat for the past two days. But he will eat pancakes—greedily, too. Kit asks Fenno to make another pot of coffee.

Walter comes into the kitchen rubbing his hands. Fenno sees him make yet another stop at the back door and remembers that he meant to call the police—though somehow the tree seems a great deal less ominous in the placid daylight. As Walter passes Fenno, he murmurs, "We should have brought in those cushions. They are going to take days to dry out."

Orange juice, syrup, milk, butter; glasses, forks, a bowl of sugar. Quickly, efficiently, Walter helps Fanny and Will lay the table for another meal.

"Did Lucinda go out for her walk?" Fenno asks Kit.

"She told me not to wait breakfast. She mentioned a Portuguese bakery she saw when you walked her from the ferry. She wanted to find it again."

"If I miss her," says Daphne, "tell her I'm sorry. The traffic's going to be something else. All the people who would have been traveling yesterday traveling today."

Kit stacks pancakes on plate after plate.

"I'm thinking," says Walter, "we could find a decent museum today."

"What museum?" says Fenno.

"Wherever there are rich people, there are museums," says Walter. "They like having wings named after them, rooms full of art. I'll go online. But no way am I playing another game. I think I got in my lifetime ration of Uno."

"I saw Monopoly," says Will. "We never played that."

"I hate Monopoly," says Fanny. "It's all about money."

As at times is life, Fenno does not tell her. Money and real estate.

"No games for Didi," says Daphne, taking her plate from Kit and sitting beside her granddaughter.

They eat noisily and gratefully, all of them. Walter tells Kit that his pancakes are better than the ones served at his own restaurant. Fenno wonders if the Sunday *Times* will be available at the corner market or whether the storm has knocked out delivery. Daphne tells her grandchildren that when they next come to visit her in Vermont, there will be a puppy to visit as well. She and Bart have decided it's time to get a dog. She meant to keep it a secret, but she simply can't. Their responses come loudly, rapid-fire. What kind? Boy or girl? How old? They turn to their father. Why can't *they* get a puppy, one that will be a friend to Didi's puppy?

"William! Frances!" Kit puts a finger to his lips.

Walter laughs after a moment of silence. "Dogs are the best, aren't they? I think it's time for a new dog in my life, too." He looks at Fenno. "Our life."

"Before everyone makes dog plans," says Daphne, "I really have to run. I'm sorry. But I forgot to give you something." She goes into the living room and returns with the bag Fenno carried from her car two days before, the one festooned with ribbon. She hands it to Walter. "Just to say thank you."

"Completely unnecessary, but who doesn't love presents?" He holds the bag in his lap and reaches inside.

"I wish I could say that I made it, but I'm not the crafty type," she says. "Never had time for things like knitting and quilting. I don't know how anyone does."

Walter pulls something white from the bag, a fabric something, peppered with black squiggles. He murmurs appreciatively. "Delicious." He holds it against his cheek. "A blanket. *Feel* this," he says to Fenno.

Fenno is standing, about to offer tea. He sets down the pot and takes the blanket. It's exquisitely, expensively soft: white cashmere patterned with a design that becomes, as Fenno unfolds it, careful to keep it away from the table, a musical score. "How lovely. How unusual. Is it . . . actual music?"

"Mozart," says Daphne. "*A Little Night Music.* Corny, I know. It's not the piece that matters. I just love the idea of wrapping oneself in music on a cold night. Silly not to think of it last night, when we were huddled by the fire."

It's a generous house gift, surely more expensive than several bottles of decent wine. Fenno wonders if there is an element of guilt in her extravagance, a hint of what she knew she would not be able to give. It also reminds him of the gift that he's brought from New York for Kit—which he will present to him, tactfully, once his mother has left; also, once Lucinda returns.

Wind rattles the windows. Sunlight swells and dims repeatedly as a few tattered clouds fly north, stragglers orphaned by the mother storm.

"Now," says Daphne, "it really is time to say my good-byes."

The rest of them follow her out to her car. Kit looks as if he wants to say something to her, but he is silent.

"Can we help name the dog?" Fanny asks her grandmother.

"I'll certainly consult you both," says Daphne. She holds the twins against her, an arm around each. "Oh, Will, not long and you'll be taller than me."

Walter tells her how to get back to Route 6. Kit hugs her, closes her door after she's fastened her seat belt, and tells her to drive safely. He directs her as she backs the car through the gap in the hedgerow; the tourists have emerged from hiding and are once again wandering the town in hapless droves.

"Do you like books?" Walter says to the children. "I mean, lots of books? Books galore?"

"Yes," says Fanny. "Definitely."

"Some books are okay. Books about wars and presidents," says Will.

"So I found out," Walter says, "that there's a giant library sale in Wellfleet, which isn't far away. I say we head down there, check it out, have lunch at this great sandwich shop, then come back and find out if we still have a beach."

"Where would the beach go?" asks Fanny, worried.

"That was a joke," says Walter. "Although interesting things will have washed up, that's for sure. Lots more of those stones you love, I bet."

"What kind of sandwiches?" Will asks.

"Just about every kind you can think of. Plus pizza."

This sells Will on the notion of a book sale.

Kit wanders back from the street. "I wish she'd waited."

Fenno wants to tell Kit that she was generous enough, to remind him how hard it must be to share a grown child with a grandmother who shows up like some sort of religious apparition—and then, unlike an apparition, sticks around.

But where is that grandmother?

"What time did she depart on her adventure?" asks Fenno.

"An hour and a half ago. Maybe two."

"Perhaps she found a church after all."

"How about," says Walter, "Fanny, Will, and I strike out on our own adventure while you two clean up the kitchen. How many times have we cleaned up that kitchen? I'm leaning toward paper plates from now on, however eco-hostile and déclassé."

Kit hesitates. "You're sure?"

"Absolutely," says Walter. "And I need to get out of here. Does anybody else have a virulent case of cabin fever?"

Kit takes the children inside to apply sunscreen and use the bathroom. He gives them the parental homily on Walter's absolute authority and then makes sure they buckle their seat belts in the back of Walter and Fenno's rental car.

"Modern parenting," Kit says to Fenno as they wave the expedition off, "emphasizes just what a servant you are to your kids. On the other hand, having them captive in a backseat means you can have the squeamish talks without eye contact. Helps with the birds and the bees."

They stand in the sun for a moment, and then Kit begins to pick up the larger stray branches that blew down from trees surrounding the lawn. Random objects have snagged in the privet: a sodden ice-lolly carton, a length of yellow plastic cord, and a silvery plastic tiara that winks, just out of reach, at the very top. Fenno finds a rake in the shed and uses it to pry the tiara free.

The Sunday paper makes it, a few hours late, to the local sundries shop. On the front page is the usual almost-hurricane photo: Times Square emptied of its customary crowds, lashed with rain, littered with crippled umbrellas, its wet pavements a canvas for all that showgirl neon. Fenno and Kit sit at the picnic table, swapping sections. (They favor the same ones: art over sports, books over nuptials, political opinion over breaking news.) At noon, there is still no sign of Lucinda. Surely no church service, even the most liturgically tedious High Mass, would last so long in Provincetown.

Fenno realizes that the number of her mobile is programmed into his own. Walter, the professional host, insisted that they record all their guests' numbers on both of their phones. So Fenno goes upstairs and fetches his mobile from the chest of drawers. When he rings Lucinda, he becomes aware that the ringtone in his ear is echoing from somewhere below.

He hurries down to locate the gadget before it segues to voice mail. In the small den where Lucinda is staying, it rests on a shelf next to her return ferry ticket and a pair of reading specs.

"Bloody hell, she's just like me," he says to Kit when he goes back outside. "She left her phone behind. Walter's always scolding me when he tries to ring me at the grocery and hears his call going through to our bedroom."

Is this *like* Lucinda, to wander off for hours? Neither of them knows her well enough. (Supposing she jumped on one of those whale-watch voyages he'd seen her reading about, forgetting she couldn't ring them—not even having the number of the house where they're staying?)

When Walter answers, the ambient rumpus makes it clear he's at the sandwich shop. "We bought half the library! Nancy Drews, Lightning Thieves, Calvins and Hobbeses, and everything under the sun about Abraham Lincoln and World War Two! Plus I got an amazing Cajun cookbook from the nineteen-fifties! Pre-Emeril!" he shouts. "And here we are eating again!"

"Lucinda's not back yet."

Walter can't hear him.

Fenno raises his voice and repeats himself.

"Call her!"

"She didn't take her phone."

"Maybe she found her Prince Charming!"

"That is not amusing, Walter."

"Yes! The pastrami and the veggie wrap—here! Fenno? I can't talk now—sorry! Pandemonium rules!"

Fenno shouts at Walter to call back when they leave the restaurant—though what can Walter do?

He says to Kit, "You don't suppose we ring the police at this point."

"They'd laugh. Unless we have reason to believe she's senile."

Fenno walks to the gap, looks up and down Commercial. The street is now a concourse of gawkers and meanderers, even this far from the tawdry center of town. People are making up for their lost Saturday.

Kit follows him. "Too strange."

"Should one of us go and look for her?" says Fenno, though he dreads the thought of striking out into what Walter refers to as the vortex of gaiety.

"I could use the exercise."

"Though I'm the one who knows where things are. To some extent."

Kit smiles. "Half a lifetime of marriage has trained me to ask directions."

Fenno laughs, but he regrets that he did not insist on going with Lucinda. Of course, she would have refused. She is as independent as the woman he met when Mal was still alive; and, to his surprise, just as hopeful, too.

Fenno cannot relax enough to read. He scrubs the kitchen counter and puts the games back in the proper cupboard. Daphne stripped her bed and put the sheets in the washer. All right then: he adds underpants, tea towels, socks, and a faded sarong that Walter used to dam the back door against flooding. He turns the dial.

Walter rings, as promised, from outside the restaurant in Wellfleet. "So where could she go, other than church?"

"Kit's gone to search for her. Needle in a sodding haystack."

"Should I keep the children away or bring them back? They're hankering after ice cream. The line at the good place is ridiculously long."

"Do you mind?"

"Am I allowed three scoops?"

Fenno smiles. Walter is the boy-man so many of their friends long for—or do not realize they should.

"I grant you dispensation for four," says Fenno. "Then do come back."

He takes the cushions off the porch furniture. A few at a time, he carries them up front and lays them in the sun on the picnic table and benches.

In the kitchen, he opens the computer. Safari takes him straight to Walter's favorite weather site: Provincetown is to be sunny and hot for the next several days. They have one more week here, one more set of guests coming up from the city. Fenno finds himself feeling sorry that they must leave before summer ends.

Lucinda's mobile, which he left in the living room, rings. He hesitates, then realizes that Lucinda herself may be calling.

"Hello."

"Mom? I'm looking for my mother, Lucinda Burns."

"She's out," he says. "Christina? Is this Christina?"

"Fenno?" Christina's voice—which Fenno hasn't heard since he met her after her brother's death—is shrill.

"Are you all right, Christina?"

"Can I speak to my mother? Please tell me she's with you."

"She's here for the weekend."

"Yes, I know. But can you please put her on?"

"She's gone out," he tells her again. "I'm assuming she's at church, or was. She forgot her mobile."

Christina is sobbing. Bloody hell: Zeke. "Is everything—is it your father?"

"My father's fine, I'm with him now, he's fine, but Fenno, the police there—the police in Provincetown called *here*. I don't understand."

Fenno walks outside, to the street. He stands on tiptoe, scanning the tapestry of faces in both directions. Let her walk up now, laden with gimcrack souvenirs, gifts for her great-grandchildren: kites, key chains, lighthouse night-lights.

"A wave," says Christina through her crying. "A rogue wave?"

"Christina, do you need me to ring the police? I'm sorry, but I'm not understanding you."

"I'm going to the airport. I'm flying to Boston, then somehow I'll get there. I have to rent a car. But if it's all . . . A rogue wave?" Her voice rises so high that it cracks. What she says next he cannot decipher.

"Christina! Christina, I'm going to ring the police. Please stay there. I will ring you back. This number, is that the best way to reach you?"

"I can't stay. I have to *go*," she sobs. "Get there. Fly there. Catch a plane."

She rings off.

Fenno stares at the sky, its garrulous everything's-jolly-brilliant-now blue. He must ring Kit. Or Walter. Walter, then Kit. He sits on the chaise. Arranged in concentric rings, on the table beside him, are the beautiful stones. A ring of gray around a ring of pink, then subtle green, then—at the center—a single round white stone, thin as a coin, the inverse pupil of an eye. Somehow, the wind and rain did not disturb the primitive elegance of Fanny's design.

When, again and again, he reruns the day, Fenno knows that there is nothing anyone might have done to alter the course of events. And supposing he were a believer in that hokum theory about world wars set in motion by the twitch of a butterfly's wing. Then what would he blame—the tea he shared with Lucinda? The toast? The knife or even the last of that homemade beach-plum jam scraped from the jar? The children's exhaustion? Ah: perhaps the tree that failed to fall on the house in the middle of the night, sending them all to one of the makeshift refugee centers.

That infernal tree; Fenno will think about it for weeks. Even three days later, as he and Walter prepare to leave, the tree still leans at the halfway point between upright and prone. For all he knows, it will stand that way for years, ignored. Is there any evidence it hadn't stood that way to begin with? Perhaps he and Walter simply failed to notice it until the day of the storm.

She went for a walk, by herself, on the breakwater. The tide was coming in, though she would not have known that. Living inland all her life, why would she think about tides? Fenno ought to have told her, when she asked about the way to the lighthouse, that it was impassable, impossible for all but the most intrepid hikers to attempt. Why had he let on that casual strollers might venture that way? Had he gone with her, would they both have been swept off the causeway, both struck their heads and lost consciousness, as she apparently had? No, because Fenno would have declared the expedition positively daft. He would have helped her find the Portuguese bakery, shop for souvenirs.

Walter and Fenno canceled their final guests and decided to leave the Cape early, two days after seeing Kit off with his family, after putting Mal's sister on the plane that would take her mother's body to Boston and then to Vermont. On their final morning, they vacuum sand from the rental car, pack the boot, walk through the house twice (each of them once) in search of small, easy-to-miss items. The travel alarm, Walter's Swiss Army knife, a palmful of change on the bathroom shelf.

They lay a towel across the backseat, secure Felicity's cage, and, over her muttering protests, lock her in.

The weather is sadistically perfect. There is no logical reason they cannot stay through the following weekend, but they've been drained of every recreational impulse imaginable. All they would do is sit together—at the beach, at the picnic table, on the porch with its absurdist view of a half-fallen tree that no one else seems to notice or worry about—in a state of bereft numbness.

Walter has work to distract him. Fenno, envious, sees that he cannot wait to let it engulf him once they return. Since they arrived here, Walter has stayed in close touch with his staff, but he's rarely mentioned their texts and calls—until now. Now, out of the domineering silence, he will sigh and say, "The blueberries this week are bland and mealy *again*. I am so sick of pandering to the locavore mafia. Is

Maine such a dirty word?" Or "Do you know who came in last night? Sacha Baron Cohen! What do you mean, 'who'? Borat, that's who." Or "So Hugo came up with a new special this week: sushi tuna casserole. Sounds revolting, doesn't it? Well get this: it is a *hit*."

He tries valiantly to drag Fenno back into the palliative currents of ordinary life, the balm of its petty irritations. But Fenno can hardly speak, let alone sleep. He does eat. He's been doing so aggressively. One morning, while reading (or skimming and not quite absorbing) the news, he somehow opened and ate an entire bag of crisps. He is not even partial to crisps.

When the car is packed, Walter locks the front door. He waters the large planter filled with petunias and coils the hose over its saddle.

Fenno is already buckled into the passenger seat. Walter gets in and drives without any of his usual banter. ("Everyone been to the potty?" "I hosie the driver's seat!") They cruise past the Red Inn and the memorial park by the breakwater, swing right onto Bradford. Fenno looks for damage done by the storm, though none of it seems all that dire, nothing like the damage they've endured. The ubiquitous hydrangeas, buxom and bright just a week ago, are frowzy and louche, their heavy heads bowed toward the pavement. Here and there, a house is missing a shutter or a patch of shingles.

Bradford runs for long stretches without any pavement or shoulder, thus discouraging the knots of pedestrians that hinder passage on Commercial. Still, they pass a group of revelers tarted up in shiny wigs and lolly-colored gowns, as if they are off to a midday cotillion. None of the pageantry is funny anymore.

In her cage, Felicity bathes noisily in her water dish; inexplicably, it's the first thing she does whenever they take her along in a car. She will splash in the dish and then perch on its edge, shaking herself like a dog. Fenno feels the spray hit his neck, soak through his sleeve.

"Did I ever tell you how much I once worshipped Walt Disney?" Walter says, breaking the silence.

"Yes, you did," says Fenno. Tell me again, he thinks. The drive to New York will be insupportably long.

"But did I tell you that I actually wrote a whole paper about him? In ninth grade. In English class we had to do an essay called 'My Surprise Hero,' about somebody unusual whom we admired. You know, not George Washington or Golda Meir. I have this theory that my fixation was part of all the painful stuff before coming out. I think I had some unconscious notion that maybe Walt Disney was gay." Walter makes a sound approximating laughter. "You won't believe this, but it didn't even hit me until I was writing a draft that he had the same name as me. No one ever called *me* Walt. Not if I could help it."

He reminds Fenno that this was long before the Internet; he had to look up newspaper articles about Disney in the library. He called the Disney headquarters in California and managed to find a sympathetic woman in PR, willing to spend fifteen minutes on the phone with a boy in a hick town writing a paper for school. "Do you know," says Walter, "they actually sent me a set of passes for rides at Disneyland? As if Granna, at her age, could have taken me all the way from Massachusetts. I think I still have them somewhere in a box. Think they're still valid? We could make that our next vacation." After a stretch of silence, Walter sighs. "Okay, jokes verboten."

They pass the row of identical bungalows named for flowers, right at the edge of the bay; exposed as they are to the elements—the "rogue waves"—they seem to have survived the storm unscathed. Fenno realizes that he longs to see some vicious destruction, an affirmation of tragedy.

They pass Pilgrim Lake. Walter accelerates now that they're on the carriageway, the asphalt spine of the Cape. "*Andiamo*, cowgirls," he says quietly. He glances in the rearview mirror. "Home we go, Miss Monster."

After a few miles, Walter turns on the radio. "Music or talk?"

"Your choice," says Fenno. "You're the pilot."

"Copilots matter, too."

"Thank you. I'm ever grateful for that."

Walter settles on the Provincetown station: vintage show tunes. "It'll fade out pretty soon, but for now I'm good with this." Would Fenno please get Walter's sunglasses out of the glove box? Fenno does. He watches Walter adjust the glasses, scratch his nose.

"I meant that, about being grateful. And I'm so sorry about everything. The past week. Everything. I should have . . . recused myself somehow."

"Stop right there," Walter says sharply. He glances at Fenno, his expression illegible behind the shades. Fenno half expects him to stop the car, but he cruises onward, returning his attention to the road. "What happened to Lucinda isn't your fault. You have to stop with the blame. As for the stuff before, you did the right thing, like you just about always do. Except when what you do is nothing. You know what? I figured something out. By doing this thing, bringing these people together, you bucked the instinct that drives me crazy: your total resistance to risk. Your passiveness. The way you hide stuff and hide *from* stuff. You wish you'd 'recused' yourself?" Walter snorts. "Oh, honey. At times I think you're tempted to recuse yourself from life."

When Fenno says nothing—what could he say?—Walter speaks again, but he softens his tone. "And these people—Kit and his entourage? They're a part of our lives now. Not a big part, but still. For better or worse. And you know what? It's fine. Maybe more than fine. We'll see, won't we?"

Once again, hardly for the first time in all their years together, Fenno wonders how, when he's the one who relishes literature, who cherishes books—who, as Walter puts it, "scarfs down words like Wheaties at the training table"—it's Walter who knows how to narrate their lives.

Fenno wants to say, *Does this mean we're through the woods?* But that would be too straightforward. Straightforward is risky. And if he did, Walter would probably answer, *What woods?* Or even, *Forget the woods, sweetheart. We have to deal with the Cross Bronx Expressway.*

Which would be Walter's way of acknowledging that he understands what Fenno can and cannot endure when it comes to discussing emotions—though understanding will not always mean accepting.

What astonished and frightened him most, next to Lucinda's death, was the force of Kit's emotion. In retrospect, Fenno is glad that he asked Kit to return to the house before telling him what the police had confirmed.

A fisherman rowing from shore to check on his mooring saw the wave knock Lucinda off the breakwater. (Fenno pictured a spiteful hand toppling a tiny porcelain figure from a shelf.) The fisherman radioed the Coast Guard. A man walking a dog along the beach also saw her go in; had it not occurred at such a distance, he claimed, he would have dived in to save her. The Coast Guard pulled her out of the water just before noon. Her purse had wedged itself between two stones in the causeway.

After Fenno spoke with Christina, Walter was the first to return to the house, along with the children—their lips tinted blue by some newfangled flavor of ice cream designed to flout the all-natural bias of grown-ups. As they got out of the car, Walter saw Fenno only from a distance and put his finger to his lips. Behind him, Fanny emerged in the middle of reciting a poem—or its conclusion; Fenno recognized the poem.

"'O, but Everyone / Was a bird!'" she trilled with the drama singular to a young girl hoping for fame. "'And the song was wordless; the singing will never be done.'"

A beat, and then Walter applauded. When he turned again to Fenno, who walked steadily toward him, he read the look on Fenno's face as disapproval. "So it took us twenty-five minutes to get through that line," he said defensively. "Will my witnesses please confirm that fact?"

Will nodded emphatically. "Like forever."

Fanny said, "They gave us a free scoop because we had to wait so long." When Will started for the house, she shouted after him, "I get the downstairs!"

Walter faced Fenno, hands on hips, poised to become indignant.

Quickly, quietly, Fenno said, "Something terrible has happened. Worse than terrible." That's when Kit walked through the hedgerow.

He told the two of them together. Knowing that the children might rejoin them within minutes, he delivered only the brunt of the news: that Lucinda had been swept into the water and drowned.

Kit cried out, "What are you telling me? What are you saying?"

"Unless there's been a colossal error," said Fenno. "This being the place it is, I'd like to think what I heard is nothing but lunacy—and until Christina gets here, we can hope the police have bollixed everything up. But—"

"Where are my children?"

Walter clasped Kit's shoulders. "In the house. They're fine. They're fed, they're fine, we just got back. They're safe."

"Safe!" Kit looked as if he'd gone mad. He ran toward the street, and for a moment he disappeared through the privet.

Walter started after him, but Kit, reversing course, ran back toward the house. Too loudly, he called his children's names.

"Bloody bloody hell," whispered Fenno. "What now?"

Walter was already through the door. Fenno followed.

Wild-eyed, his voice shaky, Kit was telling his children to take their books and go read in their room. "It's hot up there now," Fanny complained.

"Sweetie," said Walter, "why don't you two go in our room. We have a jumbo fan." He handed Will the bag they had dropped inside the door, their loot from the book sale, and he led them upstairs.

Fenno, who couldn't bear to look at Kit, listened for the sound of the fan.

"This cannot be happening." Kit started to whimper, then to cry loudly, uninhibitedly. He sat on the couch and doubled over.

Sit beside him, Fenno ordered himself. Awkwardly, he tried to put an arm around Kit's shoulders. What could he say? What could anyone say? The policeman on the phone had spoken as if he were ashamed of the facts, as if the circumstances could have been averted; not as if this woman had heedlessly tempted fate. It crossed Fenno's mind, uselessly, that some people would level blame at the town or the Coast Guard: sue *someone* for failing to prevent or thwart such a mishap. Americans refused to see accidents as accidental. They did not comprehend that while tragedy always exacts a formidable price, it rarely incurs a debt.

Kit cried like a child, plaintively, forlornly, without any sign that he would try to take control of himself.

Fenno went into the kitchen and returned with a glass of water. "Kit, drink this. Please."

Kit paused to look at the glass of water, then resumed crying.

Where was Walter? Was he explaining to the children? Did they see Lucinda as anything more than a benevolent stranger? Fan or no fan, they would hear their father's calamitous lament through the gap-toothed bedroom floor.

Again Fenno sat beside Kit. After a moment, he drank the water himself. Perhaps he should refill the glass with whiskey. He laid a hand on Kit's back. "Walter's with Fanny and Will."

Kit sat up and wiped his eyes, though he did not cease crying. "Please call Sandra. I can't drive the children home."

"I'll do that." Crikey, thought Fenno. Bring another player into the drama?

When Walter came downstairs, he and Fenno went into the kitchen. It was four o'clock. Food, thought Fenno. Food was the only sane, dependable option he could think of. He told Walter about Kit's request.

"So call her now," said Walter. "You have their home number, don't you? You do that, and I'll search the bathrooms for some approximation of Valium. Why am I such a clean-living individual?"

Fenno opened the refrigerator.

"What are you doing?"

"Seeking solace," said Fenno. "What were we going to eat?"

"Burgers," said Walter. "Burgers and dogs. The definition of summer. Mac 'n' cheese for Fanny. I was going to make icebox cake." He shook his head. "Never mind. Pizza is what we'll be having."

Sandra, with whom Fenno had spoken only once before, quite briefly, turned out to be, like Walter, a listener. She did not ask unnecessary questions. All she wanted was his assurance that her children were fine. She would be there by noon the next day. She asked to speak with Kit. Fenno carried the phone into the living room. Kit took it, and Fenno returned to the kitchen.

Walter appeared in the doorway empty-handed. "Percocet, three years past the expiration date. And some mysterious drug prescribed to the wife, probably hormones. And a truckload of Q-tips. Come the revolution, these folks will have clean ears." He walked to the porch. "If that blasted tree had fallen on the house, this would never have happened. Go ahead!" he shouted at the tree. "Make my day!"

An hour later, Fenno found himself keeping a reluctant vigil beside Kit's inert body. Was he asleep or paralyzed with sorrow?

Shamelessly, he stared at Kit: at his flat torso, twisted against a cushion; at the pale legs that protruded from his shorts; at the unruly hair matted with perspiration, blond streaked with gray. Who was this man, really? Fenno tried to remember Mal's legs, hair, the shape of his torso before the wasting. They hadn't been lovers, but Fenno had seen Mal naked, in the helpless exposure brought on by disease. He had helped Mal clean his own body, take off and put on his clothes, climb into a bathtub, climb out again.

When he heard Kit snore lightly, he sighed with relief. And then it occurred to him that while Lucinda had felt the deep satisfaction of finding Kit after believing for so long that she had permanently lost him, for Kit it was the other way round. Kit had never known that Lucinda was there to begin with—and then, having only just found her, lost her for good, far too soon.

And that, Fenno realized, glad that Walter wasn't there to witness his own tears, is what losing Mal had been like for him—though Fenno, unlike Kit, hadn't even realized what it was he'd found until he had managed to lose it.

He went into the kitchen, unable to bear even the company of a sleeping companion. He was pouring a glass of whiskey for himself when he heard a muffled ringtone in the living room. Kit's mobile, on the floor beneath a fallen cushion. Fenno took it into the kitchen. Perhaps Sandra had decided to leave at once and needed directions.

"Kit! I just wanted you to know I got home safely. Not even too much traffic."

"Daphne? It's Fenno."

"Oh! Hello there. Thank you again." Her voice became oblique and courteous. "What a beautiful place, and how kind of you to bring us all together."

"Daphne, this is difficult to say," he began.

Unlike Sandra, she hungered to know every detail; too tired to resist, he complied. When she asked to speak with her son, he told her that Kit was out with the children, fetching pizza. "Can you call back tomorrow? I think that's best, with all that's happening here."

"That poor woman. Her poor family."

"Her daughter is on the way. The rest of us are coping." As if. "There *is* a lot to do, I'm afraid," he hinted. He could hear Walter's voice on the front lawn.

He had barely ended the call when Will opened the door. Walter entered, carrying three enormous pizzas and a plastic bag clearly containing a liter of wine. Fanny held a large box from the fudge shop. She looked at Fenno and said, as if she wasn't certain, "Six kinds?"

She understood that the indulgence was hardly a matter of reward or celebration.

Walter led the children swiftly into the kitchen, instructing Will, in a whisper, to close the sliding door.

A storm of energy, Walter set the table for four, found jazz on the radio, lit candles, poured wine and lemonade. "Fenno, would you get some pizza on everybody's plate before we expire?"

Once the two men and the two children were seated, he said, "Fanny, can I ask you a favor? We don't say grace, but I'm wondering if you'd recite that poem again."

"The one about the wild geese?" Her pride seeped through her bewilderment.

"I was thinking the one about everyone singing."

She sat up, raising her chin. She might have been admiring her young face in a mirror. " 'Everyone suddenly burst out singing,' " she began.

When she finished, Fenno said, "Siegfried Sassoon."

"Yes!" exclaimed Fanny, pleased.

"Poems by men in trenches," whispered Walter, but only Fenno heard; the children were lunging at their pizza. Walter had accomplished, more or less, what he had doubtless intended: to reassure the children that the sky was not falling—even if their father lay on the couch looking as if he had been crushed by something far weightier than a cloud.

Walter suggested to Will that there just might be a baseball game on the radio—though didn't they all despise the Red Sox? They could jeer instead of cheer. He got up and skimmed the stations until, sure enough, they were in Fenway Park. "The Orioles!" he exclaimed after listening intently for a few minutes. "All right, we'll root for them." Never mind that Walter couldn't have cared less about baseball.

Fenno had the brief illusion that here they were, parents as well as partners, having slipped sideways into a parallel existence where everything was a different, happier version of normal.

By the time Mal's sister drove up to the house with her husband, it was past midnight. She was subdued and resigned, well past hysterics. Christina and Greg had driven from Logan Airport to the hospital in Hyannis. They had identified Lucinda's body. She told Fenno

that much, and she asked if she could go to bed. Fenno showed them
to the den where, the night before, her mother had slept. He didn't
tell her this; he had already packed Lucinda's things in her suitcase
and put it in the closet off the living room. He silenced Lucinda's
phone.

They pull up in front of their apartment building in the middle of
a scalding afternoon. They spoke very little for the last two hours of
the journey, Walter dedicated to the intricacies of traffic approaching the city, both of them slipping into resignation, well aware that
normal responsibilities must resume—and that they aren't through
with the fallout of how their holiday came to a crashing end.

Double-parked, they go through the tedious relay of guarding the
car while lugging possessions up the stairwell, Felicity last of all.
Walter will return the car to the leasing agency; Fenno will open
windows and turn on fans.

Once everything is inside the apartment, he frees Felicity; she flies
her well-practiced circuit of the living and dining rooms, returns to
the kitchen, and settles in a fuss on the summit of her home cage,
empress and sentinel both.

Fenno wheels his suitcase into the bedroom and hoists it onto the
bed. He begins unpacking: soiled clothing into the hamper, shirts
and trousers into the cupboard, plimsolls on their appointed shelf.

Taking up the bottom half of the suitcase is a polystyrene bag
containing the gift intended for Kit. He had meant to bring it out in
Lucinda's presence. He was also conscious that by relinquishing it, he
might earn a morsel of goodwill from Walter.

The quilt has lived in Fenno's bottom drawer, beneath swim trunks
in the summer and waffled undergarments in the winter, ever since
his move to Walter's flat. It's a stained-glass window of silks and
velvets, a sumptuous, glittering flummery of patchwork fashioned
from remnants of party frocks that Lucinda had intended to discard.
Mal loved to tell the story of how he had chanced to be visiting
his parents at the time, how he persuaded his mother to turn them
into a bedspread rather than give them to the jumble sale funding
her church. ("Evening gowns for an establishment that promotes the

wearing of sackcloth? Mom? I'd call that a felony, a crime against beauty.")

Mal referred to it as his "insomnia quilt": invoking the kinship of sleeplessness that he shared with his mother had been the key to her compliance. He had slept—and not slept—beneath it for years. During his final months, it had covered his body while he pined with fever, clung to the telly for distraction, cursed the bone pain and nausea, and probably, when no one else was with him, wept in panic and fury at the imminence of death. The night he chose as his last, he asked Fenno to fold the quilt and put it away, worried that the messiness of dying might ruin it. Afterward, Fenno had kept it, but even before Walter, he had never been able to bring himself to spread it across his own bed. It would always remind him of a funeral shroud.

He need not share such details in the letter he will write when he ships the quilt to Kit. Not just yet, however; he'll give it a month. Which reminds him that, like it or not, he should call Kit, check in on him, this evening.

Kit slept through much of the day on which Sandra arrived, on which Christina and Greg drove hither and yon to answer questions, fill out forms, arrange transport of Lucinda's body once the coroner's office agreed to release it. Thank heaven there had been witnesses. Had there been the slightest hint of suicide, everything, for everyone, would have been ten times harder.

Fenno was also relieved that Christina had already met Kit and Sandra, and the twins, if only once. Still, the twenty-four hours they spent packed into that borrowed house with people they barely knew (and who barely knew them) were a trial for all. For Fenno and Walter, that long day swiftly and efficiently annulled the salutary effects of all the leisure and letting go they had accrued over three long weeks (as if they were building some kind of spiritual savings account!). Walter finally lost the cheerful determination bolstering his ceaseless efforts to entertain, distract, and nourish.

The last two nights, after everyone else departed, Fenno and Walter went to bed without reading or talking. They slept with a vengeance and rose quickly each morning, hardly touching. Sex seemed irrelevant, even heretical.

Death to sex, death to reading, death to plans of any reasonable sort, thought Fenno. Death to everything but death. Yet aside from whatever might happen to his relationship with Walter once everyone else had gone their separate, shell-shocked ways, his greatest concern was Kit. Before they left, Sandra treated her husband gently but firmly, forcing him to do errands with her, play cards with the children, take a family outing to a nearby beach. (No one suggested Twister.)

Wednesday morning, Sandra and Kit packed up their two cars. The twins would ride with Sandra.

"We will certainly stay in touch," Fenno said as they stood together on the lawn. He was the only one to see them off.

"I hope so," Sandra said. "I mean that."

"I'm so sorry," Kit said. "I'm just so—sorry." Fenno heard the silent obscenity omitted in the presence of children.

"We're all sorry; *sorry* is the sorriest of words for what we are," said Fenno. "But like it or not, we're tied together by that sorriness. And I don't mind that. We'll see one another; we don't live so far apart."

Sandra nodded. "We will."

Fenno said to Fanny, "Do you have your collection of stones?" The table where she had arranged them was empty.

"I took them back to the beach. I only borrowed them." She sounded as world-weary as the grown-ups.

"What about your books? Walter would be unhappy if you forgot them."

"Yes," she said primly. "We have the books." Will was gazing out the opposite window, already leaving.

The conversation had to end. They had to drive away. Fenno directed them out the hedgerow. He waved, however pointless the gesture. He hoped he hadn't lied to Kit and Sandra. If Walter, when all was said and done, declared that he never wanted to see them again, Fenno would never see them, either.

He looks at the clock on his side of the bed. Odd to think that it's been ticking away here, oblivious to his absence from home, for weeks. Perhaps he should walk to the post office and fetch their accumulated mail. No: let it wait till tomorrow. Nothing in the post could make much difference to him now.

He lays Mal's quilt on Mal's chair. He feels a stirring of anger.

Mal claimed to have "organized" the effects and remnants of his life before so deliberately leaving it behind. As it turned out, he'd done a bloody poor job of it, hadn't he? Fenno laughs bitterly.

In the kitchen, he looks inside the refrigerator: nothing but condiments. Walter is diligent about keeping it clean, free of spoiled or redundant foods. He even removed the pitcher that filters their drinking water; upended, it waits in the drying rack to be refiltered and refilled. Maybe there's ice cream in the freezer. Alas, just a pair of pork chops, a pound of butter, a package of double-A batteries, and the bin of vaporous ice that Walter will empty noisily into the sink when he returns. He will not tolerate out-of-date ice cubes.

With all the windows open, Fenno hears the ecstatic shrieks of children in the sprinkler at Bleecker Playground. Time away from this sound has made it newly notable; in a week, it will fade once more into the complex embroideries of the city's everyday clamor.

The landline rings.

"The car's returned," says Walter. "But I have to go straight to Bank Street. Two waiters are quitting this week. Grad students. I think they knew all along they were going back to school, but they swore to me they weren't. Remind me to stick with actors. So reliable and selfless."

"You want me to unpack for you?"

"No. But come for dinner at the bar. Nine-thirty?"

"Haven't you had enough dinners with me the past month?"

"Creature of habit, what can I say? Shortcake of the day is *black-berry*. I am not missing that, and neither should you. But would you please get the mail?"

"Yes," says Fenno. "I'll go now." He dreads the hot walk to the P.O., but never mind. On the way there, he'll begin to compose his letter to Kit, the one he will send with the quilt. He promises Felicity to buy her a mango on the return. Gently, he moves her inside the cage to her favorite perch, closes and latches the door. He goes to the loo for the sunscreen he just unpacked.

Returning through the bedroom, he pushes his emptied suitcase to the back of the cupboard. Before closing the door, he looks up and sees it, on its high shelf: the red box that he stole from beneath Mal's bed, the one containing letters and photographs related to Kit. The framed label, in Mal's handwriting, reads CHRISTOPHER. He takes the box down and sets it on the bed. To this day, he has resisted the urge to read the letters to Mal, from Lucinda and Daphne. There are just a few—their postmarks before and just after the beginning of Kit's life—but they are the reason that Fenno has never known what to do with this box. Whom might he betray or wound with what were obviously secrets? And of course, that was before he met Daphne. (How could he ever have imagined he would?)

For all his protesting otherwise, Fenno knows full well that he was closer to Mal at the end than anyone else. Surely Mal would have told him about Christopher if the boy's existence had not been a deeply private matter—wouldn't he? Fenno has not lied to Walter: he and Mal were never lovers, not in the technical sense. But Fenno relives, more often than he should—sometimes, helplessly, in dreams—one of their last times together: sitting on the beautiful quilt, side by side against the pillows on Mal's bed, some forgettable *Masterpiece Theatre* episode plodding along on the telly. By then Mal was so thin, his skin so easily bruised, his bones so close to the surface, that Fenno touched him only when he required help to move. That day, Mal fell asleep and slumped against Fenno, full length: his head on Fenno's shoulders, knees over knees, one translucent hand, slender and weightless as a bird's wing, curled on Fenno's belly. For an instant, Fenno feared that he had died—but then his breathing became noisy, sawlike in a reassuring way.

Fenno froze at first, though gradually, after a few minutes, he allowed himself to relax. The heat of Mal's slight body—its fever like a protest against its diminishing—bloomed through his own, till Fenno, too, slipped into sleep. He awoke only moments later, aware that he was fully aroused, erect beneath Mal's hand. Mal slept on. For an hour, until Mal awoke, Fenno stayed perfectly still, not even reaching for the remote to mute the irksome drama on the screen at the foot of the bed. He would gratefully have stayed like that for days.

Perhaps Walter can help him decide whether to give the box to Kit, letters and all. Will it seem better or worse that his father kept track of him from a distance both cold and safe? Walter will look at it more objectively than Fenno could; more wisely, too. One way or another, it's time for the box to go. It doesn't belong here. It never did.

The clock tells him there's still time to reach the P.O. before it closes. Good. He can buy a proper box for shipping the quilt.

Then he'll go to the restaurant. Walter won't have more than a few stolen minutes to sit with him at the bar. He rarely does. The all-seeing Ben will catch Fenno up on a month's worth of gossip. He will order Hugo's nightly special. (He hopes it's the Idaho trout.) He will eat blackberry shortcake.

THE TOWN WHERE SHE HAD GROWN UP, where her mother had once taught first grade and her father's hardware store doubled as an alternate town hall, was small enough that once her news was out, the sequence of humiliating encounters Daphne had to endure, however endless they seemed at the time, were finite: from her family doctor (a ghastly conversation about venereal disease) and her tactless brother ("Knocked up? Whoa") to teachers and neighbors and parents' friends and the salesclerks she couldn't avoid forever in the shops where she still had to do her everyday errands. On and on it seemed to go, this awkward continuum of faked joy, hidden panic—not regret, never regret, she would remind herself; at least not about the baby—and, from nearly everyone around her, thinly disguised pity. People were kind but distant; she almost wished somebody would go ahead and call her a slut. Now and then, she caught a certain glance exchanged by her parents, a glance whose meaning she wished she did not understand.

Yet somehow, in nearly a full round of seasons, she had eluded the one chance meeting that she dreaded more than any other. Just when she began to think that maybe she'd be spared—maybe Mrs. Patton had moved away or even died (she was, after all, a gray-haired widow)—it happened.

Kit was a few months old by then. It was a mercifully comfortable summer day, not too humid or still, and Daphne was taking a walk through town—a walk just for the sake of a walk—pushing him in his carriage, the same baby carriage in which her own mother had pushed her along the very same streets. She hadn't been paying much attention to people passing her by on the sidewalk—often, when she could get away from the house, she would slip into vague daydreams detailing Malachy's change of heart, their fates rejoined through his mother's intervention—so she had only a few seconds in which to absorb that the woman approaching her was Mrs. Patton.

Mrs. Patton had been her first cello teacher—the woman who had seen and believed in her early talent, who had persuaded Daphne's mother to drive her three times a week to Hanover for expensive lessons with a more advanced teacher, who, in turn, had sponsored her audition for the camp. As soon as they received the acceptance letter, Daphne's mother had invited Mrs. Patton for dinner. She arrived with a congratulatory bouquet of daffodils gathered from her garden. After handing the flowers to Daphne's mother, she had embarrassed Daphne by grasping her hands and telling her, tearfully, "I always hoped that one of my pupils, someday, would have a chance like this. You, Daphne, are my true musical daughter."

Daphne knew full well how disappointed her parents were in her "change of circumstances," as they phrased it in their letter to her high-school principal, but at least they had a consolation prize: a first grandchild. If Mrs. Patton had meant what she said the day she came for dinner, she had every right to be disappointed, too—without a single consolation. Daphne had been a good student in all the subjects she possibly could; to cross a teacher was something that never gave her pleasure.

They both stopped, beneath the shade of a store awning.

"Hi, Mrs. Patton."

"How are you doing, dear?" It was clear (and no surprise) that she knew about Daphne's "change of circumstances." Perhaps her parents had sent that letter to Mrs. Patton as well, to all sorts of people who'd had loftier expectations for Daphne. Maybe they had mimeographed it and asked the postmistress to slip it into everybody's mailbox, like the flyers advertising sales at Mack's Grocery. Or maybe she had posted it on the bulletin board alongside the FBI's wanted posters. (What did Daphne care, at this point?)

"I'm doing all right," Daphne said. "I'm living at home, and I'm going to take some college courses in the fall. I might major in music." She became aware that she was shaking. "I'm thinking I could maybe become a teacher."

"I'm glad to hear it. Your pupils would be fortunate," said Mrs. Patton. Then she turned her attention to Kit. She asked how old he was and if he was a "good baby." She reminisced about her own two sons as infants, and she disclosed that she had three grandchildren, one of them not much older than Kit. She said nothing about Daphne's cello playing (she hadn't played in months) or her squandered chances.

As Daphne listened to Mrs. Patton, she understood that her old teacher held nothing against her, that she was a loving woman who took things as they came. (Maybe, when her husband died, she hadn't been all that old.) Before she continued on her way, she leaned down so that her face was inches from Kit's, and she said, "You have many happy surprises in store, little boy, especially with this young lady as your mom. A lucky baby, that's what you are."

After they parted ways, Daphne realized that she could stop dreading the judgment of others. Kit was real now; the youth of his mother and her lack of a husband were very old news. She stopped fantasizing about life in a distant city or anyplace where no one knew her. If she could just find a way to move out of her parents' house—to wake up somewhere other than the same twin bed where she had dreamed so many grandiose dreams (which, in a way, she was relieved to set aside)—then she would be as free as she could hope to be.

5

What I'd Be Without You

THE TIMING OF THEIR CONVERGENCE, from three different places—three different states—is nearly perfect. Kit has just pulled his jacket from the backseat and slipped his sunglasses into a pocket when, looking over the roof of the car, he spots Christina, three rows away, unfolding her father's wheelchair.

"Can you bring along the picnic stuff?" he says to Sandra.

He calls out Christina's name and jogs across the lot, shrugging his jacket into place: uncomfortable in the afternoon heat, but his mother says he'll be glad to have it once the sun goes down.

"Were you planning on managing this by yourself?" he says when he reaches her car. Seeing Zeke in the passenger seat, Kit waves.

"The chair I can deal with," she murmurs. "Dad is the challenge."

"Heard that!" Zeke is climbing out, stiff and slow but determined. "Leave that contraption," he commands Christina. "Don't need it."

"Dad, believe me, it will make all our lives a lot easier. It's not just about you and your senatorial dignity."

"You," Zeke says to Kit. "Glad to see you." It seems to take a full minute for the older man to hoist himself to a standing position, but it's true that he can maneuver on his own two feet.

"How about," Kit says, "we use it to carry the food until you need it?"

"I won't eat on ground. Done with that silliness when I retired."

"My mother says there are picnic tables." As Sandra arrives with the canvas bags containing their contribution to dinner, Kit's phone rings. "We just got here, Mom. Where are you?"

She's already there, waiting for them in the main building.

Cars locked, wheelchair piled with cooler bags and satchels, they set off toward . . . Kit reads the sign. "'Manoir de Mélodie'? What is this, a theme park?" He intends, if nothing else, to keep the mood light. Nearly a year has passed since the catastrophe in Provincetown, but he hasn't been together with his mother and anyone from Lucinda's family since last Thanksgiving.

They move slowly, the pace set by Zeke, but they have plenty of time, and Kit is happy to stop every few paces, just to take in the variously impressive views, the fragrance of the burgeoning flower beds. The "camp," as his mother so quaintly calls it, was established in the 1930s, cannibalizing a bankrupt estate built around a dairy farm (so the website explained). Over nearly a hundred years, it's become an eclectic campus of ornate Victorian structures and clusters of low whitewashed buildings—the "studios"—with a Scandinavian reserve.

At Christmas, his mother began to describe her memories of this place, but none of her descriptions prepared Kit for the sense of studiously understated privilege—high culture merged with old money and horticultural know-how—that greets outsiders who visit the camp. The trees are tall, lustrous, and vaulted, their shadows on the far-reaching lawns magnificently wide.

The signs, by contrast, are low to the ground and meant to simulate rustic modesty, the names of the various buildings burned into cedar planks.

"You two go on ahead. Dad and I are going to visit the facilities." Christina points down a hill toward a shed sequestered by yews.

Kit hesitates, but he knows his mother will be impatient for them to arrive. He and Sandra follow the arbitrarily serpentine course of the bricks until, emerging between the embrasure of two oaks, the vista brings them to a halt. Here is the building his mother referred to as "HQ," a turreted white mansion competing for their awe with its backdrop: the satin surface of Lake Champlain.

"My God," says Sandra. "I can't begin to imagine the caretaker's budget. Forget the rest. She spent a whole summer here and you never heard about it?"

"Well," he says simply. Her question is as rhetorical as they come.

A group of people dressed up for the concert commune on the porch. Kit and Sandra sidle through their midst to enter a spacious hall, its principal furnishings a moose head over a stone fireplace, a gilt-framed mirror on the opposite wall, and a red Persian rug easily twice the size of their living room.

"I can't believe you're here; I can't believe *I'm* here!" To Kit's relief, his mother glows with excitement. She rushes to embrace them. "This place—it's all so . . . it's been so gussied up since I was here, but I guess that's a sign of the times, isn't it? The arts demand opulence now."

"Opulence or grunge," says Kit.

Bart, catching up with his wife, grins at Kit and reaches for a high five. "Dude!" he growls. Kit has often wondered whether Bart's mimicry of teenage mannerisms (always a year or two behind the times) endears him to the students at his high school or makes him an object of ridicule. Reflexively, Kit plays along.

"Word," he answers as they slap palms (uncertain what the word *word,* in this context, might actually mean).

"Word indeed. Like, can this be for real?" Bart gestures broadly.

"Where are the others?" says Daphne.

"Zeke's taking his time," says Kit. "Christina's with him."

Sandra stands before the fireplace and gazes up at the stuffed moose, its bearded chin four inches above her head, antlers reaching just shy of the coffered ceiling. "Can we—can you give us a tour?"

"Of course." Daphne takes Bart's hand. They look like people on a date rather than a long-married couple. How much does Bart know about her history here? Maybe, unlike Jasper, he's known all the details from day one—maybe since before Kit's mother left Jasper (which she did in order to be with Bart). Now that Jasper is back in Kit's life, he can't help comparing the men. He will never see them through his mother's eyes, but he is baffled by her choice. Was Bart's playfulness, even buffoonishness, something she needed? Did she think it would help restore her stolen youth? Bart has always been attractive in a sporty way: fit, hale, game for anything upbeat and social. But he has none of Jasper's wry edge; didn't she miss that? (Not that he can't see the obvious justification: here was a man who gave her another shot at being a mother—a married mother, properly paired with a father.)

"Show Sandra around," says Kit. "I'll wait here for Christina and Zeke."

"But you have to see everything, sweetheart. You more than anyone else."

"There's time. Don't worry about me."

From the porch, he sees no sign of the others. He wanders inside again, past the moose and into another large room, this one paneled in dark polished wood; no cedar-plank aesthetic here. Another massive hearth, a pool table, and a grand piano all vie for attention—losing out to a bay window facing the lake. Far more captivating to Kit, however, are the row upon row of photographs checkerboarding the walls. They are not hung chronologically, as photos of sports teams in a college gymnasium would be, and only some are posed group shots (posed on the porch of this very building). Most depict musicians in performance or rehearsal. Kit, who now defaults to a curatorial mind-set, is irritated at the haphazard quality to the display, especially at the lack of identifying captions on most—but, more irritating still, not all—of the pictures. Hastily, he scans the photos whose occupants are attired in a way that suggests "the sixties": girls in grannyish dresses that look like they belong on women braving the Oregon Trail; boys flaunting sideburns like strips of Velcro, wearing bell-bottoms and Nehru jackets (*there's* a garment overdue for its comeback). He finds a group shot dated August 1968, one year too late.

"Here you are." Christina, alone. "I've parked Dad out front. About five people got up to offer him their chairs as we approached the porch. That always puts him in a gloomy mood. Two years ago he looked a decade younger than he is; now he looks a decade older."

She pauses to assess the room. "Are we in a fairy tale or what? I can't believe Greg and I have never been to one of these concerts—or brought the girls." Then she says, "Listen. Don't look so worried. Dad's fine—as fine as he can be. What I hate is the way he refuses to take into account his effect on other people. Since the stroke, I mean. Ironic, if you consider that knowing his effect on other people was the key to his career."

"It's too bad Greg couldn't come."

"He claims he's overworked right now, but that's the status quo. Know what? Just about now"—she looks at her watch—"he's microwaving a bowl of popcorn and tuning in to a ball game. And bully for him. I think he's gone from stunned to bored over the family soap opera."

"Starring me."

Christina puts a hand on his arm. "Ouch. Sorry."

"I'm flattered you can be so blunt."

"I have a huge mouth. Speaking of knowing one's effect on other people." She turns toward the view of the lake. "Un*real*. Where's your mother?"

"Giving a tour to Sandra. And Bart."

"Ah, Mr. Chips!"

"I think his fantasies tend more toward *Breakfast Club* or *School of Rock*."

Christina sits in a morris chair beside the piano. "Where's the butler with my Pimms?"

"You hang out till he gets here," says Kit. "I'll spell you with Zeke."

Zeke sits rigidly, arms and legs symmetrically placed, in the same grave posture, with the same glum expression, as Abe Lincoln in his stone memorial. "Yo," he says drily when he sees Kit. "Daughter's left me here as ant bait."

"Don't feel so sorry for yourself." Immediately, a woman in the chair adjacent to Zeke's offers it to Kit. He accepts. Zeke's hearing has begun to dwindle, so Kit sits close when they talk.

Zeke laughs his sandpaper laugh. "Probably miffed no one's recognized me. Right?"

Kit smiles. "From your lips, not mine."

"Lucinda called me on it. The vanity."

"A sin we all suffer in spades. Don't think you're special there."

"See? Vain about my vanity." Zeke turns to Kit and smiles, victorious.

It took Kit surprisingly little time to feel comfortable (and to stop feeling guilty) around this thorny man, to recognize that his thorniness is the shadow of his former easy charm, his public radiance—a side of Zeke that Kit is sorry he will never know. But he did see Zeke at the apex of his grieving, during the arduous, awkward Thanksgiv-

ing when all the Burnses—or those remaining—came together at
the farm with Kit, Sandra, Daphne, Bart, and the twins. Predictably,
Lucinda's absence was magnified by the occasion. More than once,
Christina would murmur, "This is when Mom would always say . . ."
or "If Mom could have seen . . ." Jonathan made a show of reciting grace before the meal. When they lifted their heads, Kit looked
instantly at Zeke, who was wiping his eyes.

Kit wonders what it would feel like to be the sort of man regarded
as a figurehead, someone voted for—your name ticked off on a
ballot—by thousands of strangers who trust you to make decisions
affecting their lives. Does their trust become the unspoken foundation of your life, so that when they forget you—when your decisions
no longer affect them—you lose your sense of balance? No wonder
public figures—athletes, movie stars, rock musicians—seem to die
younger than painters, inventors, scientists, those whose success
relies on a talent for solitude.

It was Christina's idea to hire Kit for what Zeke called the family chaos project, or FCP (the F, as Christina likes to say, vacillating
in what it really stands for). This is the work of weeding through
and cataloguing the letters, speeches, ledgers, pedigrees, auction
programs, studbooks, photographs, and frighteningly plentiful paraphernalia related to the history of the farm and Zeke the Elder's influ-
ence on American agribusiness. Some of it will go to a dairy museum
in the Midwest, some of it to a Vermont historical society mounting
a major exhibition. "And please may a heck of a lot of it," said Zeke,
"go directly to the landfill."

Since December, Kit has been spending two to three days a week
at the farm. He survived the stage of inhaling gallons of dust and
aerated rodent dung in Zeke's enormous, neglected attic, bashing
his head repeatedly on the roof's raw interior as he removed box after
box, trunk after trunk, and carted them out to the barn for sorting.
There is a soothing monotony to the work—broken every so often by
the discovery of startling treasures: most notably, a 1948 letter from
Thomas E. Dewey to Zeke the Elder, floating the notion that Zeke
might be secretary of agriculture if Dewey is elected president. The
surviving Zeke—despite his age, still the Younger—held the letter
in his trembling fingers and, when he finished reading it, gasped.

"Kept that from us? Ego he had? Wonders never cease!" But Kit saw how moved he was.

For Kit, the most momentous find, irrelevant to the project itself, was a carton of his father's belongings that Lucinda had clearly saved from Mal's apartment yet hidden away. (Had she worried that others might find their preservation pointless and maudlin?)

Here was a small velvet box containing garnet cuff links and studs. Here was a perfect malachite egg, a cherrywood metronome, a fountain pen well worn above its tarnished nib, a ceramic tile glazed with a tiger, a folding travel alarm clock, a set of ornately carved wooden spoons that looked as if they were made in Morocco or Turkey. Here was a framed photograph of Mal looking vigorous, well sunned, and completely at ease in his tuxedo, laughing, with the glamorous scarlet Felicity vamping on his shoulder. Mal's left arm was bent, his fingertips concealed in the bird's feathery ruff, one of the garnet cuff links visible at his wrist. Kit held it against his chest, breathing quickly in the stifling air of the attic. Each object emerged from a shroud of yellowed tissue, a gift. At the bottom lay a trove of programs (Lincoln Center, BAM, the Metropolitan Opera) with opinionated notes tucked throughout, the critic pulling no punches in private. Out of one fell a sheet of paper torn from a pocket memo pad, a scrawled verse:

> *O Jersey-haired Gilda Duprée,*
> *Do you think we can't tell you've gone gray?*
> *Your high C is wobbly,*
> *Your chins have gone gobbly,*
> *Please say you're retiring today!*

Written beneath: *Mean, mean, MEAN! Nod to her yrs @ Gbrne, Tosca '82, etc. Mourn decline of etc. KTK her successor yyy.*

Kit had seen his father's handwriting, but not in its adult guise. Lucinda had shown him school compositions, letters from 4-H camp, the typical memorabilia of parents reaching back into a child's childhood.

Christina was the one he approached for permission to keep the box from the attic. She said, "Do you really need to ask? Mal would have laughed at your Boy Scout virtue. Except he wouldn't have called it virtue. He'd have called it something like punctiliousness or unimpeachability. Maybe his life was too short, but he got out of this burb in good order and made the most of it. Sometimes I wish I'd gone farther away than I did."

Christina makes it clear to Kit, on a regular basis, that the role of Dutiful Daughter is not one she savors, no matter how much she loves her father. She counts on Kit to be a covert "sitter" to Zeke when he's there; she visits two or three other days, and his physical therapist, Zoe, comes by twice a week as well. But once they finish the FCP, which (to meet the exhibition deadline) they must do by midsummer, Christina will have to suggest to her father that he move in with her and Greg—or to an assisted-living place. Kit has even thought about taking Zeke to New Jersey, but there simply isn't room. And Zeke still has local visitors, even some who seek his counsel, who keep him in the legislative loop. To take him away from Vermont would be to deprive him of oxygen and light.

Not to mention that Sandra has her hands full now that Kit is a virtual nomad. For the two or three nights he spends in Vermont each week, he sleeps in a bedroom that was once shared by his father and Jonathan (the one member of his new family who understands the particular nightmare of failing to get tenure, all the downhill destinations toward which it points). Quilts made by Lucinda cover the twin beds: airplanes on one, turtles and frogs on the other. Kit sleeps in the bed by the window, under the airplanes, not knowing which bed belonged to which brother. He asks fewer questions than he'd like to, mainly because Zeke is so often the only person around to ask. Zeke has barely enough energy to answer questions related to the papers and trophies Kit is sorting—though he is at his most alert when doing so. At the end of an afternoon working in the barn, Kit brings the most important or mystifying documents to the house, takes a shower, wakes Zeke from his nap, and makes the two of them a simple meal in the kitchen. Then they sit down at the dining room table (now perpetually covered with musty papers) to puzzle out the day's archival finds.

Zeke doesn't seem curious about Kit's life before they met. At first, Kit would wait, whenever they were alone together, for the older man to follow up on dropped remarks Kit might have made about grad school or his driveabout in Canada, his early years with Sandra. Perhaps it's simply a matter, again, of Zeke's limited resources—when they come together, they're doing work that requires concentration and, for Zeke, the labor of a fading memory—but Kit suspects it's more than that. Unlike Lucinda, Zeke does not reminisce about his older son, does not correlate tales of childhood quirks and talents with adult accomplishments—say, Malachy's relentless domination of the grade-school spelling bee as the earliest predictor that he would become a writer, not a musician. Zeke respects the traditions and burdens of the past (would he be living on that farm if he did not?), but he is not a sentimentalist.

Kit, too, has limited energy. In addition to the time he spends in Vermont, he now spends another two nights a week in Rhode Island. He had hoped to be finished with the FCP by May, which is when he started work at the museum in Providence. Yet even if the overlap means he can spend little more than long weekends at home, he is relieved to be taxing his mind on chores beyond home repair (his skills there shaky at best) and even more relieved to see how much happier Sandra is. She seems to have embraced her skills as a master juggler, driving like a madwoman between meetings with clients, pick-ups of children, and shopping expeditions for shrubs, groceries, and camp supplies. Without a word to Kit, Zeke sent Sandra a check with a short note directing her to spend it on "getting children out of the house." It will just about cover two weeks of drama camp for Fanny and a monthlong football clinic for Will.

But those activities have yet to begin. For this weekend, Kit, Sandra, and the twins are staying with Jasper and Loraina. Kit broke the news to his mother in an e-mail nailing down the details of their rendezvous. She did not mention it in her reply. What she did mention was that she and Bart were "still adjusting" to having the house to themselves, struggling with "the usual problems couples our age have to deal with, the textbook ennui." The new dog, advised by friends of theirs who'd "been there," was both a help and a hindrance.

But for now we're okay, she wrote. Kit felt a spasm of panic at the thought that his mother might find herself alone. Did the restlessness or resentment or the "textbook ennui" come from her—or from Bart? (Surely not from dependable, corny, "Hey dude" Bart.)

The older Kit gets, the less confident he feels judging other peo-

ple as spouses or parents. These days, driving past the home of the
Naked Hemp Society, he finds himself more curious than contemptuous about their easily ridiculed New Age ways. Why shouldn't
they nurse their babies till age four? Why shouldn't they want to
keep their children away from factory-farmed meats, from clothing
soaked in fire-retardant chemicals, from dull-witted burned-out public school teachers whose tenure is all too easily approved? Why *not*
frolic naked in the sprinkler—under the full moon, perhaps? Why
not turn one's family into a small, nurturing country protected by a
virtual moat?

Daphne produces from her basket a flowered cloth and napkins to
match. Kit recognizes them from countless picnics stretching back
into their years with Jasper. She produces as well two bottles of
prosecco.

"Mom, people are driving."

"Not me. Not Bart. We're staying at a little inn down the road."

"Lucky you." Kit thinks of the drive to Jasper's—scenic in the
daylight but sure to be long and demanding in the dark.

"You indulge," Sandra tells him. "I'll drive us back."

Gratefully, he says, "Well, maybe I just will. Indulge." It's good to
see his mother look so happy with Bart, but he worries about other
emotions this outing may inspire. At Christmas, when she told him
she had bought the tickets, she announced, "It's time to make my
peace with that place. The place where you were conceived."

Kit flinches when she speaks in such terms, but isn't this what he
gets after forcing her hand? He asked for the biological truth, and
now he's getting it, back to the very beginning. He tries to imagine,
to picture in these fields, in that imperious manor house, on that
stage glowing like a cosmic eye in the distance, not just his mother
as a teenager but the man (the boy) who was (or, his mother would
correct him, *could have been*) his father. Gradually, over the past year,
Malachy Burns has been coming into focus for Kit. He will always
be, to some extent, a blur—from so many angles, his image remains
obstinately shadowed, hopelessly smudged—but he is no longer a
phantom. And there are so many shapes that phantom might have

taken (a lascivious older man, a drunken acquaintance in a bar, a violent stranger) that it decidedly didn't.

Christina puts cold grilled chicken, slices of French bread, hunks of cheese, and tomato salad on paper plates. She pours sparkling water for those not drinking wine. Kit decides to let himself be waited on. He sits next to Zeke and sips prosecco from an orange plastic cup. The air is acrid with the scent of the insect repellent they've sprayed on their clothing and skin—without it, they'd be miserable—but everywhere he looks, the splendor is staggering. The sun is about to set, the sky aspiring to Tintoretto. If he were seventeen in this place, he would fall in love with the first girl who crossed his path. This is Eden.

"So I should explain," says Daphne. "Tonight is a celebrities-only concert. The campers are still practicing like crazy to get up there later in the season. I thought about getting us tickets for then, but I didn't want to wait too long."

Is she alluding to Zeke, to the worry that later in the summer might have been too late for him? His doctors are impressed with his progress, but there is always the risk of another stroke.

Daphne reserved tickets so early that the program had yet to be determined. So it's only by happenstance that they will be hearing a famous pair of vocalists, a husband and wife who perform together.

"How do they manage?" says Bart. "I'm always glad I don't play an instrument. The thought of being coerced to harmonize with my wife . . ." He laughs loudly.

"But you do work together, every day," says Sandra.

"Ah, but we run different parts of the show. If we were in the same room all day, every day . . . well, Katy bar the door."

"I hear you," says Christina. "Greg and I once joined forces on a class-action suit against a paper company, a pro bono thing. All I can say is, thank God they settled. And Dad"—she looks at Zeke—"Mom used to say she'd count the minutes to the end of every campaign."

Zeke is intent on eating his chicken. Kit leans over. "You holding out okay?"

Zeke glares at him. "Day I'm *not* 'holding out,' that's the last day. I promise you." He picks up his napkin and wipes the grease from his fingers and mouth with a defiant delicacy. He surveys the trees, the people scattered at other tables, on blankets and beach chairs. "Remember this place well. We came before Mal, too. Never dreamed I'd have a child here. Seeing him on that stage? My father—man you know from all those letters—would not have approved."

"Of course he would have. He'd have been proud."

Zeke shakes his head. "When I was a child, no music in that house."

"Really?" Kit cannot imagine a childhood without music.

"Lucinda brought the music."

Kit hears the dual meaning, intentional or not. Once more, he remembers that this man is his grandfather and that the man whose papers he is reading, classifying, filing, and so preserving was—is—his great-grandfather. An invisible scaffolding to his life has begun to reveal itself, like backstage machinery exposed at the lifting of a scrim. But is Kit any different for it? Could he know if he were? On one of the first nights he stayed at the farmhouse, he stole quietly into the upstairs bathroom with a photograph of Malachy, a formal head shot that he found in Lucinda's sewing room (a room untouched since her death). Though no one would disturb him, he locked the door. He faced the mirror and held the picture next to his face. Yes: the eyes, the ears, the hairline. Maybe the chin. The mouth, no. But in this picture Malachy is younger than Kit; he cannot be anything *but* younger. What does it mean to discover your father when you are older than he would ever be? Kit worries that he is unable to feel sad enough. Too often now, he wonders what it is he *should* feel.

He glances at Sandra, who is talking to Christina about raising girls in such a shameless culture (a recurrent conversation that Kit does his best to avoid). How has she done such a successful job? Especially here, now, the last thing Kit wants to contemplate is Fanny as a teenage girl.

Daphne baked shortbread for dessert. Kit licks sugar off his fingers, tasting beneath it the bitter charcoal of the chicken.

Night is encroaching, gently, turning pools of grassy shadow from green to violet. Kit's mother was right: without the sun, he's glad to have a jacket. Collectively, their attention turns in the same direction when the cabled spotlights radiating from the stage go on, reminding them that they are here for more than a picnic. The stage itself gleams, the long piano a study in patience.

They pack up the linens and the leftover food. Kit drains the last of his prosecco and collects the disposable items in a plastic bag.

Daphne hands out tickets. "I think we have very good seats. I want to take a detour and look at the old studios. Come with me, Kit?" It's plain to everyone that she is inviting Kit and no one else.

Nervous, light-headed from the wine, he follows his mother away from the general flow of people toward the stage. They take a gravel footpath into a thicket of birches. Daphne exclaims at the fireflies.

They stop for a moment, just to marvel.

"I don't think we have fireflies," says Kit. "Where we live, I mean."

"It's just for a week or two, did you know that? Then they're done. If you don't pay attention, you miss the show."

They enter a clearing that holds a bunkerlike building, its only windows tucked along the eaves. The seams of its cinder-block construction are visible through a pristine coat of whitewash. Kit's mother grasps the door handle, clearly expecting it to open. When it doesn't, she backs up and stares at it, puzzled.

Kit points at the keypad. "Looks like you need a combination."

Cupping her hands around her face, she tries to see through the window in the door, the only one at eye level. The interior is dark. "This is where we did most of our work. I suppose they lock everything now." She laughs quietly. "Things were so open back then. We were trusted. Even if we didn't deserve it." She continues to gaze at the door, as if her wishfulness might coax it open.

Was he conceived here? Not that Kit wants to know; he most certainly doesn't. He puts a hand on her shoulder. "Let's make sure we get back in time."

But she seems reluctant to leave. "We were so *cocooned* in this place."

"Well, they worked you hard, so they took good care of you."

"No." She sighs. "I mean yes. That's all true. Though boy was the food awful! But when I think about what was going on in the world outside these walls . . . Nobody talked about the war, about politics or Haight-Ashbury or riots or . . . I mean, the fast kids—the ones who came from New York, Chicago—they joked about dropping acid. But I doubt they'd seen more than the occasional joint. And the adults here—I suppose it didn't help that most of them were foreign. What would somebody from Czechoslovakia or Vienna care about what we were up to in Vietnam?

"But you know, one of the musicians who played with me, his brother was killed in the war. He had to leave. And I remember feeling as if—as if somehow our acting so above it all, so 'exempt' from normal life, had put that brother in extra danger. Well. Silly."

Kit wonders what his mother is driving at. He says, "I'm sure it's the same now. Do you think the kids here now, this summer, ever talk about Afghanistan? The banking crisis? Rising unemployment?"

She seems to ponder this. "I'll bet they do."

"They're all online, I guess. Connected to everything that way. But only because they can't help it. It's doesn't mean they're . . . more conscientious now."

"Kit, I spend five days a week with kids this age. Everything is so different, believe me." She pauses. "I guess I just wish that we hadn't felt like we lived in a parallel universe. Somewhere the usual laws didn't apply." She puts out a hand to test the keypad by the door. She touches a few numbers. But suddenly she's the one to look at her watch and notice the time.

"Enough with the memories, right?" she says.

They head back the way they came, toward the noise of the crowd pressing toward the stage. When they reach the main path, they yield to a tight clique of teenagers passing by: confiding, teasing, and laughing; oblivious to anyone outside their bubble. They are dressed up, combed, and (where necessary) shaven, self-conscious but pleased at how they stand out.

Daphne takes Kit's arm. "Look. That was me. I was one of them." She steps into the path to follow. She speeds up to match their youthful gait, to stay close behind them.

"They are *babies*. My God," she whispers when they slow down, having hit the edge of the crowd.

"So were you, Mom." The fruity aroma of shampoo mingled with drugstore cologne emanates from the kids clustered before them.

Kit thinks of something his mother said a few minutes ago: that she spends entire days with kids this age, kids who yearn toward being (and half-believe they already are) adults. She spends most of her days with girls the same age she was when she made, and didn't make, whatever decisions led to her having a baby: to Kit.

An usher takes their tickets and leads them to the center section, fifth row. Zeke, in his wheelchair, is parked on the aisle. The others move in so that Kit ends up between Zeke and his mother.

"Oh my." Daphne holds out her program to Kit. He glances at the list of songs, many of the titles foreign, most but not all of the composers familiar: Handel, Schubert, Britten, Ravel, Bernstein. But among the familiar songs and composers are a few that take him by surprise. Maybe Sondheim isn't so unconventional (a medley from *Into the Woods*), or Duke Ellington, but they will apparently hear songs by Tom Waits, Joni Mitchell, Barry Gibb, and the Beach Boys. The famous couple will also scat-sing a handful of the Goldberg Variations.

"Wild," says Kit.

"Not your usual night at the philharmonic," says Sandra.

"These days you have to be catchy, do something exotic," says Daphne. "There was a concert like this one when I was here. Malachy said that if the program had a title, it would be 'Dare Me to Sing It and I Will.'"

Kit laughs. He hears Zeke comment quietly, "Couldn't get much closer."

"Is this all right for you?" Kit knows, because it frustrates Christina, that Zeke refuses to consider a hearing aid. He assumes that sitting close to the stage, for Zeke, is good.

"Fine," says Zeke. "Not a complaint."

Involuntarily, Kit puts a hand on Zeke's knee. "Good."

And now the pianist comes onstage, a slight, wiry-haired man in a tuxedo that, when it catches the light, looks more blue than black. Applause; silence; urgent clearing of throats. Only when it is completely silent again—or as silent as an early summer evening in the country can be—do the singers enter, from opposing directions, joining hands like a bride and groom eager to say their vows. And isn't this a lot like being in church? Aren't the spectators worshippers, devotees to a particular kind of cultural cult?

Kit turns to study the expressions on the spectators' faces: amusing and slightly absurd in their rapt uniformity. They are like small children in this moment of composure, vessels waiting to be filled with joy. They are happy. They are safe. Except that in fact—he glances to one side at Zeke, to the other at his mother—they are all just as fragile as ever.

He shouldn't have had the second glass of prosecco, yet he knows that if he closes his eyes and surrenders, he will feel the same way everyone else does. Carefree, lucky, smiled upon by fate if just for a few fleeting hours. The music will be a welcome illusion, like a salty sea on which floating takes no effort.

He looks over at the students—the "campers"—and knows that, for them, the experience is wholly different because of their aspiration. The couple onstage (singing in Italian, something bawdy and teasing) might be their teachers, the artists whose fire they hope to borrow if not steal. Yet they look as earnest in their wonder as the adults do.

Seeing his mother glance in that direction, too, Kit realizes that the summer she spent here was surely the first time in her life that she felt genuinely powerful, the way before her clear and sunny, the world her opalescent oyster. Malachy Burns must have felt that way, too.

Listen to the music, he scolds himself. Just listen. Be your ears and nothing more.

Kit had spent a long, cold, bruising day in Zeke's attic, after which he had shoveled snow off the porch and served the two of them omelets and soup. It was March, and he had been going back and forth to Vermont for nearly a month: relieved to have the work but disoriented every morning by the brilliant light, the narrow mattress, the frigid floor beneath his feet. The first thing Sandra said in her nightly call was "Someone named Bruno phoned. Do you want his number?" Being Sandra, she didn't ask who Bruno was. Having no news of her own, she called the children to speak with their dad. Kit told himself it was a good thing that Will and Fanny seemed antsy when they came on the phone; he was interrupting whatever they were doing. They didn't miss him too much.

It took no feat of recall for Kit to know who Bruno was. Bruno and Raven taught at the Rhode Island School of Design; they had ties at

Brown as well. RISD and Brown: a true job for Kit at either place would be more than a long shot—more like a laugh—but Providence was a place with a number of schools where he might talk his way into something. It helped that Bruno felt certain Kit and Jasper had saved his life. That day, thawing by the fire, stoked with painkillers inadequate to the occasion, Bruno had clung to Kit as diversion: "Talk. Tell me anything. Your story—tell me that." So Kit told Bruno his story—or the story of his work . . . his not-work, his unwork, his maybe-never-work-to-begin-with.

Bruno had begged Kit to stay in touch, and after a couple of months, after another Christmas freighted with too much thinly veiled anxiety, after a stiff drink, Kit had e-mailed his CV to Bruno. Bruno wrote back that he would "keep an eye out." Maybe he'd meant it; maybe not. Kit let it go at that.

But he had.

"So I'm pretty proud of myself, pal, because get this," said Bruno when Kit reached him from Vermont. "The museum's getting a big but crazy-random collection of outsider art, from this guy in Spokane whose mother went to RISD like sometime back around the Civil War. It's the mother's collection; the son is pretty clueless about its contents. Turns out a lot of it's tribal—Native American, but Eskimo, too. Maybe Inuit?"

"Probably." Kit waited, afraid of hs own eagerness.

"You know, I have to say, the term *outsider* gives me the skeevies. Smacks of empire mentality, don't you agree?"

"Academia as the baseline," said Kit, barely breathing.

"Right. So listen. The collection's uncatalogued. A mess, but now *our* mess. Arriving here in May. Paperwork is a guaranteed nightmare, repatriation issues up the wazoo. All the Canadian stuff. But what I hear is we'll keep most of it—the museum. So this lightbulb went on in my head—that you, with your background . . . Probably a freelance thing—you know. So I sent your CV to the curator. You have experience cataloguing? Appraising?"

Kit stood beside Zeke's dining table, covered from one end to the other with file boxes and folders, Kit's laptop an island in the flotsam. "As a matter of fact, I have a cataloguing job right now. But nothing permanent." *Nothing permanent*: how true of everything, really.

He did not tell Sandra until he'd spoken to the curator and knew that she took him seriously, would meet with him, give him a look at the collector's manifest. "It's like some eight-year-old's list for Santa," the curator scoffed. "Handwritten, torn. There's crayon! She had an eye, but . . . *eccentric* would be tactful. The son's not much better."

Since late May, his two jobs overlap. Both are ephemeral, and at times they feel mostly clerical. Highbrow scut work. Lists to make and remake, filing systems to devise, software to learn. But the very different surroundings keep boredom at bay, even amuse him. Providence is a city whose bipolar nature makes Kit feel strangely comfortable: scruffy yet elegant, it's a small-stakes fiefdom where B-list mobsters and Ivory Tower bureaucrats have worked out a symbiotic hold on power—petty power, the hardest kind to share. He works in a sleek, flashy building that flanks a pillared Greek façade—but sleeps in a closetlike bedroom he rents from a colleague of Bruno's, at the back of an undistinguished three-decker building in a Portuguese neighborhood. He eats dinner in a bleakly bright restaurant that offers ample servings of pork, cod, and potatoes for a song. Two days a week, Kit is content to live on oversalted fish and meat in sauces shiny with fat. Funny, he thinks: not all that different from Inuit food.

At the museum, he rules in solitude over a basement room kept cool, dry, and dim in deference to the sacred pampering of art. Beyond the table he uses to examine most pieces, there is hardly space to stand among all the crates and folios the shipping company constructed to contain the artwork. In the donor's house, they were exposed for decades to winter damp, summer heat, unfiltered sunlight. Never mind. Now they'll be "safe." They will be treated as if they have finally come home when, in fact, they couldn't be farther away.

Like most art collections worth preserving, this one has its standard-bearing masterpieces, its what-was-she-thinking dross, and its closeted gems. Among the gems, in Kit's eye, are the contents of a colossal portfolio: a cache of drawings by a group of artists from Cape Dorset. He's read about these artists, but this is the first time he's seen their work outside journals and art magazines.

Some of the drawings are six feet across, most of them rendered in colored pencil, the thick toothy paper and the pencils part of a grant from a famous manufacturer of art supplies. Whether grateful or bemused, the artists worked with what they were given. Some were in their seventies, some in their twenties.

Several are panoramic townscapes: meandering rows of blunt, soot-colored buildings surrounded by constellations of bundled figures driving snowmobiles and pickups. Though the images are flat, lacking any guile or subtlety, they remind Kit of Brueghel in their gull's-eye view of community life. Tiny citizens carry spears, gut fish, skin seals, but they also take out garbage, play basketball, shop, mail letters, pump gas, drink and dance in bars. The artists are clever to mix traditional and modern pastimes; this is what collectors like to see in work of this kind. *The collision of cultures.* They may not recognize their condescension, but the artists do—and if they profit, no offense need be taken.

Other artists have chosen to draw the animals they know; the animals have always been Kit's favorite subject in the art he studies. It seems to him both logical and wondrous that people unschooled in the Western tricks of sculpture can make seals, bears, whales, owls, and foxes feel so tangibly alive, or frozen in time, whether the medium is mineral, wood, or bone. (Is Kit, like the collectors he disdains, condescending to feel this wonder? Maybe so.)

In this two-dimensional medium, the animals are every bit as authentic. In one drawing, a five-foot-long whale contains, Jonah-like, a sleeping polar bear. Within the bear nests a family of seals, which in turn enclose a flock of eider ducks in flight. Confined within each bird is a man decked out for hunting. The hunters are both dwarfed and engulfed by the animals and birds. So many creatures, yet most of the picture comprises the plain white surface of the paper; only the most sinuous, minimal lines, in blues and greens and grays, define the creatures themselves. Kit has fallen in love with this drawing and wishes he could own it, see it every day. There is so much tenderness in the care with which the artist made his lines: the soft folds around the whale's one visible eye, the bear's furling claws, the strokes that give spine to each feather.

One day Bruno visited Kit in his subterranean lair. Kit was formalizing descriptions of these drawings, their provenance, their market value according to galleries in Toronto and Vancouver. Lying on the table was one of the drawings Kit now privately thinks of as Arctic Brueghel.

Bruno leaned over the drawing, issuing grunts of amusement and admiration. "Yikes. A land of no trees. No place for me, tell you that."

"It's oppressive, if trees are what you know, what you take for granted."

Bruno nodded vigorously. "You know this part of the world, yeah?"

"Not really, but I've been there. As a tourist."

"I'd be homesick for green in no time. Green-sick!"

"If you grew up in the woods," said Kit, "it feels like you've gone to the moon."

"Houses are made of what, tin?"

"Some. Asphalt shingles, fiberglass, recycled shipping crates, and salvaged boats—but they import building materials, too. It's a perfectly connected world. Well"—Kit laughed—"imperfectly connected."

"As we all are," said Bruno. "Man, as we *all* are."

They say good-bye to one another in the parking lot. Zeke fell asleep in the second half of the concert, and though he woke during the thunderous applause at the end, he is drowsing again by the time they get to the car.

"That was something, at intermission, wasn't it?" Christina whispers to Kit as he folds the chair and lifts it into the back of her car.

"I think he was thrilled, though tomorrow you can be sure he'll say something cynical about it."

Christina laughs quietly. During intermission, one of Zeke's past colleagues from the senate recognized him. Gradually, a number of Zeke's fans gathered around him. He insisted on standing and walking with them to the bar; Kit watched from afar as Zeke enjoyed their affectionate laughter, glad-handing, probably their recollections of his achievements—perhaps Lucinda's, too.

But Kit was distracted by his mother's tremulous emotions. Spotting a woman she recognized near the stage, she seized Kit's arm. "It is. It *is* her. I can't believe it." She pulled him through the crowd,

Bart and Sandra following. The woman was older but arrestingly stylish. Her silver hair was cut in a razor-sharp pageboy. She wore a purple sequined sheath—short, showing off legs that defied her age. When Daphne approached her, spoke to her, it took the woman just a moment to place Daphne as one of her former students.

"You played 'The Swan,'" she said. *Svahn.* Was she Russian? "I remember. You were an exceptional swan or I would not. I am telling the truth."

Daphne told the woman about her playing in the Dartmouth ensemble. She did not mention her teaching. Kit held his breath, then realized that of course she wouldn't say a thing about Malachy. (Had he been memorable, too?)

When they were seated again, Daphne said, "I guess she was just in her thirties then, maybe younger. We were so myopic about our teachers. Not that we weren't in awe, but we needed them to be on the way out." She smiled through the second half of the program.

"Are you sure you can drive back this late?" he asks Christina now as he closes the cargo door after securing the wheelchair.

"Please. I drive constantly, twenty-four–seven. Life of carpools, of chasing depositions from Boston to Bangor. And now Dad. I'll be driving the day I die. Probably drive myself to the funeral home."

"Tell him I'll see him at the farm tomorrow night," says Kit.

"Thank you, Daphne. That was amazing." Christina opens her door. She hesitates visibly before adding, "And thank you for sharing this piece of my brother's life. I forgot about his being here."

Daphne hugs Christina forcefully. "You are welcome. You are so very welcome." She's been tearful since the end of the concert, especially since leading them along a roundabout path, a detour on which she discovered that a building she remembered well—an old barn—had been razed and replaced.

"Oh," she said, as if someone had offended her. "Look at this. Now they sleep in real dorms. They probably have televisions. Computers. Who knows what luxuries."

"It's called progress, Mom."

"No, Kit. No." She wiped her eyes. "When I was here, the key to our work was *regress*. If there's such a thing. All we had was music."

And one another, thinks Kit.

They wave off Christina, and then, finally, Kit's mother pulls him into a prolonged hug. "Kitten," she says, "this was something we should have done a long time ago. I mean, just because this place is a part of *me*. Forget the rest."

He lets her hold him, unsure what he should say.

Walking to their car, one of the last few in the lot, Kit and Sandra look at each other and let out a collaborative sigh.

"Are you all right?" says Sandra.

"Define 'all right.' I don't think I've been all right in years."

"You know what I mean."

"Well, maybe I do. Let me sleep on that." The truth is this: every new revelation, every new relationship, brings new confusion as well. Sometimes he feels like a mouse being coaxed through a laboratory maze. There's no guessing what's been planted around the next turn, or the next.

Sandra unlocks the car. Kit asks her, as he did Christina, if she's sure she can do the driving. (Could he? Doubtful. The wine has worn off, but the entire evening has left him feeling raw, fretful, ready to howl at the moon.)

"I'm fine." She clicks in her belt, then looks at him and says, "I got it. The Rutgers job. The memorial garden."

"Oh God, that is so great," says Kit. "Why didn't you tell me sooner?"

"I just found out. They texted me sometime during the concert."

"Modern life. Did I actually call it progress?" Kit laughs. Soon, no one will be able to remember a time when there was such a thing as "between" or "away" or "off" in the context of work. (Though if he thinks of his mother back when he was a child, there were days she seemed to work—playing her cello, planning her lessons, teaching at school—from early morning till well after reading Kit a bedtime story.)

"I have to refine the design, call my plant sources, all that. And I somehow convinced them I know a lot about fountains. Because of course there's a fountain. Where there's sorrow, they almost always demand water." She drives through the gate, the exit from Eden. "But the thing is, by September, I'll be spending a lot of time there."

"You'll need me for the kids."

"Or someone."

"I ought to be back on the street by then."

"Back at home, you mean. I hope that's what you mean."

"Hope. Word of the moment," he says, trying to sound light-hearted.

"But look. Say you found a job in Providence, or Vermont—just about anywhere—I'd be fine with moving. Things change."

"Or get desperate."

"Stop. Really, Kit. The good news is, we're flexible."

"Flexible," says Kit. "I'll go with that."

"And lucky."

Sandra's father loaned them money to pay for a new roof; last year, when their situation did seem more desperate than flexible, Sandra insisted they prepare to sell the house. They talked about moving out to Oregon, staying with Sandra's parents for a while; Sandra could work at the nursery. Kit knows this is still a possibility, and it wouldn't be the end of the world—but now he feels more tightly bound to the Northeast.

"I'm poking around at private schools," he says. "But Mom thinks I should go for certification. She's all for public."

"Of course she is." Sandra's tone is hard to read. Over the past year, she and Daphne have been working hard at remaining amicable; anyone can see this.

Their car travels alone on a winding road where trees knit together above them, blocking out whatever light the stars and moon might offer. Sandra clicks on the high beams.

"What was your favorite song?" he asks. "Tonight."

"You're asking me to choose? Between Bach and Tom Waits? Ravel and the *Beach* Boys?"

"You know what? That was incredible. Maybe that was my favorite." The married singers had performed, in all its hymnal sweetness (gazing into each other's eyes), "God Only Knows." Kit stops himself from saying that this is one of many songs he knows involuntarily well, because it's one his mother taught in her class years ago, playing it over and over at home, asking him—and Jasper—for their impressions, too. He stops himself because he doesn't want to bring up his mother right now—not yet. He isn't ready to talk about the events or emotions of the evening, not even with Sandra. Instead, he says, "I read somewhere that Paul McCartney loved singing that song as a lullaby to his children."

"Easy for him. *He* could do all the harmony on his own."

Kit realizes that he is still holding the program. "Do you think we should take Will and Fanny to something like that? An outdoor concert?"

"Only if we balance it with a Giants game."

"Will should be able to find entertainment outside a stadium."

"Should. Now there's a loaded word."

Yes, thinks Kit, and how. Here it is again: worrying over how he *should* feel about recent events, rather than knowing what he genuinely does. It's as if he's living an unremitting dream, watching himself from the dreamer's distance, a witness unable to intervene. He feels a growing affection for Zeke—yet he cannot vanquish his guilt. To be with Zeke is also to be without Lucinda, who would surely be there still, with her husband, if Kit had not barged into their lives. He feels gratitude toward Fenno McLeod—yet the quilt and the box of letters and pictures, which Fenno sent with a letter telling him more about his father, only sharpened Kit's guilt. Here were swatches, *literal* swatches, from Lucinda's bright, generous, celebratory life. . . . What was he to do with this memento? He will always love his mother, yet now that he's muscled his way into knowing things she withheld—in a way, pulled filial rank on her (Malachy may once have been her lover, but he will always be Kit's father)—he feels as much sadness for her sacrifice as he does admiration. Tonight's outing only deepened that sadness. Never mind that it looks as if she's happy: as if love, whatever form it takes in her marriage to Bart, will prevail, at least for now.

Sandra's voice emerges from the silence. "Do you suppose the children will be in bed? I somehow doubt it."

"Loraina can't get enough of them, can she?"

"Don't be fooled," says Sandra. "Jasper's the one who'd change the locks."

The clock in the dashboard tells them it's ten-thirty. They have at least another hour on the road, though Sandra tends to drive faster than Kit. "I could phone and find out. Put down my disciplinarian foot," he says. "But they can sleep late. Can't they?"

"Except that now I have to get back sooner, start making calls. They can't exactly stay here with you."

Sandra always remembers the logistics. Because yes, the kids will return with her to New Jersey, while Kit returns to Zeke's for another couple of days in the sweltering barn. Another visit or two and that work will be done.

"So tell me about the garden." He saw Sandra's earliest sketches, but he's been away from home too much to have paid close attention.

"God knows if I'm up to it. Right this minute I'm terrified I'm in way over my head."

The garden is as much a recognition as a memorial—and, Sandra says (though only to him), an act of political correctness. Rutgers is hardly West Point, so the number of graduates lost in a decade of skirmishes and roadside bombs is—so far—negligible. More than three dozen alumni, however, died on September 11. The garden will be a walled enclosure, intimate in scale, though the donor has wealth on a scale that is anything but. So while the job is "small," says Sandra, she'll be free to choose unusual materials and plantings. Despite the acutely different climates, she will hunt for horticultural crossovers between the Middle East and New Brunswick. "I do have a good source of opium poppies," she says. "A client who loves to share her seeds. Garden-club insurgency."

Kit pictures the cinematic field of poppies in *The Wizard of Oz*. Jasper began reading the *Oz* books aloud to Kit as soon as he and his mother moved in. He had read them to Rory and Kyle when they were younger; sometimes, if Jasper was reading to Kit on the sofa, they would loiter about for a minute or two and listen. Jasper's deep sawtooth voice was the perfect storyteller's medium. Just last night, he read to Will and Fanny; Fanny had brought along the third *Harry Potter*. He will have read to them again tonight.

The twins are sleeping in Rory and Kyle's bunk bed, which Loraina is determined to haul to the dump. ("If we put in an honest-to-God four-poster with a mattress that doesn't reek of feral boy, maybe we could attract some actual guests!") Jasper claims, however, that having children as regular visitors is a vote in favor of keeping the room as it is, moth-eaten cowboy rug and all. Kit knows that Jasper is hoping Kyle's life will stay on the rails; maybe he hopes for just one more grandchild—this one living right around the corner.

The children were predictably delighted when they entered Jasper's house. Kit can still remember the first time he saw it. But unlike nine-year-old Kit, whose mother warned him to "behave," the twins ran up and down the stairs, peering into the various nooks with their various views, finally convening at the top, in the crow's nest. "Can we stay *here*?" said Fanny, sitting possessively on the futon that Jasper installed once Kit moved out for good.

Kit briefly considered the image of himself and Sandra sleeping in the bunks below, and while there are still too many nights when they sleep together like siblings, he said, "No, I'm afraid not. This is my room."

"How is it yours?" Fanny challenged.

"I slept here for ten years, or just about." He glanced around, possessive in his own way. Above the desk where he did his homework hung the corkboard once crowded with his collection of art cards. But for a constellation of colorful thumbtacks, it had been empty ever since.

Fanny looked puzzled. Eagle eye that she is, she had already noticed, on the stone mantel in the living room, a picture of Rory, Kyle, and Kit. "Isn't that you as a kid?" she asked. Kit had been startled by the picture; where had it come from? Since moving into Jasper's house, Loraina has been softening its edges: not all at once, as Kit's mother did, but by stealthy increments: one month a rocking chair by the fireplace, next a fresh rag rug in the kitchen . . . but it looks as if she's also exhuming artifacts of Jasper's past, a past with which she has no quarrels.

Kit was naïve to bring the children for a weekend at Jasper's without, as Sandra put it, "full disclosure." He sat on the futon with Fanny and Will. "You remember how I told you that Didi was married before Papa-da?"

Will frowned. "No."

Fanny turned to her brother and said, "She got a *divorce*. We know that."

"Right," said Kit. "Didi was married to Jasper. We lived here when I was your age."

"But Jasper's not your dad," said Fanny. "Your dad died."

Once again, Kit wondered when he would be able to explain to his children all the discoveries of the past year—all these new people in their lives, these new places they were visiting. Kit is also certain that Fanny, though she hasn't said anything, is taking note of the emotional hum that rises and falls around her father these days. He can still detect in her the wariness both children felt after his collapse in Provincetown.

Fanny and Will have friends with stepfathers or stepmothers, so this part was relatively easy to explain. (Welcome, he thought, to the era of the fragmented family as norm. What was the correct term these days? *Blended:* that was it. The Naked Hemp Society flashed across his inner screen once more. The correct term for that kind of family he knew: *intact*.)

"So why'd we never come here before?" demanded Will. "This is a cool place."

"Yeah," said Fanny.

The two of them faced him squarely, allies in their accusation.

"You know, I should have brought you here a long time ago."

Sandra gasps and briefly hits the brake, startling Kit back into the world of the dark car, the late night. She drives on, but slowly.

"What?" cries Kit.

"A deer. It's okay. Sorry. I just saw a deer at the edge of the road."

"The last thing we want is to hit a deer," says Kit. "Your car is the best one we have. Soon to be the only one, I'm guessing."

Sandra is briefly silent, then laughs. "I'm thinking about the moose up over that fireplace. How it got there. Not stalked down and shot by some Davy Crockett type but hit on the road somewhere near the camp."

"By a drunken, lovelorn conductor, spurned by his first violin. Car totaled, nose broken, moose the consolation prize."

"My God, that *place*. Some 'camp.'" Sandra's profile glows in the light of the too-many information systems showing off their data behind the steering wheel.

Kit imagines his children asleep in Jasper's house. He thinks of them that morning, running in the meadow with the dogs. Will insisted on keeping the dogs straight, knowing their names. In addition to last year's crew, there's a litter of half-grown puppies. Kit watched from the open window at the kitchen sink, waking slowly to his first sips of coffee, as Jasper taught Will how to recognize each dog by its markings. "Not long," he heard Jasper say, "and you get to know their personalities, their voices, same way you know the people in your life. I can recognize a dog in the dark just from the way he breathes, the feel of his fur."

It pierces Kit so suddenly, with such unfamiliar certainty, that the impact on his body is as fierce as if they had hit that deer five miles back on the road.

"Kit?" says Sandra.

He leans forward, his palms on the dashboard, as if bracing himself, or trying to see farther ahead than the darkness will allow.

"Kit!" Sandra slows the car, begins pulling over to the narrow shoulder. "Kit, are you all right?"

"I'm fine," he says. "Really."

But she pulls over anyway. "Kit? Talk to me, will you?"

"Let's go," he says. "There's nothing wrong."

She sighs with obvious relief. She checks the rearview mirror and pulls back onto the road.

"Sandra."

"Yes."

"Remember when you made me leave, when you told me I had to go see Jasper?"

"I never *made* you go." She's silent for a moment. "But I needed you out of the house. I thought I might go crazy, living with you like that. You were like this resident invalid. I'd have been happy to send you off on a freighter to South America—I mean, so long as you came back."

"You didn't send me to Jasper on purpose? Specifically to—"

"Kit, that was the worst it's been for us. Even worse than when we were trying so hard to get pregnant. I don't even want to remember what I was thinking. I want never to feel like that again."

Kit still has no clear prospects for a job, yet he has other prospects. And though he can't say it out loud now, not even to Sandra (perhaps, for the moment, especially not to Sandra), he knows what he ought to have known all along: that Jasper is his father—or, as Sandra said when she kicked him out (because she's wrong for once: she did make him go), the closest thing to a father he's ever had. What, exactly, is a father if not a man who, once you're grown and gone and out in the world making your own mistakes, all good advice be damned, waits patiently for you to return? And if you don't, well then, you don't. He understands that risk. He knows whose choice it is.

"Kit, are you sure you don't need me to stop for a minute? We still have bottles of water in the trunk, from the picnic."

"I really *am* all right," he says. "But I'm glad you're doing the driving."

"We'll be there in about ten minutes, I think."

Yes; right again. Because now Kit recognizes a house by the side of the road. Only the porch light is on—revealing its surface to be a glossy buttercup yellow instead of a parched, peeling white—and the slumping barn that stood behind it is gone, had probably been gone for years; but this was a landmark for Kit on the long drive home from the stuffy, antiquated inn where his mother liked to go for special-occasion dinners. Jasper always drove, Daphne beside him. Kit sat behind them, in the early years squeezed between Rory and Kyle, then alone, an only child all over again. And if he hadn't fallen asleep—if he was simply worn out from a night of rich food and public table manners, idly watching the trees and the occasional buildings pass them by—he'd know, when they passed this particular house, that he would be in bed within fifteen minutes. That house was like one of the stone inuksuks he and Sandra saw, and took so many pictures of, when they drove along Hudson Bay, newly in love, enchanted by everything unfamiliar. A signpost, a beacon.

Ahead is the turnoff. Before it was paved, the final stretch was bumpy; no one would have slept through the car's jostling over the rough dirt road ending at the house. But in the early days, even up to an age when he was really too big for such coddling, he liked to pretend he was out cold, just so that Jasper would hoist him up and carry him into the house. Kit would will his body limp and keep his eyes firmly closed while Jasper paused at the base of the stairs to secure the boy's weight against his chest and then, sometimes grunting at the effort, began the long climb—"Alley-oop and upward, my friend"—all the way to the top.

Acknowledgments

I want to begin by thanking Dana Prescott and Diego Mencaroni of the Civitella Ranieri Foundation, as well as Will Conroy and Patty Doar of the Arizona Inn. Their benevolence and sumptuous hospitality enabled me to write many, many pages of this book at two magnificent, tranquil retreats.

My friend and fellow novelist Edward Kelsey Moore, who also happens to be an accomplished cellist, shared with me a great deal of knowledge—not to mention beautiful music—essential to my inventing the life of a gifted young musician. I asked a hundred questions; he gave two hundred answers. Although many details of that invented life vaporized in final revisions, I thank Ed for hours of richly entertaining melodic diversion. The more personal experiences of two other friends also influenced my work on this book. I was deeply moved by their discussing in detail how shadow parents—those whose identities remain unknown—can exert a subtle but inexorable power over the entire course of a child's life and relationships. Without your stories, G. and G., this one would be less authentic.

As always, I am grateful to my sons and their father, who witness firsthand the ups and downs, and the middling doldrums, during the years I spend pulling together a novel. My work is invisible, and they honor it entirely on faith.

The publication of this book also marks thirteen years of equally faithful support from my agent and my editor, Gail Hochman and Deb Garrison, who have stood by me from the start of my life as a novelist. They are the best of the best, always insightful, always truthful, always there. I cannot begin to count my lucky stars.

I SEE YOU EVERYWHERE

Louisa Jardine is the older one, the conscientious student, precise and careful: the one who yearns for a good marriage, an artistic career, a family. Clem, the archetypal youngest, is the rebel: committed to her work saving animals, but not to the men who fall for her. In this vivid, heartrending story of what we can and cannot do for those we love, the sisters grow closer as they move further apart. All told with sensual detail and deft characterization, *I See You Everywhere* is a candid story of life and death, companionship and sorrow, and the nature of sisterhood itself.

Fiction

THREE JUNES

In June of 1989 Paul McLeod, a newspaper publisher and recent widower, travels to Greece, where he falls for a young American artist and reflects on the complicated truth about his marriage. Six years later, again in June, Paul's death draws his three grown sons and their families back to their ancestral home. Fenno, the eldest, a wry, introspective gay man, narrates the events of this unforeseen reunion. Far from his straitlaced expatriate life as a bookseller in Greenwich Village, Fenno is stunned by a series of revelations that threaten his carefully crafted defenses. Four years farther on, in yet another June, a chance meeting on the Long Island shore brings Fenno together with Fern Olitsky, the artist who once captivated his father. Now pregnant, Fern must weigh her guilt about the past against her wishes for the future and decide what family means to her. In prose rich with compassion and wit, *Three Junes* paints a haunting portrait of love's redemptive powers.

Fiction

Seventy-year-old Percy Darling is settling happily into retirement: reading novels, watching old movies, and swimming naked in his pond. But his routines are disrupted when he is persuaded to let a locally beloved preschool take over his barn. As Percy sees his rural refuge overrun by children, parents, and teachers, he must reexamine the solitary life he has made in the three decades since the sudden death of his wife. With equal parts affection and humor, Julia Glass spins a captivating tale about a man who can no longer remain aloof from his community, his two grown daughters, or—to his great shock—the precarious joy of falling in love.

Fiction

ALSO AVAILABLE
The Whole World Over

ANCHOR BOOKS
Available wherever books are sold.
www.anchorbooks.com